DEATH OF ME

A Valarian City Novel

Erin Jacobs

AIIRY PUBLISHING CO.

CONTENTS

PLAYLIST

Death of Me – Madilyn Bailey
Just Like Jesse James – Cher
Play with Fire – Sam Tinnesz, Yacht Money
Trouble – Valerie Broussard
I Did Something Bad – Taylor Swift
Alkaline – Sleep Token
Grace – Lewis Capaldi
Power Over Me – Dermot Kennedy
Control – Halsey
Way Down We Go – KALEO
Goddess – Xana
What Have I Done – Dermot Kennedy
Breath of Life – Florence + The Machine
The Great War – Taylor Swift

For every single one of you who ever offered me support in this very long journey.
Thank you.

Also, a word of warning:
This is not a spicy book. The sex scenes are mostly fade to black. If that's not your cup of tea, totally get it! But, I hope the story of Juliette and Vincent is enough to keep you hooked anyway.
Love always,
Erin

ONE

KIDNAPPED

"You're a damn idiot, Juliette," I muttered to myself, pulling my leather jacket tighter around my shoulders. Everybody knew that being outside in the city at night was a bad idea, an even worse one if you lived on the wrong side of Valarian like I did. Walking home was practically suicide.

So, of course, that's exactly what I was doing.

Cursing under my breath, I carefully watched where I was going as I navigated the dark streets. Growing up where I had, I was used to the violence that happened around my home, but that didn't mean I wanted to be a part of it. Three near assaults in the past year were enough to teach me to keep a switchblade in my purse along with a can of mace. Getting my hands on a gun was my next task when I had the extra cash.

Glancing up at a street sign when I passed under a light, I grumbled as I realized I was still fifteen minutes from my apartment. My heels clicked along as I walked, practically announcing my presence to anyone within twenty yards. This was the last time I allowed Dante to work me this late. He had other bartenders.

Who was I kidding? I would never tell him no when he needed me. And I would also never turn down the money from a closing shift.

Sighing heavily, I cast my eyes skyward. The moon was bright, but the lights of the city nearly blocked the stars out. Though in this portion of the city, thanks to almost every streetlamp being busted, the stars shone through a little. *You have a death wish,* I thought as I hopped over a wide crack in the sidewalk. After taking only a few more steps, I was at the mouth of an alley. Out of instinct, I clutched my bag even tighter against me before glancing inside it.

I should've just kept walking.

The sounds of a scuffle reached my ears, causing me to freeze in my tracks. Straining my eyes against the darkness, I could make out the shapes of what looked like four men. One was lying down with the others surrounding him. As one of the ones standing kicked the one on the ground, my heart burst into overdrive.

A mugging. That's what this had to be.

Run!

It took me a minute to register the order my brain had screamed at me, but once one of the men's head raised and our eyes met, I regained control of my body. A small squeak escaped me before I spun on my heel and took off towards my home. When the sounds of pursuit broke through the panicked haze that had settled over my mind, I only pushed myself to go faster. However, the heels that were required with my uniform were not helping my speed. I knew that if I stopped to take them off, my assailant would only catch me, so I just pushed my legs to move faster. And prayed a heel wouldn't snap.

My street was in sight when someone roughly threw me against the brick wall of a building.

"Okay, *ow*," I hissed, shoving my hair out of my eyes as a man glared down at me.

"Going somewhere, sugar?" he breathed, cracking a smile at me as he raised a knife to my collarbone.

Letting out a huff, I shrugged. "Home," I answered, trying to control my breathing and my heart rate. *You've been in situations like this before,* I reminded myself. *Just take it easy.*

"And what did you see?" he questioned, running the cool blade up the curve of my throat.

A shiver wracked my body against my will as his buddies slowed to a stop around us. "Three shadows attacking another shadow," I responded, a wry grin curving my lip as I tried to work my hand into my purse.

One of the other men noticed my actions and ripped my bag away from me. "What're you searching for?" he asked, a teasing edge in his voice as he upended the contents of my bag onto the pavement.

"Hey!" I struggled against the hold of the one in front of me. "Let me go."

"Don't think I can do that, sugar," he told me, glancing back at the one that still had my bag in his hands. "What's she got?"

A car came rolling down the street. Headlights washed over the three men in front of me, giving me a clear view of each of them. The one that held me was blonde and the other two had darker hair. The blonde and I locked eyes, and his flickered with surprise as he took me in anew.

"Nothing of importance," I snapped, drawing the other's attention back to me as the car continued past us. No one stopped attacks around here. It was everyone for themselves. Or maybe they just didn't see me. That excuse let me keep a little faith in humanity.

"I beg to differ," the man said from the ground, brushing his fingers over my makeup bag until they rested on my wallet. He flipped it open and my earnings for the night tumbled out. In the dim light from the moon, I could see his eyes widen as he took in the multitudes of cash. "Stripper?" he questioned, raising his gaze to mine before it trailed over my body.

"Bartender," I spat, glaring at him as he pocketed it all. "Don't even think about it," I said, once again struggling against the blonde's hold.

"Easy now," he chided, pressing the knife harder against my neck.

"I worked hard for that money," I stated, feeling my anger spark. My heart was pounding so hard in my chest I was positive he could feel it against the forearm he was using to hold me against the wall. "Rent is due in a few days, and I'd really rather it not be late."

"Juliette Gracen," the one searching through my things said. My head snapped in his direction at the mention of my name. "What a *sweet* name."

"Don't even start with me," I seethed.

"What do we do with her?" the last one asked, finally speaking up. "She saw us all clear as day when the car went by."

"C'mon!" I whined, slumping against the wall. "I've gone through enough shit lately. Just let me go."

"Well, Lucas?" the one with my purse asked, letting me know the name of the blonde.

"Should we take her to Vincent?" Lucas questioned.

"*No*, we shouldn't take me anywhere," I said. Turning my head, I sent a lingering glance towards my street. I had been so *damn* close.

Lucas laughed at me. "Sugar, we don't know if you're smart enough to keep your mouth shut."

"Totally am," I said, offering a bright smile. "You think I live in this city without knowing a couple of things?"

"Obviously. Luke, she's got a knife and mace."

"Could you please quit going through my stuff?"

"I vote we take her to Vince," the quiet one said.

"Me too."

"That makes it unanimous," Lucas stated, hauling me away from the wall by my arm.

"Can't a girl catch a break?" I muttered under my breath.

"This is your break. If you weren't a girl, we would've killed you already."

"Comforting. Can you at least make sure your friend puts all my stuff back?"

Lucas nodded. "Brandon, shove everything back in her purse and then catch up." The one who had stolen my money rolled his eyes before stooping back down to replace everything inside my bag. When I stumbled over my own two feet, I had to focus on what I was doing so that I wouldn't face-plant onto the concrete.

"An entire night's work down the drain," I grumbled, jutting my lower lip out into a pout. Something in the back of my mind told me it was wrong that I was getting used to this kind of circumstance.

"You're calm," the blonde said, glancing down at me as he continued to drag me along beside him.

"Calm, huh?" I scoffed.

"You're not screaming," the quiet one said, startling me by speaking from directly beside me.

"Used to it, I guess," I replied, shrugging my shoulders.

"That's disturbing."

"Do you see where we are?" I questioned, raising my eyebrows at him.

"Good point." And with that said, we fell into a tense silence. I wanted to ask who Vincent was, but something told me to just keep my mouth shut. For once.

The one named Brandon didn't take long to catch up, but when he did, he held my purse out for me to take. "I kept the knife and mace," he informed me.

"Just don't stab me with my own weapon and we'll be good," I said, hiking my bag up onto my shoulder. I kept the fact that I was going to punch him in the face the first chance I got to myself. Jerking on my arm, I tried to rid myself of Lucas's hold. He glanced down at me. "It's cold," I said, attempting to shake his grip again.

"Run and I'll just catch you," he threatened, his hand releasing.

The minute his touch left me, I wanted to bolt, but they had weapons. Not just knives, but I had seen a gun tucked into the quiet one's waistband. They may have been going easy on me because I was a girl, but I was willing to bet I'd be dead if I tried to run. Instead, I just pulled my jacket tightly around my small frame as I trotted along between Lucas and Brandon.

We passed the alley where I had first seen them, and it took everything in me not to look and see if the fourth man was still there or not. Somehow, I kept my gaze focused forward. Before long, we came to a black SUV. Lucas pulled a set of keys out of his pocket and beeped it unlocked before opening the back door and all but shoving me in.

"Ladies first," he teased when I spun around to glare at him.

Huffing indignantly, I scooted to the far side of the car and placed my bag in my lap. Brandon climbed in beside me. Lucas positioned himself in the driver's seat and the one whose name I didn't know fell into the passenger seat. Lucas cranked the engine over before pulling out onto the street. I internally groaned when I realized he was driving even farther away from my apartment. A familiar song floated through the air, and I leaned my forehead against the heavily tinted window.

The men spoke amongst themselves, and I didn't even bother to try listening in. There wasn't any part of me that wanted to know what they were talking about. All I wanted to do was go home, take a shower, and then go to bed. But of course, apparently even that was too much to ask for. They referred to me a few times, but I pointedly ignored them. Brushing my mocha hair out of my face, I reached back and removed the ponytail holder. Slightly massaging my scalp, I prayed that the headache that was forming would go away now that the pressure was relieved.

"We're here," Lucas called a few minutes later as the SUV rolled to a stop.

"Wonderful," I muttered as he opened my door. He grinned as he held out a hand for me to take. Rolling my eyes, I placed my hand in his and allowed him to help me down from the vehicle, which I realized sat higher from the ground than I expected. When

I looked up, I huffed. I recognized the place. It was no secret that this small warehouse was home to one of the most ruthless gangs in Valarian.

Lovely.

Two

BAD, MEET WORSE

Lucas took hold of my arm again as he began dragging me towards the warehouse from where we had parked in the back. "How you hanging in there, sugar?" he asked, glancing down at me.

"I've come up with fifteen ways to kill you already," I quipped, forcing my voice to come out as sugary sweet as possible.

Brandon and the quiet one erupted into laughter as Lucas shoved through the door to the warehouse. "We're home!" he yelled, hurting my ears.

"Make that sixteen," I said, causing the other two to go into another laughing fit. I really didn't think what I was saying was all that funny.

"Vincent!" Lucas called, towing me past the curious stares of the other people scattered around the open room.

"Back here," came a deep voice from what seemed to be an office space in the far-left corner of the building. Lucas's grip on my arm turned to iron and his face hardened.

"Do you have to act all macho in front of the boss man?" I questioned, wincing when he squeezed my arm even tighter.

"Try not to be as snippy with him as you've been with us," he said, pushing the door of the office open before dragging me inside with him. "He's not as nice."

"Nice?" I asked, crossing my arms over my chest once he released me. "Your friend just stole close to three hundred dollars off me."

"And who do we have here?" the same voice from earlier asked, causing me to pivot to face him.

Dark green eyes snared me in a trap so absolute, I forgot how to breathe for a moment. It was like staring into the deepest depths of a forest; where the trees were so close together that barely any sunlight filtered through. When I regained control of my breathing, my eyes flickered over his face. He had a strong jawline covered in stubble and dark, tousled hair. My eyes almost rolled to the back of my skull. Of course, he was attractive. Devastatingly so. The kind of man designed to bring me to my knees.

Because why not?

"None of your business," I spat before I could help myself. The minute the words were out of my mouth, I winced. I really needed to gain a filter. He arched one dark eyebrow at me as he stood from behind the desk. The fact that he towered over my measly frame was clear, even with at least five feet of space separating us. When he crossed to stand directly in front of me, I had to crane my neck back to meet his gaze.

"Are you sure about that?" he asked. Even though his voice was soft, there was a dark undertone to it that sent a shiver skittering down my spine.

"Yes," I replied, never moving my gaze from his.

"This is Juliette," Lucas said, causing me to whip around to him. "She saw us deal with Roberts."

"Did she now?" the one that could only be Vincent asked.

"Thanks a lot, Lucas," I said, narrowing my eyes into angry slits.

"Don't come up with a seventeenth way to kill me," he teased with a wink before holding his hands up in a gesture of surrender.

"I'm working on an eighteenth."

"Juliette, huh?" Vincent asked, drawing my attention back to him.

"That's right," I replied, pulling at the collar of my jacket as heat seeped into my skin under his scrutiny. My eyes grazed over the black t-shirt that he was wearing. It couldn't cover the tattoo that snaked down his arm, nor the one that was poking out from the V-neck collar. Something in my gut told me he was someone that I should be afraid of. *Very* afraid of. Power damn near radiated off of him. But when I raised my gaze back to his green eyes, I just felt irritated. I wanted to go home. "So can I go now?" I asked, gesturing to the door.

His eyes zeroed in on the tattoo on the back of my hand before raising to meet my gaze. "I think you should have a seat first," he said, pointing to the one of the two armchairs on the opposite side of the desk from where he sat down. He moved with such controlled grace. "You're dismissed, Luke," he added, nodding at the blonde that I had temporarily forgotten was there. I didn't turn my head, but when I heard the door shut, I knew Lucas was gone.

"If you're going to kill me, just get it over with."

"Sit."

I plopped into the chair closest to me. "Happy now?"

"Not particularly," he said, crossing his arms as he leaned back in his chair. "I have to figure out what to do with you."

"I'll tell you the same thing I told blondie," I started, hooking my thumb in the direction Lucas had vanished. "Just let me go home. I'm used to the shit that goes on around here. I'm not going to say anything."

"Blondie?" he asked, arching his eyebrow again.

"Lucas, whatever." I waved him off.

"Well then, in that case, do you know who I am?" His eyes studied me as I crossed my legs and met his steady gaze. Something told me he didn't miss much, and my already flushed skin burned underneath his attention.

"Vince."

The smallest of smiles graced his lips. "And more specifically?"

"Not a clue," I said, shrugging my shoulders.

"I'm the leader of this gang," he informed me. There was a beat of silence as we just stared at each other, neither of us daring to break eye contact.

"Is that supposed to intimidate me or something?" I asked with raised eyebrows, shedding my jacket. I was sweating.

Maybe it was time to admit to myself that, despite what was coming out of my mouth unchecked, I was more afraid of him than I thought.

"It should," he said with a nod. He studied my arms, and I brushed my fingertips over my tattoos as his eyes traced them. "That's... surprising."

"Like I haven't heard that before," I muttered, leaning back as I kicked my feet up to rest on the edge of his desk.

"You could at least attempt respect," he snapped, his calm demeanor crumbling. His eyes darkened as they narrowed on me.

Lowering my feet back to the ground, I held my hands up in a gesture of surrender. "Chill out, Vinnie," I soothed, though the minute the nickname fell from my lips I wanted to take it back.

"Do not call me that," he spat, narrowing his eyes. I met his stare head on, his reaction sparking something inside me.

A grin to rival that of the Cheshire cat curled my lips as I leaned forward. "And why not, *Vinnie?*"

"Because I could kill you in an instant," he said, snapping his fingers to punctuate his sentence. He had leaned forward as well, leaving only a mere foot of space between us over the desk.

"I'm shaking," I taunted, wishing for all I was worth that I would just shut up. The low and dangerous undertone in his voice was back, causing that same shiver to slither down my spine. Something akin to a growl rumbled in the back of his throat as he glared at me. He closed his eyes and sighed through his nose.

"Most people would be on their knees by now," he told me a few moments later, leaning back once again. When his eyes met mine, they were calm and clear.

"Begging for their lives?" I asked, disgust seeping into my tone. "I'll pass."

His eyebrow arched again before he raised a hand and ran it through his already tousled hair. "Tell you what, for right now, I'll let you go."

"Why does it sound like there's a 'but' at the end of that sentence?" I asked, slumping down into the chair.

"*But*," he continued. "If I find out you've said anything to the police about what you've seen, I'll kill you myself."

I winced at the mention of the police. He didn't need to worry about that. "Whatever you say, Vinnie," I replied, cursing myself once I saw the dark look on his face.

"In fact, I'll come with Lucas to take you home."

Resisting the urge to slap myself, I stood and grabbed my jacket before moving towards the exit. Vincent beat me there, holding the door open for me. My eyes narrowed at him, but I made to brush past him. The sheer size of him dwarfed the doorway, and it forced our chests to touch as I scooted past. The heat that surged through my body at the small contact made my breath catch. Every head in the room snapped in our direction as we emerged together, and I had to fight the urge to shrink back into a corner. Instead, I raised my chin and trailed after Vincent as he headed for Lucas.

"So, what's the verdict, sugar?" the blonde asked once we reached him.

"I get to live," I said with a thumbs up.

"Nice ink," a semi-familiar voice said from behind me. Jumping, I whirled around to find none other than Brandon standing there. Before I could even think about what I was doing, I pulled my fist back and let it snap for3ward.

"Shit!" Lucas exclaimed as several of the other men's jaws dropped.

"What the hell?" Brandon yelled, blue eyes blazing as he glared at me.

"That was for dumping my purse and robbing me. So, like I said, rent's due in a few days. Give me my money back or I'll make sure you never have children," I threatened. He grumbled something unintelligible before digging his hands into his pocket and bringing out a handful of cash.

"Here," he grunted, thrusting the money my way. Grinning, I took it and stuffed it back into my purse.

"My knife and mace?" I questioned, faux innocence lacing every word.

"Damn, that really hurt," he muttered, cradling his nose as he reached into his back pocket and pulled out the items. A line of blood trickled down his chin, and I had to smother the twinge of guilt.

"If it helps any, I wasn't thinking. Otherwise, I might've asked nicer," I said before I returned everything to my bag.

"So, do you always randomly punch people?" Lucas asked, drawing my attention away from Brandon.

"I've been mugged and kidnapped all in the same night. I needed to hit something," I defended, shrugging my jacket on.

"Come on," Vincent said, grabbing my arm before beginning to drag me along with him.

"Sorry, Brandon!" I called over my shoulder. He just waved as Vincent shoved me out into the night and slammed the door shut behind us.

"Punching my men isn't scoring you any brownie points," he told me, grabbing my arm again.

"Manhandling me isn't making me want to punch *you* any less."

"You'd know if I was manhandling you," he murmured, lips brushing my ear with his words. Another shiver ran down my spine, though this one wasn't born of fear. Out of the corner of my eye, I saw Lucas wince.

"Just take me home," I said, fighting the unwelcome blush that wanted to tint my cheeks.

"Happily," Vincent replied, straightening up before towing me back to the black SUV. He opened the door, and all but threw me inside when we got there. As I unceremoniously crumpled onto the leather seat, Lucas got in the driver's side while Vincent climbed in the passenger.

"How do you deal with him?" I muttered, my question aimed at Lucas.

However, it was Vincent that answered me, meeting my eyes through the rearview mirror. "Because unless he wants to risk his life, he kind of has to."

"I don't believe I was talking to you," I said, the fake innocence once again present in my voice even though my lip curled. Lucas laughed, but one look at Vincent had him trying to disguise it as a cough.

"Just because I'm being nice to you, doesn't mean I won't change my mind and kill you right now," Vincent warned.

"Calm down," I said, even though fear seized my heart in its grasp. I knew he was serious, but I waved him off all the same. A heavy sigh sounded from the front, and I was guessing it came from Vincent.

"So," Lucas started, causing me to refocus my attention on him. "What's a girl like you doing on this side of town, anyway?"

"A girl like me?" I parroted, raising my eyebrows as I tried to dodge the question.

"You know exactly what I'm talking about," he replied. "A pretty thing like you doesn't normally hang out down here."

"Circumstances don't really favor people by looks." My voice was sharper than I intended, but I didn't bother to apologize for it.

"What's your story, sugar?" he pressed. "You look familiar, now that I think about it."

"Drop it," I deadpanned, crossing my arms over my chest. "After tonight, you're never going to see me again. So, there's no reason to get into it."

Please, let him be wrong about the looking familiar part.

Lucas's brow furrowed, but his attention focused back on the road. Neither of them spoke to me again, so I turned and stared out the window. My life story wasn't any of their business. And my words were true. There was no way I was going to the police, so the chances of us ever running into each other again were slim.

"How far do you live?" Vincent asked, breaking the silence that had descended over the car. Trying not to roll my eyes, I focused on the outside world enough to see that we were passing the alley where I had first spotted the three gang members.

"You can let me out here," I said, already placing my hand on the door handle.

"I don't think so, princess." There was venom dripping off the pet name, and it made me bristle.

"Excuse me?" I asked, my eyebrows raising as I turned to face him.

His eyes narrowed on me in the rearview. A muscle ticked in his jaw. "I told you if you go to the police, I'm coming after you. My life will be easier if I know where you live."

"Leave it to me to get caught up in a bunch of gang shit," I muttered to myself. "Keep going and then turn onto Dixon. I'm the third building on the right."

"Quite the mouth you've got there," Lucas teased, maneuvering the car according to my instructions.

"If you had worked with my boss for as long as I have, you'd understand," I said, a wry grin forming on my face at the thought of Dante. If he found out about this, I'd never hear the end of it.

"Who's your boss?" Vincent asked as the car rolled to a stop in front of my building.

"Oh no," I started, shaking my head as I scooted over so that I could get out on the sidewalk. "You know where I live. I'm not letting you know where I work, too." I had a sneaking suspicion they already knew, even if they hadn't placed it. Tuxedo wasn't under the radar by any means. It was one of the most popular clubs in the city. It surprised me they hadn't figured it out by the uniform alone.

Jumping out of the car, I didn't spare either man a glance as I hastened across the sidewalk to my building. However, I hadn't made it ten steps before a hand on my wrist had me careening back into a hard chest. Glancing up with wide eyes, I took in the ghost of a smile that passed across Vincent's face.

"I'll walk you in," he said, nodding at my building.

My eyes narrowed in suspicion, but I allowed him to follow me all the same. Digging my keys out of my purse took longer than I would have liked, thanks to Brandon messing everything up. Vincent held the door open for me as I crossed into the lobby. Not that it was much of a lobby, more like a small area before the hall leading to the first floor of the apartments. Cursing once I reached the last door on the right, I knelt in front of it to better search through my bag.

"If I ever see Brandon again, I'm going to kill him," I grumbled. Laughter erupted from behind me, and I tilted my face up to lock Vincent with a glare.

"Why do you have it out for Brandon?" he asked.

"He stole my money, and I'm pretty sure he kept some of it, and completely screwed up how I had my bag organized. I can't find my damn keys." I ran a hand through my hair, and then the hand that was still in my bag clamped around cool metal. "Never mind," I said, pulling the keys out before standing. Another soft chuckle escaped him before he stepped closer to me.

"Remember what I told you," he warned, the heat from his body radiating into mine.

"No po-po. Got it," I said, unlocking my door before swinging it open.

"You're a strange girl, princess." He leaned against the wall as I stooped to pick up my purse.

"Don't call me that, Vinnie," I replied, stepping into my apartment before turning back to him. If he wanted to play the nickname game, I could play too. He opened his mouth to reply, but the deep growl from behind me cut him off. "Chill out, Dex," I called, causing the threatening sound to cut off.

"Dex?" Vincent questioned, arching one dark eyebrow as he craned his neck to get a look inside my dark apartment.

"You think I live alone?" I asked, opening my door farther as I whistled through my teeth. The harsh sound split the air, but the rustling from the couch told me all I needed to know.

"A Rottweiler?" he asked, surprise coloring his tone as Dexter stepped out beside me.

"You got it," I said, kneeling to wrap my arms around the best dog anyone could ever ask for. Dexter pulled his lips back and bared his teeth at Vincent until I rested my hand between his ears. Vincent grunted before shoving off the wall.

"Just keep your mouth shut and you won't have to see me again," he reminded me before turning and walking towards the front door of the building.

My eyes trailed down to his backside, and I admired it for a moment before I snapped myself out of it. *Scary gangbanger, Jules,* I told myself, retreating into my apartment and shutting the door before locking it. *Bad idea,* I chanted in my head as I tossed the keys onto the end table.

Dexter whined to get my attention. I sighed and made my way into the small kitchen, tossing my bag onto the couch along the way. Once there, I dug around in the cabinets until I found his food. I poured out a generous amount before dumping it into his bowl. When I set the bowl on the ground, he almost knocked me over in his rush to get to it. Shaking my head at him, I left him to his dinner as I crossed through the living room to my bedroom.

I didn't waste time before shedding my work uniform. The white tank covered with a black vest was constricting, but when you work at a bar called Tuxedo, you deal with it. The next things to go were my heels, followed by the high-waisted shorts, and finally the hose. Before long, I was going to have to talk Dante into something a little more practical. The uniforms were cute, and they definitely helped tips, but they could be smothering on busy nights.

My phone let out a loud beep from the other room. Groaning heavily, I pulled on an oversized t-shirt and trudged back out into the living room. I flopped down onto the couch and dug my phone out of my purse. I blankly stared at the screen for a moment. It had still been on vibrate from work. However, it let out another annoyingly loud beep in my hand, so I unlocked it and opened my messages.

Three texts each from my boss and my best friend. And one from a number I didn't recognize. Dread twisted my stomach as I clicked on the unknown number.

Brandon got your number out of your phone. I'll be checking in, princess.

Another groan slipped past my lips as I let my head fall back against the couch. Hadn't he *just* said I wouldn't have to see him again? The idea to text him back and tell him to leave me alone floated across my mind, but I figured maybe just this once silence would be better. After checking the other messages to find that Dante and Devyn were just worried about me, I assured them both I was fine before checking the time. It was nearing five in the morning.

Wonderful.

Dexter padded his way into the room with me, sitting next to my leg. His warm tawny eyes intently watched me as I slid my phone back into my bag. "Is this your way of telling me to go to bed?" I asked.

He let out a soft bark in response before trotting off to the bedroom. Laughing at my human-like dog, I heaved myself off the couch and followed him. Once I reached my room, I realized Dexter had already made himself comfortable on the bed. Rolling my eyes, I climbed in beside him. Shoving him over, I nestled down into the blankets. He made a grunting sound before scooting closer to me so that his big head was right next to mine.

"Night, Dex," I murmured. The softest of whimpers slipped past his lips as he licked my cheek. Giggling, I reached out and scratched between his ears. The rhythmic sound of his breathing was the last thing I remember before falling asleep.

She was going to be trouble.

Vincent hadn't had a reaction to anyone like he had with Juliette in years. He was used to fear or respect. He didn't run into many people who challenged him. Not anymore, at least. Yet she had. It had stirred something he had assumed was dead.

He drummed his fingers against his knee as they drove through the city. He could feel Lucas's eyes on him, but his second said nothing. Vincent was trying to figure out why he felt like tonight wasn't the first time he had met Juliette. There was a spark in her honey-brown eyes he *knew* he had seen before. It was driving him insane as he sifted through his memories.

Then it clicked.

The first time he had seen those doe eyes looking at him from across the bar, just a few weeks ago. She had stolen his breath then, and tonight had been no different.

"She works at Tuxedo."

"What?" Lucas asked.

"That's why she looks so familiar. That's the bartender uniform from Tuxedo."

Lucas knocked his head against the headrest. "I can't believe I didn't put that together before you did. We're in there all the time."

"Did anyone see you bring her back to the warehouse?"

"Not that I know of," Lucas said, running a hand over his face. "But you never know who has eyes on us anymore. Why?"

"Until we're sure she's safe, and not going to say anything, I want someone watching her."

Lucas didn't turn from the road, but his eyes flicked to his boss. "Are you sure that's necessary?"

"She's an innocent. I don't want her getting hurt because of this. Especially not with her working in that bar, of all places." Tuxedo was neutral ground for all the gangs in Valarian. Dante Simms had made sure of that. If anyone else recognized her and thought she was involved with Vincent or his gang, it would be too easy for them to find her.

Lucas didn't push the subject. He knew the exact reason Vincent was worried someone would target Juliette. The other gangs in Valarian had been looking for a weakness in Vincent for years. They'd jump at any opportunity to strike. Even if Juliette wasn't a part of their world.

"My rounds have me on this side of town tomorrow. I'll keep an eye on her."

Vincent nodded his agreement, and they didn't speak of her again.

THREE

THE BLONDE STALKER

"Good lord, Dex," I whined the next morning when I woke up. "You need a diet." He made a snuffling sound in response before flailing around and getting to his feet. Once he was off the bed, I stretched and got up as well. The slight whining echoing through the apartment let me know he was ready to go out for his walk. "Hold your horses," I muttered, forcing myself into a standing position before searching for pants through the laundry I had yet to put away.

After locating a pair of jean shorts, I shimmied into them and slightly tucked my shirt into the waistband. Better to look like I dressed like a bum on purpose rather than I had just rolled out of bed and left. Which was exactly what I was doing, but why be technical?

Pulling on a pair of socks along with my beat-up converse, I made my way into the bathroom. Dexter was patiently waiting by the door, but I just shook my head at him. Once inside the bathroom, I brushed my teeth before grabbing a ponytail holder and throwing my hair up into a bun. Scrunching my face up at my reflection, I wiped away the eyeliner that was smudged under my brown eyes as I crossed over to Dexter. His tail wagged excitedly when I clipped his leash onto his collar.

"Ready to go?" I asked, smiling when he rose to his feet.

Taking his leash in my hand, I grabbed my purse from the couch. After locating my phone and shoving it into my back pocket, I tossed the bag back to its previous place and picked up my keys from the table behind the door. "C'mon," I told him. His whole butt shook with how hard he wagged his tail as I opened the door.

After locking up behind me, we made our way out into the blaring sunlight. One thing I had learned since having Dexter was that few people wanted to mess with the girl with the Rottweiler. It was nice. Few people were out around this area this early in the day, so the walk to the small city park was peaceful.

My phone vibrated in my pocket, and when I pulled it out, Devyn's face was smiling back at me. Shaking my head, I let Dexter lead me as I answered her call. "Good morning, sunshine!" I chirped.

"So, what happened last night that you couldn't text me back?" she questioned, and I could just imagine the way her pierced eyebrow would raise.

"Nothing," I said. "My phone was just still on vibrate."

"Uh-huh, sure."

"You're not my mother, Dev," I muttered, stopping as Dexter sniffed along the mouth of an alley. "No, no, Dex," I said, gently tugging on his leash.

"Where are you two?" Devyn asked, and I could hear the jingling of her keys in the background.

"Devyn," I whined, knowing that she would come whether or not I wanted her to.

"Don't sass me, bitch," she said. "You're going to the park, right?"

"Right."

"Meet you there." And she hung up without as much as a goodbye.

"Well, let's hurry, Dex," I said, tugging on his leash.

"You know it's not safe for a pretty thing like you to be walking the streets," a familiar voice called. A loud groan escaped me as

I turned around to face the blonde, who was hanging out the window of a black SUV.

"Are you stalking me now?" I questioned, a teasing edge to my voice as I reined Dexter in closer to me.

Lucas laughed as he shook his head at me. "I do rounds every day. I'm actually surprised that we haven't run into each other before."

Dexter moved to stand directly by my side, and he bared his teeth at Lucas. "Calm," I soothed him, reaching down to scratch between his ears. "We probably have," I said, redirecting my attention back to the blonde. "You just never had a reason to notice me before."

"Sugar, I would've noticed you," he informed me, his gaze leisurely running over me from head to toe.

Clearing my throat, I placed a hand on my hip as I met his hazel eyes. "Well, if you're done now, I have somewhere I need to be." And with that, I turned and continued down the sidewalk with Dexter trotting along beside me.

"Where're you going?" he asked, rolling the car forward at a pace that matched mine.

"Park."

"Let me give you a ride."

"I told you, we're not going to be friends, Lucas."

"You also said we'd never see each other again."

"I still haven't ruled out stalking."

His boisterous laughter reached me before he sped the car up, only to pull onto the sidewalk directly in front of me. Dexter went rigid as Lucas swung himself out of the vehicle. When he came closer, Dexter stepped in front of me. He let out a warning bark, a growl rumbling down the leash in my hand.

"I'm not going to hurt her," Lucas said, stooping down until he was at Dexter's level. The dog studied him but didn't move. "Mind helping me out?"

I ran my hand down my face with a huff before tugging against Dexter's lead. "Back down, Dex," I said. He positioned himself at my side in response. "Now, what do you want?" I questioned, meeting Lucas's gaze.

"Let me give you a ride," he repeated.

"I'm not some damsel in distress," I snapped, crossing my arms over my chest. "I'm perfectly capable of getting around on my own."

His shaggy hair fell in front of his eyes as he mirrored my stance. "C'mon, Juliette," he said, the tiniest hint of a whine creeping into his voice. "Just get in the car."

"Why should I?"

"Because I'm asking nicely."

My eyes narrowed, but there was something like worry shining in his hazel eyes. Throwing my hands up in exasperation, I marched around to the passenger side of the SUV and opened the back door for Dexter. He cocked his head when I patted the seat. "Up, Dex," I ordered. He didn't waste another second before he jumped into the car and made himself comfortable. Sighing at him, I shut the door before hauling myself up into the passenger seat. Lucas was already backing the SUV out onto the street when I kicked my feet up onto the dash. "Are you going to make this a habit?" I asked.

"I might," he answered, flashing me a grin as he headed towards the park.

"Please don't," I muttered. "Does this have anything to do with Vincent?" I asked, barely keeping the anger from my voice.

"I'm not sure what you mean," he said, softly laughing. As well as dodging the question.

"Lucas," I pressed. "Did Vincent tell you to watch me?"

He puffed out his cheeks before slouching down in the seat. "How'd you figure it out?"

"I'll kill him," I grumbled, "and you weren't exactly subtle."

"You're threatening a gang leader's life?" Lucas teased, his grin fitting itself back on his face.

"You bet your pretty blonde ass I am."

He burst into a fit of laughter and nearly drove us off the road. "You think I'm pretty?" he choked out. Against my will, my cheeks tinged pink.

I *really* needed to gain a filter between my brain and my mouth.

"Shut up," was my brilliant reply.

"You're not so bad yourself, sugar."

"Nineteen ways to kill you."

He just shook his head at me as he effortlessly pulled into a parking space. "I'd love to see you try."

"I'm not going to say anything," I told him, turning to get out. "So go do your rounds or whatever. I don't need a babysitter."

His eyes followed me as I opened the back door and let Dexter out of the car. "Juliette," he called as I made to turn. When my gaze met his, he jerked his head in a gesture asking me to go to his side of the car. Rolling my eyes, I tugged on Dexter's lead as I rounded the SUV until I was standing at Lucas's window.

He blew out a breath. "Vincent asked me to keep an eye on you, but that had nothing to do with making you ride with me. There was an exchange going on not too far from where I spotted you. The parties involved aren't like us. They don't care about collateral damage. I didn't want you getting caught up in something else."

My shoulders dropped as I felt some of my ire slip. "Thank you."

"Promise me you won't do anything stupid," he said, a pleading tone in his voice. "I'd really hate to watch Vince kill you."

"I promise." Even though his words should have scared me, I just shrugged.

"I'll see you around, Juliette," he said with a grin before he pulled away. I gave a half-hearted wave as I prayed he was wrong. Not that Lucas was necessarily a bad guy, excluding the fact that he had held me at knifepoint, but I just wanted to be done with anything to do with the gang.

"So, who's the hunk?" an annoyingly familiar voice asked from behind me.

"Don't start, Dev," I warned as I turned to her. She crossed her arms over her chest before arching a single eyebrow at me.

Why could everyone do that except me?

"Excuse you?" she questioned. Sighing, I had to divert my attention to her face so that her sunflower-yellow tube top wouldn't blind me. With the sun and the shirt, Devyn's rich brown skin glowed. Only she could pull off such a bold color and look like she just walked off a runway. She brushed her black hair out of her eyes, which were gilded bronze in the sunlight and glaring at me.

Dexter didn't hesitate to pull me towards her, happy to see a familiar face. "It's nothing," I assured her as she switched her attention from me to my dog.

"Didn't look like nothing," she cooed as she scratched Dexter's ears.

Groaning, I motioned for her to follow me to a bench. Once we reached it, I tied Dexter's leash to one of the metal legs before I collapsed onto it. Devyn daintily sat down beside me. "Just don't freak out on me too much, okay?" I muttered, launching into the story before she spoke. Her eyes about bugged out of their sockets when I told her about meeting Vincent.

"Wait," she said, holding up a hand to silence me. "Vincent, as in Vincent *Monroe*?" she squeaked.

"I guess," I replied with a shrug.

She fanned herself with her clutch. "He's come into Tuxedo a few times while I've been working. That is the finest man I've ever laid eyes on."

My eyes rolled of their own accord. Leave it to Devyn. "He's a dick."

"He spared your life. Not someone I'd want to hang around, but he didn't kill you. Guess he couldn't off someone with such a pretty face," she teased, reaching over to pinch my cheek. Glaring at her, I swatted her hand. "So, who's the blonde?" she asked on a laugh.

"Lucas," I answered. "Apparently, Vincent assigned him to make sure I didn't go to the police."

"Those boys obviously don't know you," she muttered, referring to my absolute loathing for the VPD. She and Dante were the only ones that knew why the idea of a cop made my stomach roll.

"Tell me about it," I grumbled. The shudder that I had been suppressing ever since the first mention of the police the night before wracked my frame.

After that, she filled me in the new man in her life. From her description of him, I didn't see him being able to last more than another week. Devyn, bless her heart, had to be the worst person with relationships I'd ever met in my twenty-six years of life. Her list of qualities 'Mr. Right' had to have was so long I doubted she'd ever find someone to fill the role. Until then, she'd work her way through every man she could sink her two-inch talons into. And she'd drag me along with her for however long I was willing.

"You're not even paying attention to me, are you?" she accused, smacking my arm with her clutch.

"Ouch," I mumbled, coming back to the present. "Not really."

"I'm going to start slapping you across the face every time you ignore me," she threatened with narrowed eyes.

"I don't think I'd make a lot of tips if I constantly had black eyes," I teased, repressing my grin when she huffed in irritation. She swung the clutch again, but I was ready and able to bat it away with plenty of time.

"I hate you," she grunted, heaving herself off the bench. "Let's go."

"Why?"

"Dex just did his business, so unless you want to clean it up–"

"To home we go!" I exclaimed, cutting her off as I unwound Dexter's lead from the bench. Devyn burst into a fit of laughter as we hastened away from Dexter's offense. That was the only thing I couldn't stand about having a dog. Cleaning up after him.

Normally I would grin and bear it, but I had left the bags at home like an idiot.

"Where do we want to go?" she mused as we strolled down the familiar streets.

"No clue," I replied with a shrug.

"Shopping?"

"Rent's due. I'm broke."

"Lunch?"

"It's not even noon yet."

"Way to shoot down every idea I have," she huffed, crossing her arms.

"Well, come up with some better ones."

"Sometimes I wonder why we're even friends."

"Because you wouldn't have a job without me," I chirped. I could see the urge to strangle me plain as day on her face and had to suppress the laugh that wanted to escape. The number of times I covered for her ass whenever she called out was astronomical at that point, and she knew it.

"Just because you have Dante wrapped around your pretty little finger, that doesn't mean anything," she said. She was trying to sound serious, even though I could see the smile twitching at the corners of her mouth.

"We have a dysfunctional relationship," I informed her, not wanting to comment on her arguably false statement. Dante saw me like a younger sister. I was someone he had taken under his wing years ago. He had given me a job when I had absolutely nothing else. That job turned into my home and my family. Sure, Dante let me get away with a lot, but he let Devyn get away with even more.

Not that she'd ever admit that.

"You better believe it, bitch," she replied, slinging an arm around my neck.

We bickered back and forth throughout the rest of our journey. The jabs were lighthearted, and I silently thanked whoever was running things that Devyn had crashed into my life. She was the sister I never had, and as much as we wanted to kill each other most of the time, I wouldn't trade her for anything.

"How did that happen?" I asked aloud, my eyebrows drawing together when I realized we were back in front of my building after all our walking.

"Habit." Devyn shrugged before kneeling to Dexter's level. "And this guy probably had something to do with it,' she cooed, wrapping her arms around his sturdy neck. He licked her face, and she squealed.

"Well, I'll see you later, Dev," I said, beginning to walk into the building.

"Get your ass back here," she teased, grabbing my wrist before pulling me into a bone-crushing hug. "You really need to stop attracting the crazies."

"Dev," I choked out, forgetting how strong she was for being so lithe.

"I'm serious," she grumbled, releasing me before taking a step back.

"Yes, ma'am," I agreed with a stiff salute.

"I'm not working tonight. You know Dante doesn't trust us together."

"I wonder why that is," I mused, a wry grin tilting my lips that she didn't hesitate to mirror.

"Later," she dismissed with a wave.

"Be careful," I half-heartedly called, knowing she would be. She flipped me off without even turning around as she crossed the street. "Love you, too," I muttered, pulling Dexter along with me as I made my way back to my apartment.

Four

Unwelcomed Visitors

"You're early," Dante commented as I breezed through the back door.

"Nothing better to do, and Dex likes to make me late," I said, hanging my leather jacket on one of the many pegs by the door to the cooler.

"Ain't that the damn truth?" He let out a small grunt as he moved another case of beer, muscles straining against the white t-shirt with the club's logo he wore.

"Keep being mean and I'll sick him on you."

"That dog loves me, Jules. It won't do much good," he replied, his warm grin lighting up his face.

"Don't remind me." Sometimes I swore the dog loved Dante more than me.

"So," he started, wiping a rag over his sweating forehead. "A little birdy told me you got caught up in some gang shit."

"Devyn?" I deadpanned. He nodded. "Damnit, I'm going to kill her."

"I've told you before if you stick around a little later, I'll drive you–"

"Save it," I said. "I'm alive. That's all that matters."

"Vincent Monroe is not a guy to mess with, Jules."

"Obviously. Why does everyone know who this guy is but me?"

Dante grinned at me, his blindingly white teeth setting off his umber complexion. But there was something in his eyes when he said, "Because you choose to be naïve." And then it disappeared faster than I could put a name to it.

"I do not," I denied with a huff, jumping down from the counter I had perched on. "I just don't care."

"And that's the kind of attitude that could get you killed." His tone caused me to pause.

I knew Dante had been in a gang once. Knew that he had fought tooth and nail to extract himself from that life. If there was ever anyone whose warnings I needed to heed when it came to dealing with Vincent and the gang, it would be my boss's. However, the arch look on his face when his eyes met mine was enough to grate on my nerves.

"Whatever," I ground out, glancing at the clock. "I'm starting early." I didn't wait for a response before pushing through the swinging door and out into the bar.

Tuxedo was one of the busiest clubs one could find in Valarian City, but I loved it. From the flashing neon lights to the overpowering scent of alcohol, it was a second home. Making my way behind the bar, I nudged Anthony with my hip as I passed him. The other bartender on shift cast a playful glance my way as I moved to my side of the u-shaped bar.

"You're early, Jules," he called over the din.

"I just love this place so much, I can't stay away," I replied.

He laughed, rolling his hazel eyes at me before turning back to the crowd of women surrounding him. Anthony was a ladies' man, and he made a lot of money because of it. With his dimpled smile, rugged features, and charming personality, it was easy to see why people just flocked to him. He just screamed 'take home to meet the parent's material.' I almost hated working with him. Mainly because at the end of the night, I felt guilty taking half of the tips when he earned most of them.

"Whiskey neat," a loud voice reached me over the roar of the music.

"One of these days, I'm going to start giving you house whiskey unless you specify," I said without looking up. I made the drink before sliding it down the bar into the awaiting hand.

"Sure, you will."

"Looks like I'm not the only one here early," I observed, trailing after the drink to its owner.

Chris just shrugged before tossing half the drink back. "It was a long day," he grumbled, running a hand through his dirty blonde hair.

"Why do you even come in here?" I asked, gesturing around to the grinding bodies on the dance floor. The man worked for one of the most prestigious law firms in Valarian City. If I had the job he did, the last place I'd go to unwind would be a nightclub fit to burst with debauchery. But Chris had been coming into Tuxedo for close to a year, and he was one of my favorite regulars. Beneath the suit and the aristocratic features, he was also one of the sweetest people I'd ever met.

"Familiar faces, I guess," he answered, nodding at me, and then behind me. Tossing a glance over my shoulder, I spotted Dante emerging from the back room. "And the service is always good, so I can't complain."

"Just keep those generous tips coming and I won't have a reason to either," I teased, moving back to get a beer from the tap for someone farther down the bar.

Chris just shook his head. "You're ridiculous, Jules," he told me, raising his glass in my direction.

"Hey," I said with a shrug as I walked backwards. "You're one of the main people paying my bills."

Mostly, I served regulars and the few people that ventured to my side of the bar. But most people went to Anthony, especially on the slower nights. He just had this aura about him that drew people in. I'd hop in if he needed me, but through the week, he usually had little use for my help. As I stood off to the side conversing with Chris, I didn't notice the new person plop himself down next to the easy-going lawyer.

"Jack and coke," the person ordered, voice a touch louder than necessary.

Something sparked in the back of my mind, but I ignored it as I spun back to our assortment of liquor and snatched the Jack Daniels off the shelf. "Single or double?" I questioned without turning around as I filled the glass with ice.

"Double."

After the drink was mixed, I moved to hand it to the man. When I gave it to him, his hand wrapped around mine, causing my eyes to snap up to meet his.

"Am I ever going to get away from you people?" I groaned.

Brandon grinned before taking the drink from me. "Not any-time soon."

Chris just raised his eyebrows before laying down a fifty and sliding it my way. "See you tomorrow, Jules." He gave me a small wave before making for the exit, leaving me to give the newest nuisance the entirety of my attention.

Brandon's eyes just about popped out of their sockets before I took the money and deposited it into the cash register. Once I had the change in hand, I placed it in the tip bucket. "So how many times have you banged him?" he asked. My cheeks heated, though it was from anger more than embarrassment.

"None," I snapped, glaring at the impish grin on his face. "Now go away."

"You're not going to hit me again?" he teased, a mischievous glint in his eyes.

"I'd get fired if I did that, otherwise I might break your nose," I replied, trying to sound sweet. I doubt it worked. A call from farther down the bar caught my attention, so I left Brandon to take the order. After serving a beer to the poor kid who looked like it was his first time in a bar, I returned to the irritating member of Vincent's gang.

"How'd you learn to punch like that anyway?" he asked as I wiped down the bar.

"Practice. Are you my new tail?" If they were just going to swap out which one of the cronies was monitoring me, my life was going to get a lot more complicated. Dodging Lucas was one thing. Never knowing which one of them I needed to dodge? Entirely different problem.

"Nope," he replied, causing me to whip my head up in time to see him wave me off. "We actually come here all the time. Vince, Luke, and a couple others are back there," he informed me, jerking his thumb behind him. Peering over his shoulder, it wasn't hard to locate Vincent and the rest of them in one of the corner booths. The gang leader in question was already watching me, and when our gazes locked, I narrowed my eyes before refocusing on Brandon. "They sent me up when we saw you working because they have a bet going on about how long it'll take you to deck me again."

At that, a grin broke out across my face before I chuckled. "Well, they're going to be disappointed. I'd rather not lose my job." Hearing my name being called, I twisted to see Anthony was trying to get my attention. Sending Brandon an apologetic look, I moved towards the other bartender. "What's up?"

"Massive order, and they specifically asked for you," he told me, handing me a small scrap of paper covered in his messy scrawl. Glancing up, I saw a familiar head of blonde hair making its way back to the gang's table. Huffing, I shoved a few stray tendrils of hair out of my face.

"I've got it, no problem."

"Thanks, Jules."

I waved him off before setting to work preparing the ten or so drinks. Most were easy, just a bottle or a glass of beer. It was the mixed drinks that took me time to make. But before long, I had every drink on a tray. I just had to make my way past the dance floor and back to where the men sat.

Bracing myself, I held the tray over my head. Thanking my lucky stars that I had been a cocktail waitress and maneuvered the same dance floor hundreds of times, I expertly moved past the grinding bodies. Right before I reached the edge of the dance floor, someone stumbled forward. Gasping, I held the tray higher and spun out of the way just in time. Letting out a deep breath, I finished my walk to the booth.

"If this was your idea, I'm on my twentieth way to kill you," I all but growled at Lucas as I set the tray on the table.

The blonde just grinned at me before holding up his hands in a gesture of surrender. "Wasn't me, sugar."

I flicked my ponytail over my shoulder before crossing my arms. "Just don't make me have to kick you all out," I muttered, spinning to make my way back to the bar.

"You think you could make me leave, princess?"

His voice made my spine lock up. Ever so slowly, I turned back to face him. Vincent's forest green eyes looked borderline black as he studied me. From this distance, I couldn't tell, didn't *want* to tell, if it was because his pupils had blown out as they ran over me, or if it was just a trick of the neon lights.

"Maybe not me," I admitted. "But I'm sure Dante would be more than happy to."

He flashed that heart-stopping grin of his for the briefest of seconds before it was gone. "I'd like to see him try," he all but purred, leaning forward on the table.

"Don't tempt me," I said, leaning forward like he had pulled me into his orbit. My hands wrapped around the edge of the table, knuckles turning white as I braced myself.

Tension sizzled in the air as our gazes locked. Something about Vincent set me on edge. Maybe it was the obvious air of danger that surrounded him, or maybe it was just his irritating arrogance. Either way, he caused my already poor brain-to-mouth filter to become practically nonexistent. Something in me wouldn't let me back down from him. Call it stupid, but my pride begged me to challenge him.

"Juliette!"

Wincing, I broke eye contact to twist my head in order to see Dante sending me a hard look. The reproach on his face made me want to roll my eyes. I pushed off from the table. "I know where to find you if you sneak off without paying," I threw over my shoulder as I walked away.

"I told you–" Dante started, taking my arm once I had stepped back behind the bar.

"Don't start with me," I hissed, wrenching my arm free. His hold had been gentle, and I broke it easily. "I'm not sixteen any-more, Dante. I can take care of myself."

"Don't pull that, Jules," he said. "You know I worry about you."

"Well, don't. I'll be okay," I assured him, laying a hand on his tense arm. He relaxed under my touch before raising a hand and running it over his shaved head.

"Just be careful," he grumbled.

Rolling my eyes, I pushed up on my tiptoes and still had to hop in order to place a light kiss on his cheek. "Yes, sir."

"Get back to work," he ordered, rolling his own eyes before disappearing into the back once again.

"So do you mind filling in your favorite co-worker?" Anthony asked, tossing a towel over his shoulder.

"Nothing to tell."

He pouted. "Now you're lying to my face?"

"Absolutely," I answered with a sly grin.

That was apparently not the right answer, because for the next hour he would pester me to tell him what was going on every time we came within five feet of each other. Finally, around the eightieth time he'd pressed, I couldn't stand it anymore. Glancing around to make sure no one was watching, I picked up a plastic shot glass and chucked it at his head. He let out a girlish yelp before rounding on me.

Blinking, I held my hands up in surrender as he advanced on me. "What's wrong, Jules?" he taunted.

"You have customers, Anthony."

It was all in vain because he just kept getting closer. "Say you're sorry."

"Sorry."

"Nope."

"Anthony, I'm so, so sorry," I apologized, jutting my lower lip out into a pout as the small of my back met the edge of the bar. He stopped his approach as the sound of a woman shouting his name reached us.

"Buy my end of the night shots and we'll be even," he said, pointing at me with all the 'no-nonsense' mom vibes he could muster.

"Deal," I agreed without hesitation. I didn't have a clue what he had been planning to do, but I had no intention of finding out.

After that, the night was pretty much business as usual. My regulars came and went, and every few minutes I found my gaze darting towards Vincent and the gang. They didn't seem to cause any trouble, which I was thankful for. Dante and Devyn had both acted as if they knew Vincent. Which would mean he had to come in often enough for him to have blipped on their radars. That or his reputation preceded him. Either way, I was happy they were behaving themselves.

How had I never noticed them before? At my request, Dante scheduled me almost every night. Wouldn't I have seen them at least once? The question gnawed at the back of my mind, but I couldn't come up with any answer other than I simply hadn't been paying that much attention.

Which was an unsettling realization. What else had I been missing?

FIVE

STUBBORNNESS AT ITS BEST

"Five hundred, seventy-four dollars, and eighty-two cents, bitch," I proudly announced, slapping down the last bill onto the stack.

"Looking at it, I never would have thought this place gets as much traffic as it does," Anthony said, beginning his job of splitting the money between us.

"Me neither," I admitted, leaning back on my hands. When I had first stumbled into the club years prior, I had thought it would be a hole in the wall because of the rather nondescript building that housed it. What I didn't know was that I had happened upon one of the most popular bars in the city. The rest was history.

Tuxedo was officially closed for the night, and there were only a few stragglers and Vincent's gang left in the entire building besides the staff. As I counted the money, I had hoisted myself up to sit cross-legged on the bar. Now all I wanted to do was stretch out on it and go to sleep.

"Jules, how many times do I have to tell you to stay off the bar?" Dante grunted as he came over to us.

"Until you actually mean it," I replied with a winning smile.

He narrowed his eyes at me. "Don't sass me. I could fire your ass at any time."

"But you won't," Anthony pointed out, a smug smile adorning his face when Dante turned to glare at him.

"Who asked you?"

Anthony's response was to hop up on the bar beside me. The look on Dante's face made me bite my lip to hold in my laughter.

"Boys," I chided, clucking my tongue before nudging Dante with my foot. "Behave yourselves."

"Speaking of behaving," Dante started, his gaze sliding over to the back booth where Vincent and the others were still sitting. "Time to get the last of the customers out."

Tilting my head in Vincent's direction, I let out a soft sigh. "I'll do it," I said, swinging my legs around as I hopped down to the floor.

"Jules, we have secur–"

"I'm a big kid now," I sang as I walked backwards, winking in response to the irritated look on his face.

When I reached the table, a drunken Lucas offered me a broad grin. "Where you been all night, sugar?" he whined, his voice coming out slightly slurred.

"Working," I replied, feeling the corners of my mouth twitch as his brow furrowed.

"Now, why would you do that?"

"Because some of us have to be upstanding citizens," I told him, reaching over to tap his forehead.

"Is there something you needed, princess?" Vincent questioned, drawing my attention to him.

"Closing time, boys," I said, clapping my hands together before gesturing around the bar. "It's time to pay and hit the road."

"And if I don't want to?"

My temper sparked, and I barely controlled what I said. "Vincent, please don't be difficult about this," I asked, crossing my arms across my chest as I met his stare head on.

The smallest hint of a smile tilted his lips upward. "Begging now, are we?"

"Go pay your bill, or I will make you," I threatened, a sugary sweetness coating my voice to take the edge off. Dante kept a gun in the back. The look on Vincent's face if I came out with it would be priceless. The thought of it was almost enough to have me heading to the back to grab it.

Almost.

He arched one dark eyebrow at me as our gazes held. "Really now," he mused, leaning back in his seat as the rest of his group let out an audible breath along with me.

"Really," I answered, offering him a smile before standing straight again.

To my utter surprise, a short laugh escaped him as he shook his head. "Here," he said, tossing a pair of hundreds at me. "That ought to cover it and tip."

"I can't take that!" I exclaimed when I found my voice.

"And why not?"

Somehow, during the few moments we had been bickering, they had all stood and were making their way towards the door. As I glanced around, I noticed Vincent was the only person left in the entire bar besides Anthony, Dante, and me.

"Because," I sputtered as I redirected my attention to him and tried to shove the money back into his hands. Tried and failed. "I didn't earn it, and I know for a fact that your bill couldn't have been much more than a hundred."

"Take it, princess."

"I don't need your money," I ground out.

He shook his head, and the smallest smile played at the edges of his mouth. "If you say so," he murmured, turning and walking away from me before I could say anything else.

"Vincent!" I yelled, contemplating the merits of stamping my foot like a child.

His laughter reached me, but I knew he was already gone. Seething with uncalled for anger, I wadded the bills up in my hand before marching over to the cash register.

"So…" Anthony said, trailing off as he saw the look on my face. "That seemed to go well."

His attempt to lighten the mood worked like a charm. I let out a huff before responding with, "Not even close."

"What're you doing?" he asked, inching closer to me. He peeked over my shoulder as I got change for the money Vincent had left.

"Divvying up another tip." He stayed silent until I turned around and handed him his share.

"You don't have to do this, Jules," he muttered, staring down at the cash. "That was your table."

"And I take half of your well-earned tips every night," I reminded him, waving the bills in his face. "Just take it."

"Somebody owes me a shot," he said, changing the subject as he jammed the money into his pocket.

"Dante!" I hollered, my voice echoing around the now empty bar. "Two shots of tequila!"

"Calm down, Jules," he grumbled as he came out of the back with the chilled bottle of Patron in his hand. "I'm one step ahead of you."

Grinning, I laid out enough money for three shots and pushed it in his direction. "This'll cover it."

"Jules–"

"She owes me," Anthony cut in.

Dante just shook his head before taking the money and shoving it into the jar we kept under the bar for our 'employee drinks' tab. Without another word, he grabbed three shot glasses and poured the clear liquid into them until it was nearly spilling over the top. "Bottoms up," he stated, lifting his glass as Anthony and I picked ours up as well.

The glasses made a quiet *clink* as they met, and we all tapped the bar before tossing them back. The familiar burn warmed my body, but a chill ran down my spine despite myself. "God, why do I let you two con me into this?"

"Because you love us," Anthony teased, reaching for the bottle again.

I stopped him with a firm smack on the back of the head. "You're driving."

He cursed before rubbing his neck. "You're right."

"Get going," I told him, patting his shoulder. He grunted before shoving away from the bar and telling us both goodbye.

"That was sweet of you," Dante commented once Anthony had left out the back.

"You're not the only one who looks after the staff," I replied, shrugging as I pocketed half of the money Vincent had left. "I'm taking off too."

"Jules, if you wait twenty minutes, I can drive you."

"The air clears my head and makes it easier for me to sleep," I said, speaking over the end of his sentence as I shoved through the door into the back room.

He was right behind me. "I'll take you."

"Dante," I whined, taking my jacket from the hook before shrugging it on. "I'll call you when I get home, alright?"

He glared at me for a moment, but sighed as he ran a hand over his shaved head. "Fine," he relented. "But I mean as soon as you lock your door behind you."

"Yes, Dad," I teased, jumping up to peck his cheek before I pushed the back door open and maneuvered my way out into the night.

The walk home was blissfully uneventful. No gang activity. It was perfect. The moon was high in the sky, and my heels beat out an even rhythm along the concrete. Tuxedo was in the busy downtown area of the city, which was partially to blame for why so many people came to it. It was also why my walk home totaled close to an hour. Anyone else would have taken Dante's offer, but my words had been true. I slept better after the long walk home, but more to do with exhaustion than the not-so-fresh air.

Plus, I was used to the city streets. The rundown buildings and cracked sidewalks were familiar to me, and no matter how much happened to me on them, I still felt safe. Not safe in the sense that I wouldn't be attacked, we all know how probable that was, but more because they would always be there. The same steady buildings that I had grown up with and explored still towered over me. They still stood tall year after year, impervious to the weight of the world. At least for the moment. The thought steadied my heartbeat until all the tension drained from my body.

Lost in my thoughts, I hadn't even realized I had made it to my building until I stepped inside. Shaking my head, I walked down the hall to my door. The minute I turned the lock, I could hear the soft padding of feet. Once the door was open, Dexter greeted me by all but knocking me to the floor.

"It's good to see you too," I murmured, wrapping my arms around him before moving farther into my apartment. When I had shut and locked behind me, I made a beeline for the kitchen so that I could feed him. Then I performed my nightly ritual of stripping out of the uniform before changing into an oversized t-shirt.

Collapsing onto my bed, I was fast asleep before Dexter even made his way into the room with me.

SIX

RUDE AWAKENINGS

The blaring of my phone from the floor woke me up. Groaning, I sat up and squinted at the bedside clock. I had barely been asleep for an hour. Realization dawned on me, and a string of profanities fell from my mouth as I all but dove for the phone. Pulling it out of my uniform pocket with fumbling hands, I prayed he wouldn't be too angry as I answered the call.

"Hello?"

"I'm going to kill you, Jules!" Dante exploded, the volume of his voice hurting my ears. "I told you to call me. I've been worried sick."

"I fell asleep," I admitted, biting my lip as Dexter poked his head over the edge of the bed to stare at me where I sat on the floor.

He let a sigh of relief slip free, and I could practically see him running his hand down his face. "I thought they got you again," he mumbled, and I didn't have to ask to know that he was talking about Vincent.

"He said he wouldn't hurt me," I reminded him, hoisting myself up just to fall onto the bed beside Dexter.

"And you trust him?"

"Don't really have a choice in the matter, do I?" I snapped, feeling bad for it as soon as the words left my mouth.

"Just be careful, Jules."

"I will. Can I go back to sleep now?"

His soft chuckle sounded through the phone. "Goodnight, Juliette."

"Night, Dante," I murmured, ending the call before pitching the phone back onto the floor. "Stupid, overprotective boss," I grunted. Dexter sniffed at my hair before licking my cheek. Shoving his face away from mine, I turned so I could press my back against his warm body. Before long, I was out again.

The next time I woke up, it was to the pounding on my door. After glancing at the clock and deciding that nine was a decent time to get up, I groaned and heaved myself out of bed. As I trudged out into the living room, Dexter was trotting right along beside me. While I probably looked like death warmed over, he was all bright eyed and bushy tailed.

Lucky dog.

Reaching up on my tiptoes to look through the peephole, another groan slipped through my lips. "I'm going to kill you," I threatened Devyn as I swung the door open.

She just grinned at me. "It's good to see you too, Jules," she greeted, shouldering her way past me on her way to the kitchen. The bag she placed on the counter, along with the coffee she set beside it, immediately lifted my spirits.

"You shouldn't have," I teased, picking up the cappuccino before taking a hesitant sip. Once I was sure that I wouldn't burn my taste buds off, I took a longer drink.

"I needed an excuse to come yell at you."

"About?" I asked with a wince, already knowing where this was going.

"You need to let Dante give you a ride home." Her voice was hard as granite as she crossed her arms over her chest.

"I'm not a child," I grumbled, digging into the bag to get the jelly doughnut that was calling my name.

"It doesn't matter, Jules," she all but yelled, flinging her arms up in exasperation. "You shouldn't be walking home that late."

"You do it."

She glared at me. "I also only live like three blocks away from the bar. Not on the other side of the city."

"Why don't you and Dante just get together already? Since you like gossiping so much, I think it'd be a grand match."

"Don't change the subject on me," she said, as the faintest tinge of red blossomed across her cheeks.

"I'm just curious," I returned, trying to fight the smile that wanted to overcome my face.

"Drop it," she ordered, closing her eyes before sighing through her nose. "You need to take better care of yourself."

"I'm saving up my money for a gun," I said, shoving the rest of the doughnut into my mouth. She gaped at me for a moment, but I think it was more to do with my eating habits than what I had said.

"How you stay skinny, I'll never understand," she grumbled, rolling her eyes before reaching her hand into the bag and pulling out her own doughnut.

"Well, if that's not the pot calling the kettle black," I teased, moving to sit at my small two-seater table.

"What time did you get home last night?"

"Like four," I grunted. "And then Dante called me an hour later and woke me up."

"Should have let him–"

"Devyn," I warned.

She muttered something under her breath, and I had a feeling it was something I didn't want to hear. "I'm just trying to look out for you," she murmured, peeking up at me through her long lashes.

"Don't pull a puppy-dog face," I groaned. "I can't take the puppy-dog face."

"You mean this?" she questioned, jutting her lower lip out.

"Stop!" I exclaimed, reaching across the table to smack her arm.

She laughed as Dexter ambled his way into the room with us. Sending me one last teasing smile, she crouched down to his level and started cooing to him. Rolling my eyes, I scooted past her and made my way back to my room. Knowing Devyn, she would want to go out at some point soon. Might as well get dressed to save some time. Once I was in the confines of my bedroom, I switched out my oversized t-shirt for a pair of dark wash jeans, an off-shoulder black top, and my converse. Once again, I threw my hair up into a bun before heading back to Devyn.

"You read my mind," she said as I emerged.

"As usual."

Dexter's ears perked up when he heard me pick up his leash. Devyn waited in the hall as I took him out to do his business and stretch his legs a bit since I had been an idiot and not done it the night before. He went right to the couch and made himself comfortable when I let him back into the apartment. I stuffed my keys and phone into my pocket, since I didn't feel like lugging my purse around with me. Devyn's foot tapped softly as she waited for me to lock the door behind us, and then we made the short trek down the hall and out into the sunshine.

"So, plans?" she asked.

"None."

"Loser."

"Love you, too."

For a while we walked in silence, but we quickly made our normal rounds to our favorite shops. We took our time, just enjoying the day together. But before long, we each had bought a couple of things and our stomachs started making themselves known. Devyn's made it sound like she hadn't eaten in a month, and I had to repress a snicker as it rumbled again. We hauled our bags with us as we headed to Tuxedo to bum some food off Dante.

Of course, it seemed like I couldn't go anywhere since getting kidnapped without seeing Vincent or his gang. And true to form, when we were a couple blocks away from the bar, a black SUV rolled past us, came to an abrupt stop, and then backed up until it was level with us. The tinted window rolled down to reveal a grinning Brandon, with Lucas riding shotgun.

"Hey, sugar," Lucas called, waving at us.

"Friends of yours?" Devyn asked.

"Stalkers," I muttered, grabbing her hand and picking up our pace.

"Should I be worried about you?" she asked as we burst through the back doors of Tuxedo.

"They're harmless unless you witness something you shouldn't," I told her, bending at the waist to brace my hands against my knees. I was out of shape.

Unfortunately, even our haven of a workplace couldn't save us from Lucas and Brandon. The back door burst open behind me, sending me flying face first into the floor.

"Oh, Jules!" Devyn exclaimed. The only response I could manage was a pain-filled groan.

"Shit," one of the boys said before I felt strong hands lift me. Spinning me around, I found it was Brandon who had helped me up. He cupped my face, thumbs running along my cheekbones and over the bridge of my nose. "Well, on the bright side, nothing's broken."

"Bright side my ass," Devyn growled, slapping him without a second of hesitation. "You threw her onto the floor!"

Brandon looked only mildly shocked at the abuse, but he barely even glanced at her before returning his attention to me. He applied light pressure against my cheeks, and I flinched when he pressed the spot directly below my left eye.

"Tender?" he asked, voice soft. I nodded. "It'll probably bruise a little, but nothing major."

"You sound like you know what you're talking about," I said, ignoring Devyn as she lit into Lucas about the proper way to treat a woman. I just prayed she wouldn't start beating him with her clutch.

"I take care of most injuries with the guys. Used to want to be a doctor," he told me, letting his hands hover around my face before they dropped to his sides. "Consider that payback for the punch."

Devyn whipped around to face us at that. "Punch?"

"I nearly broke his nose for trying to steal my money the other night," I told her, mock punching Brandon in the arm for good measure. Devyn opened her mouth to say something, but I cut her off. "Now, is there something you two wanted?"

"No, this time I'm actually just stalking you," Lucas piped up, grinning at me.

"Hey girls, I didn't know you were–" Dante's voice cut off as he came into the room. Turning to face him, I saw him scrutinizing the two strange men in his kitchen. To their credit, they had the wherewithal to look sheepish. "Jules?" he asked, raising an eyebrow at me.

"Why do you automatically assume this was my fault?" I fired back, outraged by his assumption, even though it was right.

"I recognize that one from last night," he said, pointing at Brandon.

"*They* were just leaving," I said, huffing as I pointed to the door. "Bye boys."

Lucas was going to protest. I could see it in his eyes, but Brandon grabbed his arm and pulled him towards the exit. "Make sure to put some ice on that eye, Jules," he told me with a wink before dragging the blonde out the door with him.

Cursing Brandon to the fieriest pits of Hell, I faced Dante. His nostrils flared in anger, and I winced at the sight.

"*Why* do you need to put ice on your eye, Jules?" His tone was much too measured for my liking.

"Dumbass hit her with the door and she fell on her face," Devyn muttered, arms crossed.

"An accident?"

"An accident," I verified. "They wouldn't hurt me."

"And just *what* makes you say that?" he asked, stepping toe to toe with me so that I could feel the worry-fueled anger rolling off him.

"Gut feeling."

His eye twitched.

"You're forgetting that I lived that life. I know these men. I know what they do. But I'm not going to keep going around this with you. I know you're going to go off and get yourself into trouble, no matter what I say. You're like a fucking magnet for it," he seethed, the volume of his voice rising slightly the more he talked. At that point, I was trying to keep a level head. Dante was only worried about me, but that didn't give him any reason to talk to me like I was an errant child.

"Dante, I'm a grown woman–"

"And that means you can take on a Vincent Monroe, of all people?" he spat, cutting me off.

I took a deep breath, trying not to blow up at him like I wanted to. Now was not the best time to reason with him. It would have been the equivalent of trying to explain to a bear why you woke them from hibernation a month early.

"Are you done yet?" I asked instead, keeping my tone light even though I'm sure my glare could've cut glass.

His chocolate eyes blazed, but he begrudgingly nodding. "For now."

"Can we have food now, you hormonal mother hen?" Devyn asked, breaking the tension that had built in the room in a way that only she could.

"Help yourselves. Make sure to be on time tonight. Jules, you're working with Anthony again." Then, with a last lingering look that I was surprised he didn't pair with a shaking finger, he went back out into the club.

"You were absolutely no help," I told Devyn. The minute the words were out of my mouth, I knew they probably weren't the smartest thing to say.

Her eyes narrowed into slits. "If you're such a *grown woman,* you shouldn't need my help."

Groaning, I let my head fall into my hands. "Not you too."

"The blonde one admitted to stalking you."

"He was kidding!" I said, flailing my arms out. I probably looked like I was trying to fly.

"Are you sure about that?"

"Devyn."

"We just want you to look after yourself."

"You saw how worried Brandon was when he hit me with the door. They don't want to hurt me. Just let me deal with my own damn problem, okay?" I asked her, hoping the pleading in my voice would get through to her.

She pursed her lips at me. "Fine, but don't think I won't mace those dumbasses into next week if they ever hurt you."

"You could probably maul them with those claws of yours," I grumbled.

"You're just jealous," she said, beaming as she waved her canary yellow talons in my face.

"Totally," I replied, sarcasm lacing the word.

She rolled her eyes at me, and then we searched for food. It didn't take us long to start a batch of wings to share. In the back of my mind, I wondered how often I was going to run into the boys. Also, I thought about whether Lucas was kidding about the stalking thing. I was almost positive that he was, but then again, I didn't know him all that well. Hopefully, it would stay that way.

SEVEN

SNEAKS AND WEASELS

"I'll be fine," I told Devyn, all but shoving her out my front door.

"But–"

"Leave!" Dexter growled at the snap in my tone.

"I'm going, I'm going. We work together tomorrow night, by the way," she said before flouncing out of the apartment.

I sagged against the door once I shut it. Devyn had insisted that we walk around more after lunch. We had, but that left me with only an hour to get ready for work and make it there in time. Which wasn't possible. Shifting myself into high gear, I ran into my bedroom and changed into my uniform. Leaving my hair in its bun, I moved into the bathroom and swiped some mascara over my lashes and lined my eyes. Glancing in the mirror, I decided it would have to do.

Purse in hand, I hollered a goodbye to Dexter and locked my door before barreling for the door to the street. Once I hit the pavement, I slowed down a little because running in heels, let alone heels on concrete, was never the best idea for me. I needed to just start leaving the damn heels at work and wearing my converse back and forth. Hastening along at a brisk pace, I made my way through the streets in the dimming light.

Damn Devyn and her constantly making me lose track of time. I despised being late. And somehow, I always managed it when Devyn was involved. Thank the heavens Dante knew exactly how she was. Hopefully, even after our little spat earlier in the day, he'd let it slide since it hadn't happened in a while. But I wasn't holding my breath. He could be a vindictive little shit sometimes.

The sound of an engine behind me caught my attention. Stopping, I waited for the familiar SUV to roll to a stop beside me. For the first time, it elated me to see it.

"Lucas, you couldn't possibly have better timing!" I exclaimed as the heavily tinted window rolled down when I reached the car.

Forest green eyes met mine once the window was out of the way. My smile dissolved in an instant. My mouth fell open and the slightest of smiles tilted Vincent's lips.

"Happy to see me, princess?" he asked.

"I thought you were Lucas."

"Obviously."

"What're you doing here?"

"I'm on my way to Tuxedo," he said before his eyes ran over my clothes. Something lit in his eyes, and I had to smother the desire to preen under his attention. "Looks like you are too."

Scary gangbanger, Jules, I reminded myself again.

Glancing behind him and farther back in the car, I realized it was empty. "You're alone?"

"Business meeting. I'm the only one they need to talk to this late in the game."

"Not in my bar," I said, narrowing my eyes at him.

"Nothing too bad," he replied, that ghost of a smile flashing across his face again. There was a twinkle in his eyes, like he knew something I didn't. "C'mon, get in."

"I'll walk." The words were out before I could even consider them. I would take being late for work over being alone in a car with Vincent any day.

"We're going to the same place. I'm just trying to save you a long ass walk."

Biting my lip, I glanced down the near empty street. "I–"

"Juliette," he snapped, cutting me off before I could even offer an excuse. "Get in the damn car or I will get out and put you in it myself." That same dark authority that always coated his words made me round the car and climb into the passenger's seat. Rolling his eyes, Vincent shifted the car into drive and maneuvered back out onto the road. Soft music that I couldn't really discern floated through the car. It sounded like a piano. Before I could ask him what it was, he spoke. "Was that so hard?"

"Considerably," I said, mirroring the snip in his tone.

"You're quite stubborn. Did you know that?"

"No, I hadn't noticed."

"Just like that," he muttered, driving through the streets with such ease I suspected he had them memorized.

"Not used to being challenged?" I mocked.

I was feeling pretty good about holding my own against him until he went silent. After two beats of it, the gears in my mind went into overdrive. Was that the wrong thing to say? Had I finally pushed too far? Was he going to drop me in the middle of the river and watch me drown? Would he smile while he did it? Several minutes passed with more and more ridiculous questions circling through my skull. And still he had said nothing. Biting my lip, I watched as the worn-down buildings of my neighborhood transitioned to the immaculate high-rises of downtown.

"Not at all," he finally murmured, just when my internal freak out was nearing its peak. Nodding, I kept my mouth shut. Testing my limits with him anymore than I already had was not high on my list of things to accomplish for the day.

The rest of the ride was quiet. When he reached the club, he pulled around to the back and parked in the spot closest to the staff entrance. I muttered a hasty thank you and escaped from the car. Hoisting my bag up onto my shoulder, I ignored the sound of his door shutting. However, I wasn't able to ignore the hand on my arm a few seconds later. Vincent eased me to a stop before turning me around to face him.

"What?" I rasped, the tiniest amount of fear seizing my heart.

"This has been bothering me the whole ride," he muttered. Furrowing my brow, I blinked up at him. He seemed to hesitate before raising a hand to my face. Before I even knew what was happening, I flinched.

He froze.

"I think that's the first sign of fear I've seen from you."

"I don't trust you," I retorted, finding the side of me that tended to get me into trouble.

"And you shouldn't, but you can believe me when I say I'm not going to hurt you. I just want to know who already has," he said, voice low as his long fingers grasped my chin. He tilted my face up to his before brushing his fingertips beneath my eye.

It'll probably bruise a little. Brandon's words from earlier floated through my mind.

Shit.

"It was Brandon," I told him, though I wasn't really aware of what I was saying. How was I supposed to work with a black eye?

"Brandon hit you?"

The deadly calm in his voice caused me to whip my head up to look at him. Quiet fury flashed across his features, and his forest eyes were blazing. His hand that was still hovering by my cheek fell to his side before clenching into a fist.

Double shit.

"No!" I exclaimed. "No, it was an accident," I rushed out, trying to backtrack over my words. I launched into the story of running into Lucas and Brandon earlier in the day. I didn't even want to know what Vincent would have done to Brandon if he thought he intentionally hurt me.

But then again, why would he care? Hadn't he threatened to kill me just days ago?

Visibly relaxing, he ran a hand through his already tousled hair. "I don't condone violence against innocents," he said.

"So, we're just going to ignore the fact that I was *innocent* when the boys hauled me halfway across the city the other night?"

"The information you held posed a threat."

My eyes about rolled to the back of my skull. *Men.*

"Well, I'm fine. I can't believe I didn't realize it had bruised."

"It's barely noticeable, princess. I wouldn't worry about it, especially not with how dimly lit the club is."

My eyes cut to his. Then why had *he* noticed it?

"Would you quit with the princess crap, Vinnie?" I huffed, deciding not to question it.

"There she is," he murmured, the barest hint of a smile tugged at his lips. I would be lying if I said it didn't make my heart take a stutter step.

"Juliette!" a familiar voice called. I flinched for the second time in the past ten minutes.

"Coming, Dante!" I hollered back, not daring to turn around and see the scathing look my boss was, without a doubt, giving me.

"Do you need a ride home too?" Vincent asked me.

"I can walk."

"I'll be waiting for you here at close."

"Vincent," I said, my voice strained when I met his eyes. "You are the only person I should worry about in this city. You're the one threatening my life."

"Don't argue with me. I'll bind and gag you if I have to."

Despite my best attempts at trying to fight it back, a blush blossomed across my cheeks. It took everything in me to keep my mind out of the gutter. Especially when, judging by the look on his face, I could tell he had only phrased it like that to get a reaction out of me.

Asshole.

"Fine. You can give me a ride home."

Rolling his eyes, he turned me around so that I could see the pinched look on Dante's face. He looked like he had eaten something sour, with the way his mouth and nose were screwed up.

"I'll be here," Vincent breathed in my ear, causing an increasingly familiar shiver to wrack my frame.

Shaking my head, I made my way closer to my boss. With each step I took towards Dante, a little more of the tension in his face fell away. When I was within arm's length, he grabbed my wrist and pulled me into a bone-crushing hug.

"Could you try not to give me a heart attack?" he grumbled in my ear.

"I'm fine."

"Get your ass in there and start working before you're late," he said, releasing me. Trying not to roll my eyes at him, I pulled away and nodded. When I turned to head inside, I groaned. It was as if Vincent was purposely trying to give Dante a coronary. He was waiting for me by the door, holding it for me.

"What're you doing?" I hissed as I brushed past him.

"Going inside," he replied.

"You're not allowed back here," I told him, gritting my teeth together. I slammed my purse down with more force than necessary and pulled up my time clock on the computer.

"Oh, well." And with that said, he breezed through the door and out into the club.

I was cursing him under my breath when Anthony came into the kitchen.

"What was he doing back here?" he asked, eyeing the door Vincent had just vanished through.

"Please don't ask," I told him, shoving my purse to the ground, hoping to vent a little of my frustration. Thankfully, there was nothing breakable in it.

He held his hands up in a gesture of surrender as he caught me up on what had been happening for the past few hours. In the grand scheme of things, it was nothing outside of the usual. But I knew how much Anthony hated being in the bar on his own until I got there, so I let him ramble on. "And then she threw the olive at my face!"

"Well, she is a regular, Anthony. You should know she hates olives."

"She's one of *your* regulars," he accused as we emerged back out into the club.

"So sorry," I teased, taking up my position at one end of the bar. Anthony stuck his tongue out at me before going around and filling all the orders that had come in while he had been in the back with me.

As I worked, I couldn't stop my eyes from searching for Vincent. It wasn't my fault. How was I supposed to *not* worry about the fact that he was conducting business, more than likely *illegal* business, in my place of work? As stupid as it sounded, I felt responsible for Vincent if he was here. If any of them were here. Not as if I could make any of them listen to a damn word I said, but still. It didn't take too long to find him. He was in the same booth he had occupied the night before.

The man that sat with him looked like the definition of bad news. Tattoos outnumbering Vincent's and mine combined spiraled up his throat, and there were even a few on his cheek. He had slicked his silver-streaked, black hair back to the point of it looking greasy. His face was like a weasel's. Long nose, pinched mouth, beady eyes that looked shrewd even from where I was standing. He was older, maybe late forties to early fifties. Physical appearance aside, he screamed old money. His suit had to be tailored with the way it fit his slim frame, and the watch on his wrist looked expensive. It wouldn't surprise me to if it was real gold.

What did I expect, though?

As if sensing my gaze, Vincent's eyes shifted to scan the bar until they found mine. He arched an eyebrow at me, just barely, only enough to let me know he had caught me. Scowling, I glared at him for a moment before his lips twitched and he returned his attention to Weasel Face.

"Jules?" Anthony asked, right next to my ear.

"Shit," I gasped out, dropping the glass I had been drying. It shattered into pieces beneath me. "Double shit," I muttered.

"Oops."

I turned my glare on the bartender behind me. "I'm going to kill you," I threatened half-heartedly, heading to the kitchen to grab the broom and dustpan.

Anthony held his hands out for it when I returned. "It was my fault. I got it."

"Thank you." He only sighed in response, but gave me a nod all the same. Trying to help, I headed to his end of the bar to pick up some of his orders while he cleaned up. Some customers looked disappointed that he was busy, and they were borderline nasty with me because of it. So, when I returned to my side of the bar when Anthony finished, I was not in the best of moods.

"Bad day?" Chris asked when he plopped down, as he did every night. Having one of my own regulars made me smile. I poured his whiskey and handed him the glass.

"You have no idea," I replied, slumping against the counter in front of him.

He returned my grin as he sipped his drink before loosening his tie. "I feel your pain."

"I still don't understand why you come in here," I told him as I scooted down a few seats to take another order.

"How many times am I going to have to tell you I come in to see you?" he replied, rolling his eyes at me.

"I guess until it registers."

"I guess I just need to bite the bullet and ask you to go out with me for you to take the hint. Huh, Jules?"

"What?" I asked, blinking at him.

His smile lit up his face as he chuckled. "You really think I've been coming in here, specifically to *you* lately, for no reason?"

"Err..." I trailed off. I was a fish out of water. "Yes." I guess now that he mentioned it, he had been one of Dante's regulars at the beginning. But then I had to cover a shift one day and Chris and I just hit it off. He was so easy-going, so easy to talk to. It had been simple to fall into a comfortable rhythm with him.

"Well, now you know."

"Chris, look–"

"Hey, princess," a smooth voice interjected.

"Yes, Vinnie?" I replied, stepping down the bar to position myself in front of him instead of Chris. For once, I was relieved to talk to the nuisance.

His eyes narrowed the smallest fraction of an inch. "Can I get two glasses of Johnnie Blue on the rocks?"

"You're asking?" I teased with arched brows. The retort that I could tell was just on the tip of his tongue was lost as I turned my back on him to pour the scotch. "Here you go," I said, my voice filled with faux exuberance when I slid the glasses in front of him.

"Thank you," he said through a plastered-on smile. He slid three fifty-dollar bills my way, and I didn't have time to call him back before he was gone. Why did he insist on over-tipping me? Seething, I changed out the money and put the sixty dollars extra directly into my pocket. If he was true to his word and took me home that night, I would leave it in the car when I got out.

"You know him?" Chris asked, his gaze following Vincent back to his corner booth with Weasel Face.

"Most of the time I wish I didn't," I told him, shaking my head before I wiped down the bar. I was just looking for a reason not to get too close to Chris for fear he would bring the previous conversation back up.

The lawyer shrugged and slid a fifty across the bar. "As always, it was a pleasure, Jules." He tipped an imaginary hat at me. "I'll see you tomorrow."

Depositing the bill he had given me into the register, I stuck the rest in the tip bucket. That had been unexpected, but I was hoping he would never mention again it. I adored Chris as a regular, but that was all I could ever see him as. A friend. Plus, it wasn't like I could have any kind of relationship at that moment in time. How was I supposed to explain the gang members that followed me around on a daily basis?

Something told me that piece of information would not sit well with any man. Let alone one of the top lawyers in the city. The thought alone made me choke on a laugh.

The rest of the night quickly passed. Weasel Face only stayed with Vincent for about another hour after the drinks. I kept track. Then, throughout the night, I could feel a particular set of eyes on me, but I studiously ignored him. I had a plan. Hopefully, I could figure out a way to walk home as well.

So, as people filtered out of the bar, I slipped into the kitchen. "I'll be right back to help clean up!" I called to Dante as I darted out the back door.

The lot was empty save for Dante's truck and the black SUV I knew belonged to Vincent. Glancing around, I pulled the three twenties out of my pocket and made my way to the driver's side. Gently picking up the windshield wiper, I stuck the bills underneath it. Satisfied they wouldn't go anywhere unless purposefully removed, I smiled and turned to head back into the bar.

And ran smack into somebody's chest.

"*What* do you think you're doing?" Vincent asked, his voice not sounding amused in the slightest.

I rubbed my throbbing nose. "Nothing," I attempted, batting my eyelashes at him.

The effort was pointless. "What did you just stick under my wiper blade?"

"Nothing." He grunted in response and reached around me. The heat of his body soaked into mine, and I had to lean away from him in order to resist the urge to do the exact opposite. And why did he have to smell so good?

"This is nothing?" he questioned, holding the twenties up for my inspection.

"That's exactly what that is."

"Stop playing dumb, princess."

"Stop over-tipping me," I said with a shrug.

He shook his head before folding the bills and sliding them into his back pocket. "Fine. Now I suggest you go finish up your shift so I can take you home."

"Stop trying to boss me around," I grumbled, shouldering my way past him.

He didn't make another comment as I slipped back into the kitchen. Muttering curses under my breath the whole time, I returned to my place behind the bar and helped Anthony wipe it down. Before too long, I was counting the money out as I did every night. But trying to plan a way to dodge the car ride was still distracting me. I would much rather walk than be stuck in the car with Vincent again. He had pushed me to my limits of dealing with him for the night.

"How'd we do?" Anthony asked, bringing me back to the task at hand.

"Four eighty-eight even," I told him, sliding his half over to him.

"Shots?" he asked, pocketing the money.

"None for me tonight," I told him, sliding him the money to cover his. "I've got a massive headache. I just want to go home."

"You okay, Jules?" he asked, coming over to place his hands on my shoulders. "Something's had you wound up all night."

Taking a deep breath, I tried to will the tension to drain out of my body. "It's just been a rough day," I told him with a grin, taking my half of the night's tips. "Now, if you'll excuse me." We said goodnight as I made my way to the back door, stopping only long enough to grab my purse. Hollering out a goodbye to Dante, I braced myself and stepped outside.

Part of me had hoped he would've tired of waiting.

Raising his gaze to meet mine, Vincent pushed off from where he had been leaning against the passenger side door of the SUV. He wordlessly opened the door for me and held it until I had hoisted myself up into the seat. Once he shut the door and was rounding the car, I tossed my purse onto the floorboard and buckled my seatbelt. Exhaustion hit me like a wave, and I leaned my forehead against the window. The car purred to life beneath me as Vincent cranked the engine over. He pulled out onto the road and began the drive to my apartment. Once again, it struck me how easily he maneuvered the streets, but I didn't feel the need to comment on it. My guess was that he had been on these streets much longer than I had. It didn't take all that long before we reached my place. Vincent pulled the car to a stop at the curb, and I took a moment before unhooking my seat belt.

"Thank you," I said, taking hold of the door handle.

"Are you okay, princess?" he asked, his voice startling me.

"I'm fine," I replied. He didn't look convinced. Sighing, I heaved myself out of the car. "Just stressed and tired, that's all." With that, I shut the door and turned towards my building.

The whirring noise behind me caught my attention before Vincent called out to me, "Forgetting something?"

When I turned back to him, I saw he had my purse in his hands. Mentally face-palming, I walked back to the car and reached through the window to get it. "Thanks, Vincent," I muttered, taking it from him.

"Don't mention it," he replied. "Just go get some sleep. You look like hell."

"Well, thanks," I said as the window rolled up, even though I knew he couldn't hear me. Rolling my eyes, I headed into my building. When I was in front of my door, I reached into my bag for my keys. What met my hand wasn't the usual cool metal of my keys. Instead, it felt like crumpled paper. My brows pinched together as I pulled them out.

Three twenty-dollar bills floated to the ground.

I was going to kill him.

EIGHT

A NEW VENTURE

"Fat ass," I grumbled as I woke up, shoving Dexter off me. He made an indignant snuffling noise before crawling to the edge of the bed. Glaring at him, I rolled over and eyed the alarm clock sitting on my nightstand. It was ten on the dot. How did that even happen?

Groaning, I threw my blankets off and immediately regretted it. The cold air washed over me and caused a series of shivers to skitter down my spine. Apparently, I had forgotten to turn the air conditioning off the night before. Dexter's eyes followed me as I left the bedroom. Once in the hallway, I switched off the air and enjoyed the silence left in the apartment after the fan quit running. A small smile tugged at my lips as I headed to the kitchen. As soon as the sound of dog food hitting plastic rang through the still air, I heard a *thump* come from the bedroom that signaled Dexter getting up. He trotted into the kitchen only a few seconds later, and I started a pot of coffee as he ate.

Once the coffee maker bubbled, I filled Dexter's water bowl as well. He glanced up at me for a split second before returning to scarfing down his food. I couldn't help but laugh at him; he was acting as if he had never eaten. Which was nothing new, but it made me giggle every time. Shaking my head at him, I left the coffee to brew and crossed through the living room back into my bedroom. I rummaged through my dresser until I found a pair of destroyed jeans and a faded band t-shirt, and then I tossed them onto the bed along with my undergarments. Satisfied with my outfit for the day, I headed to the bathroom.

I let the water warm up as I stripped out of my t-shirt and underwear. After I tossed them into the hamper that sat in the corner of the room, I stepped into the tub and pulled the tab for the shower. The hot water hit me and caused a content sigh to slip past my lips. The heat eased the tension that had built up in my shoulders over the past few days and I couldn't help but to revel in the feeling for a just a moment. Before I was ready, I felt the slight temperature change in the water that signaled the iciness that would hit me within the next few minutes. As fast as I could, I washed my hair and my body. As I let the conditioner sit in my hair, I debated whether to shave my legs. Deciding I might as well get it over with, I grabbed my cream and razor.

I ended up having to rinse my hair in cold water, but at least I was fully awake when I stepped out. I wrapped my hair in a towel and one around my body. When I emerged back out into the living room, the rich smell of fresh coffee enveloped me. Another smile fitted itself onto my face as I hurried into my room to get dressed. It took me four tries to get my jeans on because my foot kept going through the hole in the thigh instead of the one it was supposed to. Huffing, I sat down on my bed to fight with the wretched things that I loved so much, but my entire body went rigid when I heard a knock on my door. It wasn't a dainty knock, so I knew it wasn't Devyn. Not that she didn't pound on my door occasionally, but it was never with as much force as was being hammered upon my poor door.

There was a moment of silence before three heavy knocks sounded again. Cursing, I hurried to pull my shirt over my head and threw the towel that had been around my hair onto the bed. Making as little noise as possible, I dashed into the kitchen and grabbed the sharpest knife out of my chef's block. If whoever it was broke down my door, I would not go down without a fight. I didn't think someone would knock before trying to rob me, but what did I know? I crept closer to the door, holding the knife at my side. Dexter walked right next to me, a low growl rumbling in his chest as he picked up on my anxiety.

"Juliette, are you in there?" a familiar voice called.

"Oh, for fuck's sake," I spat, dropping my tense stance and crossing to the door. Swinging it open, I glared into Lucas's sparkling hazel eyes as he smiled at me.

"Morning!" he chirped.

"What the hell are you doing here?" I asked, crossing my arms over my chest.

"Why do you have a knife?" he countered, eyeballing the blade that dangled from my hand.

"You were pounding on my door like a crazy person. I was scared."

"Oh, I'm sorry," he apologized, eyes softening. "It's just this thing has been ringing off the hook and it was driving me nuts. Vince said it was probably yours."

When I looked down at what he was holding in his hand, I saw my phone. Sighing, I took it from him with my free hand. It had to have fallen out of my purse the previous night. "Thanks, Lucas," I muttered, moving back from the door. "Do you want to come in?"

"Sure, but not for too long. Is that coffee I smell?" he asked as he stepped into the apartment and closed the door behind him.

"Just started a pot," I said as I made my way back to the kitchen. Lucas followed behind me, and Dexter watched him from his perch on the couch. "You remember Lucas, Dex. Calm down."

The dog was all but glaring at the new male in the apartment, but he settled down into the couch and quit growling. Lucas stopped at the dining table, and I poured both of us a cup of coffee. "How do you like yours?" I asked, turning to grab my creamer from the fridge. "I've got this, regular milk, and sugar."

"Just black is fine."

"How boring," I teased, but he grinned at me when I handed the cup to him.

"Thank you."

"No problem," I replied, checking my phone. Sure enough, there were multiple missed calls from both Devyn and Dante, and quite a few texts as well. Groaning, I sent them each an identical text letting them know I was fine and that my phone had just been dead. Sure, it was a little white lie, but they could deal with it. I was not about to listen to their speeches if they found out why I really hadn't answered their phone calls.

"So..." Lucas trailed off as he took a seat at my small table. The poor thing looked dwarfed compared to him.

"So, what?" I asked.

"How did your phone end up in the car?"

"Oh, please," I grumbled, rolling my eyes as I poured the creamer into my coffee before going to sit across from him. "Your pain in the ass of a boss insisted on driving me home from work last night. I was exhausted. I must not have realized it fell out of my purse."

He pouted. "That's not what I was imagining happened."

"Sorry to burst your bubble," I said, laughing. I took a sip of my coffee and let the warmth of the liquid soak through my veins. If I was going to make it through the day, I would need it. I was debating calling Anthony to cover my shift, but I had something else on my mind as well. There had been too many instances of me running into some nasty situations. While I had always been lucky enough to scrape myself out of them, I needed something more. I needed to know how to work a situation to my advantage because I wasn't delusional. I was small. But I was sure with the proper trainer, I could even the odds at least a little.

Lucas snapped his fingers in front of my face. "You there?"

"Yes," I griped, swatting at his hand. "Just have a lot on my mind."

"Anything to do with us?"

"*Everything* to do with the lot of you," I grumbled.

"Sorry," he replied, sounding genuinely upset that he was part of what was making my life so difficult.

"It's okay," I said, smiling despite myself. Lucas reminded me of a golden retriever, and I couldn't stand the defeated look in his hazel eyes. "I'm a big girl. I'll get it figured out."

That seemed to brighten his spirits. "If you say so." He checked his watch, sighed, and tossed the rest of his coffee back in one swig. When I raised my eyebrows at him, he just shrugged. "Speaking of figuring things out, I have to get going. Vince sent me out to do more than just return your phone. I'll see you soon, sugar."

"Don't count on it."

"Oh, I am," he teased, reaching over to muss my still wet hair. I glared at him, causing him to burst into a fit of laughter. "I'll tell Vince you say hi."

"Don't you dare," I said, voice low as my eyes narrowed.

He shrugged again before standing. He stretched his arms over his head and headed for the door. "You never know with me," he threw over his shoulder before slipping out into the hallway.

"Asshole," I muttered before getting up to collect his mug. Shaking my head, I took both of our cups into the kitchen to wash them. Once they were both clean, I placed them back into the cabinet and headed into my bedroom. There, I took my stash of cash out and counted out how much I needed to pay the rent. When I had the correct amount, I reached into my nightstand and pulled out an envelope and filled it with the cash. I sealed the envelope and wrote *Rent from Juliette 1B* on the front. Thankfully, my landlord had always been understanding about me paying my rent in cash. Heaving myself off the floor, I left the apartment, mounted the stairs, and made my way up to the fourth floor. I knocked on the door to 4D and only had to wait a few moments before it opened.

"Mornin', Jules," Kyle greeted.

"Good morning," I replied with a smile before handing him the envelope.

"Would you like to come in?" he asked, and I could catch the scent of tea brewing on the stove. He grinned, running a hand over his full head of salt and pepper hair. He took the envelope from me and opened the door a little farther.

"Not today," I told him, a grin pulling at my lips. "I've got to get going."

"Don't be a stranger, Jules." He shook his head at me with a smile in his eyes before he shut the door. Kyle was in his late fifties, and he was one of those blessed men who just looked better with age. However, *I* counted myself blessed he was one of the best landlords I could hope to get in this part of town. He always understood if I needed a few extra days to get the cash together to pay him. There was a part of me that was still convinced that had something to do with the fact that he had always been sweet on my mother. The cancer took her before anything could ever start with them, but I think he always looked at me like his last tie to her. And since I was never one to look a gift-horse in the mouth, I had jumped on the opportunity when he offered me the apartment.

A small smile slipped onto my face as I turned away from the door and made my way back down to my apartment. I walked in only long enough to exchange my slippers for socks and converse before I was on my way again. Dexter whined at the door, and I knew he wanted to go with me. However, I had no idea where I was going or how long I would be, so he had to settle with just being taken out to do his business. After I had him back in the apartment and it securely locked up, I walked towards the downtown area.

I knew that there had to be a studio around there somewhere that taught one-on-one self-defense courses. Not that I had any-thing against the large group classes that the gym closest to me hosted, but that wasn't what I wanted to learn. With Vincent and his gang hanging around, I needed to know a little more than how to spray someone in the eyes with mace or kick them in the nuts.

It didn't take me too long to locate a small gym that advertised personal trainers. Crossing my fingers, I walked into *24/7 Gym* and strolled to the front desk. For having such a mediocre name, the studio itself was nice. I could see multiple rooms lining the halls that had different classes going on in them, and then at the very end of the hall was the room with treadmills, weights, and the like. There were two people at the front desk when I walked in. The girl behind the desk was looking at her computer and trying not to make it obvious that she was ogling the man standing in front of it. He looked up when I approached the counter and raised an eyebrow at me.

"Can I help you?" he asked, putting down the folder he had in his hands before angling so he was fully facing me. The girl gave me a cheery smile before fully focusing on the screen in front of her. Her badge said *Sherry,* and I filed that piece of information away as I gave the man my attention.

"I hope so," I said, biting my lip. "I need a personal trainer and I saw the advertisement." My thumb jerked in the direction of the flyer posted against the front door.

"I'm one of the trainers here. What is it you're looking for?" he questioned, his eyes roaming over my body. If it were any other time, I might have felt a little violated by how closely he was scrutinizing me. However, after so many years working in a bar, I was well versed in knowing when a man was checking me out. The man in front of me was doing nothing of the sort. His eyes were calculating and analytical, sizing up what he had to work with.

"Self-defense," I replied, crossing my arms over my chest.

"We have a class–"

"I really don't think that would work for me."

This time, both eyebrows reached for his hairline. The receptionist laughed, then unsuccessfully tried to cover it with a cough when she caught the scowl he was sending her. "Oh, really?" he questioned, turning his tawny eyes back to me.

"Really."

A grin pulled at the corners of his lips as intrigue sparkled in his gaze. "Well then, let's see what you've got. Follow me." And just like that, he headed down the hallway, not even bothering to look back to see if I was following him.

"Is he always like this?" I asked the girl.

Her blonde ponytail bobbed as she nodded. "Jack co-owns the gym, so he can be a little full of himself. But he's also our best trainer. You landed a good one." She beamed at me, extending a hand over the counter to me. "I'm Sherry, the day receptionist. If you decide to start a membership here, just see me on your way out."

"Thank you," I said, taking her hand. Her grip was stronger than I was expecting, and her eyes danced when she saw the surprise that flitted across my face.

"Like I said," she started, settling back into her seat. "He's the best. You might want to get going."

Nodding, I scurried off down the hall to catch up with Jack. That was not what I had been expecting in the slightest. He had stopped at the second to last door on the left and held it open for me, ushering me inside. *He* really wasn't what I had expected either. There was no way he could be much older than me, and he wasn't hard to look at. It was easy to see why Sherry could barely focus around him. He had light brown hair and the natural tan many people would kill for. When his eyes met mine, the warm tawny color hit me again. Like fine-aged brandy. Then I realized he was speaking, and I had to focus on his words.

"... your name?"

"Juliette," I replied, hoping that I had correctly deduced what he was asking.

"I'm Jack," he said, extending his hand my way. When I shook it, his callouses scraped against my palm, a nod to the many hours he probably spent here. "Now, why don't you enlighten me on why the class wouldn't work for you?"

"Well..." I trailed off. *How should I go about this?* "I work really late hours at a bar, and I walk home a lot. Because of that, I've gotten into a few not-so-great encounters in the past few months.

I'd like to feel comfortable in kicking someone's ass if they tried anything."

"Alright," he said, grinning at me. "That's a valid argument. I'll take you on. We can start now."

"But I'm not wearing–"

"Are you going to be wearing gym clothes on your way home from work?" I shook my head. "Exactly. So, let's get started."

Sighing, I pitched my purse over into the corner of the room. This was going to be interesting.

NINE

THE DINER FIASCO

"Ow! Damnit," I cursed, letting a string of other profanities fall from my lips as Jack pinned my arm behind my back.

"You were distracted."

"You distracted me."

"That was the point."

I huffed and blew my hair out of my face. "Whatever."

"Juliette, you have to pay more attention to what I'm doing. Otherwise, this is always going to happen. Or worse." He made his point even clearer by twisting my arm harder, causing a shooting pain to rip through my shoulder. I hissed at the sensation and tore myself out of his arms the way he had shown me. Before I really thought about it, I threw a punch at his chest as hard as I could. I was pissed. Jack let out a small grunt at the impact.

"Shit, are you okay?" I asked, dropping my fists and hurrying to his side. A flicker in his eyes alerted me to his intent, and I sidestepped him when he lunged for me.

"Much better," he applauded when he turned back to face me.

"You're tricky," I said with narrowed eyes, but I couldn't help the smile that overcame my face.

"And you're a quick study," he replied. He walked over to the far side of the room to a mini fridge that I hadn't noticed earlier. Bending down, he withdrew a bottle of water and held it up in question. I nodded, and he tossed it to me. When I caught it, I ripped the cap off and drank. "Slow down," he told me as he raised his own bottle to his lips. "You don't want to shock your system."

Nodding again, I capped the bottle and set it next to my feet. "Thank you," I said. "For all of this."

"No problem. It's always nice to get some new people in here that are actually willing to follow instruction."

"Are we done for today?" I asked, grinning as I rubbed my knuckles. His chest was hard.

"Yeah, but I want you back in here in a few days."

"How much do I owe you?" I questioned, making my way over to my purse.

He followed me and placed his hands over mine when I brought out my wallet. "Nothing for now." His warm eyes met mine as he grinned. "Consider today a consultation. You can have your next few lessons on the house. If you want to continue seeing me after the start of the month, we'll talk money."

"I'm not going to not pay you," I stated, narrowing my eyes again. I didn't need charity.

"Think of it as a trial basis, okay?" he reasoned, taking a step back from me. "A trainer-trainee relationship like this can never work out if there isn't trust. I know you don't trust me, so I don't want your money."

"How do you—"

"You lied to me about why you're here," he said, his voice so matter of fact that it took me aback. "Whatever, or whoever, you're afraid of, you need to feel comfortable telling me. I can't coach you on proper techniques if I don't know the full situation. Fighting off someone you care about, on any level, is a lot different from fighting off a stranger."

"I don't care about him."

"So, it is someone specific?"

Shit.

"No." He still looked skeptical. *Double shit.* "I'll think about it, okay?"

Jack searched my face but backed off all the same. "Then I'll see you on Thursday, if that works for you."

Hiking my bag up onto my shoulder, I nodded and headed for the door. I threw him a quick goodbye and then slipped out. I turned to wave to Sherry once I was in the lobby, but she was nowhere to be seen. When I stepped outside, the sun was warm on my face, and I heaved out a breath before heading home. I was exhausted. Muscles that I didn't even know I had were sore. There was no way I was going to be worth a damn at work that night, and I knew it. Between the physical exhaustion from the training and the mental exhaustion that was the entire past week or so, I would be moody and, more than likely, end up scaring people away. It took a few minutes rummaging around in my purse, but I finally dug out my phone. Anthony was my first contact, and I hit the call button.

It rang until I was almost sure he was going to ignore it before his gruff voice said, "Hello?"

"Mornin', sunshine!" I chirped.

"Jesus, Jules," he grumbled, and I heard some shuffling around and I assumed he was getting out of bed. "What time is it?"

"Not sure," I said, pulling my phone away from my face. My eyes about bugged out of my head. "It's two." Much later than I expected. No wonder I was so sore.

"It's too early!" he wailed, and I could picture him throwing himself back down onto his bed. He was so dramatic.

"Don't be such a baby."

"I'm not a baby."

"Are you sure?"

"Is there a reason you called?" he groused.

"Of course. I was going to see if you would cover my shift tonight."

"Jules!"

"Anthony!"

"Tonight's my night off!"

"I know," I said, a little defeat slipping into my voice. "But I really don't feel the greatest and I'm supposed to work with Devyn —"

"I'll cover for you," he stated, cutting me off.

"Well, that was easier than I thought."

"Jules, if you're not feeling good, Dev is the *last* person you need to around."

I smiled at that. "Thank you."

"You owe me."

"Whatever, I'll bring brownies in next time we work together."

"Sounds like a fair trade."

"Thanks, Anthony. You're the best," I said, a broad grin stretching across my face.

"Don't I know it? Talk to you soon, Jules." With that, he hung up.

My day was looking a whole lot better. I slipped my phone back into my purse and resisted the urge to skip home. Not only would I embarrass myself, but it would probably hurt thanks to my overworked muscles. I was in such a good mood that I should have known it wouldn't last.

"Juliette!"

I froze. Turning slightly, I saw Brandon and the member of Vincent's gang, whose name I had never learned, heading towards me. I debated making a break for it, but decided against it. They had no reason to hurt me, or anything negative. In fact, I knew they harbored no ill will for me. Shaking my head, I raised my hand in a wave and allowed them to catch up to me.

"Still stalking me?" I teased once they were within earshot.

"Of course not," Brandon told me, grinning as he slung an arm over my shoulder. "This one is strictly coincidence."

"Sure."

"It is! I'm offended."

Rolling my eyes, I addressed the other man. "In all the nastiness that night, I never caught your name."

"I'm Arkin," he replied, an easy smile slipping onto his face.

"I would say it's nice to meet you—"

"Don't be rude, Jules," Brandon scolded me.

"Who gave you permission to call me that?" I asked, my nose wrinkling.

"Me, duh."

"You're obnoxious."

He shrugged. "Whatever you say."

Huffing, I turned on my heel and continued home. Laughter sounded behind me, and then I heard the pursuing footsteps. Why was I not surprised? Slowing to a halt, I let Brandon and Arkin catch up again.

"What's up?" I asked.

"Where are you going?"

"Home."

"You hungry?"

"No." However, my stomach rumbled at that exact moment and made a liar out of me.

"Come to lunch with us," Brandon offered, a grin stretching across his face.

"Your treat?" I questioned, my voice layered with faux sweetness.

"Of course."

I blinked. "Well if you ins—" Before I could even finish my sentence, Brandon had my hand in one of his, and his phone in the other. He dragged me in the opposite direction of my apartment before putting his phone to his ear.

"Meet us at the Rev Diner!" he ordered, his voice chipper.

"That had better not be Vincent," I threatened, thinning my eyes at Brandon's back as he continued to tug me along.

Arkin chuckled from beside me. "I wouldn't put anything past him."

"Between him and Lucas," I grumbled.

"Yeah, they're hard to deal with sometimes."

"You'd think they were related."

"They are."

My head whipped to stare at Arkin. "What?"

"Brandon and Lucas are cousins. But they grew up together, so they're more like brothers."

That made so much sense. Finally, I zoned in enough to catch the very last of Brandon's conversation with whoever was on the other end of the line. "Don't argue with me. Just be there in five minutes." And with that, he punched the end button and shoved his phone into his pocket. He glanced back and caught my glare. "What?"

"Who was that?" I asked.

"Nobody," he replied, a cheeky grin overtaking his face.

"Brandon." I tugged on my hand to remove it from his grasp.

"Juliette," he whined right back.

Scowling, I jerked my hand out of his with all I had. "I think I'm going to go find my own food."

Arkin thwarted my attempt to escape when he stepped in front of me. "C'mon, don't let him get under your skin. It's free food."

"Fine," I grumbled. He had a point. I turned around and continued with them. It didn't take us too much longer to reach the Rev Diner, and once it came into view, my stomach tied into knots. I did not want to see Vincent. The three of us trooped in and found a booth at the back of the restaurant. The sixties themed diner brought a smile to my face but did little to ease the tension in my stomach. Sure, Vincent had been nothing but nice in all of our recent interactions, but he still made me nervous. So, when I spotted a familiar blonde making his way towards us, all my stress drained in an instant.

"Lucas!" I exclaimed, tempted to jump out of my seat next to Arkin and hug him.

"Well, hello to you too, sugar," he said, grinning as he slid in across from me, next to Brandon. "Twice in one day. Lucky me."

"Shut up," I said, laughter bubbling out of my mouth. "I was worried it was going to be the other one."

"Not today," he replied, reaching for a menu. "He's busy."

"Looks like you're stuck with just us," Brandon threw in.

"I'm still irritated with you."

"Why?" He pouted.

"You wouldn't tell me who you were calling."

"You're a child."

"And you're not?"

His blue eyes sparkled with amusement. "Touché."

At that moment, our waitress arrived and took our drink orders. She was a sweet girl, and I was going to make sure the guys left her a good tip. Throughout the rest of lunch, they kept me busy by taking turns asking me things. Naturally, I interrogated them just as hard. They laughed at me when I asked if their gang had a name, so I took that as a no. I pouted the longer they laughed at me.

"It's not that funny," I snapped, throwing a fry at Lucas.

"Yes, it is."

"I don't know about the inner workings of gangs, genius," I grumbled, taking an angry bite out of my burger. He still had a smug smirk on his face. After I swallowed my food, I threw another fry at him. "All I know is you like to abduct young women."

"Hey, now," Arkin said, dodging a fry when Brandon threw it at him. "That was a one-off occurrence."

I snorted. "Sure."

"Cute," Lucas commented, throwing my fry back at me.

"No one asked you."

He threw the tomato he had pulled off his burger at me. It smacked me in the face before I dodged it. Without thinking, I tossed it back. To my horror, it landed dead center on his white t-shirt, staining it pink. My face paled when he turned an accusatory glare on me.

What had I done?

"Now guys," Arkin started.

"Shut up," Brandon and Lucas chorused, both of their eyes trained on me.

"I'll wash it," I said, giving him a smile. *Please behave,* I pleaded in my head.

"Do you promise?" he asked, lowering the hand that was filled with fries.

"Pinky promise!"

"Too bad," Brandon cried, his voice gleeful as he launched his attack.

They instantly pelted me with fries. Arkin, bless his heart, tried to help me deflect some of them, but it was no use. When they were out of ammo, I gazed around at the mess we had made. A little voice in the back of my head was muttering about what a waste that was, but a bigger part of me was more worried about what was going to happen to us. All four of our heads whipped to the front of the restaurant where a very tall, very round man was *very* red in the face.

Long story short, we got kicked out.

"Look at that, Jules. We didn't have to pay for lunch at all," Brandon said, draping an arm around my shoulders as the four of us made our way down the street.

"I also didn't get to *eat* at all," I grumbled, batting his arm away.

"Are you still going to wash my shirt?" Lucas asked, tugging at the pink spot on his chest.

I sighed. "Of course. I'll also order pizza as long as you guys swear you won't trash my apartment."

"Deal," they agreed in unison.

I didn't believe it for a second.

TEN

SO MUCH FOR A NIGHT OFF

When I unlocked my door, a malicious thought crossed my mind. I swung the door wide and motioned for the guys to enter ahead of me. Brandon and Arkin both grinned while walking right in. Lucas just smirked at me. I scowled in return, remembering that he had been there this morning. He knew all about Dexter. But when I walked in, I was pleased that my wonderful dog had the other two backed into a corner with his teeth bared. Lucas burst into a fit of laughter, and they both glared at him.

"A little help here, Jules?" Brandon asked, eyeing Dexter. The dog let out a sharp bark when Arkin went to move forward. I laughed before walking up to him and resting my hand between his ears.

"Easy, Dex," I soothed. "They're friends." Dexter immediately sat back on his haunches and wagged his tail.

"Amazing," Brandon commented, kneeling in front of Dexter. The Rottweiler eyed Brandon but allowed the attention. It didn't take him long to roll onto his back, begging for his belly to be rubbed.

"As you can see, he's actually just a giant teddy bear," I said, shaking my head. And I had paid an arm and a leg for professional training when I adopted him, but they didn't need to know that. I headed into my bedroom to dump off my purse. After depositing it on the bed, I pulled out my phone and shoved it in my pocket. When I turned to walk back out into the living room, I ran smack into someone's chest. "Okay, ow," I muttered, glaring up at Lucas. He grinned at me before shedding his jacket.

"Here you go," he announced, pulling his t-shirt over his head. When he tossed it at me, I didn't even bother to catch it. We had a short, staring contest before I relented and snatched the shirt off the ground along with a basket from the closet.

"You're an ass," I said as I shoved past him on my way to the bathroom to grab the rest of my white clothes. I didn't want to waste a full load of laundry on one shirt.

Lucas trailed behind me. "That's not nice."

"I'm not nice."

"That's a lie."

"And what makes you say that?" I questioned as I tossed a few bras, some underwear, and my white t-shirts into the basket. My aim was to make him uncomfortable, but it wasn't working. He watched with a teasing glint in his hazel eyes, and I huffed. My cheeks heated before I shoved past him.

"I've been around you for more than five minutes. This the laundry?" he asked, gesturing to the folding doors in the hall.

"Yeah." I nodded, deciding to roll with his subject change.

He pulled the doors open and took the basket from me. Rolling my eyes, I started the washer and added soap. When there was enough water, I took the basket from him and dumped it in. After I evenly deposited everything, I set the basket on top of the washer and shut the doors.

"Food?" he asked, a grin overtaking his face.

"Food."

"What took you two so long?" Brandon whined when we reemerged. His eyes zeroed in on Lucas's bare chest, and a sly smile crossed his face. "Oh, I see."

"Don't be an idiot," I scolded, smacking the side of his head as I moved past him. "Pepperoni okay with everyone?" I was refusing to acknowledge the hurt expression Brandon was giving me.

"That's fine," Arkin told me, smiling as he shook his head. "If you get three larges, we'll throw in."

"Sounds good," I said, pulling out my phone. The guys explored the apartment as I placed our order. Once I finished, I watched them as they examined the few pictures on my walls. They were like children in a museum. Smiling to myself, I plopped down onto the couch. Dexter wasted no time in jumping up beside me and laying his head in my lap.

"Who's this?" Lucas asked, pointing to the picture of me and my mom taken a few weeks before she passed.

"My mom," I told him.

"She's pretty."

"I'm sure she would appreciate that." I couldn't help but laugh. Of course, Lucas would be the one to compliment a woman who was obviously on her deathbed. Mom had hated the fact that I kept that picture. She had said it made her *look* sick. She had been impossible.

"How long on that pizza?" Brandon asked, throwing himself onto the floor. "I'm *starving*."

"Maybe you shouldn't have started a food fight."

"That was you."

"Don't even," I quipped.

He huffed, and the other two laughed at his expense. A wry grin formed on my face. Leave it to me to be hanging out with the same men who had kidnapped me only a few days prior. No matter what they had done, they had more than proven that they weren't going to hurt me. They were easy to get along with and they made *me* feel at ease. Even if Brandon and Lucas relished getting under my skin, they meant well. If it wasn't for the whole gang thing, I could see us being friends.

Who was I kidding? The gang thing didn't bother me. It was the *leader* that bothered me.

As if cued by my thoughts, Lucas's phone started ringing. My head whipped up, and I didn't have to be a genius to figure out who was calling because of the grimace that crossed his face.

"Hey Vince," he said, a casual tone to his voice that sounded fake even to my ears. "No, Brandon and Arkin are with me. At a friend's place." His eyes traveled to me, and a coy smile formed on his face. "Yeah, you know them."

"Don't you dare," I hissed.

"From where? Oh, she's a bartender. Warmer. Oh, you almost had it."

"Juliette says hi!" Brandon hollered.

My eyes snapped to his. He smiled. In return, I glared at him as hard as I could. If looks could kill, he would be nine feet underground. However, looks couldn't kill, so he just continued to give me that same obnoxious grin.

"Vince wants to talk to you," Lucas said, appearing in front of me with the phone.

"No." I vehemently shook my head, the movement causing Dexter to jump down.

"Hear that? She doesn't want to talk to you." Lucas's expression went blank before he took the phone away from his ear and glanced at the '*call ended*' flashing on his screen. "I think he's on his way here."

Groaning, I sunk even farther into the couch. "I hate you. I hate all of you."

"He's not that bad," Arkin said, falling onto the couch beside me.

"My apartment can't take all this testosterone," I grumbled.

"And you don't hate us," Brandon piped up, his voice matter of fact as he sat next to me as well, sandwiching me between him and Arkin.

"Yes, I do."

Dexter whined at my feet, placing his head on my lap. I knew he was jealous he wasn't on the couch. A small laugh left me as I scratched behind his ears. At least I knew he would never betray me. With little else to do, I reached forward and grabbed the remote. Turning on the TV, I flipped through the channels before giving up. I didn't know what they liked to watch. I tossed the remote to Lucas and had to stifle a laugh when it hit him in the head. He gave me a half-hearted glare before running through the channels himself. Finally, he came to rest on *The Godfather*, and I had to bite my cheeks to keep from smiling.

"What's so funny?" Arkin asked.

"Nothing."

Thankfully, the knock at the door saved me. I heaved myself off the couch and out from in between Brandon and Arkin. Crossing my fingers behind my back, I opened the door. A relieved breath escaped me when I saw it was just the pizza.

"Gracen?" he asked, checking the ticket on the top box.

"That's me," I said, reaching for the boxes. "How much?"

"That'll be $47.59."

"Just one second," I told him, taking the pizzas into the kitchen and setting them on the table. When I made to get my purse, I noticed Brandon was already at the door. He slipped the kid a handful of bills and told him to keep the change. I scrunched my face up. "I said I would get at least some of it," I scolded when Brandon came up to me.

"I owed you lunch," he said, shrugging. Then he rubbed his hands together like a cartoon villain. "Now let me get a hold of this pizza."

"Wait!" I exclaimed, snapping the box shut when he went to open it. He raised an eyebrow at me. "Paper plates. On top of the fridge."

"Yes, Mom," he muttered, brushing past me to grab the plates. Once he returned with them, I allowed him to stack his plate with three pieces. Arkin and Lucas weren't far behind, and they each took three pieces as well.

"Sheesh, pigs," I muttered under my breath as I took the last piece out of the box. One down.

"Heard that," Lucas told me, even though his words were garbled.

"You're disgusting."

They all just laughed at me as they settled in to watch their movie. I sighed for what felt like the hundredth time in an hour as I went to sit on the floor with my back against Brandon's legs, since they had all sat on the couch. Something made me feel like they were hiding out. Why else would all three of them be fine with sitting in my apartment, eating pizza, and watching a movie? I felt like I was babysitting. When I glanced at the clock, I realized it was how late it had gotten.

We were almost at the end of the movie when someone started pounding on my door.

"It's unlocked!" I hollered, not bothering to get up. The last thing I felt like doing was moving. The door swung open, and Vincent stood there, looking confused as he surveyed the room. Each of the boys lifted their hands in greeting, but I barely spared him a glance. I was sure we were quite the sight.

"Don't you all have work to be doing?" Vincent asked, his voice low.

"I'm doing my job," Lucas said, patting me on the head.

"You're still watching me?"

"Doesn't this make it less stalker-ish?" he asked, hazel eyes sparkling with amusement.

"Whatever." My eyes traveled to Vincent, and he arched an eyebrow at me. I motioned for him to come in. "C'mon then. Don't just stand there. Go get a piece of pizza and claim some floor space."

He shook his head but shut the door behind him all the same. He ambled into the kitchen before opening the third box and helping himself to a slice. The boys and I had knocked out the second pizza when we got seconds. On his way back, he stopped to scratch Dexter behind his ears. The dog's tongue lolled out of his mouth as he leaned into Vincent's touch.

Traitor.

Vincent looked like he wanted to tell one of the others to get up, but he just shook his head and sat down next to me on the floor. He was unnervingly close. Of all the spots he could've taken, he was close enough that I could feel the heat radiating from him.

"You need to get some more seating," he told me.

"I never in a million years planned to have this many people in my apartment at one time."

"Something tells me you might have to get used to it," Arkin said, startling me.

"So how did you all end up here, anyway?" Vincent questioned, his eyes roving over his men. "Since you all have other things to do." As he spoke, his eyes strayed to Lucas, who was still missing his shirt. His eyebrows arched, but he just shook his head and didn't comment.

"Well, you see..." Brandon started, scratching the back of his neck. A heavy sigh fell from his mouth before he launched into the story about running into me, going to lunch, and getting kicked out. Vincent's lips twitched into that ghost of a smile when he found out we had started a food fight, but other than that, he had no expression.

When Brandon finished, Vincent turned his forest green eyes on me. "You're quite the distraction, aren't you, princess?"

"Shut up," I told him, barely resisting the urge to stick my tongue out at him.

"What were you doing on that side of town anyway?" he asked, ignoring me.

"None of your business."

"We'll see about that," Vincent murmured, narrowing his eyes at me. A darkness fell across his face. Something told me whatever it was he had to say, I didn't want to hear it.

"Oh, please," I spat, shoving myself off the ground and heading towards the kitchen.

Stupid men.

With more force than necessary, I snatched the two empty pizza boxes off the table and made for the front door. Whistling through my teeth, I called for Dexter. He trotted over to me, wagging his tail as he gazed up at me. I bit my lip. I hadn't exactly thought my plan through. There was no way for me to clip his leash with both boxes in my arms, even if I had thought to pick it up. I cast a pleading look at the boys, hoping Lucas or Arkin would help.

Fate wasn't on my side.

Vincent heaved himself off the floor and picked up the lead on his way over. When he reached us, he clipped Dexter's leash onto him. He opened the door, motioning for me to go out first. I narrowed my eyes before shouldering my way past him. A low chuckle sounded behind me before I heard the jingling of Dexter's tags as they followed me outside.

"I wanted to take these out to get away from you, you know," I said once we reached the dumpster. I tossed the pizza boxes in and held my hand out for the leash.

"And here I thought you just didn't want a dirty apartment," he responded, placing the lead in my hand. A shockwave ran up my arm from where our skin brushed, but I did my best to ignore it.

"I cannot handle having you all here at once."

"I'll be more than happy to kick them out."

"That means you have to leave too," I reminded him, allowing Dexter to drag me into the grass a bit so that he could do his business.

"Sure thing, princess."

"Stop calling me that."

"No." He shook his head at me, a small smile appearing for a split second before it was gone again. "But really, what were you doing on that side of town? No wonder Lucas couldn't find you."

"Lucas doesn't need to follow me," I snapped. "If I haven't gone to the police yet, I'm not going to. For god's sake, Vincent. Your men are in there having dinner with me. Watching a movie. Obviously, I'm not all that bothered by what happened the other night."

"That's what worries me."

He said it so low I almost didn't catch it. I shook my head at him, massaging my temples to stave off the oncoming headache. The last thing I needed was a gang member tailing me around. I could take care of myself; I was making sure of that with Jack. Whistling for Dexter so that we could go back in, I breezed past Vincent on my way back inside.

When I reentered my apartment, I went rigid. My eyes trailed over the upturned coffee table to the brawl that was going on in the kitchen. From the snippets of conversation I could hear, it seemed like Brandon and Lucas were fighting over the last slice of pizza. *Literally* fighting. Lucas's fist slammed into Brandon's jaw, and I winced. That had to hurt.

A slight groan from behind me caused me to jump. "It's like working with children," Vincent muttered, slipping by me on his way to the kitchen. His fingers brushed across the small of my back as he passed me, and just that simple touch ignited a fire in my blood that I struggled to tamp down.

Christ, I needed to get a grip. Or get laid. Either would suffice, as long as I stopped having a reaction to this man.

Arkin caught my gaze and made his way over to me, shooting an amused glance over his shoulder. "I'm really sorry, Jules."

"You're fixing it."

"What?" He blinked at me.

"You heard me. You were in here, you could have prevented this. It's on you."

"But–"

"No buts," I cut him off. "Clean it."

He shook his head, not mad in the slightest. He picked up the living room while Vincent separated the brawling cousins. Lucas and Brandon both went slack in his arms, crossing their arms over their chests before scowling at one another. It all happened so fluidly, it almost looked rehearsed. Heaving out another sigh of my own, I trudged into the apartment after kicking the door shut behind me. I may not have been going into Tuxedo, but I was sure as hell going to be working.

ELEVEN

THE MYSTERY OF MOODY JULES

"Get out," I growled, glaring at Lucas.

"No," he refused, shaking his head. He was being petulant. Somehow, the night before, I had made my way to bed around one in the morning. When I had gone to bed, Arkin, Lucas, and Brandon were still there. Vincent had left not too long after separating the little spat over the pizza. Some documentary on the history channel had captivated their attention, so I had let them stay and watch it. The only condition was that they promised to lock the door behind them when they left. When I woke up that morning to find Lucas sprawled out across my couch, it was safe to say I was less than pleased.

"You were supposed to leave last night," I reminded him, running a hand through my hair. I was vaguely aware of the fact that my over-sized t-shirt rode up when I lifted my arms, showing off my black underwear, but I couldn't bring myself to care.

"And miss this?" he asked, his eyes zeroing in on the flash of abdomen he got to see before I dropped my arms. I picked up the closest thing to me on the coffee table, the remote, and chucked it at his head. He grinned from behind the pillow he used to block my assault. "Not a chance, sugar."

"I'll call Vincent," I threatened.

"You wouldn't," he scoffed, but I could see the trepidation in his gaze.

"Try me."

And try me, he did. He flopped back down onto the couch, whistling for Dexter to jump up with him. The dog didn't even hesitate. He jumped into Lucas's lap and snuggled into him, loving the attention. Feeling betrayed, I marched back into my room and scooped my phone up off the nightstand. Biting my lip, I scrolled through my text messages until I found the one Vincent had sent me the very first night we had met.

Do I really want to go down this road?

Would it get Lucas into trouble? Probably not, but I was hoping Vincent would make him leave. I knew that if I *really* wanted to, I could beg Lucas until he listened. He was just trying to push my buttons. But I also wanted to see his face when he realized Vincent was involved.

A smile was on my face after I hit the *call* button and waltzed back out to him. Leaning one shoulder against the doorframe separating the living room from the hall, I gave Lucas an evil grin as I placed the phone against my ear.

Ring, ring, ring.

"Monroe," was his curt greeting. His voice sounded rough, and I wondered if I had woken him up.

"Good morning!" I chirped. Lucas's head whipped up, and for a moment, he looked stunned.

"Juliette?" the confusion in Vincent's voice was almost comical. "Is something wrong?"

"Yes," I said, put off by the genuine concern lacing his voice. "Lucas won't leave my apartment."

A heavy sigh sounded down the line. "Give him the phone."

Lucas vehemently shook his head as I sauntered over to him. He stared at the phone in my hand when I offered it to him. "It's for you," I cooed, waving the device in front of his face.

"Hello?" he muttered after taking it from me. A myriad of emotions played across Lucas's face as he listened to Vincent. Finally, Lucas muttered something incoherent and then mashed the *end call* button before tossing the phone to me. I barely caught it.

I shot him a glare. "Don't be a baby."

"Don't be a baby," he mocked, his voice irritatingly high.

"I don't sound like that!" I stomped my foot to punctuate my sentence, but that just sent him into a fit of laughter. Grinding my teeth together, I turned and made my way back into the hall. After grabbing his shirt out of the dryer, I walked back into the living room to find him still doubled over. Pursing my lips, I dropped the shirt onto his head. It sobered him up. He grinned at me after he pulled it on.

"What?" he asked, batting his eyelashes at me.

"Out," I ordered, pointing stiff-armed to the door.

"Aw, Jules."

"Out."

He huffed, but heaved himself off the couch. "You're no fun."

"*Out.*"

"Alright," he agreed. Laughter bubbled out of his mouth as he moved to grab me. I skipped out of his reach, narrowing my eyes. He rolled his at me and the next time he tried, he managed to hook an arm around my neck. He pulled me into him and ruffled my hair. "Later, sugar," he said before he walked out the door.

"Twenty-one ways to kill you!" I yelled after him. His laughter echoed back to me even through the shut door. "Idiot," I grumbled. Dexter nudged the back of my legs. When I looked down at him, he just sauntered off back to the bedroom. A knowing smile cured my lips as I followed him. He jumped up onto the bed and just stared at me. "Are you wanting me to come back to bed?" I asked. His tail wagged. Taking that as a yes, I laid back down.

The pounding on my door later that afternoon really shouldn't have surprised me. Dexter and I glanced at the door from our seats on the couch. His ears perked up in anticipation and I paused with my spoonful of cereal halfway to my mouth. It was Devyn. I had a sixth sense about these kinds of things, and I could feel her displeasure radiating through the door. For the briefest second, I considered ignoring it. Maybe I'd get lucky, and she'd leave. But probably not. She would more than likely just start yelling until the neighbors called the cops. Groaning, I set my bowl down on the coffee table and trudged to the door.

When I opened it, Devyn arched her pierced eyebrow at me. "So, you're sick, huh?"

Glancing down at my attire, I had never put pants on, I nodded at her. "I think I might die."

"Give me a break," she muttered, shouldering her way past me.

"Come on in, Dev."

"Thanks."

Rolling my eyes, I shut the door and returned to my spot on the couch. Devyn stared down at me, tapping her foot. Once again, I paused with my spoon midway to my mouth.

"Can I help you?" I asked.

"We have to be at work in an hour and a half. You realize that, right?"

"*Fuck.*"

Kicking myself into high gear, I scrambled to place my dishes in the sink before dashing towards my bedroom. I threw on my uniform faster than I ever had and put on a full face of makeup in under twenty minutes. I was damn proud of myself.

When I finally emerged into the living room dressed and ready, I noticed Devyn was just walking in the door. She unclipped Dexter from his leash, and he meandered into the kitchen. She saw the look of gratitude on my face and smiled. "You're welcome."

"Let's go," I rushed out, waving my keys at her. I hollered a goodbye to my dog and promised myself I would take him out for a nice long walk the next day. Devyn and I locked up and began our lengthy walk to work.

The surrounding silence was so heavy I could taste it. Normally, silence wasn't something I feared with Devyn. In fact, I relished it most of the time. But I could feel the questions she wanted to ask hanging in the air. Finally, when we were nearly at the bar, I couldn't take it anymore.

"Spit it out," I snapped.

"What?" she asked, blinking at me as if coming out of a daze.

"What do you want to ask me?"

"I don't know what–"

"Don't play dumb with me, woman."

"Alright," she sighed, before reaching up to twirl a piece of her hair. "Why didn't you come to work last night?"

"I was sick."

"Juliette."

"Fine," I grumbled. For a moment, I wondered why I had been so grouchy all day, but I pushed the thought away. "I went to see a self-defense trainer yesterday. He wore me out. I was so sore I knew I would be useless at work, so I called Anthony to cover my shift."

"What else?"

"What do you mean, *what else*?"

"Nothing else happened?" she asked, her voice dripping with accusations.

"No."

"Jules, your apartment reeked of cologne."

"Oh, that." I felt the color drain from my face. Busted.

"Yes, *that*."

"I ran into the guys afterward," I admitted. "Then they came over and watched a few movies."

"The guys?"

"Yes?"

"As in the gang?

"Yes."

"As in the gang that kidnapped you?"

"Yes."

"As in the gang that is still following you around?"

"Yes."

"Jules–"

"Dev," I snapped, cutting her off. "You don't get to play Mom on this one. It was fine. They're harmless."

"Was Vincent there?"

"Yes, but I don't see what–"

"Juliette!" she exclaimed, throwing her hands up in the air as she came to a full stop. "What are you *thinking*? He threatened to kill you."

"And he *hasn't*."

She pointed a scarlet-painted nail at me. "Juliette Gracen. I swear to God, or whoever is running this shit, if you go and get yourself killed for trusting a bunch of *gangbangers*, I will personally kill you myself." I opened my mouth. "And don't you dare tell me that that's redundant." I shut my mouth.

We were stuck in a glaring match. We were so focused on each other that I didn't even realize a car had pulled to a stop beside us. I didn't recognize the black sedan, but I sure as hell recognized the brunette that stuck his head out of it.

"Jules!"

"Not the best time right now, Brandon!" I hollered back.

"Want a ride?"

"No."

"Yes."

"Ex-fucking-scuse me?" I asked Devyn, my eyes bugging out of my head. "After you literally just gave me a lecture about trusting them?"

She smirked at me. "If you're going down, I'm going down with you. And it beats walking in these damn heels."

I stared at her, dumbfounded. Shaking my head, I made my way to the car and slid into the backseat with Devyn. Arkin turned around in his seat and gave me a sweet smile. "Hey, Jules."

"Hi, Arkin," I greeted, trying my best to return his smile. However, I was so irritated I was sure whatever he saw was a sad attempt. He chuckled and faced forward.

Devyn and Brandon fell into a natural conversation like they had been friends for years. My eyes rolled as I stared out the window. Arkin was watching me in the rearview mirror. I could see him glance at it now and then. Before long, we arrived at Tuxedo and I all but dashed from the car. I was through the back door before Devyn even got out. My purse hit the floor with a *bang* and I laughed when Dante jumped and turned to look at me.

"You okay, Jules?" he asked, his eyebrows raising.

"Just peachy."

"I take it you're not feeling any better?"

"In a manner of speaking," I grumbled as I clocked in.

Devyn breezed through the door at that moment. "Alright," she started, placing her hands on her hips as she narrowed her eyes at me. "What's your problem? Your bitch levels are through the roof."

My hand ran down my face as I wracked my brain for what could have caused my irritability over the past day and a half. I wanted to face-palm when it finally clicked. "My period," I muttered.

"My cue to leave," Dante said, lightly laughing as he made his way out onto the floor. "Your painkillers are still in the office if it gets too bad tonight."

"That explains it," Devyn mused, coming over to wrap me in a tight hug. "You're always like this right before it hits. I can't believe *I* didn't figure it out."

"It's annoying. God, I feel so bad," I grumbled, returning her hug. "I'm sorry, Dev."

"No worries. I'll be twice as bad in another week or two."

I grimaced. Truer words had never been spoken.

Twelve

PIT STOP

The night passed smoothly, as it tended to when Devyn and I worked together. I adored working with Anthony, but there was just something about working with Devyn. We didn't split the bar down the middle. We were so in sync that it wasn't necessary. When Brandon came up to me at the end of the night, I gave him a kilowatt smile.

"What can I get for you?" I asked, my voice coming out a little more chipper than I had intended.

He laughed and shook his head. "In a better mood, are we?"

"Significantly."

"Well, I don't want a drink. I was just sent to deliver a message."

"What's that?"

"Vince said he'll be waiting for you after your shift."

The glass I was pouring vodka into slipped through my fingers and clanked against the counter. "Shit," I muttered, turning to find my towel to wipe up the spill. "What?" I asked Brandon, wanting to make sure I had heard him right.

"Vince is going to wait for you."

"Tell him to go home," I snapped, my earlier irritation returning in full force.

"Why don't you come on over and do it yourself?" Glancing at the corner booth where they normally sat, I saw Vincent along with Lucas, Arkin, and a few of the other men I had seen the very first night. I narrowed my eyes at him, even though he wasn't looking in my direction. Refocusing on Brandon, I shoved a few loose strands of hair out of my eyes.

"I don't have time for this right now. Tell him Dante is giving me a ride."

"Will do." He saluted me and headed back to the rest of them. Biting my lip, I decided not to dwell on the smug smirk that had crossed his face before he left.

The rest of the night went as easily as the first half. Devyn and I were both sitting on the counter after closing. Dante was glaring at us from the back, but we were both pretending we couldn't feel the holes he was burning into the side of our heads. Continuing my counting, I was happy when I finally broke three hundred dollars. The club typically only had one or two slow days a week. Since I almost always worked the weekend shifts, the slower nights were actually a godsend. They gave a reprieve from the chaotic energy that rattled the club walls on the weekend.

"Three twenty-two, twenty-seven," I told her when I had laid the last bill on the pile. Shoving it at her, I let her start her job of splitting the tips.

"You still rolling your change?" she asked me. I nodded. "Then here." And she pushed the quarter and two pennies over to me. "Keep that."

Laughing, I took them and jammed them into my pocket. Once she had finished splitting the tips, I took my half and headed for the back. When I made it to my purse, Dante came up to me.

He flicked my forehead. "Stay off the bar."

"Ow," I grumbled, rubbing the spot of his assault. "Rude."

"Shut up."

"Why is everyone telling me to shut up today?" I muttered, hiking my bag up onto my shoulder. I punched in my number to clock out and headed for the door.

"Jules, hold up!" Dante called. "I'll drive you home."

"I can walk. I'm ready to go," I told him as I pulled the back door open. "Just take Devyn home." He didn't even have time to give me a reply before I was gone.

When I faced the parking lot, I froze. Vincent was leaning against the side of the SUV, a small smile playing on the edges of his lips as our gazes met. My eyes narrowed. Deciding to try my luck, I hugged the side of the building as I headed towards the sidewalk. Maybe he'd take the hint if I just flat out ignored him. Hearing sounds of pursuit, I pushed my legs harder. I'd be damned if I let him give me another ride home. If it continued to happen, I would be indebted to him.

Owing anything to Vincent Monroe was not high on my list of priorities.

However, I should have known that he was not someone who could easily be ignored.

My back met the side of the building as I was pushed against it. It should have hurt, but Vincent was surprisingly gentle.

"Where do you think you're going, princess?" he asked, forcing me to meet his eyes. He was so close to me, toeing the line of crowding me, but something told me if I protested, he'd step back.

So why wasn't I?

"Home," I said, trying to ignore the warmth that sank into my skin from just being in his proximity. This man was going to be the death of me.

"You're not walking."

"You're not taking me."

"I thought Dante was supposed to be giving you a ride." I scowled at the smug look on his face. He *knew* I had been lying. That I was going to make a break for it. "Guess it's a good thing I stuck around."

"Vincent," I groaned, slumping against the wall. "Would you leave it alone?"

"No, c'mon." His voice broached no argument. He took my arm in a firm grip and steered me back to the SUV.

Relenting, I allowed him to hoist me up into the passenger seat after he had opened the door for me. I settled into the now familiar leather seat with a sour look on my face. Vincent got into the driver's seat and cranked the engine over. We didn't speak as he drove. The only sound in the car was the soft notes of a piano. He seemed to favor it. Sighing, I allowed my eyes to flutter closed as the car continued to move.

It took me a while to figure out that I had been in the car way longer than I should have. Peaking one eye open, I noticed we were on the opposite side of the city. We were close to the gang's warehouse. Straightening in my seat, I turned to Vincent. He ignored me, or at least didn't seem to notice the change in my demeanor. I let the silence continue for another few minutes before I spoke.

"Vincent?"

"Hmm?"

"Weren't you supposed to be taking me home?"

"I said I would," he responded, his head nodding. "But I have to swing by the warehouse first. I've got some business to attend to after I drop you off."

"It's three o'clock in the morning."

"And?"

"And it's *three o'clock in the morning*. What could you possibly be doing at this hour?"

"Illegal things."

Well, duh, Jules, I thought, resisting the urge to smack myself. Before I could open my mouth again, Vincent maneuvered the SUV into a parking spot outside the warehouse I had been to the first time I had met him. Vincent got out, and I followed suit. There was no way I was just going to sit in the car. Not around here.

Vincent held the door open for me, and I had to shield my eyes from the lights. Since I wasn't a prisoner this time, I surveyed the room. It was large, and someone had clearly converted one side into a lounge area. There were two couches and a few chairs arranged in a semi-circle, facing a large TV. Cards, cigarette packs, ashtrays, and the like littered the coffee table. My gaze traveled to the staircase at the far end of the room that I was guessing led to the apartments over our heads.

"You coming, princess?" Vincent called.

It was then that I realized he had never stopped walking. He was already at the door to his office, standing at the threshold. He fixed me with that steady gaze, and when I failed to answer, he raised his eyebrows at me and cocked his head to the side.

"You look a little lost, Jules," a voice said from behind me.

I yelped. When I spun around, I met Arkin's shimmering blue eyes. Before I could even think about what I was doing, I hauled my arm back and punched him in the shoulder.

"You asshole!" I hissed.

"Ouch," he said, rubbing the spot. "That hurt."

"Good!"

"Juliette."

"Oh, shut *up* already!" I snapped, whirling back to face Vincent before stomping towards him. "I'm coming." Snickers erupted from around me, and I finally took the time to realize that we had an audience. There were people scattered all around. They all seemed to be entertained by my outburst, especially the pretty red head lounging on one of the couches. Her sapphire eyes sparkled as they met mine, and she winked at me. Wincing, I glanced back at Vincent. Just as I suspected, he didn't look as amused. The color drained from my face as I came to a stop in front of him.

A muscle along his jaw was twitching.

"Inside," he ordered, that dark authority coating his voice, rolling off him in waves. I nodded and moved past him.

When he closed the door, I felt the temperature in the room drop.

"I'm guessing 'I'm sorry' would be pointless, huh?" I asked, squeezing my eyes shut.

"Just a little," he bit out.

Oooooh, Vinnie's mad.

Shaking my head, I tried to rid myself of my obnoxious thoughts. If there was ever a time for me to filter what I said to him, it was now. Biting my lip, I looked anywhere but at him. His office was nice. I hadn't noticed that the last time. Small, but cozy. His desk was the dominant feature in the room. A rich mahogany that looked like it was religiously polished. But what really drew my attention were the two bookcases on the left wall. They were jam-packed with books. The range surprised me. Everything from a gun manual to a special edition set of *Lord of the Rings*. The smallest hint of a smile blossomed across my face. And then I remembered what my dumbass had just done, and the butterflies flooded my stomach all over again.

A deep sigh reached my ears before I heard him move. Taking my chances, I peeked in his direction. He was rooting around in his desk. His furrowed brow cast a heavy shadow over his cheekbones, making him look even more intimidating than usual. He finally straightened when he had a few papers in one hand and a gun in his other.

"Are you really going to need the gun?" I asked, cursing myself because my voice came out so soft. There was no way I was concerned about his well being. *None.*

"Hopefully not," he replied. His eyes raised to meet mine and one side of his mouth quirked up into a grin. "Don't worry about me, princess. I'll be fine."

"I'm not worried."

"Sure."

"I'm not."

The smug look on his face made me want to smack him. He tucked the gun into the waistband of his jeans at his back and placed the papers in a pocket on the inside of his jacket. He made his way over to me and placed his hands on my shoulders. I couldn't look away from his eyes even if I had wanted to.

"Try not to undermine me in front of my men anymore, okay?" he asked, his voice whisper-soft, yet filled with a dark promise that caused a shiver to wrack my frame.

I was choosing not to examine that too closely.

"I'm sorry," I murmured, breaking eye contact. "I'm just–"

"Exhausted and irritable? I noticed." He brushed his thumb along my cheekbone. "How's this feeling?"

"Better," I murmured. His touch was so enticing. The urge to lean my cheek into his palm was overwhelming, and it took everything I had to fight it. To finish responding to him. "The bruising was so faint it was basically gone this morning."

"Good." He pulled away from me, heading to the door. He motioned for me to go ahead of him. "Let's get you home."

Nodding, I headed out into the main part of the warehouse. Curious stares met me as I emerged, and I wanted to stick my tongue out at all of them. Once Vincent was standing by my side, however, everyone found something else to be interested in. Except for Arkin. He made his way over to us with a smile on his face.

"You okay, Jules?" he asked, worry crossing his brow.

"I'm fine," I replied, giving him a thumbs-up. "Just ready for this day to be over."

"Let's go," Vincent said, taking my bicep in his strong grip as he steered me to the exit. I waved goodbye to Arkin and then followed Vincent with no fuss. I was tired and my bed was calling my name. As long as Vincent actually took me home, I would go without complaint. When we stepped out into the night air, I took a deep breath. Vincent didn't take the time to stop. We made it to the SUV, and he once again helped to hoist me into the passenger seat.

As he rounded to the driver's side, I didn't spare him a glance. I just rested my forehead against the glass. I was so tired.

"Dexter's gonna be so mad at me," I mumbled, letting my eyes flutter closed.

"Why's that?"

"There's no way I'm going to mange walking him tonight," I replied just as a yawn broke free.

We fell silent after that. It didn't take me long to be lulled to sleep by the warmth of the heater and the soft hum of the engine.

"Princess, we're here. I need your keys."

"What?" I groaned, lifting my hand to rub sleep from my eyes. Then I realized my feet weren't on the ground. "Why are you carrying me?"

"You were asleep," he said, as if it were the most obvious thing. "Can I get in your purse for your keys?"

"Sure."

My eyes fluttered again as I felt him shift me around with ease. Before too long, I heard my keys jingling. My door swung open, and he stepped through, kicking it shut behind him. Vincent had only been in my apartment once, but he maneuvered through it like he had it memorized. Dexter, the little traitor, didn't even growl at Vincent as he walked past him. He opened the door to my bedroom and made his way over to the bed.

"No," I protested as he laid me down. "Dexter–"

He shushed me, cutting me off. "I got him."

I blinked up at him. One of his rare full-blown smiles graced his lips as he gently pushed against my shoulder, easing me back down onto the bed. My room was dark, but a slice of moonlight broke through the blinds. It lit his face up, softening the harsh lines I was growing used to. There was a sparkle in his dark eyes as his hands trailed down my body. He was barely touching me as he grazed over my hose-clad legs. His eyes stayed locked on mine, and in my sleep-induced haze, my breath hitched in my throat. His smile turned teasing as he pulled my heels off for me. Then, as I continued to watch him from beneath tired eyes, he eased my legs under the covers and pulled the duvet up to my chin. His eyes flicked over my face.

"What're you doing?" I questioned around a yawn.

"Get some sleep, princess. I'll take Dexter out."

He didn't need to say much more. After that, the warmth the covers created pulled me back under.

Vincent was fairly certain that Juliette was asleep before he even made it out of the bedroom.

He stood in the doorway, allowing himself the chance to admire her. To imagine, for just a moment, that she was someone he could keep. But he knew she wanted nothing to do with him, or his world. And he'd be damned if he dragged anyone else into it against their will.

Shaking his head, he drew the door shut as he entered the hall. Dexter lifted his head, staring at Vincent from his spot on the couch. Vincent knelt, patting the floor to call the dog to him. There was no hesitation before he trotted over. He set his big head on Vincent's knee as his tail wagged.

"You keep her safe, you hear me?" Vincent told the dog, rubbing behind his ears. "I'll do my part too. But she likes to disappear. She's been spotted with us, and I won't risk anyone trying to hurt her to get to us." To get to him.

Never again.

Vincent clipped Dexter's leash onto his collar and took him out for a long walk. He kept an eye out for anyone who could be a threat to the brown-eyed woman who made his heart beat a little faster for the first time in years.

THIRTEEN

MINOR SLIP UPS

"Fuck," I breathed as my back collided with the floor mat. *Again.*

"You're not focused," Jack chastised, taking my hand in his to pull me to my feet.

"*You're* not focused," I muttered, brushing off my leggings.

He rolled his eyes at me. "Again."

I took my stance in front of him with a bone-deep groan. We had been at it for what felt like hours. He had barely let me take a break to breathe. For some reason, Jack seemed to think I was getting jumped every night. I guess I could tell him I had a very dangerous, blonde puppy dog tagging along everywhere I went, but I decided against it. If I thought too hard about it, it might summon him to find me. It had taken a lot of maneuvering to escape the building without him noticing.

Waking up the morning after Vincent drove me home had been disorienting, to say the least. I knew he had taken me home that Tuesday night over two weeks ago. I also knew that I had been completely out of it. For some reason, I was convinced that he had been sweet and caring. That he had taken Dexter out for me. It just made no sense. Vincent didn't care about me, let alone my dog. Why would he have gone out of his way to do something nice for us?

But then again, I couldn't ignore the fact that Dexter hadn't tried to wake me up in the middle of the night to go out. Meaning he had to have gone outside.

Lost in my thoughts, I missed Jack's movement. He swiped my legs out from under me with little effort. My back slammed the mat with a resounding *whack* as my breath left me.

"Juliette," Jack growled, clearly getting frustrated with me.

"Shut up," I spat, blowing my hair out of my face without getting up. He wasn't nearly as irritated with me as I was. I couldn't turn my brain off to focus for the life of me. What Vincent had done had plagued me the whole two weeks, and well into every session with Jack, too. I couldn't understand his motives. Someone like Vincent Monroe didn't just take out a girl's dog without some form of ulterior motive. I sure as hell didn't believe he was taking me home out of the kindness of his heart, either. Which he continued to do. He wanted something from me. I just couldn't figure out what.

Jack's hands gripped my waist as he hauled my unwilling body into a standing position. He set his hands on my shoulders, ducking down so that he could catch my eye. "Jules, what's wrong?"

"Nothing."

"Haven't we had the talk about trust already?"

"I'm just distracted."

"You don't say."

"Fuck off," I growled, swatting his hands off me before going on the offensive. He wasn't expecting my attack, and I had him on the floor before he could catch his bearings. He blinked up at me, and I struggled to contain my grin.

Something in his eyes flashed, and in an instant, I was the one on my back.

"Once again, you're distracted."

I shoved him off me. "I just said that," I snapped. Huffing, I allowed myself to fall flat on the mat. It was a day for the books: one of the least productive days ever.

"Get up."

"No."

"Now."

"You're not my boss."

"No," he said, sitting down beside me. "However, I am someone who's trying to help you. I'm just not sure if you really want it."

A sigh heaved its way out of my mouth. Everything in me wanted to throw a tantrum. Why couldn't I just forget about Vincent? I only needed to get him off my mind for the duration of the training session. Otherwise, nothing was going to be accomplished. Jack was trying so hard to help me, and I couldn't absorb anything. Except for the stinging pain in my back every single time I hit the mat.

"It's a guy," I said before I could stop myself.

"Is he a threat?"

Oh, buddy. If you only knew.

"No," I said anyway. "I just can't figure out what he wants."

Jack crossed his legs and leaned back on his arms. One of his eyebrows quirked. "What do you mean?"

"He takes me home from work. And he's just always *there*. I mean, I guess it's nice that I don't have to walk all the time but–"

"These don't sound like bad things."

"That's the problem." I rolled onto my side and met his warm, tawny eyes. "He's not the kind of guy to do things for someone with no benefit to himself. So, I don't know what he wants from me."

"Maybe he just wants *you*."

I held his gaze for a solid six seconds before I burst into a fit of laughter. Not just any kind of laughter, either. It was the bellyaching, knee-slapping, I-should-have-abs-after-this kind of laughter. Jack looked at me like I was psychotic. And maybe I was, but that was single-handedly the funniest thing I had heard in a long time. When I finally quieted down, he rolled his eyes and stood. He hoisted me up by my elbow and steadied me.

"Feel better?" he asked. Covering my mouth with my hand to hold in another fit of giggles, I nodded. I needed that. "Good. Let's go."

And he was on the attack again.

We went at it for another thirty minutes. But my head was finally clear. I could dodge or deflect almost everything he threw at me. When I pinned him down on the mat again, he tapped out with a wicked grin on his face. We finished up and he walked me to the front door since Sherry was out for the day.

"Thank you," I threw over my shoulder as I was about to leave. "I really appreciate everything you're doing for me."

"Just be focused when you get here next time."

I mock-saluted him and walked out.

As I hoisted my duffle onto my shoulder, I began my walk home. It was getting close to when I needed to get ready for work, which sucked. A deep breath left me as I set myself at a brisk pace. I was going to have to take Dexter on a long walk the following day to make up for not spending a lot of time with him. I had been in a such haze. Between the endless cramps and my brain hyper-focusing on a certain gang leader, I had been next to useless the past couple of weeks.

"What are you doing here?" I asked the minute the window rolled down. Lucas smiled at me. I had spotted the SUV from a block away. We stared at one another for a few beats before he shrugged.

"I was waiting for you to make yourself known. Where are you coming from?"

"None of your, or *his*, business," I seethed. "Tell Vincent I don't need a damn babysitter."

"Do you really think that's going to work?"

"Then lie to him. Tell him you're watching my every move. But leave."

"He'll figure it out."

"He's not omniscient."

"What?"

I rolled my eyes. "He doesn't know everything. You'll be fine."

"You and I *both* know he'll figure it out," he reiterated.

He was right. I didn't want to admit it, but I knew it was true. I just didn't know how to feel about it. Was Vincent still worried I would go to the police? It had been so long that it wasn't like they would believe me. Roberts, or whoever he was, was probably holed up somewhere nursing his wounds. If he was even still alive. A shiver raced down my spine at the thought, and I had to shake my head to clear it. There was nothing to be done about it anymore.

"Guess you're stuck with me, sugar," Lucas said, his voice breaking me out of my thoughts.

"Twenty-two," I muttered before turning on my heel and marching towards my apartment. It wasn't like I could even sick Dexter on him. The ungrateful pup seemed to be quite fond of the gang members that used my apartment as some kind of haven. Lucas's laughter followed me until the door to the lobby fell shut.

Asshole.

I took my time getting ready for work. If Lucas was going to just camp outside the building, he could take me. Having a ride to work cut the commute in half, which doubled the time I had to get ready. I used part of the extra time to take Dexter on a short walk. It wasn't enough to make up for what I owed him, but it was a start. He trotted along beside me as I let my mind wander again. A certain pair of forest eyes flitted through my mind, and I had to stop myself from physically shaking my head like an etch-a-sketch to remove the visual. Damn him.

When I was finally ready for work, I crouched down to hug Dexter goodbye. He licked my face, and I laughed, tightening my arms around his muscular neck. "I love you," I said, scratching him behind the ears. "Be good." Phone and keys in hand, I pulled the door shut and locked it. My heels clicked along the tile in the lobby before I headed back out into the waning daylight.

I froze.

The black SUV was gone.

Of *all* the times for Lucas to listen to me, it had to be this time. I bit the inside of my cheek as I contemplated what to do. There was no way I could make it to work on time if I attempted walking. Devyn didn't have a car. Dante was already at the club. I didn't have Lucas's number.

But I had Vincent's.

The thought formed before I could stop it, and others swiftly followed it.

He was probably busy. I didn't want to see him. I definitely didn't want to start *asking* him for favors. That would go against everything I was trying to accomplish by cutting him out of my life.

The phone rang as I held it against my ear.

"Monroe," he answered on the second ring. His voice was gruff, and I heard something slam in the background.

"Bad time?" I asked, running my fingers through my hair.

"Juliette? What's wrong?" he questioned, his voice taking on a lilting softness from one heartbeat to the next.

"Why do you always assume something is wrong when I call you?"

"Because I know you're not just calling me to chat."

"Touché. So, I got myself into a little bit of a situation."

"Spit it out, princess."

I huffed. "Lucas was outside, so I took my time getting ready for work because I was going to make him take me. Now he's gone, and if I walk, I'm going to be late as hell."

"Lucas is gone?"

Shit. "Yes, but it's not his f–"

"I'll be there in five." And he disconnected the call.

Double shit.

I stared at my reflection in the blank black screen. Did I get Lucas in trouble? I figured he left because he had been needed elsewhere, not because he was actually *listening* to me. I pressed the edge of my phone against my forehead and tapped it a couple of times. *Stupid, stupid, stupid.* If Vincent was at the warehouse, that meant he was at least twenty minutes away. *At least.* So where was he that he could be here in five? What was I pulling him away from?

Must not have been important.

Sure enough, a black sedan came skidding to a stop in front of my building barely five minutes later. The passenger side door was nearest me, and it swung outward. Vincent looked at me from where he leaned across the center console. His eyebrows arched before he straightened. I assumed that was my cue to get in. My legs were wobbly as I made my way to the car. I didn't enjoy being around Vincent when he was angry. We hadn't known one another long, but it was enough time for me to realize that the erratic twitch in his jaw wasn't a good thing.

"Vincent–" I started.

"He had orders, Juliette," he stated, cutting me off. "He's supposed to be watching you. It's as simple as that."

"I told him to leave."

"Sorry to break it to you, princess, but you do not outrank me." His voice was so tight and controlled that a shiver skittered down my spine. The darkness that always reminded me just how dangerous this man was, rolled off him in waves. I bit my lip but kept quiet. There was nothing I could say to him.

We drove in silence for a while, only the soft notes of a piano filling the car. When we were about halfway to work, I noticed him relaxing his white-knuckle grip on the steering wheel. The twitching in his jaw stopped and he let out a deep breath. Almost unconsciously, I reached for him, and my hand landed on his forearm. He went rigid again for half a second before all the tension left him. His eyes cut to me.

"Don't kill him," I said, letting one corner of my mouth lift in a small smile.

His lips twitched. "I'm not going to kill him. But he's definitely in trouble."

"I'm not going to the cops. I think you know that by now. There is no reason for him to be watching me anymore." He stayed silent. "I'm serious. You can trust me."

"I don't know about that," he grumbled, shifting his grip on the wheel so that my hand slipped off his. It fell limply back to my side. "He's staying with you."

Why? The thought floated through my brain, but I refused to voice it. If Vincent still planned on killing me, I didn't want the verbal confirmation. I didn't need it. I was afraid of him enough as it was, even if I tried to pretend that I wasn't. There was a small part of me that still screamed for me to stay away from this man.

I took my seat belt off before the car even stopped rolling when we pulled into the parking lot of the bar. He caught my arm before I had the chance to hop out. Our gazes met as I turned back to him. There was something like heat in the endless green of his eyes. His touch was gentle, and warmth bloomed in my chest. I couldn't look away from him.

"What?" I asked when I couldn't stand the silence any longer.

"I'll be here at close."

My eyes rolled. "I can walk, Vincent."

"Not gonna happen, princess," he responded, releasing me not only from his touch but also from whatever hypnosis his eyes had drowned me in as well.

I huffed. He was impossible. Instead of arguing with him, I just hauled myself out of the car. It took everything in me not to turn around and look at him as I crossed to the bar's back entrance. The sound of the car driving off only sounded once I had stepped through the threshold and into work.

FOURTEEN

SMALL FAVORS

Dante eyed me as I walked in. I held up a single finger when he opened his mouth.

"Do not start," I said.

"Who dropped you off?" His tone was casual enough, but there was a sharpness in his eyes that I recognized. Mother hen mode: activated.

"How do you know I didn't walk?"

He nodded towards the small bank of monitors along the back wall that were hooked up to our security cameras. We could see the tail end of Vincent's car leaving the frame of the camera that overlooked the back entrance. My teeth snagged my bottom lip. How was I going to get out of this one?

"Bet it was the gangbanger," Devyn cooed, sauntering her way into the room.

"Would you shut up?" I grumbled, narrowing my eyes at her.

"Jules, how many times do I have to tell you to stay away from him?" Dante asked. His eyebrows drew together in worry, casting deep shadows over his molten brown eyes.

"Calm down, both of you." Walking over to the computer, I threw my purse down and clocked in. "I would have been late if he didn't bring me." There was no use in denying it now. They both knew that there was no one in my life that could have dropped me off besides Vincent.

Wow, that sounded pathetic.

My words were jumbled and unintelligible as I walked out onto the floor.

"I'm not going out with you," I said. A small chuckle fell from my lips as I handed Chris his last drink at the end of the night. He had gotten absolutely hammered, which was something I had never seen before. He was usually so composed. But he had told me his day had been shit, and he needed me to get him drunk. I thought I had performed my job very well. I almost felt sorry for him.

He pouted in response to my answer to his question. "But why not?"

"Because I don't date my customers."

"Jules, all you do is work. If you don't date your customers, you're gonna stay single forever," Devyn piped in from across the bar.

The look I sent her was scathing. "I don't need any men in my life."

"You mean to say you don't need any *more* men in your life."

"Devyn," I warned.

"I didn't take you for the polyamorous type, Jules," Chris said, his voice slurring. His brows pulled together as he contemplated what Devyn had said. Bless this poor man.

"I am absolutely not," I assured him, shooting Devyn another dirty look. "I just have a lot going on right now. And, honestly, I don't see you like that, Chris."

"Figured as much," he grumbled, resting his cheek on his hand. "I think we could be good together."

"She doesn't," a new voice cut in.

"The fuck are you doing here?" Devyn asked, coming to stand directly beside me. "We don't like you." She brandished the shot glass she was cleaning like a weapon.

My eyes rolled of their own accord. I was choosing to focus on my irritation with my best friend instead of the way my heartbeat changed pace when Vincent walked up. And I was *definitely* not reacting to the fact that the two words he had snapped at Chris sounded mildly possessive. That was certainly not the reason I was pressing my thighs together.

I needed serious help.

"What're you doing here, Vincent?" I asked, surprised at how even my voice came out.

His forest eyes stayed focused on Chris as he answered me. "Closing was over an hour ago. I wanted to make sure you didn't dart off on your own."

"Just got pulled into conversation. I told you I didn't need you to take me home."

"You're not walking."

"I think that may be the only thing we agree on," Dante threw in, appearing out of nowhere.

"Dante," Vincent greeted, cutting his eyes to my boss for the briefest of seconds before he returned to glaring at Chris. Chris, to his credit, was glaring back at Vincent with all the venom he could in his inebriated state. It took me a moment to realize that they might know each other, being on opposite sides of the law and all. *Men.*

"Alright, Chris. Your total is seventy-four dollars."

"Jesus," he breathed, digging into his pocket for his wallet.

"You said you wanted to be drunk. Doesn't help you drink the fancy stuff." Shaking my head, I counted the drawer. Chris slapped three fifties down onto the counter and slid off his stool. "Hey, where're you going?" I hollered after him.

"Home?" he called over his shoulder. He was stumbling. His blonde hair stood up at odd angles, and his tie was cockeyed. Shoving past Vincent, I hurried after the lawyer. I whipped him around to face me. His hands came to rest on my waist as he re-balanced himself. A sweet smile slid onto his face as our eyes met. "Aw, are you worried about me?"

"Of course I am, you idiot," I muttered, reaching up to straighten his tie. "You're not driving yourself home."

"Can drive."

"Not even close. Give me your keys."

He fished around in his pockets until he came up with his keys. He begrudgingly placed them in my outstretched hand. But now I faced a whole new dilemma. I didn't want Chris to drive home, but I also didn't really want to drive and be stuck with his car. My eyes widened as an insane idea passed through my mind. Biting my lip, I turned to Vincent. His gaze zeroed in on where Chris's hands were still resting on my hips. It was a long shot.

"Vincent?" I called.

His eyes snapped to mine before narrowing. "No."

"You don't even know what I was going to say!"

"I'm not giving him a ride home. Call a cab."

"It's too late."

"That's ridiculous."

"Then at least follow us and then take *me* home?"

"No."

"Please?" We locked ourselves in a staring match. That muscle in his jaw ticked a few times before he closed his eyes. He blew out a heavy breath through his nose before he opened them again.

"Fine."

Dante and Devyn exchanged skeptical glances, but I pretended I didn't see. I didn't care what was going through their minds right now. I had just won an argument with Vincent Monroe, and I was feeling proud of myself. A smile broke out across my face, before I turned back to Chris.

"Problem solved."

Neither man looked happy as I finished closing with Devyn. We all said goodbye to one another as she got in the car with Dante. Once they were gone, I turned back to Vincent. He was side-eyeing

Chris, and Chris ignored him to focus on me. My eyes rolled again. *Idiots,* I thought as I pressed the unlock button on the fob in my hand. A sleek, silver sedan winked at me from the back of the lot. I felt the two men following me as I made my way over to it. I opened the passenger door with a flourish, giving Chris a cheeky grin. He rolled his eyes at me before climbing in. As I rounded the car and reached for my door handle, someone else's hand closed over it first. Vincent opened the door for me, and our eyes connected.

There was so much lying in wait in the depths of his eyes. So much that I didn't want to linger on. At least not right now.

"Be careful," he warned. I saluted him, snapping the tension that had built around us before I slid into the car. He slammed my door and a small giggle bubbled out of my mouth in response.

The drive to Chris's was relatively silent other than his directions. But as he directed me into a more upscale neighborhood, he shifted his gaze to me. I kept my attention ahead, but I could feel the weight of his stare.

"What's up?" I asked as I pulled into the driveway he pointed out. The house was modest. Almost picturesque, with the white picket fence surrounding the manicured lawn. I almost snorted. It was smaller than I would have thought for a man of Chris's status, but even with the little I knew about the lawyer, it made sense.

"Vincent Monroe, huh?"

I winced. "So, you know him?"

"VPD has been trying to pin that man down for years, but nothing ever sticks. I may not work in the DA's office, but people talk. He's dangerous."

"Chris–"

He held his hands up to cut me off; the gesture placating. "It's not my place, I know," he said, blowing out a breath. He ran his hand through his blonde locks. Our gazes met, and he gave me a soft smile, eyes warm. "But if you ever get tangled up in anything to do with that world, you come to me. Okay?"

"You're corporate law."

"I'd make an exception."

High beams flashed in the rearview mirror, and I had to restrain the laugh that wanted to bubble out of me. Without a word, I flung my door open and heaved myself out of the low car. Chris mirrored me and looked at me across the roof of the vehicle. I tossed him his keys, and he caught them effortlessly in his hand. Glancing at the SUV sitting behind us, I held up a finger to Vincent. His eye roll was almost palpable, but he nodded before focusing his attention on his phone.

My gaze caught Chris's, and I gave him a grin. "Thank you," I said, crossing my arms on the roof and propping my chin on them. "If it ever comes to something like that, I'll keep it in mind."

"Good. Night, Jules."

"Night."

Chris made his way up the walk, and I watched him until he was safely inside the house. Then I turned back to the force of nature sitting in the car at the end of the drive. His eyes were already on me. Something in me told me I was going to get it once I was in that car, but I appreciated what he had done so much that I would welcome it. For a split second, I almost considered telling him that Lucas would be fine to keep tailing me.

Almost.

I had to jump a little to get into the SUV without Vincent's help, which caused me to scowl once I got settled in the seat. He eyed me but didn't comment as he braced his hand on the headrest behind me, turning to look out the back window as he reversed out of the driveway. My mouth went dry at the sight of him. With the weight of his attention elsewhere, I allowed myself the chance to ogle him.

He was so beautiful. Not the kind of beauty one would find on a runway. No. Vincent was the kind of beauty that only existed in chaos. In the eye of a storm or in the aftermath of a lightning strike.

That muscle was twitching along his jaw, cluing me into just how much this whole interaction had affected him. But as he turned back to the road in front of us, his eyes caught mine. I'm not sure what he saw on my face, but I watched the tension wash out of him. His jaw unclenched, his shoulders dropped, and that ghost of a smile played at the edges of his full lips.

We were silent for a long time. Chris lived in the complete opposite direction that I did, meaning Vincent had gone even more out of his way than usual to see us both home. I worried my bottom lip between my teeth before digging around in my purse. When I found a twenty, I slipped it into the cup holder. A hand shot out, grabbed the money, and stuffed it back into my purse before I could blink.

"Vincent," I said, trying to put the money back in the cup holder. "Take the money."

"Not on my life," he said.

I huffed. "Then how am I supposed to repay you?"

His eyes twinkled as a grin to rue that of the Cheshire Cat tilted his lips. "I'll take an IOU on that one."

"Nothing too extreme." My eyes snapped shut. I knew I was going to regret those words.

"Sure thing."

I didn't believe him for an instant.

When we pulled up in front of my apartment, I turned in my seat to face him. "Did you talk to Lucas?"

"He's suspended."

"I didn't realize you were a principal."

He shot me a dark look. "He won't be getting his cut of any profit for a bit. Arkin will take over his job of shadowing you."

"That's a bit extreme."

"No."

"Vincent–"

"Closed subject, princess."

We held one another's gaze for a moment. I wanted to tell him to ease up on poor Lucas, but I knew he wouldn't. If there was one thing I had learned about Vincent, it was that we were incredibly similar in how stubborn we were. He had decided, and I would bet that there was next to nothing that I could do to convince him. Letting out a bone-deep sigh, I threw my door open and slammed it behind me.

I only saw his headlights pull away from the curb once I inserted my key into my door.

Lucas was sitting in Vincent's office when he got back to the warehouse.

"Why are you in my chair?" Vincent asked, narrowing his eyes at his second in command.

The blonde grinned at him. "Are you really assigning Arkin to stick with Juliette?"

"Until further notice, yes."

"She hates being tailed. She's not going to the cops. What's the endgame here, Vince?"

Vincent clenched his jaw. He had known this line of questioning was inevitable. Knew that his men would want to know why he was using up the manpower to have someone with Juliette as often as possible. But it wasn't their consciences that would bear the weight if anything happened to her. There were still people out there who were loyal to the other gangs, his rivals. Ever since he had taken over, there had been people gunning for his throat.

"I need you with me to hammer out everything with this deal with Henry Kline," Vincent finally said, turning his eyes back to his friend. "Until I know for sure no one will make the foolish decision to go after her for her association with this gang, I want someone close by."

"I thought you suspended me?" Lucas's voice was coy, and there was mirth sparkling in his hazel eyes.

Vincent rounded his desk and shoved Lucas out of his chair. The blonde dissolved into laughter and sprung to his feet within seconds. That grin didn't leave his face as he settled himself in the chair on the opposite side of the desk. Vincent rolled his eyes before sinking into his own seat.

"From Juliette, yes. But not from this deal. This is the biggest exchange we've worked on in years. If we can secure it smoothly, we can let the dust settle a bit. The VPD have been amping up their efforts to put me behind bars lately."

Lucas tapped his fingers against his knee, his eyes searching Vincent's face. He knew there was more to the story. Vincent had lost so much in building this gang, and he knew his friend carried that guilt with him. But he didn't think that was the only reason Vincent couldn't let this thing with Juliette go. Lucas had seen it with his own eyes. Juliette had gotten under Vincent's skin, and the gang leader had burrowed under hers as well.

Lucas couldn't wait to see what happened when they both just admitted it.

FIFTEEN

RECOGNIZING THE INEVITABLE

Just like Vincent had said, Arkin was the one sitting in front of my apartment building the following morning. And every morning after that.

Didn't he have anything better to do? Couldn't he be a little more inconspicuous?

My eyes rolled as I let the curtain in my bedroom fall closed. It overlooked the street in front of the building, so I could see Arkin plain as day when I peeked out. One would think the word *discreet* was a common thing in a gang member's vocabulary. Apparently not. Or maybe he just didn't care about hiding when I knew he was out there.

Dexter came trotting into the kitchen when I poured his food into his bowl. He pushed his entire body into me as he walked past like a cat. The coffee pot bubbled as it finished brewing, and I got a mug out of the cabinet. I needed some normalcy. The gang had encroached on my life. The only time I felt wholly separate from them was when I was with Jack. Training with him had become my haven.

It still blew my mind that none of the men had ever figured out where I went when I vanished. I mean, I did my best to sneak out either early in the morning, or when I knew Arkin had been called away. He only ever realized I was gone when I returned, and he would just give me a disgruntled look when I walked back through the front doors.

Vincent was anything but happy with the missing time.

He questioned me about it from time to time. But I continued to dodge the interrogation and keep him from finding out about my self-defense training. Not that it was some big secret I had. But my time at the gym, training with Jack, was *mine*.

On the other hand, I had become a little reliant on Vincent and his car. Devyn and Dante hated it, but they were warming up to the gang. I was guessing in Dante's case it had something to do with the amount of money Vincent and the guys had been pouring into Tuxedo throughout the past few months.

Had it really been that long?

The night I was 'kidnapped' seemed like a distant memory. The guys had become a staple in my life. They were always there. If not just Arkin, then Brandon and Lucas sometimes came over too. Lucas had told me he didn't blame me for ratting him out. He was just trying to do me a favor and picked a terrible time for it. Somehow, they had become important to me, and I missed them if I went too long without seeing them.

It was crazy how life worked sometimes.

A knock on my door pulled me from the recesses of my mind. Dexter's head raised, and he let out one soft bark, but nothing more. Just from his reaction, I had a feeling I knew who it was. Immediately, I grabbed another mug to pour coffee into. Then I took both cups to the door and fought the battle with how to hold them and also unlock the door. I was an idiot for not thinking about putting them down first. After only spilling a little of the coffee onto my arm, I walked back to the couch and sat down, placing both cups on the coffee table.

"Come in!" I hollered a minute later. He was usually busting through the door the second he heard the lock tumble.

Lucas came in, eyes riveted to his cellphone as he shut the door behind him. He still didn't look up as he crossed the room and sat down next to me. When this had become our routine, I couldn't really say. Even though Vincent assigned Arkin as my new tail, Lucas periodically popped in to check on me. I think he knew more than any of them how much I hated having someone puppy-dog me around all the time, and it was nice to get a break to just talk with him. He fielded questions about the gang, always making sure I wanted to know what I was asking. Their life was dangerous. The more I knew about the ins-and-outs of everything they did, the more sucked into their world I became. Lucas knew exactly how to explain things so that I'd understand, but without going into the gritty details.

He reached for his cup of coffee, his eyebrows furrowing as he glared at his phone.

"Lucas, watch–" But I was too late. His fingers hit the rim of the mug and it slid backwards, sloshing hot coffee onto his hand from the force of the movement.

"Son of a bitch!" he cursed, dropping his phone to the ground as he shook his hand and then clutched it against his chest. Unlike me, he drank his coffee black. It was still just as hot as it had been when I poured it.

"Idiot," I muttered, shoving off the couch to go get some paper towels. I tossed the roll to him when I returned.

"Sorry, sugar," he said, mopping up the mess.

"It's fine. You okay?"

"It was more reactionary than anything. It didn't hurt too bad."

"You know you're allowed to feel pain, right?"

"Shut up." Dexter came in and licked Lucas's hand. The blonde smiled before rubbing Dexter behind the ears.

"What were you so focused on, anyway?" I asked, nodding towards his phone.

"Don't worry about it."

Why do men think telling a woman *'don't worry'* will actually make her stop worrying? It has the exact opposite effect. At least on me.

"Lucas."

"It's nothing."

"Mhmm."

"Really."

"Sure." Eventually, he was going to wear down. I had learned how to play this game with him, and I always came out on top.

"It's nothing!"

"Okay."

"Vince is worried about this deal we have going," he admitted.

Bingo.

"What's wrong?"

"Something just feels fishy. To all of us. But we have no proof. And it's with someone we've done business with time and time again. Not sure what's wrong."

"You guys know better than anyone to go with your gut."

"It's a big payoff. We'd be able to slip onto the back burner for a while. Gets the cops off our asses if activity dies down."

My lip curled at the mention of the police, but I shook it off. "Just be careful."

"Always am," he responded before picking up his coffee and blowing on it.

He stayed with me for a while longer. We made small talk, and I just enjoyed having his company. It wasn't exactly the normalcy I had been craving, but it was close. When he left, he made a comment about telling Vincent I said hi.

"Twenty-three!" I yelled after him as I chucked a pillow. It hit the front door after he shut it. Even though his laughter was muffled, I still heard it.

Arkin waved when Dexter and I stepped out into the sunshine. I waved back and headed off. Dexter needed to stretch his legs as badly as I did. The thing about training with Jack was that it was making me want to be all-around more active. Days that I wasn't training with him, I was itching to get out of the apartment. Half the time, I had to restrain myself from going for a run. Part of me wasn't willing to run these streets. Even with Dexter and Arkin, I still wouldn't feel completely safe.

There was an ulterior motive for my walk. I had finally saved the extra money to buy a gun, and I was excited. It had been my goal for so long. Because my knife and mace hadn't stopped me from getting kidnapped. Then again, if I had shot Lucas, he probably wouldn't be one of my best friends.

There was a tug in my chest. Even if they drove me nuts, I didn't want to think about a life that the gang hadn't infiltrated.

That Vincent hadn't become a part of.

No. Damn him.

Even if I didn't want to admit it, the gang leader intrigued me. And he was the first person to catch my attention in a very long time. The last serious relationship I had been in had an awful ending. It was a long time ago, but it still stung now and then. Apparently, being upset over the sudden death of your mother was unacceptable. That man had abandoned me at one of my darkest points, which had only caused me to sink even lower. Dante and Devyn were thankfully around back then. I wasn't sure I could've pulled myself out of that depression without them.

Not to say that Devyn hadn't attempted to send me hurtling back into the dating game full force. But no one had ever kept my attention for more than a couple of weeks.

Not until this stupid man wormed his way into my life.

Scary gangbanger, Jules, I reminded myself. Which was definitely part of what was so interesting. Vincent couldn't be too much older than I was. So how did he get to the position he was in?

Did I even want to know?

Probably not.

My mind continued to run circles around itself until the gun shop came into my field of view. The shop had a shooting range in it as well. One that I had frequented for a while before the gang came into my life. I had wanted to make sure that I was comfortable with a firearm before I purchased one. When the bell over the door jingled, Marco looked up at me. A smile cracked across his weathered skin as he straightened. Marco reminded me of old action-movie heroes. He had a head full of thick, steel gray hair, and a beard he kept trimmed close to his skin. He crossed his beefy arms over his chest, his flint-colored eyes crinkling around the corners.

"Long time no see, Jules," he greeted, his voice booming throughout the empty shop. His eyes snapped down to Dexter. The dog's tail wagged. "And Dexter! How ya doin' ya little shit?"

"Hello to you too, Marco," I said, a chuckle falling from my lips.

"What can I do for ya today?" he asked. He reached down behind the counter to grab the jar of treats he kept there. Marco was a sucker for anything furry on four legs.

"I think I want to practice with the Glock a little more. I've finally got enough to buy it."

"Told ya I would've just given ya a discount months ago, girl."

"And I told you I would make it. And look, I did."

The old man rolled his eyes at me before pulling the gun I was comfortable with from the case. He set it, the ammo, headphones, glasses, and the key to the range out on the counter for me. I traded him Dexter's leash for the paraphernalia. Making my way back to the range, I glanced over my shoulder just in time to catch the sight of a black SUV rolling to a stop outside the shop.

I unlocked the door to the firing range and stepped inside. Thankfully, it looked like I was the only one there. Walking down the aisle, I selected a booth and set everything down. When I was all set up, headphones and glasses on, I took my stance. The weight of the gun in my hands was familiar and caused me to smile. Letting out a breath, I fired off a few shots. I was no marksman, but I was proud of myself that they were at least all within the black silhouette. Time fell away as I tried to hit the bullseye.

Eventually, a prickling awareness crept up my spine. I slowly lowered the gun to the counter before turning around and slipping the headphones off.

Even though something in me was expecting him to be there, I still jumped when my eyes met Vincent's.

"Don't just sneak up on me like that!" I exclaimed, placing my hand over my hammering heart. He leaned against the wall behind me, arms and ankles crossed. He was the picture of ease with his long legs stretched out in front of him. His lips twitched as he pushed off and came over to me.

He invaded my space. For the first time in a while, I realized how much taller than me Vincent was. Besides being in the car, I kept my distance from him to try to curb the way my heart liked to kick-start in his presence. Without my heels, when he stood directly in front of me, I had to take a step back to meet his eyes. That step caused the counter to press against the small of my back, but I tried to ignore it. The man in front of me took up every ounce of my focus.

For the first time, I noticed his nose sat slightly crooked, like it had been broken more than once. There was a scar running from the top of his left eyebrow to almost his hairline. Neither of these facts surprised me, and they certainly didn't change how attracted to him I was. I knew he was dangerous; the scars were just more of a testament to that.

"Are you done staring?" he asked, causing my eyes to snap back to his.

Shit. "Yes."

"What're you doing?"

"What does it look like? Practicing my shooting. Why are you here?"

"Arkin told me you walked into Marco's Guns. Of all places."

"And?" I crossed my arms to put a little more distance between us. "How is that any of your business?"

"Guns in this city are my business. Who do you think supplies Marco?"

My face paled. "That's illegal."

The look he gave me said: *no shit, Sherlock.* "Yes. And he wouldn't be able to stay in business if everything here were from us. There are just a few special things he gets from us that a few special people know about and that this is the place to get them."

"I don't want to know anymore," I muttered, dropping my gaze from his.

"Facts are facts, princess."

I knew that. It still didn't mean that it wasn't a shock. I had been coming here for close to a year. I could have run into Vincent at any time.

What would have happened had we met under different circumstances?

My eyes found his again. More than likely, I never would have spoken a word to him. Drooled over him a bit? Absolutely. But looking back on how everything had changed since meeting him, I couldn't picture my life without them. The guys were my *friends*. I couldn't imagine them, or this infuriating man, not being there.

His eyes softened, as if he could read my thoughts. And it wasn't like I had a good poker face. My emotions were probably laid out for him to see like a bad hand. He raised his hand to my face. It was a simple touch, just a brush of his fingertips along my jawline, but it sent the most pleasant shiver down my spine. Goosebumps erupted over every inch of my skin. In that instant, I wanted to kiss him so badly that something inside me ached.

Realizing I had feelings for a man like Vincent Monroe was a hard pill to swallow.

Sixteen

TIME WITH VINNIE

Vincent took a step back, giving me room to breathe, and the spell broke.

"You're a shit shot," he said.

"I am not!"

"No, you're not." There was laughter in his voice and his eyes glittered. Of course, he delighted in riling me up, the prick. "But you're not great either. Here," he placed his hands on my shoulders and spun me around to face the target. "Pick up the gun."

Doing as he instructed, I readied myself. I slipped the headphones back on without covering my ears, took my stance, and raised the gun. Vincent knocked my feet farther apart with his foot and brought his arms around me so that he was holding the gun as well. He steadied me and murmured instructions in my ear. I could barely hear him. From the moment he had pushed my legs apart, I was imagining a very *different* scenario that could include the same movement. Wondering what it would feel like if he just bent me–

Fucking hell, Jules.

My blood was pulsing through my veins and raising my body temperature to fever levels. Shaking my head, I forced myself to concentrate. He gave me a few more pointers, slipped the headphones over my ears, and then stepped back.

I fired.

It wasn't a bullseye, but it was the closest I had gotten. When I glanced back at him, the small touch of pride on his face was enough to make my stomach flip. He nodded his head at the target. I gave him a smile before refocusing on the task at hand. Each bullet I fired was closer and closer to the center. On my second clip, I hit the bullseye three times in a row. I laid the gun on the counter as another grin emerged. A light chuckle left Vincent's lips when I bounced on the balls of my feet. His laughter reminded me *he* was the reason for my improvement. Without stopping to consider, I spun on my heel and jumped, my arms slipping around his neck.

He stiffened for a second, and then his warm arms wound around my waist. His hold was firm, yet still gentle. He radiated strength, and it was like a balm over my frantic heart. Something clicked, and it was the safest I had felt in a long time. Longer than I cared to admit. For just a moment, time ceased to exist. I couldn't tell you how long we stood like that and just held each other. I think it took both of us by surprise.

Vincent withdrew from me, save for the hands he kept on my shoulders. He said something, but I couldn't hear him. I removed the headphones and tossed them onto the counter.

"Better," he repeated. His smile was edging on smug, and it made me want to smack him. Which felt much more normal than the warmth that was still meandering through my chest.

"Thank you."

"Don't mention it. Clean up and meet me out front." He didn't wait for me to acknowledge him before he started walking away. I rolled my eyes. I didn't know why him being bossy was surprising. It was what he did.

After I had gathered everything, I made my way back to the front. The first thing that caught my attention was that Vincent had squatted down in front of Dexter. He was petting him, but his focus was on Marco. Dexter stood when he saw me, causing Vincent's hand to slip. Both men turned towards me.

"Still like the way it shoots?" Marco asked, a broad smile stretching across his face.

"Yes. Remind me how much it was again?" I knew I had enough. I had rounded up so I would be sure, but the exact price was escaping me.

"Covered."

"What?" My voice went flat as my eyes cut to Vincent. That had better not have meant what I thought it did.

"The gun is yours. I handled it."

"Marco, give him his money back. Right now."

"Can't do that for ya, girl. He's kind of got a hand in what I do here."

The glare I shot Vincent was acidic. "I've been saving up for months to have the money for this gun. I have it, so I don't need your help."

"Suck it up, princess," he told me, rolling his eyes. "What's done is done."

My eyes narrowed. "I'll get you back for this."

"Sure."

We said our goodbyes to Marco and exited the shop. I tugged on Dexter's lead and headed back to my apartment without so much as a goodbye to Vincent. I was beyond pissed at him. How dare he do something like that without at least speaking to me about it first?

"Princess," he called, his voice lazy.

I picked up my pace.

Dexter let out a small whine as he looked over his shoulder. Of course, he liked Vincent. It was almost impossible not to. As much of an asshole as he was, his sweet moments were incredibly charming.

Bad Jules, I scolded myself. *Just because you've realized you like the asshole doesn't mean you have to stick up for him.*

A firm hand on the crook of my elbow jerked me to a stop. I was so focused on my thoughts; I hadn't even heard Vincent's footsteps as he came up behind me. He whirled me around to face him, and his forest eyes were fierce when they met mine.

"What do you want?" I fired off before he could open his mouth. I knew my eyes were blazing just as hot as his.

"You forgot this." He handed me the gun, and I scrunched my nose up at it. I couldn't even consider it mine. I hadn't paid for it. "Take it."

"No."

"Don't tell me no. Take the damn gun."

"*No.*"

Something akin to a growl rumbled in the back of his throat. "Juliette, you wanted this for a reason. Now. Take. It."

"I don't need your help, Vincent."

He jerked my purse away from me. I made a sound of protest, but the glare he sent me caused me to fall silent. He placed the gun inside it, along with two extra clips I had failed to notice, and then slid it back onto my shoulder. He let his hand rest on top of the strap. The heat of his touch radiated through the thin fabric of my shirt, and it took every ounce of resolve I had not to squirm. Our eyes held, and slowly, his hand slid around to the back of my neck. My breath hitched in my throat as he pulled me forward, bending down until our noses were centimeters away from one another. His gaze had me enraptured, and I had forgotten how to breathe. The reason I was angry with him retreated to the very back of my mind until I couldn't even find it anymore. Why was I mad at him? What had he done?

"I didn't even pay for it," he breathed.

Oh, right. He hadn't let me pay for the gun. What a stupid thing to be mad over.

"The gun you wanted is one that I specifically supplied Marco with. At the end of the day, it's mine. I'm the one the money comes back to. I don't want your money, princess. So just take the fucking thing."

"Okay."

His eyes widened the smallest fraction. He held me close to him for another moment before nodding and stepping away from me. I felt his absence like a bucket of ice water.

This is stupid.

"Glad to see you coming around. Now c'mon," he said, nodding towards the SUV. "Let's go."

"Go where?"

"I'm hungry. And I'm guessing you and Dexter are, too." The dog in question let out a small bark at the sound of his name. Vincent's lips twitched at the corners as he knelt to scratch my dog behind his ears. "That's what I thought."

That was how we ended up back in my apartment with Chinese takeout. Dexter was looking dejectedly down at his dog food, so I opened a fortune cookie and tossed it to him. If the dog could roll his eyes, he would have.

"Don't look at me like that," I muttered, turning my back on him before he could start begging. I tried my hardest not to give him table food too often. His stomach was easily upset, and I didn't want to deal with him vomiting or having diarrhea. One of Vincent's rare, full-blown smiles graced his face when he caught my attention. "What?" I asked, my forkful of rice halfway to my mouth.

"Nothing, princess."

"Liar."

"No."

"Whatever," I huffed.

We ate the rest of our food in silence. Vincent had won the argument about paying when we had gotten the food. It was a coin toss. He called heads; I called tails. When it landed heads up, I couldn't stop myself from pouting. He had already gotten me the gun for free. I didn't need him to buy my food too. However, a deal was a deal.

I stood and picked up a couple of empty containers. Vincent grabbed his and followed me into the kitchen. We tossed the garbage into the trash and then I placed the few things we hadn't eaten into the fridge.

"Do you want anything?" I asked him, still holding the door open.

His gaze raked over me in a way that made me shiver. He saw it and his lips tilted. "Do you have any beer?"

"Unfortunately, no."

His eyebrows arched, and he pushed off where he was leaning against the counter. He invaded my space for the umpteenth time that day. He bent down and examined the meager contents of the fridge over my shoulder. His body molded flush against mine and suddenly I couldn't think straight. My breath had snagged in my throat. The only thought that remained in my head was the fantasy I had cut short at the gun range.

He hummed, and his chest rumbled against my back. "What a shame," he murmured, before standing straight and stepping away from me. My stomach clenched in the most pleasant way, and I had to take a deep breath. If he didn't stop pulling this shit, I was going to end up doing something we would both regret. After a few more deep breaths and some time to compose myself, the thought was still in my head when I turned around.

Vincent wasn't as far away as I had thought. He was directly behind me, and I ran into his chest when I tried to move.

"Can I help you?" I asked, crossing my arms to put some distance between us.

"I've gotta head out," he said. His voice was harder than it had been moments before. He wasn't looking at me, instead his gaze stayed locked on his phone screen.

"What's wrong?"

"Nothing."

"Vincent." His eyes met mine. That muscle in his jaw twitched, but his eyes lost a little of their rigidity. He slipped his phone into his pocket, then reached for me. I let him draw me into him. One hand settled on my hip as the other cupped my cheek. I blinked at him, waiting.

"Something's gone wrong," he told me, running his fingertips along my jaw before tracing them down my throat. "The men need me."

"What happened?"

"I know you don't actually want to know. Everyone's fine. I'm going to be fine, but I have to go."

"Be careful."

"I always am," he said. His eyes clouded over for just a moment, then they steeled. He pressed a feather-soft kiss to my forehead. Our eyes locked before he withdrew from me.

Dexter whined at the door when Vincent left.

What the hell had just happened?

Seventeen

FIRST STEPS

"You're oddly aggressive today," Jack commented as I slammed my fist into the punching bag again.

"Shut up," I grumbled, throwing my gloves to the ground.

My intensity had impressed Jack when I arrived. I had already gone on a run before coming in, so I was buzzing by the time we started training. Apparently, I had too much energy to go at him, so we had started out with the punching bag. What felt like an hour later, I still felt as wired as I had when first stepped into the studio.

I think Jack could see it in my eyes.

"Anything you want to talk to me about?"

"No." Definitely not the fact that for the first time in weeks, Vincent hadn't driven me home the night before.

That definitely was not bothering me one bit.

"Jules."

"I'm fine."

He rolled his eyes at me, which resulted in my blood igniting. I had him on the floor before he could blink. From the look on his face, I wasn't the only one surprised at the ease with which I pinned him. He stared up at me but made no move to throw me. Instead, he adjusted so that he was lying flat on his back. As I straddled his stomach, I could feel the blush crawling up my neck. It didn't help that he let his hands settle on my hips. His tawny gaze caught mine, and I froze.

"You sure?' he asked, his voice soft as cashmere.

"No." I slipped off him and fell onto my back beside him.

"The guy?"

"Isn't every girl's problem a man in some way?" I grumbled, throwing my arm across my eyes.

He chuckled. "You might have a point."

"I don't wanna talk about it."

Jack took the hint and hauled himself to his feet. He reached down and took my hand before pulling me up as well. He used more force than I expected, and I stumbled into his chest. His hands steadied me, but instead of stepping away from me, he gripped my chin with gentle fingers and tilted my face up. For half a second, his eyes searched mine. My brows rose of their own accord, but I made no move to step away from him. The shake of his head was almost imperceptible when he released his hold. Even though he wasn't touching me anymore, neither of us moved.

"I need you to trust me if this is going to work. We've talked about this." His voice was low, and I could swear that there was pleading in his eyes.

"I trust you as my trainer," I told him, taking a step back and raking my fingers through my hair. "This is different. And he really isn't anyone to worry about."

"Are you sure?"

No. "Yes."

Jack looked as skeptical about my statement as I felt. The thing was, I didn't even know what I was feeling, so how could I even begin to explain it to him? How was I supposed to tell him I had developed feelings for a man who had kidnapped me?

Okay, so maybe he wasn't the one who had technically kidnapped me, but it had been *for* him. And that sounded creepy.

There was absolutely no way to explain this situation to Jack without sounding like I was some kind of victim of Stockholm Syndrome. Which, maybe I was.

I was making my own head hurt.

It had been over a week since the incident in my kitchen with Vincent. I shouldn't still be thinking about it. More than that, I shouldn't have been *so* bothered by walking home last night. But I had grown accustomed to his company. Scrunching my eyes closed, I rubbed my temples.

"You good?" Jack asked, and I felt him step closer again.

"Fine," I replied, taking an equal step back. I hadn't imagined the warmth in Jack's eyes every time he looked at me, and I had enough on my plate without adding him to the mix.

When our eyes met again, he just shook his head. "Go home for the day. Do some yoga when you get a bit of free time. It'll help you unwind. Have a drink. Take a bubble bath. Something, woman."

"Sir, yes, sir," I said with a mock salute. A smile twisted my lips despite my mood. His grin matched mine as we said our goodbyes. I promised to be more on my game the next time I came in. Sherry waved to me as I exited the gym, and I winked at her before I slipped out the door.

The sky was dark with clouds when I left the studio. The oncoming rain was so heavy in the air I could feel it. My lip curled as I ducked my head and trudged on. After a while, I checked my phone. A missed call from Devyn and four from Vincent.

That brought me up short.

Why had Vincent called me? What on earth could have happened?

There was no way he was apologizing for the night before. He would have just texted, not called *four* times. I worried my lip between my teeth. It was probably nothing. Vincent's overbearing ass probably just wasn't used to people not being at his beck and call.

Should I call him back?

My phone rang in my hand, making my decision for me.

"Hello?"

"Where are you?"

"Well, hello to you too, Vinnie."

"Not funny, Juliette." My whole body seized up. That was obvious distress in his voice. "Where are you?"

I glanced up at the street signs above me to find that I was a good mile from the gym. So, I gave him my location. He ordered me to stay put and disconnected the call. I was dumbstruck. For once, I just did as I was told. I leaned against the brick store face behind me and waited.

The rain came down in a curtain. One second, I was dry, the next it soaked me down to the bone.

He had better hurry, I thought.

It wasn't too much longer that the black SUV rolled to a stop in front of me. I pushed off the wall and headed towards it. Before I could even reach for the handle, Vincent was around the car. He hadn't even bothered to turn it off, and his door was still hanging open. My eyes widened as he pulled me against him with a force he had never used with me. He crushed my body against his so hard I thought my bones would give way. He buried his face in the crook of my neck as one hand tangled itself in my hair and the other banded across the small of my back. Utterly at a loss, it took me a minute to react to him. As his warmth enveloped me, I forgot about the rain and wrapped my arms around him as well.

"Vincent, what–"

"They found a body," he said, cutting me off. He pulled back just enough to press his forehead against mine, but didn't release his death grip for an instant. "The cops did. Short, brunette, in her twenties. Three blocks away from your apartment. I went by this morning when the news broke. You weren't there. You weren't answering your phone. The men couldn't find you." His voice was strained as his eyes bored into mine.

"You thought I was dead?"

"The one night I don't take you home. The one night the guys are too busy with this deal to do it. The *one night* Arkin or Lucas wasn't with you." He shut his eyes, let out a deep breath through his nose, and pulled me impossibly closer. "I was terrified."

The admission was so quiet I barely heard it.

But I did, and suddenly I wasn't so cold.

"I'm okay," I murmured.

"Answer your phone next time." He pulled back enough to cup my face in his hands, running his thumbs across my cheekbones. The tenderness in his eyes took away from the bite in his tone.

"Okay." The urge to roll my eyes was so strong that I barely contained it. My sass was the last thing he needed right now. I had never seen him so distraught. I just couldn't fathom why. There was no way he felt the same way about me as I did about him.

Right?

"I'm taking you home. Get in," he ordered as he swung my door open.

This time I did let my eyes roll, but I got in all the same. For just a moment I worried about the seats, but then I remembered he was just as wet as I was. The ride home was silent. Not even the familiar melody from a set of piano keys distracted from the constant hum of the rain. When Vincent finally parked the car, neither of us moved. Instead, we just sat within the safety of the car. I wanted to say something to him. Reach for his hand. Anything. I just didn't know what to do. I never thought I would see him in the state he was in.

Eventually, I slipped out. He followed me. After beeping the SUV locked, he placed his hand on the small of my back as we walked. It confused me to find my apartment door unlocked when we reached it. Dexter was waiting patiently inside. Nothing seemed too out of place, but I could tell that someone had been inside my apartment while I had been gone. My eyebrows arched at Vincent.

"I told you I came by earlier."

"And you *broke in?*"

"You need better locks. The locksmith is coming by in the morning."

"Dexter is usually more than enough of a reason for someone to stay out." I glanced at the traitor, knowing he must have let

Vincent have free rein while he was here. "Maybe I need a better guard dog."

I was in my bedroom before the realization dawned.

"*What* locksmith?" I asked, popping my head out into the hallway to glare at him where he stood in the center of the living room.

"The one I hired. He doubles in security, so I also told him to install a security system."

"Vince–"

"Juliette," he snapped. "Just... Don't fight me on this."

I harrumphed before slipping back into my bedroom to strip out of the wet clothes. I bit my bottom lip after changing out of my wet clothes. Leaving Vincent in his equally wet clothes sounded like a terrible idea. Rummaging through my drawers, I came up with a pair of basketball shorts and a shirt that I had stolen from an ex. I had had them for so long, I couldn't even remember who they had originally belonged to. But they were the best I could do, so I hoped they fit.

When I entered the living room, I tossed him the clothes. He arched a brow at me, then shook his head like he had thought better about whatever had crossed his mind. With no warning, he undid his belt. I whipped around to face away from him.

"A little warning next time!"

"Don't act like you don't want to look." His tone was back to normal, so I focused on that instead of the fact that he was right.

When he finished changing, I turned around. In an instant, it was glaringly obvious that the previous owner of the clothes and Vincent did not share the same physique. The t-shirt stretched across his chest and shoulders like a second skin. The shorts fit better, but I was trying to distract myself from the fact that I could see every outline of hard muscle that corded Vincent's body. This man was a storm waiting to be unleashed.

I took all his clothes, underwear included, and threw them into the dryer. He could wash them himself when he got home. He was sitting on the couch with Dexter in his lap when I finally made it back to him. That was when the true dilemma arose. It was my night off. What was I supposed to do with him?

"Come here," he said, his voice soft.

My thighs clenched. I ignored *that* reaction, but listened to his words all the same. My steps were slow, but eventually I sat on the opposite end of the couch to him with my back against the arm. For a few moments, I just studied him. I still wasn't sure how to take his admission earlier. I wasn't sure I was even supposed to have heard it, but I did. Something told me not very many things scared a man like Vincent Monroe. And the thought of me being gone? That was enough to *terrify* him.

"This isn't about me going to the cops anymore, is it?" I asked before I could stop.

Our eyes met.

The silence that followed spoke volumes. As if sensing the tension, Dexter jumped down and went into the dining room. Without him, the space between Vincent and I yawned open. He reached for me, and his grip on my wrist sent electricity firing into every nerve ending. He had me straddling his waist in a movement so swift it didn't register until it was too late. We went from being so separated to so close in a blink. His hands slipped underneath the hem of my t-shirt and his fingertips grazed along my hips just above my waistband. My breathing hitched and one of his full-blown smiles broke across his face.

Goosebumps rose as his heat sank into me. His touches weren't hesitant. In fact, they bordered on reverent. The soft strokes were rewiring my pulse to beat in time with each swipe of his thumb. It was like he was trying to reassure himself that I was still there.

Still alive.

He cupped the back of my head and drew me even closer.

"No," he responded, reminding me of my question. His eyes wandered to my lips.

I was the one that closed the distance between us. Fuck all the warning bells going off in the back of my mind.

He was so gentle with me. The care with which he handled me shouldn't surprise me anymore, but it still did. His lips moved against mine in a smooth rhythm, soft and urgent all at the same time. When I came up for air, his mouth didn't leave me. It just trailed a line of burning kisses from my jawline, down the column of my throat, and then repeated the journey back up. Every ounce of attraction I had for him burst forth from the recesses of my brain to demand my attention. I was aching for him.

He was still being so careful, and I was sick of it. When his mouth closed over mine again, I pulled his lower lip between my teeth and bit down. Maybe a little harder than I should have.

He let out a low hiss and constricted his arms around me until I could feel every inch of his body. At least I knew he was just as affected by me as I was by him, if the stab against my abdomen was any sign. He returned the bite in kind, and I dug my nails into his shoulders. He wrapped my legs around his waist, and the friction drove me mad. It repositioned his erection so that it rubbed directly against my core, and I almost whimpered.

Almost.

He stood in a fluid movement and carried me through my apartment as if I weighed nothing. My head was still reeling when he dropped me on my bed.

His gaze was scalding as it raked over me. He moved slowly to grip the bottom of my shirt. When I made no protest, he slipped it over my head and tossed it into the far corner of the room. His ghost of a smile pulled at his lips as he reached forward to flick the silver bars that ran through each of my nipples. I swatted his hands away and scooted back on the bed. His brows arched at me as he simply followed my retreat, crawling to hover over me.

"What?" I snapped under his scrutinizing. "Did you expect me to only have tattoos?"

"Kind of," his voice was just as heavy as his eyes, and it was almost my undoing.

"Sorry to disappoint."

"If you think I'm disappointed, you are sadly mistaken." He settled onto me, his body a comforting weight as he pinned me to the mattress. He flashed me a wicked grin before reclaiming my mouth in another head-spinning kiss.

Most of our clothes joined my shirt in a matter of minutes. The only thing separating us was the pair of shorts still on his body. His forest eyes searched mine as he paused. I knew what he was waiting for, and I nodded. His hands slipped lower until my back arched off the bed, only pressing me impossibly tighter against him. His fingers were teasing, just like the light dancing in his eyes. By the time he sank two of them inside me, his thumb rubbing maddeningly sure circles over my clit, I was a pathetic mess beneath him. The ease with which he worked my body was ridiculous. His eyes never left me, and he studied every reaction. Every twitch and tremble that his touch elicited. The moans that left my mouth didn't sound like my own, and when I finally fell over the edge, his mouth muffled my scream. I was panting as I tried to regain my bearings. He had this smug smile on his face that I wanted to smack off of it.

I almost did, but he caught my wrist and pinned it to the bed.

His free hand roamed down my body, gently stroking every dip and curve. Our eyes locked, and his lips tilted into that rare smile of his. He bent down and pressed a gentle kiss to my forehead before he met my gaze again.

"Are you sure you want to do this?' he asked.

His question threw me off guard. "What?"

"Princess, if you want to stop, I need you to tell me now." There was laughter in his voice, but I knew he was serious. I took a second to come back to my senses and all the nagging thoughts that I had pushed away earlier came back full force.

And Vincent Monroe missed nothing.

He pulled back from me but took me with him. He cradled my naked body against his chest, tucking my head beneath his chin. A sense of safety wound around my heart, and my eyes fluttered shut as I relaxed into him.

"Okay," he murmured. He held me until the aftershocks wore off and then kissed the top of my head. His hold loosened enough for me to slip from his lap, and he went to find our clothes. He picked all of it up and brought me my shirt and shorts before pulling his shirt back on.

Putting on my clothes, I felt more exposed to him than I had naked.. Cheeks flaming; I tried to move past him, but he caught my hand before I could get out of the room.

"What?" I rasped.

"What're you doing?"

"Going to the living room?"

"Don't hide from me."

My shoulders slumped. "I'm sorry."

"Don't be. C'mon, let's watch something."

And that was how I ended up curled up on Vincent's lap on what I thought would be a regular Thursday. I didn't know where the events of the day left us, but I knew I didn't regret a single second. Somehow, Vincent and I's lives had become entangled more than we, or at least I, had ever dreamed. There was no denying that I felt something for him, but there was nothing to be done about it. He was the leader of one of the most notorious gangs in Valarian. Who knew what he was up to when he wasn't with me? Which led me to my primary concern of the night: how *was* he with me?

"Don't the boys need you?" I asked when the sun disappeared below the horizon.

"I took the day off."

"Can you do that?"

"Princess, I do what I want. I'm the boss."

He had a point.

EIGHTEEN

SECURITY MEASURES

It shouldn't have surprised me to find my bed empty the next morning.

The last thing I remembered was Vincent covering us both with a blanket while we were on the couch. It must not have taken long before I fell asleep. There was a slight sting that he wasn't there when I woke up, but the note left on the nightstand lessened it.

I got a late-night call that I had to deal with. Stay safe. Arkin will be with you. For my sanity, don't lose him. I'll call you. – Vincent

It made me smile, if nothing else.

My morning was relatively mundane until my doorbell rang around noon. Dexter began growling at the door, and I had to calm him down before I cracked it open just enough to see out into the hall. Vincent's words from the night before came rushing back as soon as I saw the man in the uniform. I rested my forehead against the door for a moment before I opened it.

The man was older, probably around mid to late fifties. He gave me a warm smile as soon as the door was fully open. "Ms. Gracen?" he questioned, extending his hand.

"Juliette," I corrected. "And you are?"

"Fred. Just here to install some new locks and security for you as requested by Mr. Monroe."

My eyes rolled of their own accord. *Mr. Monroe* would never hear the end of this. With a deep sigh, I swung the door open and allowed him to come in. We made small talk for a while, but before long, I ventured off to my bedroom. Dexter eyed the man before trotting after me. No sooner had I fallen into the covers than my phone buzzed. I stared at Vincent's name for a moment before I answered. I almost didn't, but after the previous day, I knew that wouldn't end well.

"Hello?"

"Arkin said the man for the security installation finally showed up."

"Hello to you too. I'm doing great. Just have a random stranger installing a whole lot of junk around my front door. So glad you asked."

His deep chuckle sounded down the line and caused my heart to take a stutter step before returning to normal speed. "How are you, princess?"

"Stop calling me that."

"Never."

"Is that all you wanted? To confirm that he was here?"

"No. I also wanted to apologize for dipping out last night. I know I keep you in the dark about what all we do, but it's for your own good. I handled it."

"I would rather not know," I confessed.

"That's what I figured. When do you work tonight?"

"I have to be there at six."

"I'll be there at five."

"I can walk–"

"Juliette."

I blew out a breath. "Why so early?"

"I have some stuff to do on that side of town, and I'll already be over there."

"Alright." No sense arguing with him. If I had learned anything, it was that. We hung up shortly after.

It didn't take Fred much longer to finish up with the installation, either. He, thankfully, took the time to show me how to use the system instead of just letting me try to figure it out with the manual. It was easier than I thought it would be, but I still thought it was unnecessary. I would probably never use it, but if it made Vincent feel better, then I would let it stay.

For now.

Needing to get out of the house for a bit before getting ready for work, I hooked Dexter up to his leash and headed out. The air was truly turning as we headed into fall. I took a deep breath, welcoming the change. The weather in Valarian tended to not really know what it wanted to do, so there was no telling if the cooler temperatures would stick around. But I was going to enjoy them while I could. Dexter seemed to be in the same frame of mind as he all but dragged me out of the house. A small giggle bubbled from my mouth as we moved along the familiar path to the park. The city was oddly quiet, but I relished it. There was something about the stillness and the familiarity of my surroundings that made me feel at ease.

When we got to the park, I took Dexter up to the dog run so I could let him off his leash. The minute I unclipped him, he bolted. We were the only two there, and he took the time to run the entire perimeter. Shaking my head, I made my way to a bench and sat down. The dog run was in one of the more secluded areas of the park, filled with old, overreaching trees. I took a deep breath and slowly released it. The fresh air was a much-needed relief. I was trying not to examine what had happened the night before too closely.

I lost the battle quicker than I thought.

My thighs clenched together as I remembered Vincent's hands roaming over my body. It disarmed me how easy and right it had felt to be with him in those moments. Or at least until I had let my brain take over and get the best of me. But there were things to consider with Vincent. Things that made the idea of an actual relationship with him next to impossible. The most obvious being the fact that he ran the gang. I would be in a constant state of worry about him, about all of them. There would always be secrets between us because I didn't *want* to know the extent of what they did. I knew enough about that world to know that should anything ever happen, the less I knew, the better. How could we build anything on a foundation of half-truths?

But then again, didn't I *already* constantly worry about those idiots?

Did I even *want* a relationship?

The last one I had been in hadn't been the best. And it wasn't like I had anything to base what a healthy relationship should look like off of. My parents had separated when I was three years old. As much as they loved each other, they were smart enough to understand that they wouldn't work in the long run. They were best friends and would have died for each other. But whenever they tried throughout the years, they could never make the relationship thing work. Then they both died before either of them could find something better than what they had together.

Devyn was no help with her serial dating rivaling my own.

I was reading too much into it. Yes, Vincent and I felt an attraction to each other. And sure, we cared about one another, but that didn't have to mean anything. So, we had one fun night, that I had cut a little short. Stupid, now that I was looking back on it. Maybe once we got it out of our systems, we could move on from this dance we were doing.

Who was I kidding? There was no way I was ever going to forget about Vincent.

Dexter's loud growls silenced my line of thinking. The hairs on the back of my neck stood on end as my eyes swept my surroundings. Before I could go into full defensive mode, I spotted the reason Dexter was so worked up. A familiar form was standing in front of the gate into the dog run, an overexcited husky prancing around his legs.

Jack.

A smile split my face as I stood and waved. Recognition flashed in his tawny eyes, and then they swiveled back to inspect the hulking mass of Rottweiler that was standing between us. "Easy, Dex," I cooed as I came up beside him. Jack stepped through the gate with his dog as Dexter's growls subsided. The husky pulled him closer to us, tail wagging a mile a minute. Once Dexter focused on the other dog, his hackles lowered, and his whole butt shook.

"Hey, Juliette," Jack greeted as he unclipped his dog's leash. It took about twenty seconds for the two dogs to run off, already best friends.

"Hey. I didn't know you had a dog."

"Not exactly something that comes up in training sessions," he replied, an easy laugh falling from his lips. It was different seeing him like this. I was used to his wife-beater and sweats from the gym. Now, he was wearing a blood red flannel unbuttoned over a white t-shirt. His dark jeans hugged him in all the right places, and he had his usually mussed brown hair hidden beneath a gray beanie. I liked the look on him.

"That's true," I admitted, a smile breaking across my face. "Boy or girl?" I asked, nodding his dog as Dexter gave chase.

"Girl. Her name is Arya, and she's a brat."

"Aren't they all?"

He laughed as we made our way over to the bench I had originally been sitting on. "What has you out here?" he asked, raising a brow at me.

"Dexter just needed to stretch his legs, and I needed the air."

His eyes drifted over my face for a moment. "You've been pushing yourself pretty hard lately. Has something else happened?" Concern pulled his brows together, and I had to bite back a laugh. *Something* had happened. But not another bad altercation, which I'm sure was where his head had gone.

"Nope," I said, trying to ignore the fact that I could feel my cheeks warming in the cool air.

"Keep your secrets then." A wry smile twisted his lip as he folded his hands behind his head and leaned back on the bench. "When are you planning to come in next? I haven't seen you on the schedule yet."

"I forgot to book it with Sherry," I muttered, rolling my eyes skyward. "Would tomorrow be okay?"

"Fine by me. I'm booked up in the morning, so it'll have to be an afternoon session. I know we don't do those very often, so is that going to work for you?"

"Sure thing," I said, but I wasn't nearly as certain as I sounded. I knew that somewhere in the background, someone was keeping an eye out for me. Ditching Arkin was easy when I did it in the morning. Typically, I could wait until he dozed off, or dip out before he got there. Leaving in the middle of the day might prove a little more difficult. No matter what, I wouldn't miss a session in the gym. It was my one break from the havoc Vincent wreaked on my mind.

My phone vibrated in my pocket. *Speak of the devil,* I thought as I glanced down at my phone. The text message from Vincent was short, just reminding me he would be there at five. Which was only thirty minutes away.

"Shit," I said out loud as I stood up. "Dexter!"

"What's wrong?" Jack asked.

"I lost track of time. I've got to get home and ready for work."

"Are you still walking back and forth from the bar?"

"No," I said offhandedly. "A friend gives me a ride now."

"Oh." There was something in his voice that made me face him after I had clipped Dexter's leash on. His eyebrows furrowed, and he was worrying his bottom lip between his teeth. He looked up, and when our eyes met, he let a smile slip onto his face, erasing the odd look as if it had never been there. "That's good then. Just stay safe, Juliette. Okay?"

"You can call me Jules, Jack. Between your training and my mace, I should be just fine," I teased. "I'll see you tomorrow!" He waved as I headed for the gate. Dexter growled low in his throat when he passed Jack. At least he hadn't completely given up on protecting me, since he never seemed to make a peep around any of the guys anymore.

Thankfully, having a stand-in bodyguard was about to pay off. As I hit the sidewalk, the black SUV slowed to a stop and Arkin rolled the window down. "Need a ride?" he asked.

"For once, absolutely," I replied. I opened the back door and got Dexter loaded up before I hopped into the passenger seat. I glanced back at Jack as we pulled away, but all I could see was his back as he watched over Arya.

"I could have given you a ride here, you know," Arkin stated, pulling my attention back into the car.

"I know. But I wanted to walk. I needed to clear my head."

"Everything okay?"

There was a tinge of genuine worry in his voice, and it made me smile. "Don't worry about me. I'm fine. And I was fine yesterday. Just have a lot going on right now."

"I'll bet," he replied, his voice low.

My eyebrows raised. "What's that supposed to mean?"

"Who was that with you at the park?" he asked instead of answering me. His tone was light enough, but something about it seemed off. Especially for Arkin. Out of all the guys that I had met, he was the most easy-going. He never really questioned what I did. But this had piqued his interest?

"He's a friend of mine," I hedged. I had fought so hard to keep my training with Jack away from the guys. This was the one thing I had that they hadn't encroached on just yet.

"Is that who you go to see whenever you disappear?"

"Sometimes." He hummed in response, keeping his eyes on the road. "Why?"

"No reason."

"You're lying."

"Well, it's just..." he trailed off, biting the inside of his cheek.

"Arkin."

"Is he your boyfriend?" he blurted.

And it all made sense.

"No." I laughed. "It's not like that."

The tension in his shoulders eased.

We pulled up to my apartment, relieving me of having to have any more of that conversation with him. I thanked him for the ride home, unloaded Dexter, and all but dashed into my apartment. I could understand where he was coming from. Something told me that the men weren't oblivious to what was happening between Vincent and me. I highly doubted that anyone was buying the 'making sure I didn't snitch' excuse any more than I was.

Now, the question was just how long would it take until Vincent found out about Jack?

I groaned out loud as I got ready for work. It was a bridge I would just have to cross once we came to it. No matter what, it was none of their business. Sure, I liked Vincent. But that didn't mean that he needed to know my *every* move.

I managed to throw myself together in the nick of time. As I was pulling my shoes on, three quick raps sounded on my door.

"It's unlocked!" I hollered, running into my room to grab my purse. Vincent was standing in the living room with his arms crossed when I reemerged. I took a moment to let myself appreciate the absolute masterpiece that he created. His leather jacket stretched over his broad shoulders in a way that made my mouth water. His dark jeans hugging his muscular thighs was a definite bonus. When I finally dragged my eyes all the way back up his lean frame, the look he gave me could have burnt a hole through steel. "What?" I asked.

"I just had a security system installed, and you didn't even try to use it. Did you?" he asked. His voice was deep, shrouded in a darkness that made the hairs on the back of my neck stand up.

"Oh," I rolled my eyes all the same. "I'll get better. I just knew you were coming."

His eyes narrowed, but he didn't comment on it any further as he gestured towards the door. "Let's go. Just make sure you engage it on our way out."

"Sir, yes, sir," I muttered, brushing past him to the system panel. While he was saying goodbye to Dexter, I engaged the system the way Fred had shown me. Vincent and I breezed out the door. He was quiet as we made our way to the SUV. As always, he helped to hoist me into the passenger seat before rounding the car to get in. As the engine cranked over, I bit my lip.

What was up with him?

I decided not to question the issue, and just prayed it had nothing to do with me. Sometimes Vincent was so mercurial that it grated on my nerves. Part of me wanted to bring up the night before, but a bigger part of me didn't want to hear what he had to say about it. For all I knew, he regretted it and that was why he was being so withdrawn.

Right, a little voice in the back of my head scoffed. *That's why he went out of his way to come get you and pay for a security system.*

Fair enough.

"Are you hungry?"

I jumped when Vincent finally spoke. A smile curved the edges of his mouth as I regained my composure. "No, I'm fine."

"When did you eat last?"

"I haven't."

"Juliette," he said, rolling his eyes at me. Without waiting for another word from me, he pulled into the next fast-food restaurant he saw. "What do you want?"

"Vincent–"

"You need to eat. It's a weekend. You're not going to have time to grab anything at work."

I hated that he was right. I reluctantly gave him my order. We did the coin toss to see who would pay again.

I lost. Again.

He had the same smug ass grin on his face as the last time when he placed the coin back into his jacket pocket. Something was up, and I waited until he parked to strike. When he was rooting through the bag to grab my food for me, I leaned across the console and slipped my hand in his pocket.

He froze, those forest eyes sliding to me.

"What're you doing?"

In response, I just gave him a sweet smile and removed my hand. One of his brows quirked as he watched me examine the coin.

"You filthy little cheat," I hissed as I turned it over again in my palm.

Heads on both sides.

A warm chuckle fell from his lips as he snagged it from me. "I don't like to lose."

"We're not doing coin tosses anymore."

"Fair enough," he said, not seeming sorry in the slightest. I huffed out a breath of irritation, but the wide grin on his face dissolved my frustration in an instant. I took the sandwich he offered, and we ate our food while familiar piano notes floated from the radio.

When we finally pulled into the parking lot of Tuxedo, my teeth snagged my bottom lip. I had been entertaining the idea of asking Vincent to let Arkin have a break the following day. However, I didn't know how to do it without raising suspicion. The car rolled to a stop, and I still didn't move. Vincent turned to me and raised a brow.

I let out an exasperated breath that blew my hair out of my face. "I have a favor."

"Okay."

"It's not really for me. But I think you should give Arkin the day off tomorrow. At least from watching over me." Vincent's stare was completely blank. My lips pursed. "I'm off tomorrow; it's got to be boring as hell just sitting outside my apartment all day. I won't be doing anything."

"What's so important tomorrow that you don't want Arkin to see?"

"What are you talking about?"

"You can't lie to me, princess," he said, a smile threatening to pull at his mouth.

"I'm not."

"Watching for signs of deception is part of my job description," he told me, leaning across the center console to invade my space. "Now, what are you trying to hide?"

"I'm not hiding anything," I snapped, nostrils flaring. "I just don't need the guys reporting my every move back to you anymore."

"We've discussed this," he stated, voice flat as the muscle in his jaw twitched. "We both know you're not going to the cops." I winced. "They're there to protect you."

"I don't need protecting."

His eyes rolled. "You consistently walk alone when I'm not around. Not to mention what lead to us meeting in the first place."

"Vincent–"

"Look," he said, cutting me off. "I know it's not the best arrangement, but there's a high chance the guys have been seen with you. That *I've* been seen with you. It won't take much longer before that starts getting examined by other parties. It puts my mind at ease to know that you're safe."

"You're impossible," I said, my cheeks heating. He said it so casually, it had caught me off guard. How had I never considered that being around them could put *me* in danger?

"So are you. I'll see you at the end of your shift." His eyes scanned the lot, and then he leaned forward and pressed a tender kiss to my forehead.

When I got out of the SUV, I glanced around the parking lot as well. It was desolate, save for Vincent and me. As he waved and pulled away, I couldn't help but think that he had been making sure we were alone before he kissed me.

Nineteen

STRESS COOKING

"Look who it is. I thought you'd died."

"Shut up, Dev," I muttered, throwing my purse into a corner. She sauntered over to me as I clocked in. When I went to move, she boxed me in.

"What's going on between you and the banger?"

"What are you talking about?"

"Don't play dumb with me, Jules," she said, raising her pierced brow. "You've barely spoken to me in days. And now, you come in here after he drops you off, all blushy and glowing. So, spill."

"Glowing," I scoffed, shoving past her. "You're delusional."

"Whatever, don't tell me." I could all but hear her rolling her eyes at me. "It's fine."

The one thing I always appreciated about Devyn was that ninety-nine percent of the time, she let things go when I wasn't ready to talk about them. She didn't question my apparent 'glow' for the rest of the night. However, that may have been in part because Vincent had been right. The bar was absolutely slammed. Devyn and I barely had time to breathe, let alone talk about my love life.

"Jesus Christ," she exclaimed once we had herded the last patron out the front door. "That was insane."

"I'll say," I muttered before grabbing the tip jar and hopping onto the bar. Dante's glare was a physical weight, and as usual, I didn't bother acknowledging it. I upended the jar onto the bar and counted the money, monitoring Devyn as I did. Now that the storm had passed, it was only a matter of time before she descended upon me.

It took about three minutes.

"You in a talking mood yet?"

"No."

She pouted. "Fine. Then since tomorrow is a Saturday we both have off, let's go out. I'll get some liquor in you and then you'll talk."

"Telling me your plan beforehand isn't very smart," I told her, a smile breaking out across my face. She was ridiculous.

"Pfft, I got this."

My eyes rolled as I refocused on splitting the tips. It was quiet for a time as Devyn continued to break the bar down. I knew she had a multitude of questions bubbling just beneath the surface, but I was glad she kept them to herself. I didn't even know the answers to anything she was liable to ask. Once I had split the money, I slid Devyn her cut. Dante meandered his way out of the back as I slid off the bar.

"How'd you all do?" he asked, flicking my forehead. I rubbed the point of assault and shot a glare at him.

"Great," Devyn chimed in as she counted out her part.

"Good. You all did an amazing job tonight. Thank you," Dante said, pulling both of us in for a hug.

"What do you want?" we chorused. While Dante appreciated all of us, this kind of display always lead to a favor.

He chuckled before releasing us. His eyes slid to me before he began talking. "We have a party reservation for next weekend. I would like to put you two on the schedule for it."

"I'm down," I automatically said. Party reservations were always big money.

"Count me in, too," Devyn agreed. But then her eyes narrowed. "Why did you think we wouldn't want it?"

"Well..." he trailed off, his eyes cutting to me again. "The reservation is under Lucas Moore."

"And?"

"That's Monroe's right-hand man."

"Ah man, not the bangers," Devyn groaned, slumping against the bar.

"They're not that bad," I said. They both just raised their eyebrows at me. "What? Think of the money."

"I just wanted to run it by you both first. Especially you, Juliette."

"Oh, she doesn't care," Devyn quipped. I glared at her. "What? Don't think I haven't noticed just how much time you've been spending with him."

I held my hand up as Dante opened his mouth. "I love you both, but that's enough," I said. Shaking my head at them, I grabbed my money and headed into the kitchen. I didn't need to be mothered. I knew how dangerous Vincent was, how dangerous they all were. But I also knew that I was safe with them. Devyn followed me into the back and hovered as I collected my things.

"Can I help you?" I snapped.

"Don't take that tone with me," she responded, rolling her eyes. "I just want to make sure you're not walking."

"I'm not," I said, softening my voice. She arched her brow at me. I waved a hand at the security monitor. Her eyes widened at the picture of the black SUV idling right outside the back door. A familiar dark figure was leaning against the passenger door, ankles and arms crossed as he waited.

"You have some explaining to do."

"I know. I'll talk to you later. And yes, we're still on for tomorrow." Not bothering to wait for her to answer, I clocked out and walked out the back door.

"Took you long enough," Vincent called as I approached him.

"I was getting the third degree. No big deal." He chuckled as he opened the door for me. Once I was in and situated, he still stood with the car door open. We were the same height from where I sat, so I had full access to the depth of his forest eyes. They seemed darker than normal, troubled. My fingers brushed across his cheekbone with the same feather-light care he always took with me. "What is it?"

"Nothing for you to worry about, princess," he murmured, catching my hand in his.

"That's not what that face says."

"Let's get you home."

Once he was in the car, the quiet stretched between us as it usually did, wrapping around me like a soft blanket. My forehead pressed against the cool glass of the window, bouncing slightly as the tires moved over jagged streets. I wanted to push him more on whatever was bothering him. I hadn't seen that clouded look in his eyes since the night he stopped at the warehouse to pick up his gun. Could it be something to do with the deal they had brewing?

Did I even want to know?

The answer was no; I didn't. But if there was something that I could do to ease Vincent's mind, I would. He was there for me whenever I needed him. The least I could do was return the favor. I worried my bottom lip between my teeth as the SUV rolled to a stop. Vincent killed the engine. We sat there for a moment before I shoved my door open. I was halfway up the walk to my building before I heard the other door slam closed. Vincent caught up in time to hold the door open for me. I paused in the entryway, meeting his gaze. The wall was still up behind his eyes, so I just slipped past him.

My keys rattled against the sideboard when I tossed them on it, the only sound in the quiet apartment. Dexter didn't even stir from his place on the couch. The incessant flashing of the alarm panel reminded me that I needed to disengage it before moving on. Vincent moved past me as I did so, and I briefly wondered what he was doing. Shaking my head, I did what I needed with the totally unnecessary security system before brushing by him on the way to my room. After stripping out of my uniform, and all but moaning once my hose were off, I went to find Vincent. He had stopped at the same picture of my mom that Lucas had commented on what seemed like forever ago.

I stepped up beside him to look at the picture as well. Mom's eyes looked tired. *She* looked tired. She had her arms draped lazily around me as we smiled at the camera. We took the picture just two weeks before she died.

"You look like her," he said, his voice breaking the silence that had blanketed the room.

"Thank you," I breathed. It was one of the best compliments I had ever received. Even when the cancer had drained her to the point she could barely move, my mother was one of the most beautiful people I had ever known. I always thought I looked more like my father, even though there was no mistaking the fact that I had my mother's doe eyes, even if they weren't green like hers.

"Do you mind telling me what she was sick with?"

"It was ovarian cancer. She hated doctors, so by the time she actually went and they found it, it was too late."

"I'm sorry, Juliette."

My eyes watered at the tenderness in his voice. I hadn't talked about my mom in years. The visceral longing for one of her hugs took me by surprise. My chest hurt, and I had to take a deep breath to stop myself from breaking down into sobs. Without a word, Vincent pulled me into him and wrapped me in his arms. He was warmer than I expected, and I buried my face in his chest. He always made me feel so small. But there was a safety in his arms, wrapped in that sandalwood scent, that I couldn't deny.

We stood like that for a while, neither of us saying anything as I got my breathing under control. Eventually, I pulled away from him with dry eyes.

"Thank you," I said again, swiping at my eyes to make sure my makeup hadn't migrated down my cheeks.

"You don't have to thank me. I know what it's like to lose family." His eyes had gone cold again, so I decided against asking about it. If he wanted to tell me, he would.

"Are you hungry?" I asked instead. I needed an excuse to move, to *do* something. He still hadn't said anything about why he had followed me in, but it didn't seem like he had any intention of leaving.

Not that I wanted him to.

"A little. Did you want to order something?"

"No. I need to stay busy. I'll cook."

"You can cook?"

"Shut up," I said, laughing as I shoved him away from me and headed into the kitchen.

"Can I help?"

"Sure, but I wasn't thinking anything too fancy. I think I can manage spaghetti on my own."

"You never know. You might overcook the noodles."

My eyes about touched the back of my skull as I began getting everything out of the cabinets. Vincent didn't enter the kitchen, he just leaned one shoulder against the wall and watched my every move. I could feel his eyes on me like a second skin. A smile played with the edges of his mouth, and I had to restrain a smile as well. I enjoyed having him here. Dexter came in and pressed himself against Vincent's leg, temporarily taking his attention off of me.

Cooking, no matter how small, had always been something I could do to calm myself. I had grown up watching my mother do it, which was probably where I got it from. My mother had been the stereotypical stress baker. I knew that if I got home from school and smelled something sweet, Mom probably had bad news.

She had been baking the day she broke the news that my father was dead.

I shook my head, forcibly trying to steer my mind in another direction. That was the last path I needed to venture down. I couldn't face that darkness again. Not now. Not with Vincent here.

As if they could sense the shift in my mood, both Vincent and Dexter turned to look at me. Vincent noted the pain I was sure was obvious on my face and moved to stand behind me. He wrapped his arms around my waist and bent to set his chin on my shoulder.

"Walk me through what you're doing."

"You've never made spaghetti before?" I asked, my voice sounding tight even to my own ears.

"Of course, I have. But indulge me."

So, I did. I talked through every single, tiny step I was taking. And as I did, the knot unraveled inside my stomach. The more I explained the simple recipe to Vincent, the better I felt. Cooking and speaking took all my focus, so before I knew it, thoughts of my parents and their deaths had completely left my mind. When I set both steaming plates on my small dining room table, I felt at ease. Our gazes met across the table, and the wall behind Vincent's eyes was down once again. This time, when the silence stretched between us, it was as calm and comforting as I was used to.

"Would you like to tell me why you're here?" I finally asked as we were placing the dishes in the sink.

"What do you mean?" he asked.

"Don't play coy," I said. "You're trying to tell me that there is absolutely no reason you came in tonight, uninvited?"

"You didn't exactly tell me to leave."

"Vincent."

"Fine." He blew out a breath and slumped against the counter. "I had a shit day. Negotiations with this deal are a complete pain in the ass."

"Still not seeing where I come in."

His eyes cut to me, and the intensity of his forest gaze made a shiver run down my spine. He reached for me, and I let him pull my body flush against his. His fingers traveled up the column of my throat before tangling in the hair at the nape of my neck. He used that grip to angle my face up towards his and leaned down until his lips brushed against mine as he spoke.

"I wanted to see you, to give a good end to my shit day."

And then his lips met mine with a ferocity that shocked me. I gasped, giving Vincent the chance to sweep his tongue into my mouth. A soft moan slipped free, and my body molded to his as if it were meant to be there. Somehow, he pulled me impossibly closer. His hold on my hair released, but his hands didn't leave me. Instead, they moved to grip the back of my thighs as he hoisted me into his arms. I wrapped my legs around his waist, assuring myself that this time I wouldn't be the one to stop.

Twenty

INTERRUPTIONS

And it wasn't me.

It was the blaring of his phone. He ripped his mouth from mine and a string of profanities fell from his lips. He whipped out his phone with enough aggression that I thought it might break.

"Monroe," he barked as he pressed the device to his ear. I stifled a laugh as I tried to disentangle myself from him. But his arm was ironclad around my waist, and he was not letting go. My eyebrows hitched as his furrowed. I couldn't hear the other end of the conversation, but from the look on Vincent's face, I didn't want to. "I'll be there in thirty." And with that, he punched the end button and slipped his phone back in his pocket. His eyes locked on mine for a moment before they went unfocused.

"Vincent," I murmured, placing my hand on his cheek. "You need to go." It wasn't a question. I could tell from the look on his face.

"Mhmm."

"So go."

"Will Dexter be alright by himself tonight?"

"What?" I blanched.

"Come with me. The guys need me, but only at the warehouse."

"I don't know if that's such a good–"

"Juliette," he cut me off, eyes boring into mine. "I told you I wanted to spend tonight with you to give a good end to my shitty day. Apparently, my shitty day isn't over yet. So, please, come with me."

"Alright," I heard myself saying before I even really thought about it. I mean, when was the next time I was actually going to hear Vincent say *please*? "But can't I bring Dexter with me?"

"Is he going to eat my men?"

"No." Dexter chuffed next to me, acting offended that Vincent thought he would misbehave like that. "He's met quite a few of them, anyway."

"Good point. Get his stuff together. Let's go."

And that was how Dexter and I ended up loaded into the SUV, making the cross-city drive with Vincent. There was a warmth in my chest that I couldn't ignore, no matter how much I wanted to. It was something I never could have considered a few months ago, before I had known Vincent. If someone had told me I would get abducted only to end up developing feelings for the one responsible, I would've laughed at them. I mean, there wasn't a shred of sense about it, but it was there all the same. The smile that tugged at my lips couldn't be helped, and I shook my head as I looked out the window.

"Penny for your thoughts?" Vincent asked.

"Just thinking about how insane this is," I said, motioning between us.

"How so?" he asked, his brows pulling together to cast a dark shadow over his cheekbones.

"You threatened my life the first time we met," I reminded him.

"Oh right. That."

"Yes. *That.*" Despite my eye roll, there was a broad grin on my lips.

One of Vincent's full smiles split his face as he chuckled. He switched the familiar piano notes on, and they sifted through the air as conversation lulled. I sighed and settled into my seat for the rest of the ride. It didn't take long, and before I knew it, Vincent was helping me unload Dexter. The dog in question bristled, sniffing along the sidewalk as we headed into the warehouse. The lights were brighter than I expected, and I had to squint as my eyes adjusted. When they did, I had to fight the urge to shrink behind Vincent.

Dexter growled so low I couldn't even hear it; I could just feel the vibrations through his leash.

I had never seen the warehouse so full. There were people everywhere.

One familiar head of blonde hair turned to look at me, and a smile broke out across his face. "Juliette!" he yelled, causing every head in the room to snap in our direction.

This time, I did take a step back to stand at Vincent's side.

Vincent's familiar, taunting smile played with his lips as he settled his hand on the small of my back, barely applying any pressure as he ushered me forward. I reined Dexter in, holding him tight to my side as he continued to growl. Once he spotted Lucas making his way over to us, he bolted away from me so fast I couldn't keep hold of his leash. The bark that he let out sounded anything but friendly as he tackled Lucas to the ground. A few of the men I didn't know jumped to their feet. However, it barely took them a moment to realize that Lucas was only in danger of being licked to death. The blonde's laughter reverberated off the walls as he wrestled Dexter off him.

"Dex," I scolded. The dog's head dropped, but he removed himself from Lucas. The tense atmosphere evaporated from the room in the same instant Dexter sat on his haunches beside me. Lucas was still laughing when he pulled me into a hug.

"Long time, no see, sugar," he said, lifting me off my feet as his arms constricted.

"Hello to you too, Lucas," I forced out. He set me back down, and I sucked in a lungful of air. "Did you miss me?"

"Always."

"He's intolerable. The sooner he picks your detail back up, the better," Brandon inserted, materializing like smoke beside Lucas.

"You'd be bored without me."

"I would be *sane* without you."

As the cousins continued their bickering, I caught Arkin's gaze from across the room. He smiled and made his way over. Dexter's tail wagged, knocking into my leg hard enough to bruise. Arkin's calm demeanor washed over me as he knelt in front of Dexter, scratching him between the ears. As much as I loved Lucas and Brandon, I was glad I had Arkin around to balance out their crazy. Just as the thought crossed my mind, Brandon lunged at Lucas and snagged him in a headlock. They tumbled to the ground mere inches from me, and Vincent pulled me closer to him as they rolled.

"Sometimes I feel like a babysitter," Arkin muttered, staring at the other two with obvious disdain on his face.

"Why do you think I keep you around?" Vincent asked. "I'd lose my mind dealing with them by myself."

"Your words are hurtful, Vince," Lucas said, disentangling himself from Brandon before standing up.

"And you're a child," Vincent replied, his voice cold. The muscle in his jaw twitched.

"Hey," I murmured, placing my hand on his arm. "They were just messing around."

He blew out a deep sigh and let his eyes roll skyward. When the tension dropped from his shoulders, his eyes found mine. I could see the battle warring within their forest depths. He still felt frustrated after being summoned back here. Hell, I was too, but I wasn't about to let him take it out on the guys.

"We're going to wrap this up quickly," he stated, refocusing his attention on the three men in front of us. "Get everyone on the same page while I get these two settled."

The men nodded before breaking off and going to round up everyone in the warehouse. Vincent's hand returned to the small of my back, and he led me to the staircase on the far side of the room. Just as we were about to go up, I cast one last look over my shoulder.

Then I wished I hadn't.

While I had expected to see the guys attempting to corral the multitude of people, I hadn't been ready for them to fail, because all the attention was still on us.

The more correct phrase would have been on me, but I was choosing to ignore that fact.

One person in particular caught my eye. I had noticed her before, her burgundy hair making her stand out in the crowd of men even more than being one of the few women I had seen. There was an upward tilt to her sapphire eyes as they watched Vincent and me. Her attention lingered on the hand he still had on my back. Our gazes locked, and a slow, secretive smile spread across her lips.

Before I could think too much about it, my line of sight was cut off as we ascended the stairs. When we emerged at the top, we were at the end of a hallway that must have stretched the entire length of the warehouse with doors lining either side. I made a move to venture down the hall, but Vincent pulled me back. I glanced back at him, and he motioned to the second staircase I had failed to notice. When we made it to the top of those steps, there was only one door. My eyebrows raised, but I kept my mouth shut as Vincent pulled out his keys. He swung the door open and motioned me inside.

Once he flipped the lights on, I had to keep my mouth from falling open a little. I wasn't sure what I was expecting Vincent's home to look like, but the immaculate, industrial style loft before me was not it. The red brick walls warmed the chill of the metal fixtures and the dark wood floors, and the overall color palette was rich earth tones. The wall directly across from me was nothing but windows, and it gave an incredible view of the city. Drawn to it, I let Dexter's leash fall from my hand and moved to stand in front of the windows. We were far enough outside of downtown that all the lights of the city simply looked like a mirrored reflection of the stars in the sky.

"Wow," I breathed.

"Not what you expected?" Vincent asked, drawing my attention back to him. He had just unclipped Dexter from his leash and was hanging it on the hooks attached to the back of the door.

"Not at all," I admitted. "Did you do all of this yourself?'

"No," he said, a soft laugh falling from his lips as he moved to stand beside me. "My sister did. She was an interior designer. She said if I was going to run a gang like a 'big boss man,' I should live like one."

"Was?"

"She's gone."

I glanced at him out of the corner of my eye. He had clenched his jaw, and he was gazing out the window. But he didn't seem to be seeing anything. Part of me didn't think he had meant to disclose that much about himself, so I wouldn't press it. He had said he understood familial loss, and now it made sense. Silently, I ran my hand down his arm and entwined my fingers with his. He looked down at our hands and just stared for a beat. His ghost of a smile tugged at his lips, and he squeezed my hand.

"What was her name, if you don't mind me asking?" I questioned after a few moments of silence.

"Alana. She would have liked you."

"Thank you. I think Mom would have liked you, too."

That made one of his genuine smiles break over his face. He used our entwined hands to whip me around and pull me flush against his chest. My eyes fluttered closed as he leaned towards me. I could feel his breath on my lips when the knock sounded on the door.

"We got everyone together, Vince!" Brandon called, pounding harder. I could hear hushed laughter through the heavy wood.

"They are literal children," he seethed, eyes cutting to where the sounds of their amusement were dying out. A small laugh fell from my own lips as I placed my hand on his cheek.

"Something tells me you're going to have to get used to it." I strained up onto my tiptoes to place a quick peck on his cheek. "Go, I'll be here."

He nodded. Before he left, he gave me a brief rundown of how his overly fancy TV worked, then pulled me into a bruising kiss. There was a sparkle of mischief in his eyes as the door fell shut behind him. Dexter sank to his haunches beside me as we stared at the closed door. The smallest whine slipped past his teeth as he leaned against me.

"I know."

He followed me as I sank into the brown leather sofa. He circled a few times before laying his head next to my feet. With a heavy sigh, I flipped the TV on and cycled through the channels until I found a familiar psychological thriller and huddled deeper into the couch.

"Let's make this quick," Vincent said when he reached the main room of the warehouse. Lucas stepped to his side, Brandon and Arkin falling in close as well. As Vincent took his place at the head of the room, the other members fell quiet. "Now, what happened?"

"The shipment was late again," Angelica said, sprawled out like a cat on one of the couches. Her red hair splayed out against the arm of the sofa, and she had her legs draped across one of the other member's laps. "That's the third one in a row."

Vincent pinched the bridge of his nose. There was no reason for this to keep happening. And with it being all the shipments tied to the Kline family, it made him even more uneasy. Henry Kline was one of the oldest leaders left in the city. He knew everyone and had dirt on each and every one of them. It was the only reason Vincent still associated with him. If he hadn't been such a valuable asset when Vincent first took over, he would have killed him.

"Aren't you supposed to be in charge of keeping them in line, Angel?" Brandon snarked, his eyes sparking as they zeroed in on her.

Vincent had never figured out why Brandon and Angelica fought like cats and dogs, probably because they were essentially the same person, but he didn't have time to entertain it tonight. Before the red head could open her mouth, Vincent sent her a scathing glare. She curled her lip at him, but settled back against the arm of the couch, flipping Brandon off instead of responding.

Lucas snickered, but tried to disguise it as a cough when Vincent turned to him.

"Angel, I need you to figure out if Kline has any hand in what's happening. We've been doing business with him for years, so I doubt they're doing this on purpose. But if they've turned on us, I don't want to be caught off guard."

Angelica nodded. Next to Arkin, she was the best in the gang at acquiring information. It was one of several reasons she was such a high-ranking member, what she meant to Vincent aside. Her eyes dropped to her phone as she started typing away, and he left her to it.

"We also need to go over what we're going to do about the rest of the Kline deal, if everything is still on the up and up," Lucas said, drawing Vincent's attention.

Vincent cursed softly before falling into a seat. Of all the nights for shit to hit the fan. He ran his hand over his face and nodded for Lucas to continue. The sooner this meeting was over, the sooner he could return to Juliette.

The tinkling of keys jolted me awake. There was a dull ripping sound as my sweating skin separated itself from the leather. I winced before running my hand over my face. Rubbing at my eyes, I searched for the source of the sound. The door opened just as I sat upright from where I had slouched over when I passed out. Vincent's eyes immediately found me, and a smile broke out across his face.

"Don't even," I warned, holding up a finger.

"Sleep well?" I chucked one of the throw pillows at him. He laughed and swatted it out of the air. "Is that a no?"

"I hate you. I hope you know that."

He made his way over to me, picking up the fluffy missile as he went. Flopping down next to me, he kicked his feet up onto the coffee table before pulling my body flush against his. He draped his arm around my shoulders with a content sigh, his head falling back against the couch as his eyes closed.

"I'm going to appoint Lucas as the new head of the gang," he muttered.

"*What?*" I asked, whipping my head so fast my neck cricked. *Ow.*

One eye slid open as he grinned. "Not really. But, man, do I want to sometimes."

"Oh." My heart rate settled. "Anything I can help with?"

"With the men? No. With me? Yes."

"Like what?"

There was a flash of heat in his gaze, hot enough to burn, but it was gone the next time he blinked. "I'll tell you in the morning. We're both exhausted. Let's just get some sleep." He pulled me up with him as he made his way to the small spiral staircase I had once again missed.

This man was full of surprises.

Twenty-One

FADE TO BLACK

Dexter trooped after us as we emerged into a beautiful master suite.

Vincent's sister had known exactly what she was doing. The room was just as immaculate as the first floor, but the bedroom felt more like what I would expect from Vincent. It was outfitted in deep shades of grey and accented with a shade of green that reminded me of his eyes. The bed was a massive four-poster style and took up residence on the left side of the room. Two doors were located to my right, leading to what I assumed were the bathroom and closet. Vincent vanished into the first of the two doors, and the warmth from the electric fireplace drew me closer to it. A large flatscreen TV hung above it, and I could see the bed's reflection as I warmed my hands. That was where Vincent found me when he reemerged a few moments later with a bundle of clothes in hand.

"You can change in there," he told me as he pressed them into my grasp and gestured to the far door.

Nodding, I moved into the bathroom without so much as a word. I hadn't realized just how tired I really was until that moment. I was so tired, I barely even paid attention to the beautiful white marble that surrounded me. Instead, I focused on taking my clothes off. It felt like peeling off a second skin as I shimmied the pants down my legs. Once I was standing in just my underwear, I finally took in what I held. It was just one of his shirts, though it was a favorite if the faded lettering meant anything. The words on the front had faded to the point I couldn't read them anymore, but I was guessing it had once been a band tee. When I slipped it over my head, it reminded me just how much larger Vincent was than me as it fell past mid-thigh. The shirt was soft, and it smelled like him. The dark scent wrapped around me, the aftereffect of whatever cologne or body wash he used, but there was also something there that was distinctly him. Since he hadn't given me any pants, I was glad for the length of the shirt. I unclasped my bra, slipped my arms from the straps, and dropped it with the rest of my clothes before taking them with me. There was no way I was sleeping in that death contraption.

Vincent was sitting in a large chair by the window to my right when I emerged. The window wasn't floor to ceiling like the ones in the main area of the apartment, but it still gave the same breathtaking view. He had his fist pressed against his mouth, but it fell to his side when he faced me. In the dark, his eyes looked black. Or maybe it was the way his pupil swallowed the green as his eyes raked over me.

A flush crept up my neck to settle in my cheeks at that look on his face. My weight shifted from foot to foot before I held up my clothes. "Where would you like me to put these?" I asked, my voice coming out in a low rasp. I cleared my throat. No matter how close Vincent and I had gotten, I still didn't like him knowing about the effect he had on me. But the smile toying with the edges of his lips said he knew *exactly* what he was doing.

Asshole.

His movements were languid as he rose from the chair. He all but stalked towards me, and I refused to budge. There was no way I was going to back down. Not when I had promised myself, just hours earlier, that I wouldn't chicken out again. Heat pooled low in my belly when he came to a stop in front of me. His gaze bored into mine and my thighs clenched in response. Wordlessly, he took the clothes from my hands and tossed them into the chair he had just vacated. His hands met my hips, drawing me forward until the heat of his body sank into my skin. My eyelids fluttered closed at the contact, and a content sigh fell from my lips.

Suddenly, I was wide awake as my body hummed under his touch.

"Juliette," he murmured, his voice a low rumble that I felt in my chest. His hands moved to my hair, tangling in it as he angled my face up to his. "If you don't want this, tell me right now."

He was giving me an out. Big, bad Vincent Monroe. Who was known for being ruthless, who wanted me so badly he was straining against his jeans, was giving me plenty of time to make my decision.

Lucky for him, I had made it before we ever set foot inside of this apartment.

"I want this," I breathed. Raising up on my tiptoes, I closed the microscopic distance between us and pressed my lips to his. He groaned into my mouth, one of his arms constricting around my waist like a coiling snake. "I want you."

His lips didn't stay on mine for long. They migrated down my cheek, across my jaw, before trailing a burning line down the column of my throat. By the time he nipped the soft spot where my shoulder met my neck, my chest was already heaving. His hands found the back of my knees and he yanked me up into his arms, wrapping my legs around his waist. His mouth met mine again with bruising force as he walked us over to the bed. I barely had time to register how soft the mattress was before the hard planes of his chest were pressing against my own. The two feelings were drastically different, and I arched into him, craving the heat of his skin.

Something akin to a growl rumbled in the back of his throat as he all but ripped the shirt off me, discarding it into the chair with the rest of my clothes. I couldn't help the breathy laugh that escaped me when his eyes came back to mine.

"Why did you even have me put it on?"

"I had planned to wait until morning to seduce you," he said, one arm snaking under the small of my back to press us as close together as possible.

"You failed."

"Princess, this is one loss I will gladly take." And then his lips were on mine again and no more words were needed.

There was nothing gentle about the rest of the night. Both of us had been denying ourselves, denying our attraction to each other, for far too long. Vincent showed me exactly how ruthless he could be, barely giving me time to breathe as he made my body shatter for him over and over again. On his tongue, his hands, his cock... it didn't matter. I lost count. By the time he threw the condom away and brought back a warm washcloth, I couldn't even move to help him. A soft laugh rolled through him as he wiped me down. He pitched the cloth into a hamper on the far side of the room. The bed dipped when he crawled into bed beside me and pulled my back flush against his chest.

"Are you okay?" he murmured, pressing a kiss to the back of my head.

"Mhmm." His laughter vibrated against my back as he pulled me closer. Glad he thought it was funny that I couldn't even find the energy to speak.

"Get some sleep, princess."

As beautiful as the view from Vincent's room was, it was a pain in the ass once the sun came out to play.

I groaned and rolled into him, burying my face in the crook of his neck to block out the light. He had lazily draped his arm over my hip, and he raised it to brush my hair away from my face. His laughter hummed through me, sending a surge of heat straight to my core. My toes curled, and I feared that if I pressed myself any tighter against him that my body would permanently fuse with his. Despite that being exactly what I wanted; I blinked my eyes open.

Vincent was wide awake. His forest eyes were alight as they met mine, and one of those rare smiles broke across his face.

"Good morning, princess," he said, leaning forward to press a soft kiss to my forehead. Despite the sweet gesture, my nose wrinkled.

"Can we not start with the princess crap quite so early, please?" I grumbled, raising my hand to rub the last remnants of sleep from my eyes.

"You're never going to hear the end of it. Deal with it."

I grumbled a litany of curses under my breath as I dragged myself away from him and to my feet. Rounding the bed, I picked up my underwear from where we had discarded them. A frown pulled at the corner of my mouth as I realized they were torn.

Shit.

"Did you have to *literally* rip them off me?" I asked, meeting his eyes. Mischief was dancing in his forest gaze as it raked over me. I was suddenly quite aware of the fact that I was still naked. My nipples hardened as his eyes swept over me again, and I let out a few more choice words as I moved to grab the shirt he had given me the previous night. Before I could get it over my head, his warmth was behind me. Heat seared my cheeks as the bare skin of him met my back. I could feel how hard he was, and there was a pulsing between my thighs that I wanted to give into more than anything. His arms came around my waist and with the smallest tug, he had plastered me against him once again.

However, I knew how late we had finally fallen asleep. Dawn had been cresting through the windows, so I knew it had to be at least noon, if not past it. I had an appointment to keep.

It took every ounce of willpower I had to disentangle myself from Vincent's arms. After I had gotten the shirt on, I spun to face him. There was hunger in his eyes, but the rest of his expression was soft. I kept my eyes securely on his because I knew if I let them drift any lower; I was going to drag him straight back into that bed and not leave it for the rest of the day.

"Do you know what time it is?" I asked, glancing around the room. There was no clock, and I had to have left my phone in the living room the night before.

"In a hurry to leave?"

"Vincent."

He held his hands up in a gesture of surrender and then walked over to the dresser. He pulled out a pair of sweats before tugging them on. I was convinced he wasn't putting on a shirt just to spite me, but I wouldn't complain. I had a full view of the tattoo that I had always noticed peeking out from the collar of his t-shirts. Even though the night before I felt like I had memorized every part of him, seeing the ink in the light of day, without the sex haze, was a fresh experience. Now I could see that what I could normally glimpse was the edges of an intricate black and grey rose design that took up the expanse of his shoulder. The swirls of smoke around it trailed down his left arm, weaving in and out of two different animal skulls. The smoke swirled in dizzying detail all the way down to the cuff of his wrist, ending so that it wouldn't be visible underneath a long sleeve shirt.

"What?" he asked, following the path of my gaze. Noticing what caught my attention, he moved until he was right in front of me, allowing me to see it in closer detail.

"What are these?" My fingers trailed over the two skulls, so similar, yet one much larger than the other. The horns on the large one closest to his shoulder arched outward, while the horns on the smaller one, below the crease of his elbow, wound back in on themselves.

"A bull and a ram," he explained. "Taurus and Aries. Me and Alana."

My throat closed, and tears pricked my eyes at the beauty of the sentiment.

"Did she get to see it?" I asked. Nodding, he took my hand before pulling me back to the bed. He sat on the edge, settling me between his legs. My hands stayed in his as he wrapped his arms around me. My back was flush with his chest, and he propped his chin on my shoulder.

"We were always close growing up." His voice was soft, and there wasn't a trace of the darkness coating it that I had grown used to. Somehow, that unnerved me more than when it was present. "We had been in foster care, but we were a part of the lucky few who didn't get separated. The minute I turned eighteen, we left and never looked back. It wasn't too difficult to get guardianship of Alana. Our foster family vouched for me. We actually had it pretty good. We were always with the first family the agency had placed us with. They were good people, but they had their own kids, too. They did their best, but Alana and I were always just kind of on the fringe of things. Though, looking back, I think that was our fault more than theirs."

"I'm so sorry, Vincent."

He shrugged. "I got the tattoo after we left. Something to represent that we would always be together. No matter what life threw at us. The skulls were her idea. She was always into astrology."

"What happened to your parents?"

"They were killed. Caught in the middle of a gang war." My breath froze in my lungs. He must have felt the sudden rigidness in my spine because his lips were on me in the next instant. He peppered a few slow kisses across the nape of my neck, only stopping once my shoulders dropped. "I came back here a few years after Alana and I were settled, and I killed the man who had ordered the hit. Apparently, killing a gang leader makes you the next one. Whether or not that was your intention."

The air left me in a *whoosh* at the new information. "So, you were..."

"Twenty-one when I took over," he finished for me, his chin resting on my shoulder again. "It's been eight years, and I spent the first half of that wrestling everyone into shape. Everyone from those days either left or swore allegiance to me. We do things differently now. And it's worked out for us so far."

I knew he was being vague for my sake. But, in that moment, it truly sank in who I had become so entangled with.

Vincent had just admitted to murder.

Granted, I had always known he was dangerous. Always knew that he was someone I needed to stay away from. But knowing the rumors of his reputation and hearing the confession from his lips were two entirely different things. And I was sure that was not the only blood on his hands.

Hands that were currently wrapped tightly around mine, as if he thought I might finally run.

"Are you afraid of me?" he asked, putting a voice to my thoughts. His tone was gentle, and I let myself relax. If there was one thing that I could appreciate about Vincent, it was that he had never hidden anything about himself from me. I had always known exactly what he was.

"A part of me has always been afraid of you," I admitted, letting the tension leave my body as I pressed into him. "Lucky for you, I'm not very good at listening to my baser instincts."

His laugh rumbled against my back. "I'm glad to hear it."

We stayed like that for quite some time. For the first time in what felt like years, I was completely at peace. But I knew that for at least today, it had to end. I had a training session, and I had to get ready to go out with Devyn. A deep groan reverberated through my chest as I heaved myself from his arms. He didn't fight me this time. While I dressed, he made his way back downstairs.

When I found him, he was busy in the kitchen. I could hear the grease popping as he cooked bacon, and the smell made my stomach rumble. Dexter was sitting just a few feet away from Vincent, eyes trained on the man's every move. Vincent took a piece of cooked bacon off the plate and tossed it to Dexter without moving his focus from the pan in front of him. I rolled my eyes as Dexter all but dove for it, acting like I had never fed him.

Ungrateful little shit.

"I try to limit his table food intake," I said as I eased into the kitchen, taking up a seat at the large island.

Vincent winced and had the good sense to look sheepish when he glanced at me over his shoulder. "I should've asked first."

"One piece of bacon won't kill him," I replied, grinning. "But unless you want to clean up a bunch of vomit off these pretty floors, I wouldn't suggest anymore."

"Noted."

After breakfast, we descended the steps into the warehouse. After the noise of the night before, the air was eerily quiet. There were still a few people mingling around, and the guys were among them, but everyone seemed subdued. Lucas's head popped up from where he and Brandon had slouched in front of the massive TV, and he waved to us. A smile touched my lips as I waved back, but it fell the minute I caught the devilish gleam in his eyes.

He hopped over the back of the couch in a fluid movement and made his way over to us. Vincent eased us to a stop, and I heard a sigh fall from his mouth. The blonde's eyes raked over us, no doubt taking in the absolute mess that was my hair. My spine straightened as he grinned, and I cut him off as soon as he opened his mouth.

"If you say one word, I'll come up with my twenty-fourth way to kill you."

To his credit, Lucas didn't even blink. "But if Vincent gets to tumble around in the sheets with you, I should at least–"

He grunted as my fist connected with his stomach. A deep groan slipped through his lips as I stepped back, shaking out my hand. I might as well have hit a brick wall with all the damage it did, but the disbelief in his eyes was worth it. My eyes cut to Vincent, but he was trying to smother a smile before it could upturn his lips.

Brandon had no such qualms about his laughter as he came up behind Lucas and clapped him on the shoulder.

"It's about time someone else was on the receiving end of her fist," he said, wild delight dancing in his eyes as he watched his cousin.

"Who the hell taught you to hit?" Lucas asked, trying not to make it obvious as he rubbed the spot my punch had landed.

"I've had a couple of talented trainers over the years," I said, breezing past him with Dexter in tow. "See ya later, boys."

A small chuckle fell from Vincent's lips as he caught up with me in time to hold the door open before we ventured out into the noonday sun. I shielded my eyes against the glare as I made my way towards the SUV. As usual, Vincent helped boost me into the seat before rounding the vehicle himself. A smile was playing around the edges of his lips, making an answering one break out across my face as well.

We were on the road before he broke the silence.

"Didn't I warn you to keep your hands off my men?"

"If I remember correctly, you just told me hitting them didn't score me any brownie points. You never said I couldn't do it."

"You're impossible."

My lips twitched. "You thought it was funny, and he had it coming. No one would argue that."

"Touche."

I had to restrain my laughter as we pulled into the parking lot of my building. Vincent helped me get Dexter out of the car and walked me to my door. As I opened it and disengaged the security system, he leaned one shoulder against the doorjamb. After two tries, I correctly entered everything. His eyes met mine, and they shone like gold filtering through a forest canopy.

"What?" I asked, arching my brows.

"You're beautiful."

"Oh." My entire face went scarlet in an instant. "Thank you."

"What're your plans for the rest of the day?"

"Just a few errands, and then Devyn and I are going out tonight," I told him with a shrug. I wasn't sure why I didn't tell him about my self-defense classes.

If I examined it further, part of me knew I didn't want to admit that I had felt so weak that very first night. I hadn't been able to fight back. Between the fear and knowing that I could never outmaneuver even *one* of the men, I had been useless. I never wanted to feel like that again.

If anyone would understand that, it was Vincent. But I wasn't ready to give up that piece of myself. Not yet, at least.

"Juliette?" My name snapped me back to reality. I blinked at him a few times, and his lips twitched at the corners. "You didn't hear a word I said, did you?"

"No," I admitted.

"I was asking if you all knew where you were going?"

"We haven't talked about it yet," I said, blowing out a breath and crossing my arms. "Though I'm sure we'll at least stop by Tuxedo. It's tradition to start there."

"Is this strictly a girl's night?"

"Considering she probably wants to grill me about this," I said, motioning between the two of us. "I would say yes."

"Then I'll tell Arkin to keep his distance."

"Vincent." I whined, tempted to stamp my foot.

"You two are going out alone. Forgive me if I want to make sure you're both safe."

"Now who's being impossible?"

A quiet laugh fell from his lips as he reached for me. Despite the scowl on my face, I let him draw me into his arms. "I know that both of you can take care of yourselves. But knowing that you have someone within earshot if something goes down would help keep my mind at ease." He pressed a kiss to the top of my head before pulling back just enough to meet my eyes. He considered the glare I was sending him before he sighed. "If it's really going to bother you too much, I'll give him the day off. Just like you asked. But promise me if you feel like something is wrong *at all*, you'll call one of us."

"I promise," I said, my heart melting. "Thank you for listening to me. I know where you're coming from, but I've survived this long without you, Vincent. Give me this one night to really tell her what's going on..." I trailed off, my brows pulling together.

"What is it?" he asked, pushing a lock of hair behind my ear.

"What *is* going on here?"

"What do you want it to be?"

"Don't answer my question with a question."

"I'm just trying to make sure I don't overstep, or make any assumptions based on last night. I know where I stand, but where is your head right now?" He met my gaze, ensnaring me. There was no shadow of doubt in his eyes, no hint of misdirection. I hesitated all the same, catching my bottom lip between my teeth. Vincent's eyes tracked the movement, and that ghost of a smile played with the corners of his mouth. "Use tonight with Devyn to figure out the answer to that question. Let me know what you decide."

"Okay."

He leaned down and covered my lips with his. The tenderness of the moment soaked into my bones so far that I turned to liquid in his hands. When he withdrew from me, our breath mingled in the space between us. His eyes all but glittered as they met mine. And, not for the first time, I let myself admire the beauty of the man before me. He dropped a peck on the tip of my nose before he headed out the doors of the lobby. It took every ounce of willpower I had not to call him back to me.

I had work to do.

Twenty-Two

WORKING OUT THE KINKS

"You're late."

"We didn't even agree on a time!" I exclaimed, dropping my bag in the corner of the room. "We just said in the afternoon."

Jack grinned, tawny eyes dancing as he stretched his arms. "You're still late."

"I'm gonna lay your ass out. Just you wait."

"All talk, but I'm not seeing any actions."

"I'm not rising to your baiting techniques, but nice try," I said, sitting down to do my own stretches before we started.

"Worth a shot." He joined me on the ground to do the stretches he always coached me through. "You ran in here like a bat out of hell. You okay?"

"Yeah," I assured him, fighting the smile that wanted to overtake my face. "I actually was feeling like I was running late, so I ran most of the way."

"Didn't you mention living on, like, the opposite side of town?"

"Yes."

"Psychopath."

A laugh fell from my lips as I stretched to touch my toes. "You're the one who encourages it."

"Good point," he hefted himself to his feet. He extended his hand for me, and I let him pull me up as well.

"What're we doing today?"

"Let's evaluate where your skills are at with everything we've done so far, and we'll adjust from there."

"Deal." I sank back into the stance he had shown me. "Don't hold back."

His grin turned wicked. "Not a chance."

He was on me before I could even blink. Sometimes, I forgot how fast the man moved. It took every ounce of focus to get the upper hand. While he had brute strength and skill on his side, I was small and quick. And those were the traits that he had tirelessly worked with me on, so I could learn to manipulate a situation to my advantage. So much so that after a few months of training, I felt like I could hold my own against him.

Today, he was quickly proving that notion to be false. Maybe he had been going easy on me all this time.

"*Ow.*" I hissed as he slammed me into the mat. "I know I said don't hold back, but *Jesus.*"

"C'mon. Weight training. Don't give me that," he said in response to the drawn-out groan that slipped through my lips. "You've still got a long way to go."

"I'm going out tonight," I told him, hoisting myself back onto my feet. "I had better be able to move after we're done here."

A huff ripped out of him as he rolled his eyes at me. He got me set up with the weights he wanted me to work with, coaching me through how to move and lift them. We fell into a rhythm. His voice became an anchor as I pushed my muscles as far as they would let me, and before I knew it, our time was up. My entire body felt like I had reduced it to jelly.

Jack tossed me a water bottle as I slumped to the floor. "How are you feeling?' he asked, mirth dancing in his eyes.

"I hate you," I muttered.

"You'll survive," he said, a deep laugh rumbling in his chest as he sank down beside me. "Are you going to make it tonight?" he teased.

"My best friend would quite literally kill me if I bailed on her, so I don't have much of a choice." The water was so cold I could feel the path it tracked all the way down into my stomach. A shiver wracked my frame as I pressed my forehead against the side of the bottle.

"Girl's night?"

"That's the plan."

"Is it just the two of you?"

"Yes, Mom."

"You're coming to me for self-defense. Your initial reason was because you were on your own a lot at night. You've improved significantly since we started, but that doesn't mean I think it's smart to go out without a little..." he trailed off, worrying his bottom lip between his teeth. "*Extra* protection."

My brows arched. "How very sexist of you, Jack."

He tossed me a dirty look. "A gun, Jules. I meant, do you have a gun?"

"Yes," I squeaked, cheeks flaming. "Sorry."

"Have you practiced with it?"

"*Jack.*"

Something flashed in his eyes, but it was gone so fast I couldn't name it. "Sorry, sorry." He blew out a breath, puffing out his cheeks. "I just worry about you."

"I appreciate it, but really, I'll be fine." I had *more* than enough people worrying about me as it was.

"Same time next week?"

"You got it."

He walked me to the door, holding it open for me. It had gotten late while I'd been inside the gym, and Jack's face was half covered in the darkness cast from the awning over the door. I went to brush past him, and his hand caught me by the crook of my elbow. When

I turned back to him, I sucked in a breath at how close we were. Jack's eyes looked molten in the waning light. They searched my face, the same way they always did. He raised a hand to my face, slowly, as if giving me the chance to pull away. When I didn't, he brushed the piece of hair that had fallen into my eyes back behind my ear. His fingers trailed the edge of my jaw before he let his hand fall back to his side.

I couldn't look away from him, and I couldn't make my lungs function.

"Be careful tonight," he said. There was an undercurrent of warning in his voice.

"I will," I whispered, my breath leaving me in a near audible *whoosh.*

Jack nodded. He took a step back and closed the door behind him, cutting off my view of him. It took me a few seconds to regain my composure, but then I turned on my heel and headed home. I wasn't sure what had just sparked between us, but I wouldn't be entertaining it. Vincent was more than enough to handle. There was a kind of safety that I felt inside the gym, and Jack was part of it. I had drawn a line between us a long time ago. One I had no intention of crossing.

Even if there was a wildness to him that sang to the part of me that tended to get me into trouble.

"You're a damn idiot, Juliette," I muttered to myself, picking up my pace.

I made it back to my apartment in record time, but still only had a little over an hour to get ready. Dexter snuffled at my feet as I hurried into the bathroom to shower. My body was an aching mess after forcing myself to speed-walk home, but it would be worth it if I could avoid Devyn's endless teasing. Turning the water to the hottest setting, I sent her a quick text letting her know I was running behind.

No surprise there, she shot back only a few seconds later.

My eyes rolled. She was just as bad as me most of the time, so she could shove it. A smile pulled at my mouth before I stepped under the water, hissing at how hot it was. It took me a second to adjust the temperature, clinging to the side of the wall like some kind of insect to avoid the near boiling water. I wanted nothing more than to let the hot water soothe away every ache in my bones after that session with Jack, but knew I needed to get a move on. I washed my hair and body quickly, and I made a last-minute decision to ditch shaving.

Dexter watched me with keen eyes as I flew through the apartment. It had been quite a while since Devyn and I had actually gone out, and I was buzzing with excitement. Even though I knew that the night would no doubt entail her grilling me on my *relationship* with Vincent, I couldn't wait.

I was swiping a second coat of mascara over my lashes when there was a knock on the door. "Come in!" I yelled, leaning closer to the mirror.

"You look like a fish," Devyn said as she popped her head into the bathroom.

"Hello to you too."

"Do you need me to take Dex out while you finish up?"

"Yes, please!" I threw everything back into my makeup bag and pitched it under the sink. "You're a lifesaver."

Devyn grinned, her blood-red lips stretching over her teeth in a blinding smile. Not for the first time, I let myself appreciate how beautiful she was. Her hair fell in a sleek curtain over one shoulder, framing her heart-shaped face. She had lined her eyes with a dark sweep of kohl, making them look even more captivating than they normally did. Her eyes were only a few shades darker than mine, but they were warm and reminded me of home. *She* reminded me of home, the only family I'd had for so long.

"Why do you look like you're about to cry?" she asked, arching her pierced brow.

"Because I love you. Leave me alone."

"I love you, too, dumbass. Don't smear your makeup before we even leave." Despite her flippant words, her eyes softened. She reached forward and touched my hand before turning to find Dexter's lead. He trotted beside her, bouncing around her legs like an overexcited rabbit.

"I'll only be a few more minutes!" I called after them, making to head into the bedroom.

"What's this?"

Turning, I saw she was staring at the security panel on the wall. Both eyebrows were about at her hairline as she tilted her head to meet my gaze. I snagged my bottom lip between my teeth.

Shit.

"It's a security system."

"Bitch, this thing costs more than this apartment. How did you..." she trailed off, realization sparkling in her dark eyes. "Did the banger buy this for you?"

"Yes."

"Why?"

Double shit.

"Can we talk about this after a few drinks?" I asked, giving her a sheepish smile.

"Oh, you better *believe* we're talking about this. Don't you dare try to distract me away from it, either." She narrowed her eyes and shook her finger at me before leading Dexter outside.

My eyes rolled skyward. And she called Dante a hormonal mother hen.

I pulled on a pair of destroyed black jeans, hopping to force them over my hips. I was standing in front of my closet, clad in nothing more than my black lace bra and jeans, when Devyn appeared in the doorway ten minutes later. I had my arms crossed, examining my closet as I tried to decide on what to wear. My bare foot tapped against the floor. I was overthinking. I knew that. But I wanted to feel *good*. Sexy would be even better.

"Wanna help?" I tossed over my shoulder.

"What shoes are you wearing?" I pointed to a pair of combat boots with a chunky heel. Something that would give me some damn height for once, but that I could also run in easily enough if I needed. And with the way my life had been going the past few months, that wasn't outside of the realm of possibility. "Are you wearing a jacket?"

"I was planning on it."

Her face turned contemplative as her eyes scanned my closet. She stepped forward, reaching for one of the pieces shoved to the very back. She held the black corset up to inspect it. It was one of the more daring tops I had since the panels along the ribs were sheer. A smile broke across her face as she tossed it to me and then continued to paw through my clothes. I didn't even bother trying to second guess her. I pitched the bra I had on into the corner of the room and slipped into the corset. Thankfully, it wasn't a traditional one with the laces, just stretchy material to give the illusion of them.

"Wear this instead of your black one," Devyn said, catching my attention as she handed me the burgundy leather jacket I had completely forgotten that I owned.

"You're a genius," I told her, pulling the jacket on. She simply grinned at me before snatching my hand and all but dragging me out the door. She barely gave me the time to engage the security system before we left. By the time we were outside, there was a silver sedan idling at the curb. I bristled, clutching my phone in my hand. If Vincent had gone back on his word–

"Who are you here to pick up?" Devyn asked the driver as the window rolled down. Letting out a breath, I realized she had called for a car. After he verified he was there for us, we piled into the backseat. The man had a broad smile on his face, his eyes crinkling around the edges. He and Devyn made small talk as we headed into the heart of the city.

"Tuxedo first?" I asked when there was a lull in their conversation.

"Yep. If we even leave at all."

She had a point. There was a reason Tuxedo was one of the most popular clubs in the city. Our liquor selection was wide enough to accommodate any taste or budget, and our staff was top-notch, if I said so myself, especially for a smaller club. I had to train for almost a year before Dante let me move behind the bar, and that was on the shorter end of training. Add that to the fact that he was picky as all hell with whom he let DJ, and we were rarely at anything less than capacity on the weekends.

When we pulled up to the front of the club, I groaned at the line that stretched for nearly a block. Devyn arched a brow at me. She thanked the driver, handed him a tip, and then shooed me from the car. The night was blissfully warm, considering the weather was taking the turn into fall. With my light jacket, I was perfectly comfortable. As I felt the bass from the club pulse under my shoes even from outside, my blood hummed in my veins.

I made to head to the back of the line, but Devyn grabbed my arm and yanked me towards the alley that led around to the back of the club. My eyes rolled. Of course, she wasn't planning on waiting in the line.

"This is an abuse of power, you know," I said as I sped up so that she wasn't dragging me behind her.

"Oh, shut up," she said, fuchsia nails flashing as she waved me off. "You know damn well you didn't want to wait, either. And this way, we can keep our purses and shit in the back where we don't have to watch it."

She had a point.

We shouldered the back door open, and all but spilled into the back room. The door to Dante's office was open and we could see him sitting at his desk. He raised his head at the commotion, and once his eyes landed on us, I could see the curse that fell from his lips. It made me laugh as I waved at him. He heaved himself up and looked like he was still muttering to himself as he walked up to us.

"How much trouble are you two going to cause tonight?' he asked, looking pointedly at Devyn.

"I'm wounded. Jules is the one fucking a gangster."

"*Devyn,*" I hissed, wincing as Dante turned his attention to me. He just crossed his arms and leaned against the doorway. "It's nothing." Devyn snorted as she shrugged out of her ripped denim jacket and hung it on the rack.

"Juliette."

"Dante," I said, my voice flat. I crossed my arms and planted my feet shoulder width apart, as if I were squaring up for a fight. Which, by the look of reproach on both of their faces, I damn well might be. "I thought we were over the warnings and bullshit."

Devyn opened her mouth, but Dante cut her off. "You're right," he said, blowing out a breath. He ran a hand over his bald head before dragging it down his face. His warm brown eyes studied me, taking in the stance and the unwavering glare on my face. "You're right," he repeated. "I've said my piece. You know how I feel about the situation. And you're not a kid anymore. I get that. But I want you to let him know that if he steps one *toe* out of line, I'll remind him just why I've never had any issues with gangs in this club."

I swallowed past the lump in my throat. Sometimes I forgot about how dark Dante's past had been before he started the club. Before he started something legitimate to get out of one of the worst gangs in the city. Forgot that I had once seen him break a bone in his arm clean in two and barely react to the pain, even though the bone had pierced his skin. A shiver raked down my spine at the memory, and I physically shook my head to clear it.

"Thank you," I said, letting my arms drop and a smile light my face.

"Don't drink all my tequila," was all he said as he dipped back into the office and shut the door behind him.

"You've still got some explaining to do as far as I'm concerned," Devyn groused. I rolled my eyes at her and moved to her side to drop my purse onto the shelf. Sliding my debit card and phone into my back pocket, I snagged the last open hook for my jacket. As cute as it was, I knew I'd be sweating within minutes of stepping out onto the dance floor if I kept it on. Devyn linked her arm with mine as we made our way out into the bar.

Anthony looked up from where he was polishing glasses. His hazel eyes sparkled as he spotted us. He moved to the swinging door that opened from behind the bar to the floor and pushed it open. As we passed him, he sketched a deep bow. Devyn shoved his shoulder, causing him to stumble into the wall. His laughter trailed us as we took up two stools on Anthony's side of the bar. I saw Ember, one of our newest to join the team, on the other side. She had fit in quickly, her tongue almost as sharp as Devyn's. She nodded her head in acknowledgement before turning back to her customers.

"How much trouble are you two going to give me tonight?" Anthony asked, leaning on the bar directly in front of us.

"Who, me?" Devyn cooed, fluttering her thick lashes at him. He just rolled his eyes and placed two shot glasses in front of us.

"Don't even pull that shit, Dev," he said as he poured a hefty amount of tequila into a shaker to chill it. "First one's on me, then you two heathens are on your own."

"We love you too," I threw in, grinning at him.

He pitched us the saltshaker and limes before heading off to take more orders. Devyn raised her shot to me, and we clinked glasses before tossing the liquor back. It burned straight down my throat before the warmth leaked out towards my fingers and toes. The lime wedge dulled the after bite, and I tossed it into my empty glass when I was done. The small breakfast I had shared with Vincent was long gone, so the shot went to work, relaxing my muscles almost immediately.

"So?" Devyn started, pivoting on her stool to face me.

"So?" I mimicked.

"Are you going to make me drag this out of you?"

"Maybe."

She huffed. "If you really don't want to tell me, Jules, I get it. Dante and I have kind of been up your ass about this whole thing. But if you tell me you're happy, I'll lay off." She paused. "A little."

"I don't even know where to start," I admitted, running my fingers through my hair.

"How about the beginning?"

So, I told her everything that she didn't already know. From the guys tailing me at all hours, to my self-defense, to the friendships I had developed with them. All the way down to the undeniable feelings for Vincent that had burrowed into my heart and grown thorns sharp enough to keep them there. I could feel my face heat as I told her every dirty detail, and mischief danced across hers in answer. When I got to the night before, her eyes had grown to the size of saucers. Once I finished, my chest didn't feel so tight. My head felt clearer than it had before the shot. I didn't know why I had hesitated when Vincent had dropped me at my apartment that afternoon.

I wanted him. He wanted me. It was as simple as that.

"I need to tell him," I said, my teeth catching my bottom lip.

"Duh."

"Excuse me?"

She held up her hands in surrender. "Look. If I didn't know for a fact that the Vincent Monroe that runs the *singular* most lethal gang in this city, and the man who is here after every single one of your shifts to make sure you get home safe were one and the same, I'd never believe you." I raised my brows at her. "But he cares about you. It's obvious in the way he looks at you."

"Because you've seen him look at me."

"I have eyes, bitch," she sniped, a smile curving her lips. "Don't think I don't watch the cameras until you all get in the car. Nothing else exists for that man when you're around. If he's treating you right, I'll lay off. I promise."

"Alright, we need another shot if you're being this nice."

The laugh that fell from her lips was rich and warm, causing an answering smile to break out across my face. While she waved down Anthony for another round of shots, I pulled my phone out to shoot Vincent a text.

I've figured it out.

It only took a few seconds for my phone to buzz with his answer. *And what's that, princess?*

I'll give you a shot, but only if you promise not to kill me.

We both know if I wanted you dead, it would've happened a long time ago.

Comforting.

You're the one with the smart-ass mouth.

I smirked. *I didn't hear you complaining last night.*

I really shouldn't have been so surprised to find out that you're such a brat. Let me know when you all are ready to head home. I'll come get you.

Devyn sat another shot in front of me, so I slipped my phone back into my pocket. Her pierced brow raised. "What was that?"

"I was texting Vincent."

"I'm never going to get used to that."

I clinked my shot against hers. "Here's to our fucked-up lives."

"Cheers."

TWENTY-THREE

FANCY SEEING YOU

Two shots later, Devyn had dragged me out onto the dance floor. I laughed as she pulled my body against hers, swaying us to the pulsing beat that seemed to merge with my blood.

How long had it been since I had let loose like this? I couldn't remember the last time if I was being honest with myself.

"Why don't we do this more often?" I asked her over the din.

"Because we both work way too much, and it's usually opposite shifts." She threw a glare at the back with her last sentence, and I had to restrain the grin that wanted to break over my face.

"He doesn't purposely keep us separated."

She huffed. "Sure seems like it sometimes."

She laughed with me as we moved to the music again. I couldn't help but notice we were drawing a few wandering eyes. Devyn had a body to kill for, and I knew I wasn't hard to look at either. But I did my best to ignore them. If I was actually going to give whatever had bloomed between Vincent and me a shot, then I wasn't interested in anyone else.

Not even the tawny-eyed man who watched me with mirth dancing in his eyes from one of the corner booths.

"*Damnit,*" I cursed, spinning so that my back was to Jack. I was fairly certain I had never told him where I worked, so it must just be fate that had it out for me.

"What's up?" Devyn asked, catching the shift in my demeanor.

"You know the trainer I told you I've been going to see recently?" She nodded. "In the booth at twelve o'clock."

Her gaze drifted around the bar, trying not to make her search obvious. But I knew the moment she saw him. Her eyes widened the slightest bit as she finished her scan, then whipped her attention back to me. "*That's* the man you're getting all close and sweaty with every week?"

"*Devyn.*"

"Does Vincent know?" she asked, ignoring the warning tone in my voice.

"No," I muttered, blowing out a breath.

"I can see why. He's hot."

"Shut up."

"Well, if you don't want him, I'm going to take a swing at it." She grabbed my arm and dragged me over to Jack's table, hissing at me to introduce them as we approached.

A grin was breaking over his face as we made it to his table, and I couldn't stop myself from rolling my eyes at him. "Fancy seeing you here."

"Hey, Jules," he greeted, holding his hands up in a placating gesture. "I swear, I'm not following you."

"You just happen to pop up where I am two days in a row?"

"Pure coincidence."

"This is the one, then?" a deep voice asked behind us, causing me to whip around. The man that was standing there was gorgeous. His dark brown skin was gleaming under the neon lights, making him look like he had stepped out of the night sky itself. Full lips pulled back to reveal gleaming white teeth in a dazzling smile. Once I picked my jaw up off the floor, he extended a hand to me, and I tried to ignore the muscles that wreathed every inch of his body that I could see. "I'm Sebastian."

"Juliette," I forced past my dry throat as I shook his hand. His grip was firm, but just as gentle as his onyx eyes when they met mine. "And this is Devyn."

"It's nice to meet you," he said, the timbre of his voice falling as he turned to her.

"Likewise," she answered, turning her head to me with a kind of *what the fuck* look on her face. I just shook my head in response. I didn't know what was happening.

"Bastian, you're making them swoon," Jack drawled, causing me to shift my attention back to him. He winked at me, which made my ears burn as the blush tried to work its way onto my face. Thank goodness it was so dark in the club.

"Well, this has been fun," I said, shaking myself in an attempt to return to reality. "But as you can see, I'm fine. And we're going." I snatched Devyn's hand and made to take off. Something about being around the two men was making the fine hairs on the back of my neck stand up. It was a reaction to the air of darkness that clung to the two of them as they settled into one of the most secluded booths in the club. The same one in which Vincent had sat with that weasel-faced man all those weeks ago. In fact, it was probably knowing this was the booth in which the gang conducted most of its meetings that had my skin prickling with awareness.

Devyn apparently had other plans. She pulled against my retreat and tossed a flirtatious smile back to the two of them. "Would you two like to take some shots with us?"

Sebastian grinned and looked at Jack, who just shrugged. Something told me he had felt the snub when I tried to dash off but was taking it in stride. As if my thoughts had summoned his attention, he settled those tawny eyes on me. My breath caught as he let them slip over me from head to toe, and I could feel his gaze like a caress. My heart thundered, and a lazy smile stretched his mouth like he could hear it.

"Don't mind if we do," Jack said. He got to his feet with the fluid grace I was used to seeing him with in the studio, and I let out an exasperated huff. So much for girl's night. Jack stopped next to me and met my eyes again. He must have seen the anxiety written plainly on my face because he said to Devyn and Sebastian, "I just need a quick word with Jules. We'll catch up."

"You sure?" Devyn questioned, glancing at me. When I nodded, she grabbed Sebastian by the hand and dragged him towards the bar. My head was spinning from the mixture of the liquor, dancing, and this strange encounter, so I lifted my hands to massage my temples.

"Juliette," Jack said, taking a step that brought him close enough to feel the heat of his body. "I'm sorry."

"For what?" I asked, my head popping up to look at him. His eyes had lost all their playfulness and the softness I was familiar with replaced it.

"I didn't mean to ambush you." He ran his hand through his hair. "This really wasn't planned. I know you were trying to have a good time with your friend tonight, so I'm sorry if we interrupted."

I snorted. "If anything, *we* ambushed you. Devyn took one look at your pretty face and all but demanded to meet you."

"You think I'm pretty?"

"Shut up," I said, all the tension leaving my body as I shoved his shoulder. I couldn't believe I had been so keyed up over *Jack*. What was I thinking? "So, you told Sebastian about me, huh?"

It was his turn to flush pink. "I may have mentioned there was a chance we could run into one of my clients while we were out."

"Uh-huh."

"How's the boy trouble?"

"I forgot I told you about that," I said with a wince. "It's sorted itself out."

"So, you're together?"

"Yeah," I replied, a small smile tilting my lips.

"Then I'm happy for you," he told me, giving me a grin of his own before slinging an arm around my neck and dragging me after Devyn and Sebastian. "Let's get that drink."

When we found Devyn and Sebastian, they had just taken their shots. Devyn's eyes glittered when she spotted me, and she handed me my shot without a word. Not waiting for any kind of go-ahead, I tossed the liquor back. I had gotten way too sober *way* too quick. As the liquor burned down my throat, I could feel my buzz kicking back in, and I let my shoulders relax under the weight of Jack's arm.

"Devyn was just telling me you all work here."

"Yep," I answered Sebastian, reaching around them to set my empty glass on the counter. I caught Anthony's gaze, and he held up a finger to let me know he'd be over in a moment. "You'd think we'd go somewhere else since we basically live here, but it's safe, you know."

Sebastian nodded, his eyes on Jack as he eased his arm from around my shoulders to take the shot his friend passed him. Something exchanged between them, but I didn't catch what it was before Jack gave an infinitesimal shake of his head. Had I not been paying attention, I would have missed it.

"What are your all's plans for the night?" Devyn asked, sizing them both up over the rim of her glass. My lips quirked in a smile. I could recognize the huntress in her eyes from a mile away. Whatever man she took home tonight, I pitied him a little.

My phone vibrating in my pocket drew me away from the conversation. I pulled it out and had to suppress my grin when I saw Lucas's name.

I know we're supposed to let you be tonight, but we want to go out. Are you at Tuxedo? the text message read. He had even thrown in a couple of pouting faces.

We're here. Y'all can do whatever you want as long as you're not infringing on what I'M doing.

You got it!

I chuckled before slipping my phone back into my pocket. When I glanced up again, I ignored the questioning look on Devyn's face in favor of stepping up to the bar to talk to Anthony.

"Are you doing okay?" he asked, eyes scanning over Devyn and the fresh additions.

"We're good. I just wondered if you'd kill me if I asked for a margarita."

"As long as you don't make me break out the blender, you're fine."

"Rocks is fine," I said, grinning at him. "I just need something to sip on instead of the shots Devyn is forcing down my throat."

"Hey!" she cried, indignant.

"Are you telling me I'm wrong?"

"No, but–"

"Make her one too, please," I told Anthony. He just shook his head at us before turning to make the drinks.

Devyn pouted. "I'm only not throwing a fit because a margarita sounds great."

"Sure."

Her eyes flicked down to my ass. Well, to my phone, if we were being technical. She moved to my side, leaving Jack and Sebastian behind us as she asked, "Vincent?"

"It was Lucas," I said, with a shake of my head. "They want to go out. I think he just wanted to make sure that if I saw them here, I wouldn't think Vincent had gone back on his word about giving us the night to ourselves."

"I don't like how likable those assholes are," she grumbled.

"Tell me about it."

"Ladies," Sebastian's voice sounded so close behind me I jumped before glancing over my shoulder. Jack covered his laugh with a cough, but those eyes glowed amber under the pulsing lights. I glared at him. "We're heading out. Care to join us?"

"Where are you going?" Devyn questioned before I could.

"We're going to head down to Black Lantern."

My blood turned to ice, and my grip tightened on the bar, bleaching my knuckles white.

"No thank you," I said as smoothly as I could. Devyn nodded her agreement before covering my hand and giving it a reassuring squeeze.

Jack's eyes tracked the movement, and after meeting my eyes, he clapped a hand against Sebastian's shoulder. "Another time then."

"Sure thing," I answered, forcing a smile onto my face.

Jack kept his eyes on me as Devyn and Sebastian exchanged numbers. He was searching my face the way he always did, and it unnerved me how much he always seemed to see. "Is Tuesday good for you this week?"

"Instead of Saturday?"

"No, on top of Saturday."

"But that'll make it two times that we meet this week."

"And?"

"*And* I'm only paying for one class a week right now."

Jack rolled his eyes at me. "We've met up more than once a week multiple times. We can talk about money on Tuesday if you really want."

I mock saluted him before they ambled away. Once the crowd had swallowed them, I slumped against the counter and tried to calm my racing heart.

"Still can't go there?" Devyn asked, her voice soft as she stroked soothing fingers down my spine.

"I'll never be able to set foot there without wondering where they found him," I murmured. "They never arrested the man that shot him." I was pretty sure he was still on the force.

"Your dad would want you to move on."

"I know. But I still freeze up any time I see a cop or hear mention of one. You know that."

"I don't think that'll ever go away. And I'm sorry I asked."

"Sorry if I cock-blocked."

Devyn laughed, swatting at my shoulder. "I've got his number if I want to meet up with them after you go home with the banger."

"I hope he hears you calling him that one day."

"I'd like to see him try anything with me."

"*He* knows Juliette would gut me if I so much as laid a finger on you," a cool voice said from behind us.

"I didn't know you were included when I told Lucas he had the green light," I admonished, glancing over my shoulder to meet Vincent's forest-green gaze. His lips tilted, and I felt every muscle relax at the sight of him.

"I'm not allowed to have a drink with my men?" he asked, quirking a brow at me.

"She's just being a brat," Devyn threw in.

"You two are *not* going to start ganging up on me," I seethed, pointing a finger between the two of them.

Vincent caught my hand and used it to spin me to face him. He took his time in looking me over. I realized he had never really seen me in anything other than my work uniform or comfy clothes.

Or naked, a small voice chimed in the back of my mind.

His green eyes darkened as he scanned me. If I had thought Jack's perusal had felt like a caress, Vincent's attention was like a brand. A searing intensity that I knew I would feel long after he was gone. My blood heated as he let out a low hum of approval. He looked at me like I was everything he had ever wanted, ever *needed,* and I had to admit that it was an intoxicating feeling. Devyn's earlier words echoed in my head as she snorted into her drink. At that, a flush crept up my chest and stained my entire face crimson. I dropped my chin to hide the blush.

Vincent pulled me into him, utterly ignoring Devyn as my chest pressed against his. His fingers slid up my throat until he had his thumb pressed against the underside of my chin, applying the slightest amount of pressure to force me to meet his eyes. The heat in his gaze made the fire in my blood bank straight to my core, and I had to resist the urge to press my thighs together. One look at the sly smirk tugging at his mouth had me realizing he knew exactly what he was doing.

Asshole.

"Can I help you?" I snapped, narrowing my eyes at him.

"I just wanted you to know I was here," he said, voice low enough that I knew it was only for me. "I'll stay out of your hair, but just come and get me when you're ready to head home."

"Okay," I replied, all the ire slipping from my tone.

"By the way," he said, leaning forward so that his lips brushed against the shell of my ear. "You look incredible."

Devyn and I stared after him as he broke away from me. He nodded to Devyn before crossing over to a far corner of the bar. I could just make out Lucas, Brandon, and Arkin at the table he stopped at. The problematic blonde gave me a broad smile before obnoxiously waving. I rolled my eyes and waved back. A smirk tugged at my mouth as I fished my phone out of my pocket and fired off a quick text.

25.

I could have sworn I heard Lucas's raucous laughter even from where we were standing, and I had to restrain a giggle of my own. Then I spun back to the bar and let my best friend have my full attention again.

"Still want to play dumb about the way he looks at you?" she asked, a shit-eating grin on her face.

"I'm going to make you buy me a drink for every time I have to tell you to shut up."

Twenty-Four

WHIPLASH

"Did you all have a good night?" Vincent asked a few hours later as he was driving me home. Devyn had stayed and help close the bar down. I only relented and left her there after Dante assured me he'd take her home.

"We did," I said, laying my head against the cool window. Blowing out a breath, I finally decided to just rip the band aid off. "We ran into my trainer while we were there."

"Your trainer?" There was so much surprise in his voice that I turned to face him.

"Yeah."

Realization flared in his eyes as he parked the car outside my apartment building. "Is that where you disappear to?"

"Maybe." The look he gave me would make any sane person drop to their knees and beg for forgiveness. I was so used to it from him, I just rolled my eyes. "Yes."

He let out a brief hum of acknowledgement before exiting the car. By the time I had my seatbelt undone and had turned to get out as well, he was opening my door for me. He stopped my exit by easing my knees apart to settle himself between them. My breath caught in my throat as he leaned forward. From where I was sitting in the SUV, we were at eye level. Vincent used that to his full advantage. His hands skimmed from my knees, up my thighs, until he settled them on the slice of skin that was open between my shirt and jeans. His thumbs slipped under the fabric of my top to rub taunting circles across my ribs. I had a front-row seat as his pupils dilated, the black swallowing green until I felt like I would fall right into them.

"And you were hiding this from me, because?" he murmured, leaning in even further to let his lips whisper across the juncture between my neck and shoulder.

"Because–" Every thought eddied out of my brain when he placed a soft kiss against the curve of my throat before proceeding to rake his teeth over the tender skin. He repeated the process, drawing the most pitiful whimper from me.

"Go on," he urged, his fingers playing with the waistband of my jeans.

"Because I was scared," I admitted in a rush, needing to get the truth out before he distracted me any further. My words hit their mark with a sniper's precision. Vincent's entire body locked up. He was so close to me, I could feel the minuscule roll of his shoulders as he pulled back to lock eyes with me.

"Of what?"

"Not of you," I said, stroking my fingertips over his cheekbone. "Okay, maybe a little," I amended at his arched brow. "But mostly, I just felt so helpless that first night. I mean, it was like four on one, but I didn't stand a *chance* if they had decided they wanted to hurt me."

His furrowed brow smoothed out as understanding flooded his features. He took my face in his hands and pressed a kiss to my forehead. "I'm sorry we made you feel like that, and I'm sorry you felt like you ever had to hide that from me. But I'm not sorry we dragged you into this world, princess." The timbre in his voice dropped as he tilted my chin, forcing me to meet his eyes. He was the only thing I could see. The only thing that existed at that moment. "Because it brought you to me. It brought us here."

I opened my mouth to reply, my eyes pricking, but he covered my lips with his, and my mind went blank. The warmth of his body drawing us together was the only thing that mattered. I twined my arms around his neck at the same time I closed my legs around his waist. Something akin to a growl rumbled in his chest, and my reaction was visceral. I couldn't get close enough to him. His fingers dug into my hips, likely leaving bruises, but I just arched into him even farther. Into that touch that was lighting me up from the inside. If someone would have told me I turned incandescent in that moment, I would've believed it.

"Let's get inside," I breathed, trying to control myself so I didn't start panting like Dexter when he smelled bacon. Vincent nodded, grabbing my hand to pull me after him. A laugh bubbled out of my mouth as he all but dragged me towards the apartment. We came to a stop in front of my door, and as I dug through my purse for my keys, Vincent pressed his front to my back. He wrung another giggle out of me when he moved my jacket aside and kissed along my bare shoulder. His kisses were feather-light, teasing, as he worked his way up the column of my throat. "If you don't give me a second to breathe, I'm never going to get this door open."

"Sorry."

"Liar."

The rumble of his laughter vibrated against my back, sending a shock wave right through me. I cursed as I nearly dropped my keys, which only made him laugh harder. I stomped on his instep and he rewarded me by letting loose a string of profanity that was impressive, even for him. My little stunt wouldn't go unpunished, but it gave me the time to actually get the door open. As it swung inward, Vincent all but tossed me into the apartment. He barely gave me enough time to disengage the stupid security system before he shoved me back into the door. He was so warm; I felt like I was going to burn alive.

And I would have done it willingly as his knee went between my legs.

Dexter let out an indignant huff from the couch, as if our mere presence were an inconvenience. He hopped down and wandered off into the other room, leaving me completely at the mercy of the man in front of me.

Vincent tipped my chin up so that our gazes met, and I was once again left defenseless in this man's hands. How had I ever denied I had any sort of attraction to him? He ran his thumb across my bottom lip; the touch displaying the gentleness I only ever witnessed him extend to me.

"Juliette," he murmured, his mouth brushing against mine as my name fell from his lips with reverence. "I need you to understand something." His eyes darkened, but not with desire. There was a storm brewing inside him, and it sobered me. Within the span of a heartbeat, all the lust drained from my body as my spine straightened, waiting.

"What's that?" I asked when it was obvious he needed a little prodding.

"Being with me, it's not safe."

"Oh, do *not* start–"

"I'm serious," he stated, a firm finality in his voice that silenced any argument I had been ready to make. His eyes softened as he brushed a strand of my hair back behind my ear. "There are people that want to kill me. There are those that have tried. Being with me, being *mine*, is going to put a target on your back. I'm not going to sit here and tell you not to be with me because of it. I'm far too selfish for that. But I need you to know the risks. If you're serious about this, you need to know what you're agreeing to. *I* need to know that the risk is worth it to you."

"It is," I said before I could think about it. But I didn't need to. I had already gone through all of this on my own. It was what had led to my hesitation earlier that afternoon. He seemed skeptical, arching his brow at me. "You, *this*," I added with vehemence, gesturing between us. "It's worth it."

"You're sure?"

"I am," I said, giving him a firm nod as I laid my hand on his chest, right above his pounding heart. It was helpful to have the physical proof I had the same effect on him as he had on me. "Vincent, you've never hidden anything from me. Hell, the first night I met you happened under less than savory circumstances. I see you, and I still want you. As much as it should, your world doesn't scare me."

"It definitely should."

"And I know that. But I've lived in this city my entire life. I know the darkness it houses. Maybe I don't know the ins and outs, but I work in the bar you all do business in. I know Dante's past." His eyebrows raised at that, and it really shouldn't have surprised me to find out that he *also* knew about the life my boss had led before starting the bar. It was the next part of this conversation that was going to be hard for me. "I've never told you about my dad."

This time, his eyebrows nearly touched his hairline. "That's quite the subject switch."

"Not really," I said, a strained laugh falling from my lips. God, I needed another drink for this. I slipped past him, missing the steadiness of his presence as I headed into the kitchen.

Vincent followed me, and all thoughts of the heat we had stumbled into the apartment with were long gone. He leaned one shoulder against the wall leading into the kitchen, crossing arms and ankles as he watched me. His attention was like a balm to my quickly fraying nerves. When Jack brought up the Black Lantern earlier, it opened up a well of grief I had buried years ago. And now, it was coming to a head, and I wasn't sure I was ready for it.

But if Vincent was being open with me, I could only offer him the same courtesy.

I had an old bottle of whiskey stashed in the corner cabinet, specifically for dire situations, and I couldn't think of a more opportune time to break it out. The amber liquid sloshed as I dragged the bottle down from the highest shelf, and I held it up to Vincent in question. He nodded, his eyes still calculating as he tracked my every movement.

I knew that of the two of us; he had been the most forthcoming with information on our pasts. Which was insane to think about. How had I never noticed how much he had shared with me before? How much he trusted me with? Not just about himself, but the gang, too. I knew so much information, I could bring them down in a heartbeat if I said anything to the wrong person. The realization was like a physical weight on my chest, and I couldn't get in a breath. The air stalled in my throat as I held the whiskey ready to pour.

I couldn't move. Couldn't *breathe.*

And all at once, I was back to that day. Walking into the home I had grown up in.

The smell of chocolate was making my heart rate go haywire before I even cleared the hallway. I knew it was bad before I set foot in the kitchen. Mom only baked when she got bad news, and she only made her triple-chocolate cake for the worst of it. So, I was bracing myself long before her silver-lined eyes met mine. Her eyes were so red and puffy that their natural sage color was damn near electric in comparison.

"What happened?" I asked, my sixteen-year-old voice coming out so small.

She didn't even try to sugar-coat it for me.

That was what the dessert was for.

"Your dad's dead."

"Hey," Vincent murmured, by my side in an instant. At his touch, I took in a strangled gasp. "You don't have to tell me anything you're not ready for."

"I'm okay," I finally said. I poured both of our drinks and spun around to hand him his. He took it with the care of someone approaching a spooked tiger. There was raw worry in his eyes, and I took a deep breath. "Ask me."

And bless this man for knowing exactly what I was talking about. Knowing that I needed the nudge, or I wouldn't get through it.

"What happened to your dad?"

"He was murdered." Vincent's eyes widened the smallest fraction, but he kept quiet. He just raised the drink to his full lips and took a small sip. He inclined his head, urging me to do the same. The whiskey burned all the way from my tongue to my stomach, but it helped me focus. Helped me continue with something I hadn't examined in almost a decade. I leaned back against the counter, pressing my glass against my forehead before speaking again. "My dad was a cop. A damn good homicide detective. His last case was a string of murders on the North side of the city. A bunch of young girls, late teens to early twenties, had been going missing. Then the bodies would show up in pieces that were almost unidentifiable. No one could figure it out, and his partner had been pushing him to drop it. But Dad wouldn't."

Because of course the man couldn't let people keep going missing on his watch. It tore him apart. Add the fact that they weren't much older than I had been, and it had hit too close to home for him.

"And like I said, he was a *damn good* detective. He eventually found out that it was a whole ring of powerful men who were responsible." A bitter laugh fell from my lips.

"Your father was *Francisco Gracen?*" Vincent asked, a touch of awe in his voice as he put the pieces together. "I remember when that bust happened. It took out some powerful players in Valarian. He was a hero."

My throat was tight. "He went by Frank."

"Juliette," his voice was so gentle as he reached for me. I let him set our glasses on the counter and pull me against him. "The stories I heard said one of the congressmen put out a hit on him."

I nodded, letting the steadiness of his heartbeat lend me strength. "What the papers didn't know to print was that his partner was in on it. The man that had been in our lives for as long as I could remember, who had come to dinner at our house, was the mole on the force. He was the one who made sure every bit of evidence for those cases ended up compromised or destroyed. And I'm positive he was the one they used to kill Dad."

God, I had never said it out loud.

Devyn and Dante had figured some of it out on their own with the small amount I had shared with them over the years. But they had never pushed for the story in its entirety.

"I think I can guess the answer to this," he started, that touch of the darkness in his voice. "But why didn't you ever come forward?"

"There was no concrete evidence, but I remember overhearing the conversation my parents had before Dad went to meet Peter at the Black Lantern. He told Mom his suspicions, and then he was dead by the end of the night. I don't have any proof, but I don't for a single second believe anyone else pulled the trigger that night. Peter was there and already had a knack for covering his tracks.

"I remember he came by to offer his condolences after the funeral. It was a miracle I didn't puke or kill him myself with the way he was watching me. I think he knew we knew. Or at least suspected. In a very well veiled threat, he made sure that Mom and I knew that if we ever said anything, we were next. As far as I know, he's been on the force ever since."

With the end of my story, that weight that had been pressing down on me lifted. I went slack in Vincent's arms, and he held me tight. He was the only thing keeping me on my feet, and if he realized, he didn't make a comment on it. He stroked his fingers through my hair, and I melted into him further still.

"So, when you said you wouldn't go to the police-"

"I will *never* trust the VPD with anything else as long as I live." I hissed. "For all I know, the corruption goes all the way to the top. That's not something I could fight. Not at sixteen, and not even now."

There were a few beats of silence, and then Vincent uttered the one sentence I truly should have expected, but that knocked the breath right back out of me all the same.

"I could kill him."

TWENTY-FIVE

LUST DRUNK

I pulled back just enough to look into his eyes. Part of me wanted to laugh, but I knew better. Knew that if I gave him the go ahead, Vincent would track Peter Vaughn down and wipe him out of existence. It was a heady kind of power, one that I had never experienced, and it scared me.

What scared me even more was that I was considering it.

What was that old saying? Evil only prevails when good men do nothing?

"You would do it." I murmured, brushing my fingertips along the muscle feathering his jaw. "Wouldn't you?"

"In a heartbeat."

"Even though he's a cop?"

There was a wicked edge to Vincent's grin. "*Especially* because he's a cop. And a dirty one at that."

At that, I did laugh. "Let's put a pin in that for now."

"*You're* actually thinking about it?"

"I would rather put him behind bars, because if I stoop to that level, I'm no better than him. But we just covered why I don't trust the police. So, if the opportunity arises, I'd be stupid to overlook it. He's hurt more than just my family." I gave him a wry smile. "The bad guy only ever has the chance to come back in the stories because the hero took the high road."

"And you're not a hero?"

"Hell no. And neither are you."

There was something like pride shining in those green depths as he stared at me. I would be a liar if I said that look on his face didn't cause my whole body to flush in response. Without questioning myself, for once, I tangled my fingers in his soft hair. He met me halfway, his arms tightening in an entirely different way than they had only moments before. Within a breath, teeth and tongue were fighting for dominance, and the lust that had banked since we entered my apartment came back with a vengeance.

I couldn't get close enough to him.

In a movement I was quickly coming to love, Vincent hitched my legs up around his waist. He walked us back until he could set me on the counter, and then he settled himself between my thighs. A low moan dragged out of my throat as the hard length of him pressed against me through our clothes. Goosebumps erupted over every inch of my skin as he skimmed his hands under the collar of my jacket, pushing it down my arms with a deliberateness that ached. I nearly growled at him.

"So impatient," he murmured, his breath coasting over my collarbone as he peppered kisses along my skin.

"Don't even start with me."

He laughed, the bastard, then continued his slow perusal. Once my arms were out of my jacket, he pitched it towards the dining room. It missed the chair, but neither of us really cared at the moment. With the lightest touch, he drew my arms back up to wrap around his neck. His eyes were on mine as his fingers closed around the bottom of my top. His eyebrows arched, and I nodded at his unspoken question. He dragged the shirt over my head with the same agonizing slowness he had used with the jacket. The cool air in the apartment swept over my skin once my shirt was gone, and my nipples pebbled in an instant. Vincent's eyes raked over the newly exposed skin, and there was a hunger in his gaze that I knew reflected in my own. My hands grasped at his jacket, but he caught my wrists before I could rid him of it.

"I wanted to take my time with you last night," he said, the darkness in his deep voice an entirely different beast than the one I was used to. "I blew that all to hell. So let me have this."

"Okay."

A blush crawled up my neck to settle in my cheeks, and Vincent's eyes glittered while he watched it. He was still moving with such restraint, his touches barely more than a tease as he brushed his fingers along the waistband of my pants. The anticipation was going to kill me if he didn't *touch* me. When he finally slid my jeans down my legs, I couldn't help the near whimper that escaped me. He knelt to yank the pants off completely, taking my underwear with them. And when he stayed there, my breath stalled in my throat.

That sense of power swept through me again. This was Vincent Monroe, one of the most lethal men in all of Valarian, on his knees.

For *me.*

That smug little smile of his danced across his face as he looked up at me. Because, goddamn it, he knew the exact brand of havoc he was wreaking on my heart. And he was relishing it. I forced myself to breathe again as he skated his hands up the back of my calves. When he reached my knees, he spread my legs apart until I was completely bared to him. My chest was heaving as he kissed up my inner thighs, getting closer and closer to where I wanted him.

"Juliette."

"Hmmm?"

His huffed chuckle caused a fresh wave of goosebumps to erupt. "Do you have a safe word?"

A startled laugh burst free. "Are you planning on me needing one?"

"Vanilla sex or the dirtiest kink, I believe you should always have one. And I'm sorry I didn't ask yesterday." The look on his face sobered me, and I forced my lust addled brain to get it together long enough to focus on what he was saying. "So, do you have one?"

"No."

"Then think of one." He squeezed my knees, an encouraging and comforting gesture. "It shouldn't be something you would normally say in the bedroom."

I rolled my eyes at him and used my foot to nudge his shoulder. "I know how it works, Vincent."

"Then pick one."

"Forest." Because as he stared up at me, those eyes of his were all I could think of.

His grin was slow as he nodded. He didn't waste another second before he was on me. He ran the flat of his tongue up the very center of me, and my blood turned molten. My head fell back to rest against the cabinet behind me, and my eyes slipped closed. His hum of approval reverberated down to my bones, and I had to grip the edge of the counter to keep from sliding off.

This man was going to be the death of me.

His mouth closed over my clit, and I lost all train of thought.

He slid two fingers into me, curling them in a dizzying rhythm. A low moan rasped out of my throat, and it snapped the tight leash Vincent had on himself. There were no more slow, teasing strokes. He was a man with a purpose, and he worked my body like he had it memorized. I tried to hold off, to prolong the pleasure he was giving me as long as I could, but I didn't last long. My release ruined me, and it took everything I had left to stifle the scream that wanted to break free. I settled for breathing his name as I floated back to reality.

He stood in a fluid movement, drawing me into his arms with a sinful edge to his smile. It felt indecent for my naked skin to brush against the leather of his jacket. But I couldn't bring myself to protest as he carried me through the apartment. My eyelids were fluttering as I rested my head against his shoulder. There was a low rumble in his chest, and it took me a moment to realize it was laughter. I raised my head and narrowed my eyes at him.

He didn't comment before he tossed me onto my bed. A startled squeal burst from my mouth as I bounced against the mattress. I hastened to get my wits about me so that I could keep an eye on him. I had seen many sides of Vincent up to this point, but the predatory gleam in his eyes as he watched me from the end of the bed was new. It was doing funny things to my heart, making it uncertain if it wanted to pound or skip a couple of beats. Our gazes held as he stripped. With each piece of clothing that fell to the floor, my mouth went dry. *Christ*, this man was beautiful. One of the great artists of the past could have carved the lines of his body. From the wide set of his shoulders to the tapered V that dipped below his waistband, Vincent was everything I could've ever imagined for myself.

All of that added to the fact that he seemed to *see* me more than anyone else ever had, and I was understanding why none of my past relationships had ever worked. This is what I had been waiting for. *He* was what I had been waiting for.

Or maybe I was lust drunk.

That was probably what it was.

"Juliette."

My gaze snapped to his at the sound of my name on his lips. His eyes smoldered into mine as he watched me through lowered lashes. The movement made his scar more prominent, and damn if that didn't make my thighs clench.

There was something wrong with me.

"Yes?" I asked, realizing he was still waiting for an answer.

"Stay with me," he murmured, moving onto the bed. He invaded my space, making sure he had my full attention before he continued. "I'm not finished with you just yet."

He was going to send me into cardiac arrest if he didn't watch it. His touch was gentle, yet still firm, as he took my face in his hands. His mouth covered mine and I let out a low moan. He took advantage of it and swept his tongue into my mouth, devouring me. I gripped his shoulders, pulling myself even farther into him.

My hands skimmed up his arms, and I traced the hard planes of his chest. I could feel the rapid beat of his heart pulsing against my palm, and it made me smile into the kiss. A guttural sound dragged out of him as I let my hands slip lower.

One moment, I almost had him in my hands. And in the next, Vincent had me flat on my stomach. The movement stole my breath *again,* and I let out a sound of protest.

Vincent's hand cracked against my ass, and my whole body went still.

Shit.

In the next breath, he was smoothing his hand over the assault, taking away the sting of it. My hips wiggled as I tried to break from his hold. Apparently, my weak attempt was amusing to him, if the laugh that fell from his lips was any indication.

"What did I say?" he asked, his voice low.

Double shit.

"I can't remember."

"You little brat," he muttered, spanking the other cheek hard enough that I was certain I had matching handprints. His calloused hands gripped my hips, jerking them up until I was on my knees with my face still down on the pillows. I tried to sit up, but a hand on the back of my neck kept me down. Heat banked in my core, and I cursed. Another of those low laughs had me clenching around nothing, and I was going to lose my mind if he didn't quit teasing me.

"*Vincent,*" I hissed.

The broad head of him nudged at my entrance, and I went still again. Waiting. Vincent took the opportunity to trail his hand down my spine, the gentle touch raising goosebumps in its wake. I glanced back at him over my shoulder, and our eyes held. There was barely a band of green left around the black of his pupils, and my heartbeat went unsteady at the sight. Vincent gathered both of my wrists in one of his hands and pressed them against the small of my back, rendering me completely helpless.

"Your safe word?" he asked, eyes dropping to where we were almost joined.

"Forest."

"Good girl."

Fuck. Me.

And so he did. Over and over again.

Twenty-Six

HIDEAWAY

"Ow."

"Quit your whining."

Peeking out from beneath the covers, I glared at Vincent, where he sat propped against the headboard. He had a sated smile on his face and mirth dancing in his eyes. The late morning sun had gilded my entire bedroom in shades of gold, but I still hadn't been able to make myself move. Waking up wrapped in Vincent's arms for the second day in a row was a surreal experience, but definitely one I could get used to. However, his morning-person attitude needed to take a back seat. Pronto.

"You weren't bent into twenty-seven different positions last night."

"It was only twenty-six, princess."

I chucked a pillow at his head, and he caught it with a laugh.

"Don't you have a job to do?"

"Lucas and Brandon have it covered for today."

"And what are *your* plans?"

"I don't have any." His eyes skimmed along the skin that he could see, which was only the tops of my shoulders. "Did you have anything in mind?"

I burrowed farther into the comforter just to spite him, and from the smirk on his face, he knew what I was doing.

"Tonight is my night to help Dante with inventory, but other than that, I'm free."

"Then I have something I want to show you."

That piqued my interest. "Oh?"

"Mhmm." I squeaked as he grabbed my wrist and pulled me into his arms, fully entangling us once again. "But first, there is something I need to take care of."

As he slid beneath the covers, I knew we wouldn't be leaving the bedroom anytime soon.

Just over an hour later, we found ourselves in the kitchen. We were both freshly showered, and I braided my hair back away from my face. Dexter sat next to Vincent in the kitchen, probably hoping he would slip him another slice of bacon when I wasn't looking. A smile graced my lips as I watched them. It was always nice to see Dexter warm up to someone new, and recently there had been no shortage of fresh faces.

"Is it bad that it shocks me how domestic you are sometimes?" I asked, my voice breaking the peaceful silence that had blanketed the apartment.

"Have you been stereotyping me?"

My eyes rolled as I slipped into one of the chairs at the dining room table. "Don't act like you haven't fit most of them."

"That's not the point."

He made his way over to me with a cup of coffee in his hand. I peaked at it when he set it in front of me, and he winked as he walked back to the stove. The heat from the mug seeped into my hands as I wrapped them around it. When I took a sip, it surprised me to find that it was exactly how I always drank it. My eyes narrowed on Vincent as he came back over and set a plate in front of me. He made bacon again and had cooked it to perfection just like the day before. He had also cut up the strawberries in the fridge and placed them on top of a fluffy pancake.

"You really didn't have to do all this," I said, eyeing him as he took his place across from me.

His broad shoulders raised in a shrug. "I wanted to. Does everything look okay?"

"It's perfect." I ran my index finger around the edge of my mug. "How'd you know how I drink my coffee?"

"I'd love to say that I've paid enough attention to just know, but I've rarely been around you early enough to see you drink coffee. I text Lucas."

A soft laugh escaped me, and I shook my head at him. "I should've known."

"He spends an awful lot of time here," he mused.

"You're the one that took him off watching over me."

"So, one would think he would spend his time doing other things."

"Vincent," I teased, trying my damnedest not to grin at him. "Are you jealous?"

"Only of the fact that Lucas seems to pay more attention to you than his actual job. But not at him being here. Not at him spending time with you. I like the men feeling comfortable around you. That they seem to see you as one of their own."

That struck a chord with me. I had never thought of it like that. Had never considered that the boys spent so much time here because, somehow, I had become a place of familiarity to them. My heart warmed at the thought, and I ducked my head to hide my smile.

"They're not so bad."

"I'll be sure to tell Lucas and Brandon you were speaking so highly of them."

"Don't you dare. They'll never shut up about it."

He chuckled, and the sound was lighter than I had ever heard it. We fell into a companionable silence as we ate. When I was pretty sure he wasn't paying attention, I studied him from underneath my lashes. There was something about seeing him like this, with his defenses down, that made something inside me settle. These stolen moments we were getting more and more often felt as natural as breathing, and that scared me just as much as it excited me. I knew it was a bad idea to always be waiting for the other shoe to drop, but I had lost the two most important people in my life in some of the worst ways. It was a hard habit to break.

But I would try. For this. For him.

If Vincent could put his feelings for me before his fear of losing someone else because of his world, then I could do the same. I owed him that much. I owed *myself* that much.

"You're thinking awfully hard over there, princess."

I threw my last piece of bacon at him. To my surprise, he caught it in his mouth. Because of course he did.

"What did you want to show me?"

"Are you finished eating?" he asked. I nodded. He collected our plates and placed them in the sink before turning back to me. "It's a bit of a drive. You up for it?"

"You haven't finally decided to kill me, have you?"

"Juliette." And that snap of playful warning in his voice had my blood running hot all over again.

"I know, I know," I muttered, standing from the table before making my way to the bedroom. "But yes, I'm in. Just let me change and take Dexter out."

I swapped my over-sized t-shirt for a pair of dark jeans and a thick sweater. As I was grabbing a pair of socks out of my dresser, I heard the front door open, followed by the jingling of Dexter's tags. A smile overtook my face as I finished getting dressed. And sure enough, when I emerged into the living room a few minutes later, Vincent and Dexter were just reentering the apartment. Vincent gave me a cool look before glancing back at the security system. That I had forgotten to engage when we got in the night before.

My eyes rolled. "*You* are the one that attacked me the minute we got it," I reminded him.

"Are you ready?" he asked, unclipping Dexter from his lead before hanging it on the back of the door.

"As I'll ever be."

"Don't sound so excited."

A smirk twitched at the edge of my lips. But I decided not to comment as we left the apartment. Vincent watched me with an eye like a hawk as I engaged the security system behind us. When I turned to head for the front doors, he snagged my hand in his. The action startled me, and I whipped my head around to look at him. He arched a brow at me, raising our entwined hands to kiss the back of mine. I had no choice but to follow him in a stupor as he made his way to the SUV.

I'm not sure why I was stunned speechless by the simple gesture of holding his hand, but it had completely short-circuited my brain. I didn't make a sound as he helped me into the car. There was a knowing glint in his green eyes as he tucked a loose strand of hair behind my ear, and my eyes narrowed in response. My ire only amused him, if the laugh that tumbled from his full lips was anything to go by. When he got settled in the driver's seat, he flipped the radio on. At the familiar sound of the piano notes he typically had playing, a knot in my shoulders let loose. I slumped into the seat, letting my eyes fall closed as Vincent maneuvered the car out onto the road. I didn't have any idea where he was planning on taking me, but I was excited.

It had been longer than I cared to admit since I had left the city. With everything I had ever really needed being within walking distance, I had never bothered saving for a car. Both of my parents were only children, so there wasn't any family to go visit. The idea of travel had always just seemed expensive, so I had never let myself entertain the idea of it. In fact, I was pretty sure the last time I had left Valarian was a vacation my parents had taken us on when I was seven. It was one of the many times they had gotten along over the years for my sake.

I had almost convinced myself on that trip that they would get back together, but it hadn't happened. They would always have love for each other, but they butted heads too much to have ever had anything stable between them. I could see that, admit that, now.

"You're quiet again," Vincent said sometime later. His voice snapped me out of the recesses of my mind, almost enough to give me whiplash, as I refocused on the present. My eyes focused on the trees slipping by outside, and I realized how far outside of the city we were.

"I was just thinking," I said. He nodded, his gaze flicking to me for the briefest second. "It's been a long time since I've been outside Valarian. Any chance you'll give me a hint of where we're going?"

"It's a surprise."

"Vincent," I whined, drawing his name out in the most annoying way I could. He just laughed, shaking his head a little as he shifted so he could hold the steering wheel with his left hand. His right slipped across the seat and settled just above my knee. He gave me a quick squeeze, and then his hand moved just a little higher. I had to focus to keep my breathing even as the heat of his touch seeped out from underneath his hand. For once, I kept my breath from catching. My heart, on the other hand, had a mind of its own as it took off at a full gallop in my chest.

"Something tells me you'll love it," he said, giving my leg another reassuring squeeze.

I huffed, but settled back into the seat. Vincent didn't remove his hand. He just focused on the road, and his thumb moved in lazy strokes, almost as if he wasn't aware of the idle movement. But this was Vincent, and this man did nothing without intention. And from the twinkle in his eye, I knew he had something up his sleeve.

The piano notes shifted into a song I had never heard before, and I closed my eyes in order to absorb it. The piece was haunting, as most of what I had heard whenever we were in the car was. But there was something about this piece, something about the way the notes flowed, that pulled at my heart.

"I've always been curious who this artist is," I murmured, letting my head fall back against the headrest.

"It's a recording of one of Alana's recitals."

And just like that, I was fighting back tears.

"When was this?"

"Back in school. She never continued it after. She just threw herself into her work. But every once in a while, we'd find time for her to play for us. There's a studio in the heart of downtown that her instructor owns, and he'd let her use one of the practice rooms whenever he didn't have class. I think he hoped she would come back to it at some point."

"She was incredible."

The softest of smiles graced his lips and his eyes shone. "She was."

Before I knew it, the SUV was making its way up a steep incline. Perking up, I all but pressed my nose against the window to see where we were. All I could see around us were towering trees, nearly blocking out the sunlight that had been blaring the whole way here. A wry smile crossed my lips as I thought, for the umpteenth time, how easy it would be to hide a body up here.

We pulled off the road onto a dirt path that the SUV barely fit on. We drove for about another five minutes before there was a break in the trees. There was a house sitting in the clearing's heart. It was a modest size, and it looked well taken care of. The white siding was clean and the bright flowers in the window boxes looked like they were thriving. Vincent killed the engine when we pulled to the end of the hard-packed dirt. There was a softness in his eyes as he stared at the house ahead of us. A porch swing was moving in the soft breeze, but other than that, there was no sign of life in the clearing.

"Vincent?"

"This was where we grew up," he told me. "Well, before we lost our parents. This was our family home. I bought it after I lost Alana. I needed something to tie back to everyone, so when I saw it was on the market, I snatched it."

My lips tilted up, and I took his hand in mine. Our fingers entwined without a second thought, and I couldn't ignore the feeling of rightness that fell over me. We gazed out at the house, and I wondered how many others knew the place existed. With Alana's playing wrapping around us, I leaned back against the seat. There was a steadiness in me. I hadn't realized how much I had missed that feeling. I hadn't felt this at peace since my mom died, and I still couldn't believe that it stemmed from the man sitting beside me.

"Does anyone else know about it?" I asked.

"A very select handful. And the only reason they do is so that if anything ever happens to me, they can make sure it's taken care of." His eyes drifted to me. "And now you."

"Thank you for bringing me here."

"I had an ulterior motive." My eyebrows lifted. "You've said it yourself. I've hidden nothing from you. And I won't. Anything you want to know about the ins and the outs of the gang, you ask. If you're in this with me, I'm not withholding information. So, if anything ever goes sideways, you come here, got it?" That darkness that always spoke to me wrapped through his words. "None of my enemies know this place exists. All the paperwork is under a fake name, so the cops wouldn't even know to look for me here."

"A safe house?" He nodded, one small dip of his chin. "Thank you."

"I want you safe, always."

The stupidest grin broke across my face, and I leaned across the armrest to kiss him. He smiled against my mouth, and when I pulled back, he caught my chin between his thumb and forefinger. The hold was gentle; I could pull away if I wanted to. But with the way his eyes searched mine, grazed over my features as if he were trying to memorize them, I had no desire to. His thumb brushed my bottom lip before he dropped a kiss on the tip of my nose and withdrew from me. He threw open his door and got out of the car.

Following suit, I hopped out and met him at the front of the hood. He slipped his warm, calloused hand into mine, and I could feel the strength in his grip as he tugged me along behind him. The scent of wild honeysuckle danced around me on the wind, followed by the heady scent of the pine trees that towered over us. As we mounted the steps up to the porch, the planks groaned with familiarity under Vincent's hulking figure. When we made it to the front door, I noticed it didn't just have a lock that you would fit a key into. It was code operated. Vincent punched it in and then glanced at me.

"What?" I asked, noting the calculating look in his eyes.

"I'm going to change the code," he murmured. He punched a series of buttons, and the panel flashed green. "That way, you and I will be the only ones who know it for now. 5-8-5-3-7," he said as he input it.

"Any significance to that?"

There was a coy smile on his lips, but he vanished inside the house without answering me. My eyes narrowed on the spot he had previously occupied. Fine then.

When I entered the house, I let my eyes wander. The inside was cozy. The tones of decorations were like what was in Vincent's apartment, but that was where the similarities ended. Where Vincent's loft was sweeping and immaculate, this place was overflowing with warmth. The living room on my left featured a collection of mismatched chairs and couches, all of which looked as though they had been well-loved. The entire atmosphere seemed suited to nights curled up in front of the fireplace on the far wall.

"How often do you come up here?"

"At least once a month. The guys and I will come up here sometimes when we need a breather or to plan. Anything that we need to hide comes here as well. There's a huge barn buried back in the trees, and we've used it for storage ever since I got access to the place."

"And the furniture?" Because there was no way this was stuff that he had bought new. I felt like I had walked into the home he remembered. The one where he must have grown up. But if the property had changed hands before he got it again, there was no way that it was that old.

"Hand-me-downs. Whenever the gang or I get something new, we transfer the old here if it's needed."

No wonder it felt like a home.

Vincent towed me along with him as he showed me the three bedrooms, letting me know which one had been who's. A Jack and Jill bathroom split the two rooms that he and Alana had occupied, and I laughed as he told me how often they had bickered over who got first dibs. It was nice to see him relive the memories of the good times. There was a sparkle in his eyes that I rarely saw when we were in the city. The same sort of peace seemed to have seeped into him that had me.

Before I knew it, we were making our way back out onto the porch. It was encroaching on the time when I would have to get ready to meet Dante at the bar. But as I went to step down, Vincent towed me over to the porch swing. The faintest smile crossed my mouth as he pulled me down with him, arranging my legs across his lap so that he was all but cradling me in his arms. He was so warm, and with the weather turning colder, I snuggled into him. The chains creaked in a smooth rhythm, and a soft sigh slipped from me. He tucked my head under his chin as he used his legs to move us.

"Thank you again for bringing me here," I murmured, keeping my voice low to keep from disturbing the quiet that blanketed the landscape.

"You're the only person outside the gang I've ever trusted enough to show it to."

My breath hitched. I craned my neck back a bit to meet his eyes. Out here, with the foliage surrounding us, I realized how right I had been in comparing his eyes to a forest. In the dimming light of dusk, they were damn near the same color as the pine trees. And with the light that was shimmering within them, even if I was being a romantic sap, I knew he was telling me the truth. But I couldn't help but prod.

"There's never been…" I trailed off, catching my bottom lip between my teeth.

His smile just widened as he used his thumb to pry my lip free. "I'm not a saint, you know that. There have been women in and out of my life. Some mattered more than others. But, no one like this." His eyes flicked down to my lips, and he brought his forehead to rest against mine. "No one like *you*, princess."

And for the first time, it hit me that the damn pet name didn't sound so condescending in my ears. I realized it hadn't for quite some time. At some point, it started sounding softer. Started being something that made me smile instead of making me want to throttle him.

With a warmth in my veins and a smile on my face, I straddled him. There was a wicked edge to the grin he gave me back before he slanted his lips over mine.

As all our clothes found a new home beneath the swing, I thanked the gods above that the house was so secluded.

Twenty-Seven

OH, VINCENT

"I've got some stuff I have to take care of with one of our deals," Vincent told me as he pulled up behind Tuxedo. "What time do you think you'll be finished?"

"It typically takes a while." I pursed my lips as I thought. "I can just have Dante take me home after." Vincent gave me a pointed look; one I knew meant he didn't believe me. I rolled my eyes. "I promise."

"You had better," he muttered, snagging the front of my t-shirt. It was one I had thrown on in a rush barely twenty minutes ago when we had returned to my apartment to let Dexter out. He yanked me towards him, and laughter spilled from my mouth as he kissed me.

"Yes, sir."

There was a deep rumble in his chest before he practically purred, "Watch it, princess."

Another giggle escaped me, and I pecked his cheek before hopping out of the SUV. Once the back door to the club fell shut behind me, I heard the engine rumble away. The smile was still on my face when I popped my head into Dante's office. He was bent over a spread of files, his face screwed up in concentration. He grumbled under his breath before running a hand over his shaved head. Curious, I knocked on the doorframe.

"C'mon in, Jules," he said without looking up, beckoning me forward.

I sank into the folding chair across the desk from him. "What's up?"

"I'm pretty sure this party next weekend is going to give me an aneurysm."

"Are they being demanding?"

"No." Dante huffed, his chocolate eyes meeting mine. "It's the guest list."

"Anything I can help with?"

"Unless you have enough pull to make them take this shit somewhere else, no."

"What's wrong with it?"

He turned the page in my direction, pointing out a few of the names. "These are some major players in the crime world. While I know this shit goes on here all the time, it stresses me the fuck out. I know all of them. When I opened this bar, I established it as neutral ground, and they respect that. But still."

"All the time?" He nodded. "Why have you never told me any of this before?" I asked. Dante had confided in me about his breakout from the gang *years* ago. Why hadn't he ever shared anything more?

"I keep the darker side of this business away from *all* of you. That way, if anything ever went down, you all could claim ignorance." He gave me an assessing look, his eyes scouring my features in a way that made me squirm. Dante may not be old enough to be my father, but damn if he didn't make me feel like a delinquent child sometimes. "Something tells me that no matter how much I try to protect you, you're not going to be able to claim that for much longer."

My cheeks heated. "What do you mean?"

"Don't play dumb, Jules," he said, a hint of amusement dancing across his face. "You have ignored every single warning I've given you regarding Monroe. And I'm not blind. I've known Vincent for a long time, maybe only in passing, but his reputation precedes him in this world. He's never had a woman at his side. Not until you."

"I'm not–"

"Oh, yes, you are."

It was my turn to huff. "Care to elaborate?"

Dante looked like he was mulling something over before he leaned back in his chair. He tapped the pen in his hand against the desk, causing the ballpoint to click in and out a few times. "I'm guessing you know about Alana?"

The name caused me to sit straighter in my chair. "Yes."

He nodded as if he had expected as much. "She was with him every step of his ascension. From the moment he killed Andras Graham until the day she died, Alana was in the gang's background. But she still helped Vincent in any way she could while staying on the legitimate side of the business. Until she was murdered."

My brain short-circuited.

Oh, Vincent.

"What?"

"You didn't know?"

My nose burned as tears pricked the back of my eyes. "He's only told me she died. I didn't know–" A sob caught in my throat. No wonder he had such a deep understanding of how I felt about losing my dad.

"I'm sorry, Jules," he said, leaning across the desk to take my hand. "I didn't realize you didn't know the entire story. I wouldn't have said anything."

"How?" I pressed, trying to take slow, steady breaths.

"I don't know the finer details. They've kept it under wraps. It's, honestly, the only flaw in Vincent's reputation. Everyone knew she was his weakness, and someone who was still loyal to Graham exploited it. Then that coward vanished. The general consensus is that Vincent put whoever it was in the ground."

"What does that have to do with me?"

"In the past four years, there hasn't been a single whisper of anyone outside of that gang meaning anything to him." His eyes implored me to put the puzzle pieces together.

"Until me," I breathed, the realization crashing into me with the force of a Mack truck.

Making sure one of the men was always with me.

Checking his surroundings before he kissed me.

"Being mine is going to put a target on your back."

"I want you safe, always."

Every precaution he had taken with me flickered through my mind on a ticker tape. My heart constricted. It had always been there, from the very beginning. Maybe it had started differently, but he knew that any association with the gang could've put me in danger. Even before there were feelings involved. It had *never* been about me going to the police. A beautifully crafted ruse to make sure I was safe. To make sure I wasn't collateral damage in a world I had wanted nothing to do with.

And now?

Now I was the very thing that could bring Vincent Monroe to heel. And if word got out, if it hadn't already, what would happen to him? To all of them?

To me?

"Breathe, Jules," Dante coaxed, squeezing the hand that he was still clasping.

The breath that *whooshed* out of me was audible. My hand slipped from Dante's as I slumped in my seat, letting my head fall back. As I gazed at the ceiling, I tried to regulate my breathing. I was going to be fine. We were all going to be fine. Vincent and the gang would never let anything happen to me.

And I wouldn't let anything happen to *any* of them if I could help it.

Something settled in my chest, my spine turning to steel as I raised myself back up. No matter what happened, Vincent and I would face it. There was a reason he hadn't told me about Alana being killed, and even if it was nothing more than not wanting to revisit old wounds just yet, I could respect that. But I would not be the next person someone thought they could use against him.

Looked like I *was* going to be doubling up on my training with Jack, because I was not about to be a liability.

Clearing my throat, I met Dante's warm eyes across his desk. There was something new in his gaze as he stared at me. It was like, for the first time, he was seeing me as something other than the girl he had taken under his wing all those years ago. As someone he didn't have to protect anymore. And that pride on his face; it was worth every fight we had regarding Vincent.

"Well, this inventory won't sort itself," I said, standing and making my way out of his office.

His laughter was of the startled sort, bursting out of him in a quick staccato as he tried to choke it back. My lips twitched, and I glanced over my shoulder at him. He flashed his teeth at me in a blinding grin. When he came up next to me, he placed his hand on my shoulder and squeezed. It was a comforting gesture, no doubt meant to let me know that he still had my back.

And then he shoved me into the doorframe before heading into the cooler.

Prick.

***

"Are you sure you don't want us going with you?" Lucas asked as Vincent tucked a gun into the back of his waistband.

"I need you to figure out why these shipments are still getting fucked up. Angelica hasn't been able to find anything incriminating Kline, so we're proceeding as planned."

"Are you sure she's not missing anything?" Brandon asked as they all left Vincent's office.

"Doubting me, Brandon?" Angelica purred as she appeared at his side.

Brandon jumped, his eyes narrowing on the redhead. Her sapphire eyes sparkled as she gave him a sweet smile. He pointed at her, and she snapped her teeth at his extended finger. Vincent smothered his laughter as he watched them.

"Stop sneaking up on people like that," Brandon hissed.

"It's quite literally my job."

Lucas wasn't as successful at holding back his laughter. He clapped his cousin on the back and steered him away from Angelica before things could get ugly. The blonde glanced back at Vincent as they headed for the door. "Call me if you need us."

"Make sure Arkin is with you," was all Vincent said as they vanished.

"So..." Angelica started, sidling up to him. "Word around the warehouse is you're settling down."

Vincent looked at her out of the corner of his eye. He didn't know if things would ever be the same between them, but he needed to bridge the abyss that had grown over the years. If for no other reason than because he missed her.

"I wouldn't go that far," he told her, jerking his chin in an order to follow him. She fell into step with him as they headed out to the SUV. He yanked his door open and turned to her before he got in. "Juliette is everything to me, but she doesn't want to have a hand in the darker side of what we do. I don't know how long she'll want to be with me, but this gang will still protect her as if she was one of their own, do you hear me? I will not lose anyone else."

He hated himself for the pain that pulled at the corners of her eyes. It had been a low blow, but he needed her to know how serious he was. She cleared her throat before crossing her arms. In the span of a heartbeat, she rearranged her features into a mask he was familiar with. One he wore himself more than he liked to admit.

"You know I'll always have your back," she said. "Consider it done."

He knew he could count on her. He always had.

He tapped the top of the car before meeting her gaze again. Angelica gave him a rueful grin, accompanied by a mocking salute. Then her hand reached out to settle on his forearm, and she gave one quick squeeze before she walked back into the warehouse.

The drive to the meeting point wasn't a long one, but it grated on Vincent's nerves all the same. He knew Juliette was safe with Dante. Just as safe as she would be under the watchful eye of the gang, but it still made him uneasy to have all of them so far from her. But it was a necessary evil, just for tonight.

He knew his unease had just as much to do with the shipment issues as being away from her. Which was half of why he had done this alone. It was a one-on-one meet, and Vincent wanted to vet the potential recruit himself.

The nondescript house on the outermost edges of the city was dark when he pulled up. It was exactly the type of place he would have expected the kid to pick. For someone who wanted to join a gang, the kid had seemed skittish to Vincent. But he would always hear someone out if this was the life they chose for themselves, because the other options in Valarian were worse.

So much worse.

Vincent and his gang were not saints by any means, but they had rules. Some of the other gangs in the city were involved in everything from drugs to human trafficking. It was something Vincent couldn't stand, and he tried to shut down at any opportunity. It was that fight that had gotten his parents killed when they tried to shut down the ring they discovered. The reason he had destroyed Andras Graham and reworked everything the gang stood for.

He killed the engine and checked the time. It wouldn't take long to see if the kid was up to gang life. He'd be able to get back to Juliette tonight, he was sure of it.

"It's about damn time you just let me drive you," Dante grumbled as he pulled up outside of my apartment.

"Only because I promised I would."

Dante shot me a dirty look. "So, *he* asks you to not walk, and you listen. But me?" He huffed, an indignant set to his mouth.

"If you stop pouting, I'll start listening to you both."

"See that you do." He leaned over and ruffled my hair, earning a glare that I was hoping was at least half as intimidating as I wanted it to be. Muttering under my breath about how insufferable he was, I hiked my bag onto my shoulder. We said our goodbyes, and once I had cleared the door to the lobby, he pulled away with a wave.

My mind kept running over everything that had happened today as I walked down the hall. The farther I got, the more I noticed that something had replaced the crisp, cheap smell of the room deodorizer used in the halls. Something cloying. The scent of copper was so potent it caused my nose to scrunch. When I finally looked up from rummaging around in my purse for my keys, I dropped the entire thing to the floor.

"Vincent," I breathed, falling to my knees beside him. "Oh, Vincent."

He grunted before cracking open his eyes. And from the pinched look on his face, it was no small feat. When our gazes collided, he looked so shocked it was almost comical.

"What're you doing here?" he ground out, teeth clenched like he could keep the pain at bay by sheer force of will.

"What am I..." I trailed off, confused. "What are *you* doing here?" He shook his head and tried to sit straighter against the door. There was a slight snuffling sound, and a quiet whine slipped out from the apartment.

Dexter. He must have known Vincent was out here.

My eyes took in Vincent's split and bloodied lip, the cut across his cheek, and the bruises decorating his face faster than I thought possible. I was cataloging every injury, trying to figure out where the worst of it was. And then the smell of copper registered again, and I looked down.

There was so much blood.

It was welling out of a spot on his abdomen. Biting my lip, I moved my hands to the hem of his shirt. He had my wrists in a vice-like grip before my fingertips so much as grazed him.

"Don't," he ordered, voice like frostbite.

"What happened?" I demanded, snapping my gaze to his. It had been a long time since he had taken that tone with me, and I wasn't about to let it return.

"Meeting went bad. Fucker stabbed me."

"We have to get you to—"

"No hospitals," he cut me off, already guessing my thought process. "Not with who I am. They'll call the cops the second I walk through the door."

Cursing profusely under my breath, I threw everything but my keys back into my bag. My hands were shaking so badly it took me a few tries to fit the key in the lock, but once I did, I swung the door inward. Dexter tried to rush into the hallway the moment he was able, but I blocked him. He whimpered again before pacing directly in front of me. I disengaged the security system in record time and then threw my purse into the center of the room. Bracing myself, I bent down and maneuvered one of Vincent's arms around my shoulders.

"You can't carry me, princess."

"No, but I can't just leave you out here to rot. So, help me. I need to get you inside." My tone brooked no room for argument. He grunted his response and then together we heaved him off the ground. Kicking the door shut behind me, I helped Vincent to the couch before easing him onto it. My muscles screamed at me to just drop him, but thanks to the hours at the gym, I had the discipline to keep hold of him so I wouldn't hurt him anymore than he already was.

Ignoring his protests, I dragged my coffee table to the couch so that I could sit closer to him. Dexter took up a vigil from the opposite end. A million thoughts came at me quicker than I could stop them as I reached for the hem of Vincent's shirt again. Taking a deep breath, I took the fabric between my fingers and lifted it away from his skin. The low ripping sound echoed dully around the room, and Vincent let out a guttural snarl. The wound pooled anew as I pushed his shirt up to the top of his rib cage. When I removed the fabric, it took the weak scab that had formed with it.

There was *so much* blood.

It pumped down his stomach from the ragged hole, the damage significantly worse than I had expected. "Lift your arms," I said as I stood.

"What?"

"Now," I snapped.

With as much of a glower as he could muster in his current state, he did as I said. I whipped the ruined shirt over his head and pressed it into a ball against the wound. Vincent grunted but placed his hands over mine in the next instant, applying pressure.

"What's going on in that head of yours?"

"Hold that," I ordered, standing again. If he wouldn't see a doctor, I was going to have to do something. He was losing blood fast, and I didn't know how long he would make it if we didn't get that bleeding under control.

"Where're you going?" he called after me.

"Figuring out what to do," I replied, snatching my phone from my bag on the way to the kitchen. With it pressed between my cheek and shoulder, I began rifling through my junk drawer to see if I had *anything* that could be of help.

"Well, hello, sugar," a familiar voice echoed down the phone.

"I need to talk to Brandon."

Lucas noticed the snap in my voice in an instant, and I could almost see him sitting up straighter. "What happened?"

"It's Vincent. Give the phone to Brandon. Now."

Once upon a time, Brandon had told me he took care of most injuries in the gang. If anyone could fix this, it would be him.

"Jules?" his voice asked less than a full second later.

"Vincent was stabbed," I said, pausing my searching to focus on the conversation. "It won't stop bleeding, and I don't know what to do."

"Fuck," he swore. "When he didn't meet us, we figured he was with you, but—"

"Brandon, focus." My hands and voice were shaking. "Please."

"Right. Where was he stabbed?"

"Stomach."

A litany of curses sounded down the line. "How much blood has he lost?"

Glancing back out to the living room, I had to restrain the cry that wanted to break past my teeth. Vincent was pale, leaning towards gray. And I could see the sheen of sweat encasing his body from here. The once-white shirt he had pressed against his gut was almost fully stained red.

"Hard to tell. I don't know how long he was here. But there's a lot of blood in the hall and it doesn't seem to want to stop even though we have pressure on it."

"We're too far," Brandon said, his voice thin. "We're over an hour away covering some shit that went down with one of the shipments."

"He doesn't have an hour," I spat, feeling my own blood freeze in my veins. I *couldn't* lose him too. "Brandon, what can I do?"

"How strong is your stomach?" he asked, a note of strained hope flaring in his tone.

"Why?"

"You're going to have to cauterize it."

Twenty-Eight

WHAT HAVE I DONE?

"I'm sorry, what?" I sputtered.

"If it's not clotting, even with you all putting pressure on it, then it has to be sealed."

There was a beat of silence as I let that sink in. And then I steeled my spine and said, "Walk me through it."

With Brandon's voice in my ear, I grabbed a small knife, a lighter, and my bottle of whiskey and headed back to Vincent. He eyed me when I sat everything on the table. His face pinched, and the muscle in his jaw feathered at a rapid beat. I still had the phone tucked between my shoulder and my cheek, but I dropped it onto the coffee table next to me and hit the speaker button. Brandon's voice echoed through the silent room just a moment later.

"You got everything?"

"Yes."

Vincent met my gaze. He nodded, barely more than a dip of his chin, and I knew he had already figured out what I was doing. Without a word, I passed him the whiskey. He lifted it to his lips, and I tried to ignore the trembling in his hands. He took a few long pulls before he handed it back to me. With a bracing breath, he removed the shirt.

Despite our efforts to stop the blood, it flowed seamlessly, as if we had never staunched it in the first place. Both of us let out a barely audible curse as I splashed a little whiskey over his stomach. Vincent winced as I flicked the lighter and held the flame to the blade. Brandon's voice on the phone became a buzzing background noise. All I could focus on was the metal in my hand. Slowly, so slowly, the knife changed colors. The color was as bright as fresh magma, and I couldn't help but look back up at Vincent. Even with everything going on, he still let a small grin break through.

"Do you trust me?" I asked, flicking the lighter off.

He nodded. "More than anyone."

"Hey!" two voices chorused from the phone.

Laughter bubbled in my throat, but I choked it down. Vincent had accomplished his goal of keeping me from freaking out. Fast as an adder, I pressed the blade into the hole in his abdomen. He hissed, the sound mixing with the sizzling coming from his skin. Dexter whined again, beginning to pace behind me. Forcing down the urge to vomit, I repeated the process a handful of times until the wound had sealed. It was over quicker than I had expected. The rancid smell of burnt flesh tickled my nose, and I nearly gagged again.

"Brandon, what now?" I called, heading into the kitchen again to grab paper towels. I doused them in warm water before heading back to Vincent. His skin had fully turned to that sickly pallor, but there was a warm smile on his face when his eyes settled on me. I sat back down on the coffee table, beginning mopping up the blood.

"Just cover it with some bandages. I'll look at it when we get back. I might need to reopen it to stitch it properly, but that should keep him from dying on us before we get there."

"I'm not going to die," Vincent grumbled, his head tilted back against the couch.

"You damn well might have," I told him, keeping my touch gentle as I got up as much of the blood as I could.

Brandon assured me they'd all meet us here as soon as they could. In the meantime, I was to make sure Vincent didn't aggravate his wound. I clicked the 'end call' button and slid my phone to the other side of the table. Once I realized the worst of it was over, the full force of what happened hit me. The adrenaline leeched from my veins, and it left a biting chill in its wake. My teeth started chattering, and I had to fight back a sob.

"Hey," Vincent murmured, a low groan slipping free as he reached for me.

"Don't move," I scolded, jolting forward to ease him back against the couch again. He snagged my waist, yanking me down beside him. His eyes were closed, and if it weren't for the sweat shining on his skin, he would be the picture of ease.

As if he could feel the worry radiating off me, he cracked one eye open. "I've survived worse," he said, somehow curling me even further into him.

"Don't tell me that," I grumbled. Pitching the bloodied paper towel I was still holding onto the coffee table, I allowed my head to settle against his shoulder. Vincent used his foot to push the table back where it belonged, and then patted the cushion I wasn't occupying. Dexter was up in an instant. Gently, the big dog laid his head on Vincent's lap. My heart was still beating out an uneven stutter-step in my chest, but I could breathe easier. The scent of blood was strong in the air, but it was almost drowned out being this close to him. I could just make out the hint of sandalwood and spice from his cologne clinging to his skin, and my pulse calmed.

For a while, we just let the silence stretch between us. I didn't even want to think about how close I had come to losing him tonight. The hardest pill I was trying to choke down was that this would not be the last time. Situations like tonight came with the territory, and I was going to have to get used to it.

"Why were you alone tonight?" I finally asked some time later, reaching between us to entwine my fingers with his.

His hand dwarfed mine, but there was more strength in his grip than I expected when he squeezed my hand. "I sent the others to deal with the shipment since I was just meeting a recruit. I didn't even consider it being a trap."

"Do you know why they did it?"

"No," he said, his broad shoulders lifting in a shrug. "Could've been for any number of reasons. Could've been a mad grab for power or someone with a score to settle. Maybe a mixture of both. Or it could've been someone that's still loyal to Graham."

"People are still loyal to him, even though he's dead?" The disbelief coloring my tone caused him to chuckle.

"That man ran the underground and the guns in this city for *years*. Some people will never let that go. There will always be people that want revenge. That would love to see me knocked down a peg or five." His eyes clouded, reminding me of the darkness that had encased him not so long ago, but that felt ages away.

A beat of silence passed. My teeth snagged my bottom lip. Like a magnet, Vincent's eyes tracked the movement.

"What're you thinking?"

"I don't want to be in the dark anymore," I murmured. I don't know which one of us was more shocked by my words. But now that I had said them, I surprised myself by not wanting to retract the statement. "If I'm in this with you, it's to the death. I refuse to lose anyone else that I love."

Vincent jolted, and Dexter huffed before getting down. The gang leader's head whipped in my direction so fast that he winced. I just blinked at him.

His gaze turned hot, branding me with its intensity. And then what I had said hit me.

Oh, no. No. Shit.

"I mean—"

Something akin to a growl rumbled in his chest, making my toes curl. With surprising speed, he had me straddling him with his fingers already tangled in my hair. The fierceness with which he kissed me seared me straight down to my bones, and I couldn't contain the moan that slipped into his mouth. I rocked myself against him, feeling the hard length of him press against me.

Vincent let out a hiss, and it was as if someone dumped ice down my spine.

Double shit.

"Where do you think you're going?" he bit out, catching my wrist as I went to scramble off his lap.

"We are absolutely *not* having sex and risking you tearing that open."

He huffed. A pout pulled at his full lips, and I was so tempted to smack him I had to curl and uncurl my fist a few times. *Men.*

At the glare I was sending him, he smoothed his features out. But there was an unmistakable light dancing in his eyes as he watched me. He intertwined his fingers with mine and tenderly brushed his lips against my knuckles.

"Did you mean it?"

I could barely think straight with the weight of his stare. Panic fluttered in my chest, trying to crawl up my throat. But there was no taking it back now.

Any of it.

"Yes," I whispered.

"Good." And despite the pain he was obviously still in, his face split into one of his rare, full-blown grins I was suspecting he saved just for me. "Because I think I've loved you since the moment you nearly broke Brandon's nose."

"Liar," I teased, leaning forward to kiss him again. We were both mindful of his injury, so this kiss was softer. A promise instead of a claiming.

"To the death, huh?" he murmured, cradling my face in his hands.

I nodded, leaning into his touch. "However slow or swift it may come."

"Are you all fucking in there?"

"Go get your men," I grumbled, pulling one of the throw pillows over my head to drown out the incessant pounding on my front door.

"They're your men now too," Vincent said, grunting when I flicked his nose in response. "And I'm injured."

I muttered a few choice words under my breath, but heaved myself into a sitting position all the same. Vincent and I had passed out together on the couch. Apparently, he was too worried about getting blood on my white sheets.

Like I gave a shit.

"I'm coming!" I hollered. Dexter picked up his head from where he was laying in the hall but didn't bother following me. If that didn't speak to how often these morons were in my apartment, nothing would.

"I didn't need to know that."

"Twenty-six, Lucas," I told him as I winged the door open, glaring at the three men crowding my doorway. "Twenty-six."

His hazel eyes were bright as he grinned at me. "Good to see you too, sugar."

"Get your asses in here," I said, rolling my eyes as I stepped aside. Lucas trooped into the living room, closely followed by Brandon and Arkin. The other boys gave me a nod of acknowledgement as they passed me. Once they were all in, I shut the door and reengaged the security system. When I turned back to face everyone, I saw Brandon had already gotten Vincent into a sitting position. Brandon was removing the bandages I had placed across the wound before we fell asleep, and I left them to it. I had seen enough of that gash to last a lifetime.

Lucas and Arkin followed me into the kitchen. "How're you holding up?" Arkin asked, his voice soft and measured.

"I'm doing better than I expected," I admitted, a small smile tilting my lips. "Thank you for thinking to check on me."

"Vincent has been through shit like this before," he said with a shrug. "But I was pretty sure you had never had to cauterize a wound."

"Is there anything you need from us?" Lucas asked, hazel eyes worried.

"If you could clean up the blood in the hall so we can avoid the cops being called, that would be amazing."

"Only for you," he teased. "Cleaning supplies?"

"Above the washer and dryer." He nodded and vanished in the direction I had specified.

"Did you all get everything sorted out?" I asked Arkin, trying to steer the conversation away from what had caused that pool of blood.

Arkin picked up on my train of thought quickly, and his baby blues tracked my movements before he nodded. "They shorted us. Not sure just yet if it was on accident or on purpose, but the rest of the shipment should reach the drop off within forty-eight hours."

"That's good."

"Are you okay, Jules? Really?"

I stopped what I was doing to meet his eyes. His gaze was steady, but worry still puckered his forehead. Sighing, I grabbed the coffee I had initially been reaching for and set about getting a pot made. I was sure we were all going to need it. The clock on the stove read it was just after five in the morning.

"As long as what I did holds up, and Brandon gives him the green light, I'll be fine." I hit the start button on the coffee pot. "But until then, I feel a little sick."

"So, finding him like that didn't–"

"Arkin," I chastised, flicking my gaze back to him. "I know what you all do. I'm fine. The only thing I was worried about tonight was losing him. If I could find the one responsible for this and stab him myself, I would." The strength in my voice startled me. Because I *would*. If I ever came across the man who had nearly taken Vincent from me, I knew I wouldn't hesitate to sink a knife into his gut as well. Or across his throat.

Lucas called for me to disengage the security system for him, and I left Arkin to man the coffee pot.

Who the hell was I turning into?

TWENTY-NINE

QUEEN

"And you're sure he's doing okay?" I asked Brandon, for probably the twentieth time today.

"Jules, he's recovering *fine*. Just like I told you," he huffed.

"Sorry," I muttered, switching the shoulder that I had the phone tucked between as I engaged the security system.

"Is that Juliette?" I heard Vincent's voice in the background, but it was muffled. "Give me the phone."

"No," Brandon said, sounding like he had turned his head. "You're supposed to be *resting*. I'm tired of reminding you that you can't fuck her brains out until those stitches come out."

I grumbled as my cheeks heated. Brandon had ordered Vincent to finish recovery at his own apartment after he had busted a couple of stitches on Monday night. *Maybe* we had been trying to ignore the no sex rule and when he started bleeding again, *maybe* we got in trouble. And Brandon put both of us under house arrest. Separately.

"Thank you, Brandon," I said, stepping out of the apartment building and hiking my gym bag higher on my shoulder.

"For what?"

"For taking care of him."

"Me?" he asked, his voice pitching higher. "Juliette, *you* saved his life. All of us should thank you. The entire gang is in your debt. If Vincent would have died, whoever shoved that knife into him would've been the one that laid claim to everything we do. But Vincent is *alive*. And that is because of you."

My heart swelled, and I had to blink back tears. "Don't let him give you too much hell."

Brandon scoffed, and I could picture the eye roll he was certainly giving me. "It's his favorite pass time."

I laughed, hearing Vincent's indignation in the background as Brandon and I hung up. A smile tugged at my lips as I made my way to training. For the first time in what felt like ages, I was alone. With Vincent down for the count until he healed, the boys were working overtime to make sure everything was still running smoothly. When Vincent asked me if I wanted someone else to play bodyguard, I told him no. While I had a better understanding of why Vincent felt better if I had someone with me, I didn't want a stranger to take over the spot. If it couldn't be one of the men I knew and trusted, I could take care of myself.

It had taken some convincing, and quite a few promises that I would have everyone on speed-dial in case anything went wrong, but I inevitably won.

I took my time getting to the gym, and when I swept into the lobby, I was pleased to see Sherry sitting behind the desk. She hadn't been around as much, something about classes getting crazy before finals, and I had missed her bubbling personality greeting me at the door.

True to form, she beamed at me when her crystalline eyes met mine. "Hey, Jules!" she chirped, spinning her chair so that she faced me more than her computer.

"Hey," I paused next to the desk. From my vantage point, I could see the door to the studio we usually used had light pouring out of it. At least I knew Jack was ready to go. "How's school?" I asked, giving her my attention again.

"The usual," she huffed, eyes rolling as she pulled a nail file out of her desk drawer. "A pain in my ass. But it'll be worth it once I graduate and can actually start helping kids."

"You're going to be an amazing teacher."

Her eyes sparkled as she raised them to mine. "You think so?"

"I don't doubt it for a second."

"You don't know how much I needed to hear that. This student teaching placement is hell."

"Sherry, if you're done chatting, can I steal my client from you?"

Sherry and I both jumped as Jack appeared behind me. I hadn't seen him approach, let alone heard him. My heart was beating double time, and I pressed my palm against it like that would make it settle any quicker. Sherry just blinked at Jack for a moment. With a playful scowl, she stuck her tongue out at him and swiveled back to the computer.

Whipping around, I punched him in the shoulder. His gaze dropped to me, laughter dancing in his tawny eyes as I hissed. It was like hitting a damn boulder. Why was every man I hung around as solid as stone?

Because half of them do illegal shit as their primary source of income.

"Jackass," I muttered, not sparing him another moment as I headed back to our studio. He chuckled, but his footsteps sounded behind me as he followed.

So *now* he could announce his approach. Wonderful.

Jack closed the door behind us, and I pitched my bag into the far corner of the room. Without a word, we met on the mat. For a moment, we just stood across from one another; both of us sizing the other up. I wasn't sure what Jack's motivation behind having me train more often was, but I knew *my* reasoning. And if he was feeling nice enough to not charge me for it, I wouldn't fight him on it. Not anymore.

His eyes sparkled, giving him away as he lunged for me. A grin spread across my face as I spun away from him with ease.

"So, it's going to be like that today?" he asked, twisting to face me again.

"Like what?" I widened my eyes before blinking a few times. "I was just doing what you taught me."

"That innocent act won't fly here."

My grin turned wicked. "Fine."

Before he could figure out what I was doing, I feinted left. When he moved to dodge, I was already sinking low to knock his legs out from under him. There was a resounding *thwack* as his back met the mat.

It was about *damn time* it was him going down instead of me.

Something dark flickered across Jack's face as he bounded back into a standing position. The light in his eyes was still there, but there was something different about it. Playful as always, yes, but darker. More predatory. I was so caught up trying to decipher what the change was that I didn't notice the maneuver until it was too late. Jack had my arms twisted behind me and my back plastered to his chest before I could even let out a sound of distress.

Forcing my brain to function, I jammed my heel into his instep as hard as I could, just like he had shown me in one of our first sessions. He hissed, his hold reflexively loosening. It was just enough for me to spin out of his grasp, and then we were circling each other again. Jack's tawny gaze ran over me. Cataloguing. Assessing. For the first time, I could tell he wasn't holding back. Maybe I was actually getting decent at this.

We played a game of cat and mouse for another thirty minutes before I finally tapped out. He had me pinned, the full brunt of his weight centered on my back to keep me down. His laughter reverberated through me as he moved off of me. My chest was heaving as I tried to draw air back into my lungs. A heavy groan escaped me, and I rolled over onto my back, letting my arms splay out at my sides.

"Ow."

"You were out for blood today," he commented, sitting cross-legged beside me.

"Sorry," I muttered, blowing my hair out of my face.

"Don't be," he chuckled. "It's been a long time since someone gave me a run for my money like that."

"You mean that?" I asked, tilting my head so I could meet his eyes.

A grin brightened his face, making him look years younger, boyish even. "I do. You've come a long way since we started."

"I had a pretty good teacher."

"Flattery will get you nowhere," he said, shaking his head before hoisting himself up. He held a hand down for me, and I allowed him to yank me to my feet as well. "How are you feeling about your progress?"

"Good," I admitted, stretching out my arms. "Definitely feel stronger than I ever thought I would, so thank you."

"It's what you pay me for."

"True," I said, trying not to roll my eyes at him. "So now what?"

"That's up to you. We can up the strength training or add in martial arts during your extra days."

"How about both?"

His eyebrows arched. "Something I should know about?"

"No."

I spoke too quickly, and from the narrowing of his eyes, he thought so, too. But this was Jack, and he had known me long enough to know that pushing wouldn't get him anywhere. He blew out a sigh through his nose and pointed me towards the free weights.

A grin twitched at the corner of my lips as I saluted him and flounced off.

Devyn kicked my knee. I nearly spat out my burger in surprise, and I glared at her before wiping my mouth with my napkin. "The hell was that for?"

"I want *details*."

"What do you want me to do? Tell you how big his dick is?" She batted her eyes slowly, looking more like a cat with every blink. "Devyn."

She cackled. "I'm kidding, mostly. But it's not every day your best friend becomes queen of the roughest, toughest gang in the city."

"Have you been watching westerns again?" She chucked one of the throw pillows at me. "What? You might as well have said rootin' tootin'."

"You're deflecting."

"I'm not *queen* of anything."

"Except this city."

"Please tell me how you figure that."

Devyn took a huge bite of her own burger, looking contemplative as she chewed. Deciding to leave her to it, I continued eating as well. She'd get to it, eventually.

After my session with Jack, Devyn called to ask what I was doing. Since my day was open, she had suggested ordering in and lazing around on the couch for the rest of the day. It hadn't taken long to convince me. After everything that had been happening lately, I needed a day to just breathe.

It took her about five minutes to start her interrogation when she got here. I had thought I had covered everything she wanted to know when we had gone out last weekend, but apparently the time apart had given her time to figure out *more* questions. And wild theories.

"The gang runs a lot of the underground crime in this city, right?"

"Yes," I said, arching my brows at her. God knew where this was going.

"So, then *Vincent* runs most of this city, right?'

"I mean to a point, but–"

"Aht, aht," she tsked, holding up a finger. "I mean, I would even argue that he was the *king* of the underground." A deep groan heaved from me as I slumped back against the couch. "Which would make you the queen."

"You are absolutely ridiculous."

"But you love me."

"That I do."

She grinned from ear to ear, launching herself at me in a hug. We dissolved into a fit of laughter that caused Dexter to chuff at us in annoyance. That only made us laugh harder, and I squeezed her tighter for a moment before nudging her back to her side of the couch. We settled in to watch a movie, and Dexter hopped up between us. He placed his head in Devyn's lap, and I shoved my feet underneath him to steal some warmth. It was just the night I needed.

My phone vibrated against my hip somewhere around the start of the second rom-com we had put on. When I squinted at the bright screen, I had to stop the grin from overtaking my face.

I miss you.

That was all Vincent had written, but my heart was swelling inside my chest. Deciding to just let the dopey smile win, I shot him back the same message in response.

"It's nice to see you this happy," Devyn said. Jerking my head around, I met her warm brown gaze. There was a soft smile on her face, and her eyes looked a little glassy.

"What do you mean?"

"Just that I haven't seen you smile like that since your mom died."

"Dev."

"I know, I know," she muttered, swiping underneath her eyes. "And I know I talked about how bad he was for you. How danger-ous. But Jules," she reached over and grasped my hand. "Anyone who can put that smile back on your face must not be all bad. And they're definitely not bad *for* you. So, I'm sorry."

"The mighty Devyn Greene, apologizing. The world must be ending."

"Don't make me take it back."
"Thank you," I told her, squeezing the hand I still held.
"Anytime, bitch."

Thirty

THE PARTY

"You look nice," Dante commented as I breezed through the back door.

"Listen, I took full advantage of not having to wear my uniform tonight," I said, smoothing my hands down the front of my black dress. It hugged my figure like a second skin, with sheer panels slashing in from the sides to show off just a bit of my stomach. My hair was down for once, and Devyn had insisted that I curl it for the party. Since it wasn't something I often did, I went for it.

"I was being serious," he said, a grin on his face as he hefted a box of liquor in his arms. He jerked his head for me to follow him. "The is the last of the initial stock for their bar tonight. You're early. You can help me finish setting up."

We trooped out into that main part of the club. Anthony and Ember were behind the main bar, and they both waved at me as we walked through. Scurrying in front of him, I held the door open onto the main floor for Dante. He gave me a look of gratitude before heading off to the far left of the club. Past the seating that adorned this side of the room, there was a hallway that led back to the private rooms. Mostly, they were rented out for things like birthdays, bachelor and bachelorette parties, and business parties. And now, apparently, gang networking.

Although I guess we could technically classify it as a business party.

I let out a derisive snort at my own thoughts, and Dante glanced over his shoulder at me. When he raised an eyebrow in question, I just shook my head at him and continued to follow him back to the very end of the hall. Holding the door open for him again, I let my eyes adjust to the darkness of the room before moving in as well. The room Lucas had chosen was one of the biggest, with a private bar and dance floor, as well as table seating. Trying not to roll my eyes, I kicked the door shut behind me and made my way to the bar.

With Devyn and I both working the party, I was guessing it would be a cinch. We had worked parties together for as long as I could remember, and they were more often than not some of our best nights. Even if there was a lot on the line tonight, I was still going to be glad to get to watch the guys let loose. They all deserved it.

Within the hour, Devyn had made her grand appearance. A smile tugged at my lips when I noticed what she was wearing.

"Did you tell me to wear this dress just so we would match?" I asked as she sidled up next to me.

"Maybe."

"Yeah, okay." The dress she was wearing was damn near identical to the one I had on. The one that *she* had selected out of the three options I had sent her earlier in the day.

Her red painted lips pulled back in an almost feral grin. "I figured if you lucked out with the bangers, maybe I could, too."

Dante dropped his head back and gazed at the ceiling. "Give me strength," he grumbled, shooting Devyn a cross look as he finished counting the money for our drawer.

Before Devyn could pop off at him, the door to the hall opened. Four men ambled in, but the one bringing up the rear was the one that held my attention.

My breath caught for just a moment. Then relief swept through me, and I knew I was beaming.

I hadn't seen Vincent in days. Seeing him up and walking without even a wince made me feel like someone had lifted a burden off my chest. That he looked utterly devastating in his black button down and slacks wasn't doing anything to help my racing heart.

The moment those forest eyes met mine, everything else faded away. I'm not sure which one of us moved first, but it only took a few steps for us to meet in the middle. My arms wrapped around his waist, and he gathered me into him. One hand slipped into my hair to cradle the back of my head, and the other constricted around the small of my back. I snuggled closer, feeling the reassuring thump of his heart under my cheek. He pressed a kiss to the top of my head, and I heard the soft rumble of laughter from his chest.

"I missed you too, princess."

"Are you feeling up to this?" I asked, pulling back enough to meet his eyes again.

"Brandon gave me the green light. He wouldn't have let me out of bed if he thought it was going to affect my *recovery.*" His eyes rolled as a smile twitched at the edges of his lips. "It's been a fight to keep what went down under wraps. If I wasn't here tonight, it would raise too many questions. It could make me look weak, and that's the last thing we need right now."

"Fair point," I muttered, scowling. I brushed my fingers over where the injury should be. I could feel one small bandage, but that was it.

"I'm okay, Juliette," he assured me, tipping my chin up so he could meet my eyes again. "I promise."

"Jules," Dante called, a lazy drawl to his voice. It broke me out of the bubble I had placed myself in with a jolt. Still fully enveloped in Vincent's arms, I glanced over my shoulder at my boss. He made a sweeping gesture towards the bar, meaning I should probably get to work.

"Duty calls," I said, twisting back to face him.

He grinned, his entire face lighting up with the movement. "Don't let anyone here tonight give you a hard time."

"Do I ever?" I asked, brows arching.

"No," he responded, leaning down until his lips brushed the shell of my ear. "It's one of the reasons I fell in love with you."

My entire body flushed, but I knew the crimson settled in my cheeks. Vincent's eyes tracked it with fascination.

"You're lucky I love you, too. Asshole," I muttered. I went to turn away, trying to extract myself from his grip. But I didn't make it a step before he was hauling me back to him. He cradled my chin, tilting his head and pressing his lips against mine. In an instant, all of my ire was gone. I melted into him, content to let reality slip away.

But only for a moment.

Someone cleared their throat next to us. When I pulled away enough to glare at Lucas, he just smirked at me. It was ten times more infuriating than the puppy-dog grin he normally gave me. I opened my mouth, but he stopped me with raised hands. "I know, I know," he said. "Twenty-seven, right?"

"I hate all of you."

"It's not nice to lie, sugar."

I swatted at him before spinning on my heel and heading over to Devyn and Dante. Devyn had a coy smile on her face as she polished a glass, and Dante looked like he was fighting the urge to laugh. Using more force than I probably should have, I knocked my hip against Devyn's as I walked past. She cursed, dropping the glass that she had been polishing.

Dante heaved a sigh at the same time the glass shattered against the floor.

"The broom is in the back," he said.

Devyn's glare was acidic. I stuck my tongue out at her for good measure before heading into the back closet so I could clean up the mess I had made. If this was any sign of how our night was going to go, it couldn't be over fast enough.

"Can you grab another bottle of tequila from the front?" I called to Devyn a couple hours later. I had just poured the last of what we had with us but, from the way the people attending were guzzling it down, my reprieve would more than likely be short-lived. "And anything else we need."

"You sure you'll be okay?" she asked.

Glancing around the bar to see that we had taken care of everyone for the time being, I nodded at her. She gave me a thumbs up before maneuvering her way out from behind the bar. As she headed for the door to the main part of the club, she snagged Brandon's arm and tugged him behind her. He shot me a bewildered look, and I gave him a smile of encouragement. If she was planning on fully restocking what we had used so far, she would probably need the extra set of hands.

A flash of blonde hair caught in my periphery. When I turned, it didn't surprise me to find Lucas leaning against the bar, his chin propped on his hand. His eyes were a little glassy, and he gave me that damned puppy-dog smile.

"What do you want?" I asked, trying and failing to keep the amusement out of my voice.

"Just wanted to see how you two were doing. Making sure no one is giving you any trouble."

"We're fine, Lucas. Stop hovering."

And hovering he had been. Excluding Vincent, one of the guys had been within ten feet of the bar all night. Having spent so much time with them, I knew they were keeping a steady eye on me. It wasn't like they were being sneaky about it. For once, I didn't fight it. I knew how tense it must make all of them to have me here, amidst the men and women that ran their part of the city. And I also knew why Vincent had been keeping his distance. Even if it killed me to be in the same room with him and not be able to be *with* him, I understood it.

Tonight was all about finding out where allegiances lied. Especially after what had happened last weekend. The last thing that we needed was for Vincent's enemies to figure out he finally had a pressure point.

While I knew I could handle myself in most situations, I wasn't sure about doing so in the face of someone who wanted to use me to hurt Vincent.

So, I stayed behind the bar and behaved as professionally as I could. I acted as if I didn't know them any more than any other patron of the bar. But the drunker the boys got, the more *they* forgot they weren't supposed to know me.

Case in point: the golden retriever posted up at my bar.

"Seriously," I told him, whipping my towel at him. He winced when it caught him in the shoulder. "Get out of here before you draw attention."

"They'll just think I'm hitting on you," he said, leaning closer with a playful glint in his hazel eyes.

"I know *someone* who would throttle you for even suggesting such a thing."

"He'll get over it."

"Get over what?" a new voice inserted.

"Nothing," Lucas and I chorused, snapping our attention to Vincent. He narrowed his eyes on his second in command, but there was laughter dancing around the edges of his mouth.

"Can I get you anything?" I cut in, batting my lashes at him with faux innocence.

He bought it about as much as I expected him to. "If you could just top this off instead of flirting with my men, that'd be appreciated."

My blood heated. There was a darkness in his voice, the same one I had grown addicted to. I knew whatever 'flirting' I had been doing with Lucas didn't faze him. It was all for show. Just big, bad Vincent Monroe putting the bartender in her place. With a tremendous amount of restraint, I kept myself from letting my eyes roll. Instead, my gaze met his. I could see the softness that he reserved just for me reflected for a moment. Letting my lips tip up in a smile, I nodded at him. His attention switched to scanning the room when I turned to grab the bottle of scotch.

With the bottle in hand, I moved back in front of him. Something in the far corner of the room seemed to have taken up all of his focus. In the seconds it had taken me to return, Vincent had masked the man I loved beneath the ruthless gang leader once again. When I went to take his glass from him, he caught my wrist with his opposite hand. In one swift tug, he had me stretched across the bar and his lips at my ear.

"I need you out of here. Now."

"Okay," I breathed, not even considering fighting against the demand. Not with that note of what I could only describe as panic laced through the order. I backed up enough to pour the drink before placing it in front of him again. "What happened?"

Lucas perked up at our shift in demeanor. It seemed as if I blinked, and he was stone-cold sober. Had the drunkenness all been an act?

"There's someone here," Vincent said. Whoever it was, his eyes tracked their movement. "Someone I thought was dead."

"Who is it?"

"Later," he said, voice murderously soft as he glanced back at me. "I don't want you anywhere near him. Get home. I'll be there as soon as I can, and I'll explain everything."

"I'll tell Dante," I said, taking the money he handed me. When I turned to cash him out, I let my own eyes take in the room. It was fit to bursting with people, and we had dimmed the lights to almost nonexistent once the guests arrived. Most of the light came from the pulsing neon above the small dance floor. Whoever Vincent was seeing, I couldn't make them out. There wasn't anyone that seemed overly suspicious to me, but I was also shorter than half of the people in the room and couldn't see very far. Once I had the change in hand, I spun back to Vincent with the same placating grin I gave to all my customers. "Your change, sir."

His eyes sparkled. Even with whatever was going on, at least I could still amuse him. When he took the change from me, he let his hand linger on mine. He entwined our fingers for half a heartbeat, giving me a reassuring squeeze before he moved away from the bar. Lucas stepped up to his side and clapped him on the shoulder. Together, they melted into the mass of people and headed in the direction Vincent had been staring.

Devyn and Brandon reappeared moments later. Sure enough, Brandon's arms were heavy with bottles of liquor. If I wasn't so wound up, I might have found it funny how easily he let Devyn boss him around.

"What's wrong?" she asked, stopping in front of me as she set down the two bottles she had carried.

"I have to go," I said, keeping my voice low as I busied myself with washing a few glasses. "Brandon, find Lucas and Vincent."

Brandon's spine stiffened as he took in the look on my face. "How bad is it?" he asked, worry lighting in his eyes.

"Someone's here," I explained, nodding in the direction the boys had headed. "They might need you. Send Arkin over here. He hasn't been hovering as much as you and Lucas. If they've got Vincent's hackles up enough for him to ask me to leave, I don't want Devyn alone."

With a nod, he finished placing the bottles on the bar and headed off to find the others. There was something to be said about him not bothering to question me. Maybe there was some merit to them being 'my men' now, too.

"Are you okay?" Devyn asked, coming up beside me.

"For right now," I said. "Are you going to be okay if I leave?"

She arched her brow at me. "I've managed worse crowds. And these men won't let anything happen to me." Her lips quirked up at the corners as she gave me a sly smile. "They'd have to answer to you."

Laughing softly, I pulled her in for a quick hug before making my way out from behind the bar. In an effort to make it look like I had a reason to leave, I took a rack of extra glasses with me. Something told me it was in our best interest not to draw any attention to one bartender suddenly leaving. Making a point to not look for any of the men, I left the pulsing music of the party behind. The main part of Tuxedo was just as crowded as the back room, and I had to maneuver myself around close-packed bodies more times than I cared to count on my way to the bar. Anthony spotted me as I approached and hustled to swing open the door separating the bar from the floor.

"Do you need help?" he asked, already making to take the rack from me.

"I'm good," I said, giving him a broad grin. "How's everything going tonight?"

"Good. It's not like working with you, but Ember's catching on quick."

My eyes strayed to the girl in question. As if she felt our attention, she glanced over her shoulder at us. As her gaze caught mine, she gave me a small smile and waved. Since I couldn't wave back, I just gave her a broad grin. She had fit in as if she had always been there, and if Anthony was singing her praises, she had to be good.

But I had more important things to worry about than our newest trainee.

"Dante in the back?"

"Yeah, he was in his office just a bit ago."

"Thank you."

Ignoring the question in his eyes, I pushed through the doors into the kitchen. The door to Dante's office was wide open, light spilling out into the dim hall in the back. The glasses clinked together as I set the rack down. Dante must have heard me, because he was in the doorway before I had even crossed the kitchen.

"Is everything okay?" he asked, eyebrows raised.

"Not sure," I admitted. I grabbed my purse and clocked out. "Vincent said someone was here. Whoever it is, he demanded I head home."

"Shit." Dante groaned, letting his head fall back against the doorjamb. "Wait here."

Curious, I did as he asked. For once.

He headed out behind the bar. From where I stood, I could just make out him talking to Anthony through the window in the swinging door. They exchanged a few words, and then Dante was back through the door and breezing past me.

"Well, let's go," he said

"Go where?" I asked, scurrying to keep up with him as we made our way out the back door.

"I'm taking you home. Heaven knows what your boyfriend would do to me if he knew I let you walk."

Silently, I followed him to his car. I was also steadfastly ignoring the way my heart skipped over the mundane term. Boyfriend. Was that what he was? My eyes rolled at my own thoughts as I climbed into the passenger seat. Whatever label we put on it, it all meant the same thing. He was mine, just as I was his.

And I wouldn't let anything threaten that.

THIRTY-ONE

EXTENDED STAY

Three quick raps on my door caught my attention a couple of hours later.

I got up off the couch so fast that my legs tangled in the blanket I had draped over them, nearly causing me to face plant. I threw the damned thing back on the couch with a curse and flew to the door. Vincent had kept me as updated as he could since I had gotten home, but I had still been a ball of anxiety the whole time.

The security panel beeped as I disengaged it, then I flung the door open.

Vincent swept into the apartment before I could utter a word, and I reengaged the system after I shut the door. Spinning to face him, I jumped when I realized how close he was. He crowded me back against the door, his fingers tangling in the hair at the nape of my neck as his thumbs pressed against the underside of my jaw. With the slightest pressure, he encouraged me to meet his eyes.

They swallowed me whole. I couldn't think past my next breath as Vincent's eyes devoured me. The feeling of his lips on mine sent a jolt of electricity through my blood, and my thoughts eddied out as I lost myself in the sensation. The urgency in his kiss consumed me entirely. It was as if he was afraid I would evaporate into thin air if he didn't keep his lips on mine.

"Are you okay?" we asked in unison when we came up for air.

I could feel the tension leave his shoulders as he chuckled. "I'm better now."

"Good." Taking his hand, I lead him over to the couch with me. We settled in together, and he pulled my legs across his lap before tucking my head under his chin. "What happened after I left?"

"We got the place cleared out pretty fast. But he was gone. It was like there was no trace of him."

"Who was he?"

Vincent paused, his arms tightening around me for a moment. Then he exhaled and ran his hand up and down my arm before continuing. "Jaxon Graham."

"What?" I choked out.

"He's the reason Alana's dead," he said, closing his eyes as if he could ward off the pain. "He ordered the hit on her. Because I killed his father and took the gang from him."

The silence that surrounded us was deafening. I grabbed his hand, entwining our fingers together in a small show of solidarity.

"I knew someone killed Alana," I said. His eyes snapped open, finding mine and swimming with questions. "Dante told me. He didn't know that I wasn't aware of the full story. But he said that as far as he knew, you had killed the man responsible."

"I thought I had," he muttered, letting out a deep sigh through his nose.

"What happened?"

He cut his gaze to me, and I could read the unspoken question in his forest eyes: Did I really want to know the full story?

I did, so I nodded for him to continue.

"We had tracked him all the way to a marina two cities over. I shot him right in the chest, and he fell into the water. When he didn't resurface, I assumed he was rotting at the bottom of the bay."

"Until tonight."

"Until tonight," he echoed, squeezing my hand. "I just want to know how no one knew he was back in the city. He was the son of

Andras Graham, and somehow, he's back in Valarian and no one thought to tell me."

"I'm sure he knew to lie low," I said, laying my head back against his shoulder. "But you'll find him. He was ballsy enough to come tonight. He must have known someone would spot him."

"Tonight was invite only, so someone had to have told him. *Someone* has to know where he is," he mused, shifting enough to pull his phone out of his pocket. It was vibrating, and I saw Lucas's name flash across the screen. "I have to take this."

"Go ahead." I made to untangle myself from him, but he just pulled me deeper into his embrace.

"What did you find?" he asked the minute the call connected. Despite everything, a smile pulled at the edges of my lips. Guess I was fully initiated. I could vaguely hear Lucas's voice on the other end, but not the words. Vincent's eyebrows lowered, casting dark shadows over his cheekbones. They exchanged a few more words, and then he hung up. He pitched his phone onto the coffee table. It hit with a clatter, skidding off the opposite side. "Fuck," he hissed, running his free hand through his dark hair.

"I take it that wasn't good news."

"The guys patrolled the area around the club, trying to find anything leading back to Graham. Nothing."

"We'll find him, Vincent."

At that, he turned to me, one of his sculpted brows reaching for his hairline. "We?"

"To the death, remember?"

"To the death." He leaned forward and pressed a kiss to my forehead. "Can you and Dexter come stay with me for a while?"

I blanched. "What?"

"I don't want to hide you. You're mine, and I want everyone to damn well know it. But, until we put him in the ground for good, I would feel better if I could personally keep an eye on you as much as possible."

"Sounding a little possessive there, Vinnie."

His eyes lit with a dark promise as he leaned into me. "Right now is probably not the *best* time to let your bratty tendencies come out to play," he said, his breath skating over the spot where my neck met my shoulder. His stubble scraped against my throat as he trailed kisses higher, causing a shiver to skitter down my spine.

"Why's that?" I asked, my voice cracking as I sucked in a breath.

Vincent's laugh caused goosebumps to blossom across my skin. Without answering me, he lightly bit down on that soft spot he knew was my undoing. The moan that it elicited was indecent, and I felt him grow hard beneath me. In an instant, he had me straddling him, my heart pounding in my chest. He didn't let me catch my breath before his lips covered mine.

The next few hours were a tangle of limbs, tongues, and promises whispered in the dark. And when we finally cuddled together in my bed, I allowed myself to absorb the silence that settled over us. Vincent had his arms wrapped around my waist, and my back flush against his chest. My breathing synced to his as he fell asleep. But my mind wandered while I idly stroked the back of his hand.

Something about tonight was still nagging at me. We had missed *something*. I wasn't sure what it could be, but I could feel it in my gut.

It kept me awake for most of the night. But no matter how many times I ran over the guest list in my head, or how many times I re-combed through the events of the night, nothing jumped out at me. I wasn't sure why I thought I could pick up on something when none of the boys could, but I still wanted to try.

Maybe I was trying to prove to myself that I could do it. That I could stand at Vincent's side and be just as in control as he was. But I knew that more than anything, it came back to my desire to protect him. As ridiculous as that notion was, it was still there. He had already lost so many people. We both had.

By the time dawn was cresting over the horizon, I still hadn't come up with any new ideas. Slowly but surely, the darkness in my room ebbed away. Cursing, I forced my eyes closed and snuggled deeper into Vincent. I needed sleep.

"What time did you say your training session was today?" Vincent asked, poking his head out of the bathroom.

"Four," I replied, glancing up from the text I had been sending to Devyn. "Why?"

"Think we can get some of your stuff over to the warehouse beforehand?"

Blowing some hair out of my face, I tapped my phone against my knee. "Are you sure that's what you want? Having Dexter and me underfoot might–"

"Don't even finish that sentence," he said, cutting me off. The glare he leveled at me was frigid, but I just gave him an equally flat stare. "Juliette, I'm serious. Until Graham 2.0 is dealt with, I need you close."

My lips twitched. "Graham 2.0?" He threw the hand towel he had been using at me. "Alright, alright. I'll pack."

Thirty minutes later, I had two bags packed with everything I would need for a temporary stay at Vincent's. Dexter had his head hanging out of the back window, and one of Alana's recitals was filtering through the SUV. Knowing how important the music was to Vincent made me appreciate it even more as we made the cross-city drive. He had our fingers entwined, and my stomach gave a pleasant flip as he raised my hand to his lips and kissed the back of it. Forest eyes found mine, and I tried not to be struck dumb by the intensity there; the fire that was always hiding in the depths of his gaze. One of many things that kept drawing me back to him again and again.

"What're you thinking?" he murmured, refocusing on the road.

"Just about how crazy my life has gotten."

"I'm sorry," he said, brushing his thumb across my knuckles. "I know the situation isn't ideal, and I'm being an overbearing ass about it, but I'll sleep better knowing you're safe."

"At least you can admit it."

He just shook his head at me. He gave my hand a quick squeeze before maneuvering the car with the other. When we arrived outside the warehouse, Vincent put his phone to his ear and trailed behind me to the back of the SUV. From the sound of the chipper voice I could hear, it was Lucas on the other end of the line. A small smile tugged at the corners of my mouth as I grabbed one of my bags and let him take the other. He slung the duffel over his shoulder and wrapped his arm around my waist before herding Dexter and me to the door. His conversation with Lucas was brief as he filled him in on the plan. Something like annoyance crossed his face before he mashed the end button.

"What was that about?" I asked, raising my brows.

Vincent blew out a breath. "Lucas is *too* excited to have you here for the foreseeable future. He's going to drive you insane."

"Maybe I *will* just actually kill him."

"Oh, really?" He grinned, pulling me close. "And just which of your twenty-seven ways are you going to use?"

"I haven't decided yet. I'm sure he'll inspire a few more once he gets here."

As we crossed through the threshold, there was a lull in the conversation. A hush fell over the warehouse as all eyes snapped to us. Gazes drifted from Vincent to the arm he still had draped around me, and then finally to my face. Their curiosity was a living entity that took up residence in the room. I pulled my shoulders back a little and lifted my chin. Sure, I had been to the warehouse a few times, but even the last time hadn't felt like this.

Something had changed. The stares felt heavier.

The last time I had accompanied Vincent through these doors, I had wanted no part of this life. Had been content to test the waters from a safe distance. It seemed like the rest of the gang knew about the change in Vincent's and my relationship from the looks they were giving me. As we passed through the room on our way to the back staircase, each person we passed met Vincent's gaze before nodding their head in a show of respect.

And then they did the same for me.

All except an increasingly familiar redhead. She perched on the arm of one of the lounge chairs. She wasn't the only woman that hung around the warehouse, but she was the only one that seemed to actually be a part of the gang, versus a member's partner. I couldn't describe it, but there was an air of authority around her; in how some others reacted to her. She had her hand braced against the back of a man's chair as she leaned over him to get a look at his laptop screen, but her eyes were on me. Our gazes locked, and I stopped moving. Vincent paused as well, and I heard a muffled curse as he realized what had caught my attention.

Her eyes bounced back and forth between us, and a slow grin spread across her face, setting those slightly upturned sapphire eyes to glittering. She brought her gaze back to mine and dipped her head, one corner of her mouth tipping up.

I returned the gesture in kind and could feel the tension leave Vincent's shoulders as we mounted the stairs.

"Who's the redhead?" I asked.

"Angelica. She handles a lot of the liaison work with the other gangs. Why do you ask?"

"I just always notice her watching me."

"She's high ranking," he told me, halting on the steps to turn and meet my eyes. "She holds just as much sway as Arkin and Brandon do. And she knows who you are. What you mean to me. And she, like all the other members, has kept her distance since you didn't want this life. But now, they're all getting curious."

"Because you told them I'm all in?"

He grinned, constricting his arm to pull me in even closer. "Absolutely, I did." He pressed a kiss to my forehead before tugging me the rest of the way up the stairs.

Once we were on the second floor and away from prying eyes, he dropped my bag to the ground. At the bewildered expression on my face, one of his broad grins broke free. He placed his hands on my hips and moved us until my back was flush with the brick. He molded his body to mine, slipping his knee between my legs.

"You do realize we only have one more set of stairs and then we'd be in private, right?" I asked, tipping my chin up to meet his gaze.

"Maybe I couldn't wait."

"For what?"

"This."

His mouth came down on mine, efficiently cutting off whatever I was about to say. He drew a moan from me by nipping my bottom lip. The bag I had in my hand slipped through my fingers before I wound my arms around Vincent's neck. His hands skimmed over my sides as they moved down to my waist. His touch was scalding as he slipped his fingers beneath my shirt, a gasp ripping free of my throat at the contact.

"Can you two *please* not fuck right outside my door?"

"Oh, for god's sake," Vincent growled. The only part of himself he moved away from me was his head. Other than that, he still had me pinned to the wall. "Go back inside."

"Is that an order?" Brandon asked, raising his eyebrows as he leaned against the doorframe. The doorframe that Vincent and I *were* barely two inches away from.

"Would you take it better coming from me?" I asked.

Brandon gave me a wicked grin. "Probably."

"Then go back inside."

"Fine." A sly smirk slid across his face as he glanced over his shoulder back into his apartment. "I have better things to do, anyway."

A girlish giggle emanated through the closed door.

"Any idea who that is?" I questioned, urging Vincent back a few steps so I could fix my clothes.

"I have an idea," he muttered, running a hand through his hair. Without offering me any other explanation, he bent down and grabbed both bags we had dropped. I didn't bother to stop him as he took my hand and towed me up the last flight of stairs to his apartment. Dexter sniffed along the bottom of Brandon's door until I called for him. The slightest whine slipped out of him as he trotted after us.

My phone pinged with a text as soon as we crossed the threshold into Vincent's.

Am I going to hear you two, or can I go back to sleep?

"*Devyn?*" I blurted, whipping my head up to look at Vincent. "It's *Devyn* down there with him?"

"He said you insisted someone watch over her."

"First of all, I said Arkin," I muttered, shooting a quick text to Devyn to let her know now she owed *me* details. "And this wasn't what I meant."

"Arkin might be down there, too."

I choked.

Mirth was dancing in Vincent's dark eyes as he watched me struggle to regain control of my breathing.

"You wanna run that by me again?" I finally got out.

"They share, sometimes," he said, shrugging as he headed for the spiral staircase that led up to the bedroom. "Although Brandon seems a little smitten with Devyn. So, maybe not this time."

"Smitten," I repeated, following him in a daze.

"And before you ask," Vincent called, causing me to realize I had stopped walking at some point. "Yes, they both know that it's *you* they're going to have to deal with should anything go sideways."

"I appreciate the thought," I said, laughter lacing my tone as I trailed him into the bedroom. "But Devyn's a big girl. She can make her own decisions and fight her own battles."

"Well, Brandon and Arkin both think you're going to skin them alive if they so much as make her pout, so I'm just going to let them keep thinking that."

"When did they become so afraid of me?"

"When I told them they should be."

"Are *you* afraid of me?"

His eyes met mine. His grin turned ferocious as he stalked towards me. Even though part of me wanted to make him chase me, I stood my ground. And as always, he invaded my space until he was the only thing I could focus on. His hands cupped my face, thumbs stroking along my cheekbones as his fingers threaded through my hair.

"The only thing I'm afraid of, princess," he murmured, leaning down to brush his nose against mine, "is losing you."

"You're quite the sap, you know that?"

"I do."

"Not what I expected when I first met you. Remember? When you were threatening to kill me?"

"How long are you going to hold that against me?"

I let an impish smile break across my face. "To the death."

"However slow or swift it may come," he finished.

When he pulled me onto the bed, I decided I didn't care if we kept Devyn and Brandon *and* Arkin up all night.

Thirty-Two

Another Training Session

"Do not walk back to the warehouse," Vincent said, his tone brooking no room for argument. My eyes rolled of their own accord as I hopped out of the SUV. Rounding on him, I let him see the glare I was giving him. "I'm serious."

"Okay, *Mom*. You're giving Dante a run for his money in the mother hen department."

"I just want–"

"Me safe," I finished for him. The look he gave me promised punishment, and as amusing as it was to push his buttons, I knew I had to let up. At least a little. "Vincent, I love you. But what are you dropping me off for?"

"Self-defense."

"With who?"

"Your trainer."

"And?"

"And he's the reason you put me flat on my ass earlier."

I beamed at him, slinging my duffel onto my shoulder. The look on his face when I had pinned him beneath me in less than sixty seconds before we left would stay one of my favorite memories for a very long time. "See? I'm going to be fine. And I know you've got a lot to do with Weasel-Face–"

"Henry."

"Whatever. I know you have a lot going on with that deal. Who are you taking with you?"

"Brandon and Arkin."

"So, as soon as I'm done, I'll call Lucas. I promise." I had a sneaking suspicion the other two were going with him to avoid me, but I'd let them get away with it. For now.

He crooked his finger at me. Arching my brows, I simply crossed my arms and leaned against the seat. Vincent smirked, and that was all the warning I got before his hand shot out. His fingers wound into the front of my shirt, and he yanked me forward. A yelp of surprise escaped as he hauled me back into the car with him.

Before I could even think about chastising him, he kissed me.

"That mouth is going to get you in trouble," he murmured, pulling back enough to snare me in his gaze.

"It usually does," I replied. I leaned forward again to peck him on the cheek, and then I disentangled from his grip. "But you're going to make me late. I'll see you tonight."

He grumbled something unintelligible as I shut the door. Trying not to laugh at his expense, I waved before entering the studio. Vincent only pulled away from the curb once I shut the door behind me. Trying to tame the smile on my face into something less dopey, I turned to the reception desk.

As I expected, it was empty. Sherry was rarely here whenever I had my rare late appointments with Jack. As much as I loved meeting with him in the mornings, I was starting to prefer the afternoon times. The gym was always quiet, and it was usually only the two of us when we met this late. It helped me focus when I knew there was no one else around.

The light was on in the studio we typically used, so I made my way back to it. Jack was in the far corner, working through a series of jabs and punches against one of the punching bags. For a moment, I just studied him. He was carrying so much tension in his shoulders, more than I had ever noticed before. His hits were short, clipped, and precise.

Frustration.

He had taught me how to recognize which emotions were the driving forces in my exercises, and how to redirect them in order to be the most beneficial. It was an invaluable skill, and I was glad I was getting to where I could see it in others as well. He was so zoned in that he hadn't even noticed my approach. Which was off for him. Jack had always reminded me of a cat. Aware of his surroundings, and ready to adapt at a moment's notice. Not to mention how light and quick on his feet he was. Yet another skill he had been helping me hone.

It was the reason I managed to outsmart him half the time.

The door creaked as I pushed it open farther. His head whipped up so fast I was sure his neck cricked. When he spotted me, he flashed a grin before waving in greeting. My own smile slipped over my face as I shut the door behind me and walked over to him.

"Rough day?" I asked, pitching my bag, phone, and jacket into a corner.

"You have no idea," he said, stretching his arms out as he faced me. His tawny eyes ran over me. Searching, assessing, and taking on that calculating gleam I was growing more familiar with. Ever since Jack had stopped pulling punches with me, the way he looked at me had changed. He still seemed to see way more than I ever intended for him to, but now and then I glimpsed predatory glee when I pinned him. Or vice versa.

"Enlighten me." He chuckled at my words. The sound was rich and warm as he motioned for me to head for the mat. Fighting not to roll my eyes, I flounced over. When I pivoted to face him, he was barely even a step behind me. My eyebrows arched before I crossed my arms over my chest. "So scared I'm going to beat you that you're resorting to intimidation?"

"Jules, you've never backed down from a fight with me," he pointed out, taking a step back. "I don't think intimidation could ever work on you."

"As long as you know."

It was his turn to roll his eyes.

"Let me see the form we went over last time." I moved into position. Jack tsked, moving forward to reorient my hips. The tank top I had on was thin, so the heat of his touch easily seeped into my skin. His fingers flexed, and my whole body went still. Raising my focus to his eyes, I saw the indecision on his face. Sucking in a sharp breath, he shook his head as he took a step back. "You need to stand like this, otherwise you'll lose balance and be finished before you even start."

"You okay?"

"I've just got a lot going on right now. Sorry if I seem distracted."

I slowly eased out of the fighting stance to cross my arms again and study him. Jack had always tried to be there for me when my brain was firing off in a thousand different directions. The least I could do was try to offer him the same. If he'd let me.

"Do you want to reschedule?" I questioned, cocking my head. "I don't want to keep you from anything."

"I think I need this more than you for once," he said, giving me a small smile. "But thank you for caring enough to ask."

"You'd do the same for me," I reminded him with a shrug.

He grunted before falling into a fighting stance, motioning for me to do the same. Despite my skepticism, I did. Jack had never pushed when there was obviously something wrong with me. When my head hadn't been in the right place because of Vincent or the gang. So, I wouldn't either. At least not with my words.

With my fists? Oh absolutely. He was going to get it.

Before he could make a move against me, I ducked low and went for his left side. It was weaker, and I don't know if he even realized I had picked up on it.

His breath wheezed out of him as he whirled on me. Grinning, I darted out of the way of his swinging fist. A look of pride flashed across his face so quickly I almost missed it. But it made my heart swell, and I was more than ready for his counter. He threw a couple more weak attacks, and I deflected each one with ease.

Well, so much for not pulling punches anymore.

Scowling, I batted away his sorry attempts to land a hit. With a growl of my own, I tackled him. The fact he even allowed me to do it was more than enough proof of how distracted he was.

"What was that for?" he grumbled, a playful glare on his face as I sat on his stomach.

"You're not even here right now," I stated, tapping his forehead. "You'd never let me get away with this if you were focused."

His laughter reverberated through me. His tawny eyes warmed, and he reached up to push a strand of hair that had escaped my braid back behind my ear. Arching my brows at his change in demeanor, I didn't move as he let his hand slip down the side of my cheek. He used his knuckle to tap the underside of my chin, and the slight twinkle of mischief in his eyes was the only warning I had before he flipped us.

My breath *whooshed* out of me as Jack straddled my hips. I glared up at him.

"What?" he asked, laughter lacing his voice as he braced his hands on either side of my head.

"You tricked me."

"You always fall for it."

"Prick," I muttered, shoving at his shoulder.

"Always," he repeated. A shadow passed over his face, settling in his eyes. "Such a shame."

My brows furrowed. "What is?"

Jack didn't answer me. Instead, he shifted so that one of his hands was resting on my collarbone. The touch was gentle, familiar, yet something was off. I had *always* felt safe in this man's presence. But a prickling awareness was raising every hair on my body on end. I just couldn't put my finger on what was causing it.

Something was different, and as Jack's hand inched closer to my throat, a terrifying possibility occurred to me. Not even wanting to consider the errant thought, I bucked my hips in an attempt to throw him.

It did nothing.

Jack settled his full weight onto me, and I was already struggling to breathe. When his warm hand closed over my neck, I knew the unease was showing on my features.

"What's a shame, Jack?" I whispered, trying to catch his attention.

"That all this time," he murmured, brushing his thumb over my feathering pulse. His eyes met mine. And I saw it. I knew. Before he even finished his sentence, everything clicked. "I had the key to ending Vincent Monroe once and for all in my hands. I've had you under me like this *so* many times. Just a little extra pressure..." He trailed off, but his hand constricted. Panic flared as he cut off my airway, and my hands flew to his. "And it's all over. I'll have once again taken the only thing he cares about from him. Just like he did to me."

All of my training fled from my mind as I lost the ability to breathe.

Fighting off someone you care about, on any level, is a lot different from fighting off a stranger, Jack's words from that very first session floated back to me, if only to mock me.

If it had just been a random attack, I might have been able to keep my wits about me. But I couldn't think straight.

Because the man that I had spent months training with, the man that I trusted and considered a friend, was so much more than I thought.

He wasn't just Jack.

He was Jaxon Graham.

And I didn't know if I was going to leave this studio alive.

THIRTY-THREE

BREAKING POINT

"Jack," I gasped, my nails tearing into the skin on his hands, leaving red welts but not breaking his hold. "Stop, please."

His tawny eyes were bright as they met mine. Something like regret flickered there, and his strangle-hold relaxed. He still kept me pinned, still kept his hand on my throat, but I could breathe. Besides sucking in greedy gulps of air, I kept my body perfectly still. Jack was making no move to get off of me, and I needed to think. Which was hard to do when you couldn't even pull air into your lungs.

"I am sorry," he said. His voice was low, and he stroked his thumb down the column of my throat again. "This was never the plan."

"Then what *was* the plan?"

"You were never a part of it. I didn't even know you were with him until last night."

My eyes fell shut. I had assured Vincent that we had been careful enough the night before. We barely interacted the entire night. No one could have possibly thought that there was anything special about how Vincent acted around me.

But Jack knew *me*. He knew my tells better than almost anyone. *Shit.*

"What gave us away?"

"Vincent and his whole inner circle had an eye on you, but that wasn't surprising. Everyone takes care inside of Tuxedo because of Dante. It was you. The way you reacted to him pulling you across that bar."

Double shit.

"I know you, Jules. You'd never let anyone manhandle you like that. Not unless you knew them. Trusted them."

And damnit if he wasn't right.

When I opened my eyes again, Jack hadn't moved a muscle. My brain was in overdrive, trying to figure a way out of this. There were a lot of things I would do to ensure my survival, but begging wasn't one of them. That singular 'please' was the only one he was going to get out of me.

"So, what now?" I croaked, trying to clear the rasp in my voice. "What do you stand to gain here?"

"I'll admit I don't have much of a plan. I never expected to care about the same person Monroe did. Alana was easy. But you..." he trailed off again, his brows puckering as he pulled them together. "I don't know what to do with you."

The sound of her name on his lips made my blood spark. How *dare* he talk about her like she was nothing? Killing her had been *easy?* I was seething, but I had to reel it in. There might be something in that admission of how he felt about me I could use to my advantage.

"Vincent doesn't care about me," I told him. "It's just a fling."

"Jules," Jack said, leveling me with a skeptical look. "Don't lie to me. It won't do you any favors."

My teeth ground together as I fought against the urge to throw him again. He'd be expecting it. He was the one who had taught me damn near everything I knew.

Fuck, how was I going to get out of this?

"Fine," I muttered, rolling my eyes to the ceiling. "Just get it over with."

"I don't *want* to hurt you."

A laugh rasped out of my tender throat. "These bruises are going to tell a different story."

"I thought I could do it. Thought I could end it right here and now, but I can't." I felt him brush another strand of hair from my face, and I resisted the desire to bite him. It might surprise him, but I needed him down for long enough to get to my phone and get out of the gym.

It was funny to think how quickly one's feelings could change. Jack had always been someone who made me feel safe. Relaxed even. But now? He'd be lucky if I didn't gut him myself.

For Vincent.

For Alana.

For *me*.

Jack shifted, just a hairsbreadth to the right, but I went for it. Snapping my head forward, I caught him in the nose. His bellow fell on deaf ears as I twisted until I was on my stomach. When he lunged for me, I slammed my elbow back as hard as I could. I scored a direct hit to his ribs, and he tumbled off me. Heaving air into my lungs, I scrambled to my feet and made a dash for my phone.

I had my contacts open when I heard the lock to the studio snap into place.

Whipping my head up, my gaze zeroed in on Jack. His chest was rising and falling in time with his rapid breaths, and those tawny eyes were murderous. Blood was dripping off his chin as it ran from his nose.

I hoped I had broken it.

"What now?" I asked, spreading my arms wide as I pressed Lucas's name. *Please let him hear me.* "You've got me trapped. What now, *Jaxon?*"

A malicious grin twisted his face into something almost unrecognizable. "So, you know who I am."

"Of course I do," I spat.

"Pity."

"You're right," I said, dropping my arms and slipping my phone into my waistband at the small of my back. "It's a pity that you turned out to be such a snake."

His laughter set a shiver loose, one that wracked my frame straight down to my bones. "Me? Jules, he killed *my* father."

"Because your father was the one responsible for his parent's deaths."

"Revenge is such a funny thing," Jack said, moving closer For every step forward he took, I tried to sidestep. I knew he was trying to force me back. Trying to get me cornered, but if I could get him to circle me, I could make a break for it. "What would have happened if you met me first? Hmm?"

"What're you talking about?"

"Vincent and I have been dancing around each other for years. But what do you think would've happened if you had heard my side of the story first? We've both done despicable things. But he's the hero in your eyes because he was avenging his family. Thing is, so was I."

"Vincent didn't kill an innocent."

Jack shrugged. "Alana was collateral. That's what happens in wars."

That startled a laugh out of me.

"War?" I asked, raising my brows at him as I took another step to the right. "Your fight is with Vincent. But you're too much of a coward to go after him directly, so you target who you think will break him the most. First with Alana, and now with me. The difference between the two of you isn't that I heard his side first.

"If the situation was different," I continued, meeting his tawny eyes. "If I was someone you truly cared about, I would never be in any danger from Vincent. He would never stoop that low. He would *never* lay a hand on me to get to you. And that makes him the hero and the better man. *That* is why people respect him. Follow him. Because even when he has to make horrible decisions, he still makes sure there is the least amount of fallout possible. He's in control of the gang because he is the *only* one worthy of leading it."

That mouth is going to get you in trouble, Vincent's words from earlier echoed in my head.

Yeah, I sure fucking hoped so.

Jack's face twisted with barely contained rage as my words hit. And just like I had wanted him to, he lunged. Ducking low, I swiped his legs out from under him. As he stumbled, I whirled until I was behind him and kicked the back of his knees. He went down, and I didn't let my conscience catch up with me. I bolted for the door, already reaching to flip the lock as I crashed into it.

Heaving it open, I didn't bother to look behind me. I had seconds, at most, before Jack was back on his feet. My phone was slipping as I ran to the exit and I grabbed it, bringing it up to my ear.

"Lucas?" I gasped out when I saw our call was still connected.

"I'm here," he responded, his voice tight. I could hear an engine revving in the background. "Where are you?"

"Did you hear everything?" My arm stung as I barreled through the front door. It smacked against the outer wall as it flew open, and I heard the crack as glass splintered. Turning to the right, I pushed my legs towards the warehouse. Jack's gym was on the east side of Valarian, not the best of neighborhoods on a good day. With twilight slipping over the horizon, the streets were left damn near deserted.

"Yes." The word was strained. I had never heard the note of darkness I associated with the rest of the gang in Lucas's voice, but it was plain as day now. "Vincent is heading back, but I'm coming to get you. Tell me where you are, Jules."

"Fallon and Crestview," I wheezed, careening around the corner I had just mentioned. "Headed to–"

I screamed.

The sound was torn out of me when I was thrown off balance. My forehead cracked against the brick wall Jack pinned me to. Stars danced across my vision as the pain lanced through my skull. His chest rose and fell in deep, panting breaths against my back. He wrenched my arm behind me and pressed hard on my wrist until my phone slipped through my fingers. His heel came down on it within the next heartbeat, severing the only connection I had with Lucas.

Fuck.

"Where do you think you're going?"

"As far away from you as I could get," I spat. Blood was running down my face, warm and sticky. Blinking rapidly, I tried to keep it from getting in my eye, but it was a useless fight. Jack shifted behind me, and I reared my head back. It was immensely stupid of him to fall for that twice. White hot pain exploded through the back of my head. I was likely to have a concussion after this, but the *crunch* that was almost drowned out by Jack's cursing was worth it. His hold slipped, and I wrenched my arms free before slamming my foot down on his instep.

When he stumbled back, I whirled around so we were face to face.

From the crooked way his nose sat, and the fresh blood streaming out of it, I knew I had broken it this time.

Good.

"You'll pay for that," he seethed, but he made no move to grab me again.

My heart splintered a little as we stayed in our standoff. I didn't know the man that was standing before me. Those eyes that had once held such mirth, usually at my expense, were now cold. Frozen over like old pond water in the dead of winter. My brain couldn't reconcile the man two feet away from me from the one who had smiled up at me from the mat not twenty minutes prior. And for *what?*

It didn't matter.

Despite what Jack was to me before today, the fact was that he was still Jaxon Graham. And for so many reasons bigger than my feelings, he needed to be eliminated.

Why didn't I keep my gun in my gym bag?

"What's the matter, Jack?" I taunted. Cocking my head to the side, I widened my stance so that I'd be ready if he lunged for me again.

His sneer made my blood run cold. "We both know that if I get my hands on you again, it's over."

"Good thing you taught me how to evade someone bigger than me."

"Something I'm coming to regret."

"Let's not forget I've handed your ass to you on multiple occasions."

"I will say that it'll be a shame to lose such a promising student."

"You could just not be a complete psychopath, you know? That is an option."

His eyes sparked with amusement before he shook his head. "I really am going to miss you."

"Wish I could say the same."

He was ready for me when I moved, but I knew he would be. When he jumped to cut me off, I spun back in the opposite direction. He stumbled into the wall, and I threw my fist into his kidney as hard as I could. I just had to keep him occupied long enough for Lucas to get here. If he could fire off just one well-aimed bullet, this would all be over.

Tires squealed on the opposite end of the street. Jack's head whipped in that direction, and a snarl curled his lip. He looked at me, and I could see the conflict raging in his eyes. I knew I wasn't strong enough to hold him. And he did too.

"Until next time, Jules."

He turned tail and ran. Vanishing back in the direction we had come. My stance relaxed, and as the adrenaline slipped from my system, I felt the tears burn in the back of my eyes. The shakes set in. A sob tickled in the back of my throat. As the first cry heaved from my chest, my knees buckled, and I had to use the wall to keep myself upright.

How hadn't I seen it?

Was I really that oblivious? That gullible?

There was a voice calling my name, but it sounded like it was filtering through water. Tears ran in hot streams down my cheeks, and I finally let myself fall. My knees stung from the impact on the concrete, but the pain barely registered. I couldn't breathe.

"Juliette? C'mon, sugar. Look at me."

Warm hands cupped my cheeks, and when I could finally focus, I saw the worry swimming in Lucas's hazel eyes. Another sob escaped, and I threw my arms around his neck. He heaved a sigh of relief before his arms tightened around me. He held me there, in the middle of the sidewalk, as my tears slowly subsided. When I had nothing left but soft hiccups, I pulled back enough to meet his gaze. He searched my face, zeroing in on the cut above my eyebrow that was still leaking blood. Reaching up, he brushed off the worst of it. His callouses scraped across my cheek, but there was reassurance in his touch.

"Where is he?" I finally got out. There was no need for elaboration.

"He's on his way," Lucas said, his voice soft, as if he were speaking to a spooked animal. "Vincent's coming."

Vincent pushed the gas pedal as far as it could go, and the SUV still wasn't accelerating fast enough.

Not again. It couldn't happen again.

They had been so careful. And Vincent had stupidly convinced himself that she would be safe with him. That he and the gang could protect her from situations just like this one.

How had Graham found her? How had he even known she was the one that would wreck Vincent all over again?

It had dumbfounded Henry when Vincent left. He hadn't offered the older man much of an excuse either; just that an emergency had come up, and he needed to go. Henry, to his credit, read the murder on Vincent's face and hadn't pushed. The others had stayed to finish the meeting in his stead, but then they'd be right behind him.

Vincent's blood boiled as he let his mind wander to the worst scenarios. It had been incredibly stupid for him to have not made sure that Graham was dead the last time. And now Juliette was caught in the crossfire, the one thing he had been trying to avoid from the very beginning.

He should have known better.

His phone rang, and he nearly swerved off the road as he snatched it off the passenger seat. Lucas's name flashed on the screen, and he jabbed the answer button.

"Tell me you have her."

"I do," Lucas said, his voice subdued.

"Is she okay?"

"She's a little banged up. Looks like she put up one hell of a fight, but she seems to be alright."

"Let me talk to her," Vincent ordered, squeezing the phone even as a little of the tension in his body released.

"Not right now."

"Lucas."

"Vince, I know. But she's shaken really bad right now. She hasn't told me anything about the attack. She won't talk to me at all. It'll be better for you both if you just wait until you get here."

Vincent took a deep breath. Maybe he did need to get a handle on his emotions before he spoke to her. And he knew Lucas would never lie to him, not about this. If he said she was okay, then she was. But Vincent would still feel better once he could see it with his own eyes.

"I'm ten minutes out."

"We'll see you soon."

Thirty-Four

PREPARATIONS

"Where is she?"

Vincent's voice boomed through the warehouse, and I glanced up from where I was sitting at his desk. Lucas had wrapped me in a blanket when we first got back. The shaking had subsided a while ago, yet the cold hadn't left. But when Vincent barged into the room, his forest eyes locking on mine, warmth finally trickled into my chest again.

"Hi," I murmured.

His chest heaved as his gaze roamed. Assessing the damage. I watched as that muscle in his jaw ticked. His focus zeroed in on the cut above my eye, and the bruises that I knew ringed my throat. His fists clenched and then unclenched. Over and over.

"Vincent," I said, rolling the chair back from the desk. "Come here."

He was across the room in three long strides. He stopped before me, sinking to his knees so that we were eye to eye. His hands cupped my face, thumbs brushing over my cheekbones with a heart-stopping tenderness. There was a still a lingering panic in his eyes as they continued to run over me.

"Lucas said you wouldn't even talk to him," he whispered, his brows pulling together.

"I couldn't."

"Are you okay?" I shook my head. "Aside from what I can see, did he hurt you?" I shook my head again, knowing what he was truly getting at. Some of the tension fell from his shoulders, and he laid his forehead against mine. "How did he find you, princess?"

My own eyes slipped closed, and I took a deep breath. Letting it out slowly, I braced myself for the conversation to come.

"Jaxon is Jack, my trainer."

There was a beat of silence. Two. And I could feel the pressure in the room change.

When my eyes fluttered open, I was looking into the same harsh gaze I had met in this room on that very first night. Murderous, unchecked rage was waltzing across Vincent's face, making that muscle in his jaw feather with a vengeance. But when he slipped his hands from my face to take my own in his grip, it was with a care only he possessed. How this man always kept that boiling anger wholly separate from me, I'd never know. But I would always appreciate it.

"Tell me everything," he breathed.

And so I did.

From the moment I first met Jack, to every training session, to running into him at the club, all the way down to how everything had devolved so quickly today. Tears pricked the backs of my eyes again, and I fought them back. Jack didn't deserve another ounce of my emotion, let alone my tears.

"He knew I was seeing someone, and he knew it was someone I had initially considered a threat. When he saw you tell me to leave, I guess everything fell into place. But only because of what he knew about me. I'm so sorry."

"Don't be sorry," he said. "Not for a moment. We were expecting someone whose eyes would be on me, not you."

"Still, how could I not have seen it?"

"Because you weren't looking for it," he reminded me, tipping my chin up. "You said it yourself. He was lying low. The last thing any of us would have expected would be for him to be running a legitimate business."

He was right, and I needed to accept it. But damn if it didn't hurt.

"What now?" I asked, injecting a little steel into my voice even as I leaned into Vincent's touch. I wasn't above borrowing from his strength when I needed it.

"Now we find him. He won't go back to the gym. Unfortunately, he's not that stupid. We'll make rounds to his old contacts, see if anyone's been spotted with him."

"Sebastian. That's who he was with at the club that night." That muscle in his jaw ticked again. "You know him?"

"Sebastian Rathbone is the one who carried out the hit on Alana."

My stomach rolled.

"I'm going to be sick," I told him, dashing from the room as fast as my unsteady legs could carry me. Knowing I couldn't reach his apartment, I made a beeline for the front doors. I was barely around the side of the warehouse before I lost the fight. Doubling over, I emptied my stomach.

Vincent was beside me within seconds. He smoothed a hand over my back, keeping my braid behind my shoulders. When I had nothing left to heave up, I stumbled to the side and leaned against the wall. Without a word, Vincent pressed a bottle of water into my hands. I unscrewed the cap and took a swig to rinse my mouth. After clearing the acidic taste, I took a few hesitant sips. The last thing I needed was to shock my system into puking again.

He pulled me into him, tucking my head underneath his chin as he stroked his hands down my arms. I hadn't even realized how cold I was.

"He was hitting on Devyn that night," I explained after I had found my voice again. "If they hadn't mentioned the Black Lantern, she might have gone home with him."

"But she didn't. She's safe and has people to look after her."

"Jack knows she's important to me." My eyes met his, and I knew he understood even before I continued. "He could go after her."

"We'll make the men aware. I'm sure Brandon will stay with her."

My lips twitched into my first smile in what felt like days. "Arkin too?"

"Maybe."

"And what about you?"

"What about me?"

"What are *you* going to be doing?"

"I'm still going to be figuring out everything with this deal." My eyebrows raised. Glancing down, his eyes settled on my throat. He raised his hand and brushed his fingertips over my skin. Even that soft touch made me flinch. I hadn't had the chance to look in a mirror since we got back, but judging from the look on Vincent's face, the bruises were every bit as bad as I thought they were.

"That it?" I teased. I could admit that he was rubbing off on me. If he had a plan for Jack, I wanted to know it.

"When I find him," he said, his voice going dark. "I'm going to take him apart piece by piece. He could've hit the warehouse. He could've come after me directly. He could've taken this damn gang back for all I care. But he came after you. He laid his hands on *you*. And for that?" His eyes met mine, and a shiver of fear I hadn't felt in his presence for quite some time slithered down my spine. "For that, he'll pay with his life. And this time I won't stop until I watch the light fade from his eyes for myself."

"Do you really think I'm going to complain about this situation?"

"Devyn," I muttered, examining the dark purple fingerprints on my neck in the bathroom mirror. "Please take this seriously. You could be in danger."

"Girl, *you* need to be more worried. I don't know how you always attract this level of crazy into your life, but it's getting a little out of hand."

Tell me about it.

"I know. For now, I'm staying with Vincent. I just wanted to make sure you keep an eye out. I can't stand the thought of anything happening to you. Least of all because of me."

I could almost feel her roll her eyes through the phone. But when she spoke again, her voice was softer. "Are you really okay? I know how much Jack has grown to mean to you."

"I feel so betrayed," I admitted, scowling at my reflection. Brandon had looked me over a few hours ago and promised me the cut above my eye wouldn't need stitches, but there wasn't much to be done about the bruising. And then he promptly ran away. Coward.

"As you should. That guy's a piece of shit and if I ever see him again-"

"Get in line," Vincent said, raising his voice to be heard as he leaned against the doorway to the bedroom.

"Am I on speaker?"

"Yes."

"Listen here, banger," Devyn started, raising her voice despite what I had just said. "This is *your* fault that she's in this mess. And so help me if she gets one more injury, I'm going to string you up by your intestines."

"Why me?" I huffed, letting my eyes roll skyward.

"Because I love you, that's why," Devyn replied. "But, I've got to go. Brandon just knocked on the door."

"Is he alone?"

"We'll get coffee and compare notes soon," she promised before hanging up.

"Compare notes?"

The question made me drop my head so that I could meet Vincent's gaze in the mirror. His eyes were sparkling, and I let a smile slip onto my face as well. Turning to face him, I moved into the arms he was holding open for me. His heat seeped into my skin, staving off the chill. He tightened his arms around me before placing a kiss on the top of my head.

"Thanks for letting me use your phone."

He chuckled, squeezing me tighter. "We'll get you a new one soon."

When I pulled back from him, I caught him glancing at the cut and bruises again. I lifted my hands, taking his face between them. His stubble was thicker than he usually let it get. It scratched at my palms as I forced his eyes to meet mine.

"Stop," I murmured.

"Stop what?" he asked. He placed one of his hands over mine, holding it still as he turned to place a kiss on my wrist.

"Blaming yourself."

"I'll try," he said, entwining our fingers. He dragged me to the bed. But the look on his face was soft, anxious.

"What're you thinking?"

"You're not going to like it."

We sat cross-legged across from each other. He bit his lower lip, and I started to worry. "Vincent?"

"You need to lie low for a while."

"Okay?" I said, my confusion making it come out like a question. "I thought that was a given."

"Juliette. That means staying away from places Graham knows to look for you."

"I'm staying here, aren't I?"

"Work, princess. You have to take a break from Tuxedo."

"Excuse me?"

"There it is," he muttered. He ran a hand over his face, a light groan breaking free. "Graham knows you work there. He knows you close a lot. It's the perfect opportunity for him to corner you."

"*How?*" My voice was threatening to go squeaky, so I cleared my throat. "Please tell me how he's going to get to me with you, the guys, and Dante around."

"It's a bar. And you have a knack for getting yourself into trouble." I opened my mouth to defend myself, but he cut me off. "What're you going to do? Work with that cut? Those bruises? You think you'll make it ten minutes into a shift without someone asking about them? And then what're you going to say?"

My blood was a roiling, seething thing in my veins.

Never mind the fact that he was right.

"You can't ask me to quit my job. I still have bills to pay, whether or not I'm living in my apartment."

"I'm not," he soothed, reaching forward to take my balled fists in his hands. "I would never. That place is a second home to you, and I know that. I'm just asking you to take a leave of absence until he's dead. If you need help financially in the meantime, I've got you."

Taking a few deep breaths, I tried to cool my anger. On a rational level, I knew he was right. The smartest thing to do would be for me to take a step back from everything Jack would be expecting. But the bar was important to me. How long would I have to give it up? Days? Weeks? Months? The thought made me sick.

"We have to find him," I grumbled, trying not to pout as I glanced back up at him.

"We will. I promise."

"Are you telling Dante why I have to bail on my shifts?"

Vincent winced. If I didn't know any better, I would think that it was genuine fear that locked up his spine. "I'll go with you to break the news."

"Oh. So, I'm allowed to go in to tell my boss I need a hiatus, but I can't work?" That muscle in his jaw ticked once. "Just trying to iron out the details of my captivity."

"Princess," he drawled, his eyes darkening as they zeroed in on my mouth. "Watch it."

"Or else what?"

He let me see one of those full-blown smiles for all of three seconds before he pounced. And then he showed me *exactly* what else I needed to be watching out for.

THIRTY-FIVE

FACE THE MUSIC

"Monroe, get out of this building. Right now."

A grimace crossed over Vincent's face as he faced down a mother hen with ruffled feathers.

"Dante, shut up," I said, glaring at him as I snagged Vincent's hand.

His brown eyes snapped to mine, narrowing before he placed his hands on his hips. "Are you serious right now?"

"Yes."

"Jules, have you looked in a mirror?"

"Yes, which is why I need a few days off."

"A few *days*?" Dante sputtered, blinking at me like I had lost my head. Which maybe I had. "That is going to take weeks to heal."

"Then I need a few weeks off."

Dante held up a hand, rubbing the other across his forehead. My guess was he was about five minutes away from an aneurysm. And not about to take the next bit very well.

"And you'll need to keep an eye on Devyn, too."

If looks could kill, my new home would've been at the bottom of the ocean. Dante looked like he wanted to wring my neck himself, and probably would have if someone else hadn't already beaten him to it. His eyes traveled to the woman in question, and she just waved her fried pickle at him before refocusing on her phone.

"How did *you* get caught up in this?" Dante asked her, speaking through his teeth.

"Flirted with the wrong guy."

My eyes widened, and I bit my lip to keep from laughing.

There was a vein in Dante's forehead that suddenly became very pronounced. His head turned slowly to stare at Vincent. Before my eyes, I watched Dante harden into a version of himself I had never seen. And somehow, I knew I wasn't looking at just my boss anymore. The man in front of us was the gang member who had thrown in the towel over a decade ago. His jaw worked a few times before he spoke.

"You've now put two women that I deeply care about in the line of fire. Do you realize that?"

"Yes," Vincent replied, squeezing my hand. "I'm taking every precaution to make sure nothing else happens to them."

"*Else*," Dante hissed, his eyes narrowing to slits. "If either of them had any sense, they never would have been involved with you in the first place."

"Hey!" Devyn and I chorused, identical expressions of outrage on our faces.

"Be quiet."

Devyn flipped him off, and I crossed my arms over my chest. "Dante, I love you, but we're going to be fine."

"Oh, that I don't doubt. Because I'm going to be coming out of retirement."

I felt more than saw Vincent's reaction. His entire body went rigid, and I twisted to glance at him. There was a look of controlled awe on his face as Dante extended a hand to him.

"Are you sure?" Vincent asked, his voice turning frigid as he met Dante's glare. "It's going to be hard taking orders when you're used to being the one in charge."

"I don't want to lead again, but I'm not sitting on the sidelines while these two are in danger."

What?

I had known that Dante had been in a gang. Had known that he still had enough respect in this city for the gangs to keep themselves on their best behavior when they were in the bar. But that was because he had been a *leader*? As in one of the rival gangs? No wonder he knew so much about Vincent and his ascension within the gang.

It was brilliant, really. The best way to keep this place safe was to still keep tabs on what was happening outside the walls of Tuxedo. To have dirt on every player on the board.

Oh, Dante and I were going to have a *talk*.

The men shook hands, and Devyn and I exchanged skeptical glances across the room. Before any of us could say anything, Ember stumbled into the back with two racks of glasses in her arms.

"Oh, shit," she said when she saw all of us. Her sage green eyes were wide as she took in the tension rippling through the air. She eased the racks onto the counter next to the sink before holding her hands up in front of her. "I'm just gonna..." she trailed off, hooking her thumb over her shoulder.

Her eyes met mine, and I nodded at the door behind her. She shot me a quick grin before spinning on her heel and darting back out into the club.

"I like her," Devyn said once the silence had stretched on too long.

"Don't corrupt her too," Dante grumbled, brushing past us to disappear into his office. He slammed the door behind him.

"Well," I said, huffing out a laugh. "That went better than expected."

"Maybe for you," Vincent replied, his eyes boring holes into the closed door to the office.

"C'mon. Let's go home."

"Gross."

"Shut it, Dev."

Her sparkling cackle followed us as we headed out the back door.

The ride back to the warehouse was silent, but Vincent kept my hand in his the whole way. It was startling how much I relied on his strength. How often I pulled from it. But I knew that there would come a time when it would be his turn to lean on me, and I would be more than willing to weather that storm with him.

When we pulled into the parking lot, Vincent killed the engine. His thumb stroked lazy circles across the back of my hand, but he made no move to get out of the car. His head fell back against the headrest and he blankly stared skyward.

"What's going through that head of yours?" I asked, keeping my voice soft.

A smile twitched the edges of his mouth as he rolled his head so he could meet my eyes. Dusk was falling, and the lack of light made his green eyes even darker than normal.

"I really have put you in a lot of danger."

"Stop right there."

"What?"

"We both know that I knew exactly what I was getting into. Not to mention, I found Jack all by myself. Before anything between the two of us even *was* anything. Sure, maybe if we would've kept our distance, nothing would've happened with Jack. But you also may not have found him until it was too late. Until he'd already made his move against you."

"I love you, you know that?"

"I do, you big sap. Now let's go inside. I have my own third degree to dole out."

A dark chuckle fell from his lips as we exited the car. Besides the five minutes Brandon had taken to look me over the night before, I hadn't seen him since finding out about him and Devyn. And Arkin had been suspiciously absent from the warehouse as well. But I knew they were supposed to be here now. And it was about time the boys and I had a heart to heart.

Or fist to nose if Brandon pushed my buttons tonight.

The light in the warehouse blinded me as usual when we stepped through. But for the first time, the weight of the eyes that fell on us didn't unnerve me. I scanned the room with my chin held high. Angelica was stretched out on a couch, and the only other person in the room I recognized was Lucas. He had sprawled out in an armchair in front of the TV, Dexter curled up on his chest.

My eyes nearly rolled to the back of my head.

Dexter was over one-hundred pounds, and he was lying on Lucas like a chihuahua. That spoiled dog had better not get the same idea with me. I wasn't built like that.

When another scan of the room came up empty, I curled my lip. Vincent dropped my hand as I marched over to his blonde second. The closer I got, the more I could hear the soft snores escaping him. When I was standing directly beside him, I almost felt bad for what I was about to do.

Almost.

"Lucas," I said, deciding to at least start off with a softer approach. There was a hitch in his snoring, like he had heard me, but not enough to rouse him from sleep. Sighing, I reached out and nudged his shoulder a few times. Dexter woke up, his eyes lighting when he spotted me. "Down, Dex."

Dexter chuffed, but got up all the same. To my utter delight, he stepped right on Lucas's junk as he jumped down. The man in question groaned in pain, cupping himself as he jerked into a sitting position. I stepped back to give him enough room to recover.

"Hey, sugar," he said, forcing a smile before wincing again.

"That's what you get. No matter what he thinks, he's not a lapdog."

"Is there a reason you woke me up?"

My hands found a place on my hips as I dipped down to meet his eyes. "Where are the other two?"

"Brandon's in his apartment. Arkin's probably around." His eyes were dancing with mischief, and I figured he was already feeling better.

"Need some ice for that?" I quipped as I headed for the stairs.

"Only if you're the one icing – *ow!*"

Whatever vulgar thing had been about to come out of Lucas's mouth was cut off by the resounding *thwack* that echoed through the room. Laughter erupted from the others, and I didn't need to turn around to know that Vincent had smacked Lucas upside the head. The thought brought a smile to my face.

When I emerged onto the floor with the apartments, I made a beeline for Brandon's door. For a moment, I just tapped my foot outside. Blowing a few tendrils of hair out of my face, I raised my hand and knocked.

"I'm not here."

"Open the damn door," I said, fighting not to laugh.

Brandon cracked it open just enough to peer down at me with one eye. My eyebrows raised. "What do you want?" he asked.

"For you to stop acting like a chickenshit, first of all."

"Fine." A laugh fell from his mouth as he swung the door open, motioning me inside. I glanced over my shoulder but couldn't see Vincent.

Guess I was on my own.

When I faced Brandon again, I realized he was shirtless. He had black sweats on, but that was it. Letting my eyes roll, I slipped past him into the apartment. Another laugh escaped him when he shut the door behind us. He gently knocked his shoulder against mine when he walked past me, and I followed him into the living room.

He pointed to the black leather couch and continued on into the kitchen that I could see through the window cut-out in the dividing wall.

"Get your buddy over here, too," I called, flopping down onto the couch. The jarring movement caused me to wince. It was easy to forget that I was pretty banged up.

"He's coming. I text him as soon as you knocked."

"So, it's true then?" I asked. He rounded the wall back into the living room with two steaming mugs in his hand. When he handed one to me, the smell of caramel wafted into my nose. My eyes narrowed on him as I took a hesitant sip. It was my favorite creamer, and he made the coffee exactly how I liked it. Brandon sat on the loveseat across the coffee table from me. "Are you trying to soften me up?"

"Lucas said it might help you not kill me."

"I'm not going to kill you," I muttered, a little exasperated.

Brandon's wry grin curved his lips, blue eyes glittering as his door opened. Arkin walked in, gray t-shirt and jeans pristine. He gave me a small smile before coming over and sitting beside me. At least he wasn't acting like I had the plague. He slipped an arm around my shoulders and pulled me in for a quick side-hug. Warmth bloomed in my chest at the small gesture. I had forgotten how calming his presence was.

"Hey, Jules. How're you feeling?" he asked, leaning back into the cushions.

"Like I got ran over by a truck."

They both laughed. "You've looked better," Brandon said.

"I will throw this coffee on you."

He sniggered, taking a sip of his own. Glancing at Arkin, he jutted his chin towards the kitchen. "There's nearly a full pot in there, if you want any."

Arkin just shook his head. And then they both looked at me expectantly.

Wanting to keep them in suspense for just a little longer, I took a long drink. This was going to be their punishment for avoiding me all day.

"Well?" Brandon finally prompted, arching his brows at me.

"Back to my original question. Is it true? Both of you?" They nodded, looking like they were waiting for a bomb to go off. "Are either, or both, of you serious about her?" Brandon raised his hand. My eyes moved to Arkin, and he scratched the back of his neck. When his baby blues found mine, he shook his head. "You don't have to tell me anything you're not comfortable with but... explain."

"Brandon and I have had threesomes before, just like we did with Devyn. But it was more of them sharing me than anything else," Arkin told me, his ears tingeing pink.

"Does she know this?"

"Yes," they chorused.

My brows rose, and Brandon continued, "I like Devyn. A lot. Bringing Arkin in was a mutual decision. Something we'd be down to do again, but I'm the one who wants to be with her."

"Okay," I said. Taking another drink, I leaned back into the cushions and let my head tip back.

"Okay?"

"Brandon, I don't know why you were so scared to tell me. Sure, she's my best friend, but she's also a grown woman. If you do anything to hurt her, there won't be anything left of you for me to even think about punishing."

There was a beat of silence before both boys busted out laughing. My smile overtook my face as I lifted my head to look at them. Brandon lunged for me, and I barely had time to set my mug on the table before he was heaving me off the couch into a bear-hug. My lungs constricted, but I hugged him back with everything I had. When he set me down again, he kept his hands on my shoulders. For a moment, we just stared at each other with dopey grins on our faces.

"Please don't be making a move on my girl. That would be a *very* stupid decision."

Vincent's voice made me jump, and I spun to see him standing in the doorway. His arms were crossed, legs spread shoulder-width apart. If it wasn't for the blinding smile on his lips, I might have taken him seriously.

"Don't worry, Vince," Brandon said, letting his hands fall as he stepped back. "She's all yours."

Forest eyes met mine across the apartment. His grin turned a little wicked before he purred, "Damned straight."

Thirty-Six

And the Hits Keep Coming

"I'm *bored*, Dev."

"It's been two weeks," she said around a mouthful of food. My nose wrinkled, and she rolled her eyes at me. "You'll be fine."

"I literally laze around the warehouse all day. Either in the apartment or down on the main floor with everyone else. But there's not much else I can do, and I'm getting impatient."

"Is he hiding anything from you?"

"Vincent? No," I grumbled, stabbing my salad with slightly more aggression than was probably necessary. "I've sat in on every meeting. I know the ins-and-outs of this deal they've got going with Weasel-Face—"

"Henry," Brandon corrected, raising his head from his phone to give me a mocking smile.

"Whatever. He looks like a damn weasel, and you all will never convince me otherwise. That slicked back hair isn't doing him any favors."

"He seems to like you," he said. Devyn shot him a dirty look, nudging his shoulder with hers. "What?"

"That man would like anything on two legs if it smiled at him for over five seconds," I retorted. Henry Kline was old Valarian money and fed Vincent a wealth of information about his predecessors, as well as the other leaders in the city, but he made my skin crawl.

"Jules," Devyn sighed, drawing my attention back to her. There was laughter dancing in her brown eyes. "What do you want them to do? We've all kept an eye out for Jack, and we're coming up empty."

"It's like he vanished into thin air," Brandon added.

I scowled at the pair. When Devyn had suggested we get lunch, I had almost forgotten that we'd need a security team with us. Vincent hadn't looked happy with the idea, but it was no secret how stir crazy I was getting. Since he couldn't come with us, we brought Brandon and a team of four that had stayed outside of the restaurant. The four extras were people I had grown more comfortable with since staying with Vincent, led by none other than a familiar redhead.

Glancing through the window, I could just make out Angelica's head of burgundy hair on one of the benches outside. She had sprawled out, taking up as much room as possible. As if she could feel my gaze, her head popped up. She gave me a two-finger salute with a sassy little smile before dropping her head back so the sun could touch her face again.

Devyn followed my line of sight until her eyes found Angelica as well. "Don't *any* of you gang bangers know how to be discreet?"

A laugh burst out of me at the look of sheer bewilderment on Brandon's face. "She has a point," I said, trying to hide my grin behind my hand.

"Angel is just sitting on a bench. She could be anyone."

"Tell that to the gun in her waistband," Devyn mumbled.

"She's one of the best marksmen they've got," I told her. "If anyone can blow Jack's brains out before we even know he's here, it's her."

"Sounds like my kind of woman."

"I bet if you ask her really nice, she'll even teach you how to shoot," I teased.

That made her light up. "You think?"

"Please don't," Brandon groaned.

"Why not?"

"Nothing gets Angel hotter than talking about guns. I dodged a bullet with Arkin. I don't want to share you with anyone else."

I smothered another smile as Devyn's cheeks tinted pink. Brandon being assigned to watch over Devyn had forced them into close proximity, something that I had worried about. Devyn tended to get bored quickly when she spent too much time with any one person. But after two weeks of Brandon crashing at her place most nights, she still went a little doe-eyed whenever he walked into a room.

Was that what I looked like when Vincent was around? No wonder she was always gagging.

Speaking of the devil, my new phone vibrated in my pocket.

How is everything?

We're fine, I wrote back.

Come home soon.

Sir, yes, sir.

The bubbles showing he was typing popped up, went away, and then popped up again. I had to bite back my smile when his reply finally came through.

I miss you. I'll show you how much once you get here.

"What'd he say?" Devyn asked, leaning across the table to get a peek at my screen.

I locked it and stuffed it back into my pocket before she got the chance. "None of your business."

"Well, from the look on your face, I have a pretty good guess. So, I guess that means it's time to get you back."

We paid for our tab and headed out the front doors. When Angelica spotted us, she stretched her arms over her head. Her back arched, making her look like a cat rousing from a nap in the sun. She was just as lithe as one as she stood and made her way over to us. Her eyes were a deep sapphire, slightly upturned at the outer corner in a way that made her seem like she was perpetually laughing at you. And judging from every interaction I had with her, she usually was.

"Did you bring me anything?" she chirped, coming to a halt beside us. She was taller than me, which wasn't surprising. But even with her attitude, she had never once made me feel like she was talking down to me. Even in meetings. There were times she caught my confusion before Vincent did, and she'd explain whatever had tripped me up. It was one reason I had agreed to have her head the team that would go with us. That, and Vincent's seemingly unfaltering faith in her.

"They were all out of every single thing you like, sorry," Brandon said, wrapping an arm around Devyn's shoulders.

Angelica pouted, and I shook my head before pulling out the coffee I had been hiding. Her entire face lit up as she bounced on the balls of her feet. When I handed it to her, she all but snatched it from me.

"Be careful," I scolded, catching her wrist before she could raise it to her lips. "It's hot."

"Yes, Mom," she muttered, gently taking the lid off to blow on it.

Devyn let her eyes bounce back and forth between the two of us. When her eyes settled on me, she arched her pierced brow., and I took the hint. "Angel, this is Devyn. Devyn, this is Angel."

Angelica let a crooked grin overtake her face as she extended her hand for Devyn to shake. "Hi! Sorry, I should probably have introduced myself."

"It's nice to meet you," Devyn said, taking her hand.

"It's just nice to have another girl to break up the testosterone."

"Hey."

Angelica's eyes trailed to where Brandon had his arm draped around Devyn, and a coy smirk played at the edges of her lips. "No offense, of course."

"I hate you. I hope you know that," Brandon told her, eyes narrowing.

"Be nice," I said, turning on my heel to head for the SUV we had borrowed for the excursion. "I don't want to listen to you two bickering like siblings all day."

Those two were cut from the same cloth, and they hated it.

They scoffed in unison, which caused Devyn and me to burst into a laughing fit. Angelica sped up, so that she was walking at my side, and she linked her arm through mine. She escorted me back to the SUV before opening the door for me. With a grin to rue the Cheshire cat, she gave me a mockingly deep bow.

"After you," she teased. A playful huff escaped me as I made to step up into the SUV.

Before I could manage it, Angelica's coffee hit the ground.

In the next instant, her hands met my chest, and she shoved me. Hard.

Off balance from being halfway into the car, I stumbled back a few feet.

"What the hell?" Devyn asked, leaping forward to grab my arm. I don't know what unspoken communication went on between Brandon and Angelica, but before Devyn could reach me, Brandon was yanking her back. Angelica dove after me, catching me around the waist. My breath flew from my lungs when she landed on top of me.

And then the car exploded.

The screams of the people around us were lost in the sound of metal shrieking and glass breaking. My ears were ringing, and I was pretty sure I could feel blood pooling beneath my head. Whether it was Angelica's or mine, I couldn't be sure. All I knew was that she wasn't moving.

"Angel?" I said, coughing as the heat scorched my lungs. We needed to *go*. "Angel, c'mon."

For just a moment, I couldn't tell if she was breathing. But then she coughed, a deep groan heaving from her as she shoved herself up. There was glass in her hair, and a cut leaking blood across her forehead. Her eyes were a little unfocused as she blinked down at me. But she shook her head, and when she met my gaze, the fog was gone.

"Can you move?" she asked.

"Not with you on top of me."

Despite the current state of events, a coy smirk tilted her lips. She got to her feet and grabbed my hand before hoisting me up as well. "Remind me to tell Vincent that I had his girl underneath me. It'll haunt him for weeks."

"Angel, can you not do this right now?" Brandon chimed in, sounding exasperated as he made it to us. Devyn was with him. Her eyes were so wide I could see the whites all the way around her irises.

"We've got to get them out of here," Angelica urged.

"No, wait," I said, raising my hand to silence them as my eyes scanned the surrounding pandemonium.

There.

On the opposite side of the square, a flash of bronze hair and tawny eyes. There was an unreadable expression on his face as our gazes met.

Jack.

"Motherfucker," I hissed, already running.

"Jules!" three voices chorused behind me.

They could catch up.

The back of my head was throbbing, and every muscle in my body was screaming at me to stop. But I pushed my legs harder. He had to have eyes on us. I hadn't left the warehouse in two weeks, and he just *happened* to find us and plant a bomb on the car? Without any of the others seeing him? There was no way. He had to have someone on the inside.

There was also no way I was going to catch him. He was blocks ahead of me, weaving in and out of people with ease. But every once in a while, he'd stop just long enough to glance over his shoulder. He was taunting me, and we both knew it. He came to an abrupt stop, turning far enough to give me a grin before ducking into an alley.

I slowed my pace. He wouldn't trap me again. And I was in no shape to fight him, either. Everything was still a little hazy, and I could barely hear anything out of my right ear. Bracing my hands on my knees, I reached into my pocket and pulled out my phone.

It was already ringing.

"Vincent," I breathed once the call connected.

"For god's sake, Juliette," he snarled, and I could almost hear the phone cracking over the white-knuckle grip I was sure he had it in. "What were you *thinking?*"

"Which part?"

"All of it. You just about died, and you went after him?"

"He headed to the East side. Have we checked there?"

I was panting for breath, and people were giving me a wide berth. Moving my stiff limbs, I leaned against the wall nearest to me. I couldn't imagine the picture I painted. Lingering bruises still ringed my neck, and now add in the aftermath of a car bomb and I was sure I was quite the sight.

Vincent was silent on the other end, but I could hear the car crank over.

"We searched everywhere, but we didn't look too hard on the East side because we figured he'd be avoiding the gym altogether. We can double check it. Can you still see him?"

"No."

"Jules!" Brandon skidded to a stop in front of me.

I just pointed in the direction Jack had gone. "Down the third alley," I told him.

"Are you okay?"

"Fine. Where are the girls?"

"I sent them back with one of the other guys. Devyn will stay with Angel until I can look her over. Now, for real, are you okay?"

"For now. Just go." He hesitated. His eyes volleyed between mine and the phone in my hand. Vincent had gone suspiciously quiet on the other end, but I could still hear the engine. My lip curled as Brandon's gaze snagged on mine. "That is an order, Brandon. Find him."

Just like the night of the party, he squared his shoulders and gave me a sharp nod. "Stay here," he threw over his shoulder as he broke into another run.

"Stay here," I mocked, leaning my head back against the wall behind me.

Everything hurt.

But my heart beat out a little stutter-step in my chest as a dark chuckle sounded down the line. "Did you enjoy that?" Vincent asked.

"Maybe a little."

"Don't get used to it."

"What was that you told me once?" I teased, wincing as a surge of pain lanced through my head. When I touched the spot that was radiating bursts of pain like electric shocks, my fingers came away red.

Great.

"You're going to have to be more specific, princess."

"Something about me not outranking you."

"You still don't." I harrumphed as I let my head fall back again. "You're just on the same level now."

A smile twisted my lips.

"Are you okay, miss?" a soft voice asked from somewhere to my left.

"I'm fine," I replied, moving the phone away from my mouth as I shifted to look at the woman beside me. She was around my age, and there was sheer worry shining in her blue eyes. Smiling, I shook my phone a little to draw her attention. "Help is on the way."

"Jules?"

The familiar voice made every ounce of color drain from my face. My attention shifted to the man coming up behind her, and if I could've melted into the brick behind me, I would have. A myriad of emotions played over Chris's features as he raked his eyes over me. The woman with him could have been his twin. She had the same aristocratic features, the same blonde hair, the same blue eyes. Eyes that were bouncing back and forth between us in rapid beats.

"Carrigan, why don't you go ahead and grab us a table?" Chris asked, not breaking our stare-off.

"Okay," she said, her gaze finally landing on me. As she passed me, she reached out and brushed my shoulder. The touch was light and probably meant to be comforting. Then she vanished into the door of the building I was leaning against.

Shit.

"Princess?" Vincent said in my ear.

"I'll see you in a bit," I told him, ending the call. I sent him my location before stuffing the device in my back pocket.

Chris looked like he had just stepped out of the courtroom. His suit was immaculate. Not a hair out of place.

God, how long had it been since I'd last seen him at Tuxedo? Not since before the party. That was for sure. My teeth caught my bottom lip. Of all the times for me to run into the lawyer, it was *now*? I could still see the smoke from the explosion in the distance. Could hear the sirens racing to the scene.

Double shit.

THIRTY-SEVEN

WAITING GAME

"*What* happened?" Chris asked, his voice low as he moved closer to me. He herded me off to the side. Out of the way of prying eyes, I realized as we rounded the corner into the closest alley. "Where have you been?"

"Would you believe me if I said I took a vacation?"

"Maybe if you didn't look like you went one too many rounds with an MMA fighter."

"Well, thanks."

He blinked at me. Once. Twice. Then he ran a hand through his hair, destroying the calm composure he had been keeping. His eyes snagged on that billowing smoke in the distance, and then they ran over me again. They cataloged the bruising, the cuts, the ash I was sure smudged my face and clothes. He blew out a breath, letting his head fall back.

"He's dragged you into it, hasn't he?"

My hackles rose, and I fought not to glare at him. "I actually got myself into this mess, thank you."

"I don't doubt it," he muttered, a smirk toying with his mouth as he dropped his head to look at me again. "Do you need my help?"

"I haven't been arrested yet, so no."

"So, the bombing that just happened in the square?"

"Are *you* a cop now?"

"No," he huffed. "But if you need legal representation, you know you can come to me, right?"

"Chris," I sighed. I opened my mouth to continue, but at that moment, a familiar SUV rolled to a stop at the mouth of the alley. Thankfully, it wasn't Vincent's Escalade we had taken today.

Vincent let the engine idle as he swung himself out of the vehicle. His forest eyes landed on Chris, and I watched the mask snap into place. His gaze was sharper, that muscle in his jaw ticking as he stalked towards us. Chris gave Vincent a nod of acknowledgement before returning his attention to me. Under the scrutiny of both men, I forced myself to straighten my spine and raise my chin. I'd be damned if I looked weak in front of them.

Although the minute Vincent's arm wrapped around my waist, I melted into him. He tipped my face up, his thumb running over my bottom lip. His eyes softened the tiniest bit, and he pressed a kiss to my forehead. By the time he faced Chris again, there wasn't an ounce of tenderness left in his expression.

"Monroe," Chris grunted, narrowing his eyes.

"Kenton," Vincent replied.

"So, you two *do* know each other." They both looked at me, brows raised. "What?"

The blonde huffed out a laugh and shook his head at me. "What have you two gotten into?" he asked.

"Nothing that you should concern yourself with," Vincent said, his voice hard and unyielding. I elbowed him in the ribs. His eyes flicked to me. He took one look at my face and rolled them.

"I can understand that." Chris pulled out his wallet. He selected a crisp white card and handed it to us. I took it, glancing at his name printed in shiny blue letters underneath *Kenton & Hutch Law Offices.* His number was there too. "I've told Jules this before, but if you both ever get to where you need my brand of help, call me. I may practice under the corporate head now, but I started my career in criminal court."

I hadn't known that.

Vincent pulled me farther into him, and I noticed Chris track the movement. The way I relaxed into the man at my side. A smile flitted across his face, and he nodded when our eyes met. I returned the gesture, giving him as much of a smile as I could with the pain still wreaking havoc on my system.

"Thank you," Vincent finally said. And to my surprise, that was begrudging respect on the gang-leaders face as he offered Chris his hand.

Chris shook it. "Well, I'm sure my sister is losing her mind with worry in there. I'm going to go tell her you're going to be alright."

"Bring her into Tuxedo some time. I'd love to meet her." I winced. "Properly."

He laughed, leaving us alone in the alley. The moment he was gone, my knees buckled.

"Easy, princess," Vincent murmured, taking the brunt of my weight as he angled us towards the car. "Let's get you home."

"No third degree?" I teased.

"It's coming. But after Brandon gets back and looks you over. I think you might have a concussion."

Vincent looked like the cat who swallowed the canary as he sat behind his desk. Brandon had just walked out, saying he was going to go make sure Angelica was still doing okay.

Because we both, indeed, had concussions.

"If you say one word," I warned, pointing at him. "I will shoot you in the foot." He opened his mouth. "*One word.*"

He threw his head back and laughed.

My scowl deepened as the sound grated on my pounding head. Picking up the closest thing to me, which was a half-empty water bottle, I hurled it at him. Still chuckling, he dodged it with plenty of time. His eyes were sparkling, and it was everything I could do to hold the frown on my face.

I lasted about another minute before my lips twitched.

"Come here."

Groaning, I made my way over to him. He rolled his chair far enough from the desk that I could settle myself onto his lap. Once I was situated, he wrapped his arms around me and tucked my head underneath his chin. Taking a deep breath, I let it out slowly as my whole body relaxed into his warmth.

We were quiet for a while, and I just listened to the hustle and bustle going on outside his office door. He was surprisingly calm, considering Jack had just tried to blow us all to bits. But I knew he would talk when he was ready, and not a moment before.

"You could have died today," he told me some time later, his voice a low rumble in my ear.

"I could die any day," I muttered.

"Juliette."

"I know, I know." I said, pulling myself far enough back to meet his gaze. Those forest eyes were dark, troubled. His furrowed brow cast shadows over his cheekbones. I ran my fingertips along the pucker between his eyebrows, and the muscle smoothed out under my touch. "We will find him, Vincent. Brandon said he had news. *You* are the one who told him to make sure Angel and I were alright first."

He grumbled something unintelligible under his breath at the same time there was a knock on his door. He called for whoever it was to come in. Lucas was the first one through the door, closely followed by Brandon. Both of their faces were grim, and they shut the door behind them. Lucas met my gaze first, and I could read the unspoken question shining in his hazel eyes.

"I'm fine," I told him, offering a small smile. Vincent scoffed, and his arm tightened around my waist.

"Glad to hear it, sugar."

"We know where he is," Brandon said.

"Where?" Vincent and I chorused.

"About two blocks from the gym. He had to have known that we would assume he would go anywhere *but* there. Or he led me there on purpose and it's a trap. Either way, we at least know somewhere that he stays. He went into the apartment and hasn't come back out yet. I had one of the other guys take over while I came back to check on the girls."

"I want a full team on that building. Now," Vincent ordered, voice hard as his hands flexed where he held me. "This ends tonight."

Resting my head against his chest, I let their plans fade into background noise. We were close. This whole mess would finally be behind us. I took one of Vincent's hands in mine, entwining our fingers together. While Lucas laid out his plan for cornering Jack, Vincent dropped a kiss on the top of my head. I could feel the relief working its way through his body. He was finally going to avenge his sister.

"Lucas, you run point. Brandon, I need you here. Text me when he shows his face again. I'll get there as soon as I can. No one makes a move on him without me."

Lucas and Brandon nodded before vanishing out the door to carry out their orders. Anticipation roiled in my blood, but I was exhausted.

"I'm going with you," I mumbled, not bothering to lift my cheek from his shoulder.

"Like hell you are."

"Vincent."

"Princess, this has nothing to do with me feeling like I need to protect you. This is your fight as much as it's mine. But you need to *rest*."

"Then bring him back here."

His muscles locked up beneath me. It caused a smile to dance across my face. As much as Vincent allowed me in, I knew he still wasn't used to the position I had taken in the gang. Still wasn't used to me meeting him on even footing in making decisions. Giving orders. Angelica wasn't the first person to call me 'Mom' in the past few weeks, and he knew it. People were looking to me if Vincent wasn't around. Sometimes even before Lucas.

Not that the blonde was any help. He was half of the reason for it. Whenever Vincent was unavailable, Lucas asked for my input before making a move.

The intricacies that came with running everything were mind-boggling. The sheer number of people that Vincent managed in one way or another on a day-to-day basis made my head spin. But I had done my best to keep up. Between the guys and Angelica, I had learned the basics within the first week, and it had only gotten easier from there. When I said I didn't want to be in the dark anymore, I had meant it. And I jumped in headfirst.

"Why?" he asked, breaking through my train of thought.

"Because this *is* my fight, too. I want to be there when it's finished."

Vincent hummed, running his fingertips up and down my arm. "Do you want to be the one to do it?"

A tentative question. But a genuine offer, nonetheless.

"This is your kill," I told him. "For Alana."

"And for you."

"And for me," I echoed, tilting my head back to give him a lazy grin. "I'll let you be my knight in shining armor. Just this once."

He rolled his eyes at me and flicked my nose. He rose in one fluid movement, keeping me in his arms. A startled squeak escaped me, but that was all I got out before we were heading for the door.

Several of the gang stood when we entered, but Vincent didn't pay them any attention as he headed for the stairs. My scan of the room let me spot Lucas barking orders, but I noted Brandon's absence. Both Angelica and Devyn were missing as well, so I assumed he was already checking on them.

There was one recent addition to the gang that still made me a little anxious every time I saw him.

But there Dante sat, immersed in a game of poker with several of the gang in a far corner. He must have felt my gaze because he raised his head. He muttered something to the group before placing his cards face down and heading for us. I tugged on Vincent's shirt, nodding in Dante's direction. An almost inaudible groan escaped him as he placed me on my feet. I swatted his chest before turning to face my boss.

Dante's nostrils flared as he took in the multitude of new bruises and cuts littering my exposed skin.

"So," I said, trying and failing to muster a smile. "I might need another few weeks off."

"You're lucky Devyn and Anthony trained Ember so quickly. Otherwise, I might fire you." I snorted. He just narrowed his eyes to slits. "I'm serious."

"Sure, you are."

He pinched the bridge of his nose. "I hate you."

"Dante, is there something you needed?" Vincent asked, impatience dripping off his words.

"Be nice," I muttered.

Despite the tension flowing between them, Dante smirked. He raised his hands in a gesture of surrender. "I just wanted to make sure she was okay."

"I'm fine," I told him, softening my voice to match his. "I just need a nap."

"They found Graham," Vincent said, pulling me to his side as he addressed Dante. "You're more than welcome to go with the team to stake out the apartment."

Dante's spine went ram-rod straight in an instant. "Consider it done. I'll text you if I notice anything."

"Stick with Lucas. He's running lead. Brandon is staying here to watch over the girls, make sure their conditions don't get any worse."

"I have a concussion, not cancer," I threw in. They both just gave me flat stares.

Dante grumbled something that sounded like *magnet for trouble* under his breath before heading for the door. Lucas's hazel eyes met mine, and I nodded in Dante's direction. With a broad grin, he met my boss halfway. They exchanged a few words, and then Lucas clapped Dante on the shoulder before leading him out of the warehouse.

"That's still going to take some getting used to."

"Tell me about it," Vincent grumbled. He sounded irritated, but when I looked up at him, there was a smile threatening at the edges of his lips.

"You like it."

Vincent led me to the stairs, and I leaned on him heavily on our ascent. His arm around my waist was a comforting weight. When we finally reached his door, he kissed my temple before swinging it open. The jingling of tags rang through the room as Dexter jumped down from the couch and came to greet us.

"I told you to stay off the couch," Vincent scolded, leaning down to scratch the dog behind his ears. Dexter's whole butt wiggled as he wagged his tail. "Guess I'll have to get over that."

"We can buy him a bed," I suggested, breaking from him to make my way up to the bedroom. The exhaustion was hitting me with the force of a tidal wave, and all I wanted was to sleep.

"It'll be fine," he said. When he caught up with me, he swept me off my feet.

"I can walk."

"Shut up." I pouted in response. "Brandon said you'd be good to sleep after the first hour. So, while we wait for an opening with Graham, I'm going to make sure you get some."

We made it into the bedroom and Vincent set me on the edge of the bed. My lids were heavy as I watched him. With painstaking gentleness, he undressed me. My boots and socks went first. He undid my jeans with deft fingers, and our gazes met when he encouraged me to lift my hips so he could slide them off. There was no heat in the depth of those forest eyes. Only concern.

For the first time since the car blew, I let myself think about how I would feel if the roles were reversed. If it had been Vincent who narrowly escaped death, only to run off in pursuit of the one who tried to cause it.

Alone.

"I'm sorry," I breathed, cupping his face in my hands. "I wasn't thinking. I shouldn't have gone without back-up."

"No, you shouldn't have. But I get it. I'm just glad you're okay, princess. I'm glad you made it back to me."

"I love you," I said, leaning forward to press my lips against his. The kiss was soft, and he kept it brief.

"And I love you. But please, try not to scare me like that again."

My lips twitched. "No promises."

Thirty-Eight

GOT HIM

"Be careful," I murmured, propping myself up on my elbows as Vincent gathered his things.

"I will be," he told me, checking his gun over before tucking it into his waistband.

"He has to know we found him."

Vincent's face was grim as he turned to face me. His eyes traced every inch of me he could see. And I knew what he was doing. Reminding himself that the reason I barely had the energy to move was because of Jack. That the reason Alana was gone was because of the man that we had been relentlessly hunting.

"I wouldn't doubt it," he finally said, coming to sit next to me on the edge of the bed. He cupped the side of my face in his hand, running his thumb along my cheekbone. "But we'll go in prepared for it to be a trap."

"I don't like not going with you."

"I know." He leaned forward to press a kiss to my temple. "But I'm going to bring him back here. I'll let you know when to head downstairs. You know where the door to the basement is?"

"Yes." A shiver wracked my spine. I had been down there only a handful of times. With the bloodstains that apparently no amount of bleach could wash away, it wasn't my favorite area of the warehouse. How they kept everything so carefully hidden from the authorities would never cease to surprise me.

"Good." He turned to leave, but my hand moved without my brain giving it permission to. He stopped, glancing down at where I was clutching his forearm. His features smoothed out, and when he met my gaze, I could see my worry reflected back at me. He covered my hand with his, squeezing my fingers. "I'm coming back, Juliette. I promise."

"You had better."

The kiss he gave me seared me down to my bones. And then he was gone.

Without him, an eerie stillness settled over the apartment. It took all of five minutes before I was kicking the blankets off of me and hunting down my clothes. Like hell I'd just sit up here and wait for them. There were things that needed to be set in motion. Prepared. And if the boys were with Vincent, I was going to make sure everything was ready when they returned.

Dexter whined as I struggled to get my boots on. My entire body was stiff, but I gritted my teeth and pushed through it. Before I could stand up, Dexter put his big head in my lap. He stared me down, and I could almost feel the refusal to let me leave. My eyes rolled. Two weeks with Vincent and my dog had completely turned against me.

"I've got to go, Dex," I murmured, scratching him behind the ears. "I'll be home soon."

He whined again, but turned and left the room. I could hear him huff as he walked down the stairs.

Drama queen.

A groan heaved out of me as I stood. My first stop was in the master bathroom. I took three pain relievers and crossed my fingers that they would kick in soon. Then I was down the stairs and out the door before I could think too hard about what I was doing.

Brandon's door opened on the second knock.

"Jules, you're supposed to be resting," he scolded.

"Where's Angel?"

"She two doors down on the right," Devyn said before Brandon could open his mouth again. She shouldered her way past him, and he grunted when her elbow caught him in the gut. "Are you okay?"

"I've been better." I gave her a smile, pulling her in for a hug. My bones protested against how tight she held me, but I just pulled her in tighter. "Are you okay?"

"Brandon pulled me away in plenty of time. My ears are ringing a little, but that's it."

"Jules," the man in question butted in. "You really shouldn't be up and moving yet. Give your body some time to recover."

"Later," I told him, already turning to Angelica's apartment. "I have shit to do."

"Like *what?*"

I ignored him, raising my hand to knock gently against Angelica's door. I could hear some shuffling on the other side, and before too long, the door opened just a crack. The one blue eye I could see glittered, and she swung the door fully open with a smirk twisting one side of her mouth.

"You look like hell," she said, leaning her shoulder against the doorframe.

"Because you look like a bouquet of roses."

She chuckled, wincing before placing a hand against her ribs. "What can I help you with?"

"How're you feeling?"

"Like I got blown up. What do you need, Jules?"

"Basement. They're bringing Jack back."

Hatred flared in those sapphire irises. Without a word, she grabbed her jacket off the back of the door and shrugged it on. In less time than it took to take a breath, she had her keys in her hand and her door locked behind her. She didn't wait for me as she strode for the stairs leading down into the main part of the warehouse.

Brandon looked like we were torturing him as he threw his hands up. "*This* is why I dropped out of med school. Ungrateful patients."

"You dropped out of med school because you were making more money with us," Angelica threw over her shoulder before vanishing from sight.

Brandon glared after her. He shook his head, turning to go back into his apartment. He glanced back at me. "I'll meet you down there in five. I just need to put some clothes on."

And for the first time, I noticed he didn't have a shirt on. My eyes trailed to my best friend. As my gaze raked over her, her cheeks tinted pink. Because that was one-hundred percent Brandon's shirt that was dwarfing her lithe figure.

"One of these days, we're going to get that coffee and have a little chat," I told her, trying to keep the sly smile off my face.

"I'm going back to bed," she muttered. But that was a glimmer of undiluted happiness in her eyes as she turned to follow Brandon. My heart warmed at the thought of her finally finding someone to instill that feeling in her.

Angelica's head popped back out from the stairwell. "You coming?" she asked.

Nodding, I made my way over to her. Her movements were stiff, just as I was sure mine were. But we descended into the heart of the warehouse. Heads lifted when we came into view, then dipped as the gazes met mine. I scrutinized who we had left.

"Pick a team, Angel," I told her, aiming for the lone door on the far-right side of the warehouse. It was almost directly across from Vincent's office. "God knows what they plan to do with him once they get him here, but we're going to need help."

She nodded before heading off to corral a few of the gang. My steps only faltered once I was in front of the door. That same shiver tiptoed around the nape of my neck, but I forced it back. As much as I hated the room at the bottom of these stairs, I needed to get down there. I had a room to prep.

Vincent stared at the nondescript apartment building. How had they missed this place? Brandon had been right. It hadn't been far from the gym, and they had thoroughly swept this area. Graham should never have been able to evade them for this long.

He *never* should have been able to plant that bomb.

Vincent's fists clenched at his side, and he forced them open. Juliette was home, and she was safe.

And she wasn't Alana.

Vincent had loved his sister, still did, but she had been too soft for this life, no matter how much she hadn't wanted to admit it. It was why they had agreed to keep her out of it as much as they could. And look what had happened.

But Juliette was a fighter, and she had been her entire life. He had to remind himself of that. Had to remind himself that she would knock him flat on his ass if he so much as suggested they coddle her. It made him smile, and Lucas nudged his shoulder.

"What's that grin for?" the blonde asked, redirecting his attention to the building across the street as well.

"Just thinking," Vincent said. "No sign of him?"

"He has to still be in there. We have the place surrounded."

They both stood in the open, not bothering to hide. Lucas was right. There was no way Graham could have gotten out of that building without them knowing, so there was no point in trying to disguise their presence. And Vincent took a sick sense of satisfaction at the idea of Graham knowing he was coming.

"Let's get this over with."

Arkin and Dante fell into step with them as they crossed the street. Vincent knew what they were walking into was more than likely a trap. But they were ready for that, too.

Brandon had seen Graham go into an apartment on the top floor. After doing some digging of his own, Arkin narrowed it down to the apartment that overlooked the back alley. There was a fire escape that aided in a back exit, and they had been watching that too. They crested the landing on the third floor and headed for the last door on the right.

"Do we knock?" Lucas asked when they stopped.

Arkin and Dante rolled their eyes at the blonde, who just grinned before he put his boot beside the knob. The others moved as he reared back and kicked the door in.

"You know, knocking *is* the normal custom," Jack drawled from inside the apartment.

Vincent was the first one through the remnants of the door. He didn't know what he had expected, but Jack lounging on the couch, looking like he had all the time in the world with a drink in his hand, had not been high on the list.

Tawny eyes met forest green in that dark room, and a million unspoken words passed between the two men.

"Are you alone?" Vincent asked, motioning for the others to spread out.

"I've been waiting for you. I wondered if your little attack dog could track me."

Vincent was glad Brandon was still at the warehouse with the girls.

"You're giving up that easily?"

Jack grinned, but it exuded more cruelty than warmth. "We have unfinished business, Monroe. I figured I'd give you the chance to meet me face to face."

"You've been in hiding for over a year. Why now?"

Something in Jack's eyes flashed, and he raised the glass of amber liquid to his lips. He took a small sip and settled farther into the cushions. The hand with the glass rested against the arm of the couch, and the other stretched across the back of it.

"How is Juliette?"

Vincent's vision tinged red around the edges, and he ground his teeth together. It took everything in him not to launch himself at the smug bastard.

Dante had no such qualms.

Juliette's boss had been searching the apartment, and it had taken him the closest to Jack. At the sound of her name on Jack's lips, Dante's fist flew. He cracked it against Jack's cheekbone and wrapped his hand around the younger man's throat. Jack choked and drew his hand from behind the couch. He pressed the barrel of the gun against the underside of Dante's chin before he let a smirk dance across his face.

"Temper, temper," he crooned, cocking the gun.

Before the sound had even echoed through the room, there were three more guns aimed at him. Jack let his eyes dance across the men surrounding him, and second guessed his decision. But he still kept his own weapon on Dante.

"Do you know who I am?" Dante asked, brown eyes furious as he glared at Jack.

"Dante Simms, my my my. Now what could I have done to earn your wrath? I thought you were neutral ever since handing your gang over."

"I was," Dante spat. "And then some moron went after my family, and I took that personally." Jack's brows pulled together, and Dante had him disarmed in an instant. It happened so fast; Vincent wasn't even sure how he had done it. It felt like he blinked, and Dante was disassembling Jack's gun before tossing it into the far corner of the room.

"You're talking about Juliette."

"I've known Jules since she was sixteen." Dante pulled his own gun from its holster and leveled it at Jack's head. "You couldn't have made a dumber move than going after her if you tried."

Vincent was waiting for Jack to make a break for it. The man's eyes flicked over everyone standing against him, and Vincent chuckled when their eyes connected again.

Jack was at a loss as he stared at Monroe. He had initially been prepared to go down swinging. There was still a grenade tucked under the couch. He could pull the pin and scatter them. It would give him time to get out. But he had to admit to himself that Vincent more than likely had more of his lackeys on the outside. Even if he took him out, he didn't know how far he could get before the rest of the gang hunted him down.

Something that Juliette had said at the gym bounced around in his head again, making him grind his teeth.

He's in control because he's the only one worthy of leading.

Jack had done unspeakable things to exact his revenge on Monroe. Had killed innocents. And he had almost let Juliette become a tally in the casualty column. He had played this all wrong. He had lured Vincent into what should have been a trap, but it was feeling like he had just served himself up on a silver platter.

And maybe he had. He was so tired. Everything he had done was to carry on his father's legacy in Valarian. He didn't know if he even cared anymore.

He needed to see her. One more time. If nothing else, she needed to know he regretted it. Regretted involving her.

He sneered at Monroe before he lunged.

Vincent cursed as Jack tackled Dante to the ground. "Hold your fire," he ordered. Arkin and Lucas just looked at him like he was crazy. "She wants us to bring him back. Alive."

They nodded, and both lowered their weapons. A smile twitched at the corners of his mouth. It was amazing to him how much pull Juliette had developed over the gang. Sure, he had told them she was his. His partner, his very reason to keep fighting. To keep breathing in order to return to her. But their devotion? She had earned that all on her own.

Vincent advanced on the brawling men. Jack was an incredible fighter; Vincent would give him that. But Dante had brute force and unbridled rage on his side. He had Jack pinned beneath him, and Vincent caught his fist as he was about to let it fall again. Dante glared up at Vincent, but his shoulders dropped before he ripped his hand free.

"You're lucky she still gives a shit about you," Dante spat, shoving to his feet before heading for the door. "I'll be in the car." Vincent and the others watched him go.

Once he was gone, the gang leader turned back to the man on the floor. Jack's chest was heaving as he pushed himself into a sitting position. His hand was inching under the couch, but then his eyes met Vincent's again. Jack let the smallest sigh slip free before pulling his hand back and moving to stand. Vincent didn't let him get his feet under him before he grabbed him under the arm and hauled him up.

He really should have seen the sucker punch coming, but he didn't.

Pain exploded with the force of Jack's fist, and Vincent felt his teeth slice into the inside of his cheek. He rounded on Jack, seamlessly moving until he had the other man in a chokehold. He spit blood onto the floor and applied enough pressure to his hold that he knew he was restricting Jack's airway.

Just like Jack had done to Juliette.

The memory of the bruises ringing her throat caused Vincent to tighten his grip further still. Lucas stepped forward and touched his shoulder. Vincent took a deep breath, and then he shoved Jack away from him, towards Arkin and Lucas.

"Tie him up and let's get out of here."

Jack fought against the other two, but it was useless. He had already expended too much energy on fighting Dante and Vincent, and he could barely pull air into his lungs as it was.

Vincent watched as the others steered Jack out of the apartment. Once he was alone, he glanced down at the edge of the couch. He knelt, reaching for the small object he could just make out hiding next to the leg.

A grenade.

Vincent's eyes widened, and he whipped his head to stare in the direction they had dragged Graham.

Why hadn't he used it?

Shaking his head, he replaced the explosive and left the apartment. He had half a mind to pull the pin and let the building crumble behind him. But whatever happened to it after they went back to the warehouse wasn't his problem.

He pulled his phone free as he crossed the street to where they had left the Escalade parked.

"You've been watching too many horror movies," Angelica said, surveying the room as the last of the guys filtered out, leaving us alone. "Or maybe too many crime dramas."

"This is exactly what it looks like every time I've been down here. Shut up."

She gave me a crooked little half smile before leaning against the stainless-steel table we had set up. The only thing I really ended up needing help with was bringing the table and chair into the room from the storage down the hall. It had been just long enough since we had anyone down here that we had put everything away. Under normal circumstances, I probably could've managed it with just Angelica. However, in both of our states, it was easier to use the others. My muscles were screaming just from the few flights of stairs.

Angelica's eyes went unfocused as she stared at the chair that was sitting under a single bulb in the small concrete room. I almost snorted. With the stains on the floor, that I was pretty sure Vincent didn't paint over simply as a scare tactic, she was right. It looked like a cheap haunted house set up. But the knives, hammers, and scissors on the table behind her were real. And if we used them tonight, the fresh blood on the floor would be too.

But there was something about that vacant look in her eyes. Something I had seen in the mirror one too many times after my parent's deaths.

"Angel?" I asked, moving to stand next to her. She blinked a few times and twisted to face me. "Do you want to tell me what's going on?"

"What do you mean?" Her voice was soft, something I didn't normally attribute to the woman standing next to me.

"You get this look in your eyes every time something about Jack gets brought up. Most of the gang hate him, for obvious reasons. But yours seems... personal."

Her eyes shuttered, and she turned away from me. Her jaw clenched tight, throat bobbing as she swallowed. I wasn't sure what to do, but I reached for her hand where it had balled into a fist against her thigh. Her spine went rigid at my touch. It only took a few seconds for her to take a deep breath, and when she let it out, she opened her palm so I could thread our fingers together. I was offering her the only thing that I could: support.

"It is personal for me," she murmured after a few minutes. "I was in love with Alana. We'd been together for two years." My heart fractured as tears filled her eyes. They overflowed, and she didn't bother to wipe them away when she met my stare. Her hand turned into a vise around mine. "He took her from all of us. She was the light in this place, and I won't rest until he's dead. Learning he's still alive after all this time–"

My phone rang, cutting her off. Giving her an apologetic smile, I answered with the hand she wasn't holding. She could borrow from my strength for as long as she needed.

"Hello?"

"We've got him." The satisfaction in Vincent's voice warmed me down to my core. "We're headed back."

"Angelica and I already have the basement ready."

"Why am I not surprised?" he grumbled, and I could all but feel him rolling his eyes at me. "How long did you actually stay in bed after I left?"

"A few minutes."

"After we deal with this, we're going to have a talk about your ability to listen."

"Oh?"

"Princess," he purred, and I heard the engine turn over in the background. "If you don't reign in that attitude, you're going to be put right back on bedrest."

Angelica's eyebrows arched, and my face went scarlet as I realized she could hear every word he was saying. "I'll see you soon."

"Is Angel staying?"

"I think she deserves to."

"So, she told you?" he asked.

"She did." I squeezed her hand. "I want her to be the first one to go at him." Her eyes went round at my words.

"I can handle that. We'll be there soon."

When we hung up, Angelica blew out a breath. She released my hand in favor of running both of hers through her hair.

"They're on their way," I told her. She nodded, squaring her shoulders.

"Thank you," she said. "I never would have had the balls to ask him for that, no matter how much I wanted it. Thank you."

"Of course."

We barely spoke after that. The more time that passed, the more my heart rate kicked up. Taking a steadying breath, I started toying with the instruments on the table. I had to get it together. This was why I had been coming down here with Vincent and the others. To develop a stomach for torture. As much as I cared for every person under our roof, I hadn't grown up in this life. I wasn't used to beating the living shit out of people to find out what they knew. To find out if they knew where Jack had gone or who his contacts were. Or how he had gotten into the party in the first place.

But I did know that when it came to Jack, I couldn't balk. Not the way I had the first time I had watched Brandon remove the skin from a man's forearm with a surgeon's precision. Jack deserved everything that was coming to him tonight. By any of our hands. And I wouldn't let my squeamish stomach deter that.

I could see the tension in Angelica's shoulders. How her eyes glittered as she ran her fingers over one of the hunting knives on the table. The blade was a wicked thing, and she touched the handle with reverence. Despite everything, a smile quirked the corner of my mouth. Something told me I was going to have to stop her at some point. Otherwise, she might just kill Jack before we got anything useful out of him. And who could blame her?

The door to the hall opened, cutting my thoughts short. The old hinges protested, letting out a shriek loud enough for a banshee. I snapped around, my head spinning a little when I came to a stop. My eyes found Vincent's first. His face frozen into that harsh mask, but my heart still beat out a stutter step as I let out a breath of relief. I knew he had been okay, but it was still good to see with my own eyes. He had a bruise blooming on his right cheekbone, but other than that, he seemed fine.

Finally, I let my gaze drift to the man he was pushing in front of him. Jack's hands were bound behind his back, and he stumbled a bit as Vincent shoved him forward. It was the first time I had ever seen them in the same proximity, and it was jarring to find that they were the same height. Vincent always seemed to dwarf me with his presence, but I had never felt that with Jack. When those tawny eyes met mine, I lost the ability to breathe.

Grief sliced through me, bitter and cold.

The pain of losing someone I had thought I had known. Trusted. It was slamming into me all over again, and I felt the sting of my eyes watering.

And Jack, damn him, that was regret. Not for the sister he had stolen from the man behind him. Not for the partner he had ripped from the woman behind me. But for me. For the friendship that he had destroyed so completely, there was no coming back from it.

He was so *selfish*.

My body moved without my permission. Before the door even closed behind them, my fist was flying. Vincent's step back barely registered. Jack's nose crunched under the force of my assault. A low curse flew out of him, but he didn't dodge as I immediately struck him in the jaw as well. More than once.

My chest was heaving. My knuckles had split, and I couldn't tell if it was my blood or Jack's that dripped off of my hand as it hung limp at my side. No one said a word as we stared at each other, neither of us daring to look away.

We were standing on opposite sides of a chasm, and we both knew it. His eyes went glassy as they held mine, but the tears never fell. Instead, that warmth that I had always taken such comfort in bled from his eyes. Slowly, so slowly, I saw the man I knew fade away for the last time. And then I was looking into the eyes of a murderer. Of a man who would kill anyone who stood in the way of what he thought he was owed. Me included.

He spat blood onto the floor at my feet, and a wry grin overtook his mouth.

"Well, well," he crooned, eyes running over me in a way that made my skin crawl. "Looks like all those hours on the mat paid off. Huh, Jules?"

"You have no idea," I hissed, eyes narrowing into slits. The door opened again, and I briefly took notice of Dante, Lucas, Arkin, and Brandon entering the room. They fanned out at my back, and I let the reassurance of their presence wash over me. "But you will."

"I'm shaking."

"You should be." I stepped forward, bringing us chest to chest. He glared down at me, but the trepidation in his face made me smile. "Because you won't be leaving this room alive."

Thirty-Nine

THE RAT

My hands shook as Brandon and Arkin took hold of Jack. They took him to the chair and tied him down. To my surprise, there was no fight in him. My eyes traced his injuries. It looked like someone had taken out quite a bit of anger on him. It made my lips twitch in a perverse sense of joy to know the amount of pain he had to be in. His eye was nearly black, and there was fresh blood dripping off his chin from my assault as well. Knowing I had more than likely broken his nose twice now almost made me giddy.

A familiar presence pressed against my back, and I leaned into him. Vincent's chest shook with silent laughter, and he reached up to cup my throat in his hand. With the slightest pressure, he encouraged me to tilt my head and meet his gaze.

"I thought you wanted Angel to go at him first?" he murmured, his breath washing across the shell of my ear.

"It was my intention." Another laugh rumbled through him. "Oh, shut up."

"Are you sure you want to be here for this?" he asked, voice softening as he spun me to face him.

"I need to be."

He nodded, cupping my face in his hands. His thumbs ran over my cheekbones as his eyes searched my face. I knew what he was looking for. He was still double checking to make sure I was ready for this. Arching my brows, I met his stare dead on.

"Alright." He pressed a kiss to my forehead before moving past me. Angelica had propped herself against the table, her lip curling as she examined Jack. The man in question leered up at her, and it was everything I could do to keep from decking him again. Angelica looked at Vincent, and he nodded.

"I take it you remember me?" she asked Jack, giving him her back as she ran her fingers over the knives on the table.

"You're Alana's bitch."

Her spine locked up, but by the time she glanced at him over her shoulder, there wasn't an ounce of emotion in her expression. There was, however, that vicious looking hunting knife in her hand. In one smooth movement, she had whipped around and driven it deep into the fleshy part of Jack's thigh.

He screamed, and it was a beautiful sound. I watched, fascinated, as Angelica picked up a scalpel and moved in between Jack's spread legs. They had tied him so tightly to the chair, the only thing he could move was his head. He dropped it back as he hissed a breath through his teeth. Angelica just laughed, running the scalpel from the inside of his elbow to his wrist. The cut wasn't deep, but it was enough to start the blood flowing.

Brandon eased up beside me, and I had to focus over the roaring that was starting in my ears to hear what he was saying.

"Did I mention Angel likes knives just as much as she likes guns?" His words startled a laugh out of me, which drew a pair of tawny eyes in my direction. The smile I gave him was dark, something I had learned from the gang leader standing just a few feet away from me.

Vincent was watching the exchange with amusement. And as Angelica began making small, precise cuts along Jack's other forearm, his grin was a mirror of mine.

We were all insane.

"So, Jaxon," Vincent said, moving until he was in Jack's line of sight. Angelica didn't stop her ministrations. The cuts she was making were deep enough to draw blood, but less than half an inch long. She had already made more than I cared to count. "Want to talk?"

"What do you want to know?" Jack asked, his voice strained as he fought not to react to the pain.

"Who's your contact?" Vincent took his gun out of his waistband and placed it on the cart. Then he leaned against the metal, crossing his arms and ankles. He was the picture of ease if you didn't know what to look for. But that tick in his jaw was back, feathering as fast as a hummingbird's wings. No matter how much he wanted Jack dead, I knew he wouldn't rush this. We needed to know who the rat was. "How did you get into the party? How did you know where Juliette was?"

"Have you ever considered that maybe she was my contact?"

I blanched.

Of all the outlandish, hair-brained shit he could've come up with. *That* was what he had decided on?

I wasn't sure what surprised me more. Jack's utterly ridiculous claim, or the laughter that spilled from Arkin. It was a boisterous sound that was completely out of place in the cold room. But his baby blues were sparkling with unshed tears from laughing so hard. Jack glared at him, barely able to turn his head far enough to see the man in question.

Arkin wiped his eyes. "Jules? That's the best you've got?" he asked, circling so that Jack could see him. "The woman that saved Vincent's life from that botched assassination attempt. That's who you're accusing of siding with you?"

Genuine shock flitted across Jack's face. So, it had been him behind it.

Vincent's lips were twitching as our gazes connected. I didn't know how Jack could think he was going to sow any discord with our group. These were our most trusted people.

My most trusted people.

"You're an idiot," I told Jack, moving to Vincent's side. "You're never going to convince my people that I would deceive them like that. But that's what you've failed to realize, isn't it?" I cocked my head to the side as his brows furrowed. And I knew I was right. "You really didn't know, did you?"

"Didn't know what?" he seethed.

"That they are *my* people. Angel, stop."

The order echoed, and she paused; her scalpel poised to make another slice against Jack's bicep. Her head tilted in my direction. Jack's eyes bounced back and forth between the two of us, and it was with no small amount of satisfaction that I watched the realization dawn on his face. I could sense his perception of me shifting in an instant, as if he had finally noticed something he hadn't before. No longer was he looking at me like I was just the gang-leader's girlfriend, but someone who stood on even footing with him.

The second most powerful person in the room.

Angelica flipped the scalpel in her hand so that she could hold the end with the blade. She offered it to me. "Did you want a turn?" she asked, sapphire eyes sparkling even in the dim light.

"Just making a point," I told her with a shake of my head. "Proceed."

She struck before Jack could take another breath. This time, the blade sank deep. He screamed through gritted teeth, writhing against the bonds that held him. It was useless. Angelica's tinkling laughter filled the room before she did it again.

"I'll ask you again," Vincent said, reaching between us to take my hand. He tucked me into his side before addressing Jack. "Who is your contact? And no useless accusations this time."

It had been hours, and I had lost count of the amount of cuts Angelica was making on Jack's skin. Once she had run out of space on his arms, she had cut his pants off at the knee and started on his legs. He was a mess of blood and skin that was barely clinging together. And he was still holding that name close to his chest. He still wasn't breaking.

"You're going to bleed out if you wait too much longer," Angelica cooed from where she was sitting on the floor, just close enough to reach the blade out and make another slice. "Death by a thousand cuts is a slow, but awful way to go."

"I think you might have surpassed a thousand a while ago," Dante muttered from the back corner, his eyes tracking Angelica's every movement. She grinned, winking at him before making a long cut along the back of Jack's calf.

"I'm not telling you anything," he panted. I knew he wouldn't make it much longer. His skin was leeching itself of color, and the blood on the floor was slowly slipping through the drain below the chair.

I touched Vincent's arm, and he turned to look at me. Our gazes held for a moment, and somehow, he read the question in my eyes. With a nod, he let me take over.

"This can all end if you tell us what we want to know," I told Jack. He struggled to raise his head, and his tawny irises were dull when they met mine. "Tell us who your contact is, and I'll have Vincent end it. Quickly."

"No."

"Then bleed out. We're done here."

With feline grace, Angelica got to her feet. She pitched the scalpel onto the table, and it hit with a metallic clatter. The sound bounced around the room as she crossed to the door. With her hand on the knob, she spared one glance over her shoulder at the man she had shredded.

"You deserve so much more, and I hope you rot in eternity for what you've done," she said, a fire lighting in her eyes as they met Jack's. His blood had splattered haphazardly across her skin, but there was a weightlessness in her walk I hadn't seen before as she left the room.

Everyone else followed her. Dante squeezed my shoulder as he walked past, and the others dipped their heads before leaving as well. When the door had fallen shut behind them, the only sounds in the room were Jack's ragged breathing and the soft drip as more blood joined the puddle on the floor. He struggled to raise his head and finally managed it on the third attempt.

"You going to stay here and watch, Jules?" he taunted. "Didn't think this was something you'd have the stomach for, considering the scared little girl that first walked into my studio."

He was trying to get a rise out of me, trying to goad me into ending him quicker, but it wouldn't work. His words were useless, and they rolled right off me as I leaned against Vincent. In fact, I let a smirk form on my face as I studied him.

He wasn't wrong. The girl I had been when I first met him would never have been able to sit here and smell the blood permeating the air. I never would have been able to pick up the scalpel Angelica had dropped and take it back to him. A small laugh fell from my lips as I stood over him. Leaning forward, I braced my hands on top of his wrists. He hissed as I applied enough pressure to dig the injured skin harder into the arms of the chair. His blood welled up between my fingers, his skin threatening to let go of the sinew holding it together, and my stomach betrayed me by twisting.

We were face to face, and he could barely keep his eyes open long enough to meet mine.

I stabbed the scalpel into his leg, directly opposite the hunting knife Angelica had placed earlier.

"You're going to tell me who betrayed us," I told him, my voice only loud enough to carry over his groan of pain.

"Why would I tell you anything when I'm going to die either way?"

"Because the other option is to continue to endure this." I twisted the hunting knife, and the scream that escaped him was music to my ears. "And that could go on for a *very* long time."

"I can handle it. We both know I don't have much longer."

"You know," I mused, ripping the knife out as I stood. Blood flowed freely once there was nothing to obstruct it. "Brandon is a phenomenal doctor. I bet I could have him cauterize every one of these wounds." Jack's eyes narrowed. "And then I know he'd be able to give you a transfusion to replace all the blood you lost."

That was panic beginning to flit across his face.

I could hear the smile in Vincent's voice as he picked up on my train of thought. "Just think how much *fun* Angel would have torturing you to the brink of death over and over again."

"No."

The word was a single breath as it fell from Jack's lips.

I had him.

I moved closer, using the tip of the knife to force his chin up so he could meet my gaze.

"Who invited you?"

"Henry Kline."

FORTY

THE AFTERMATH

"Weasel-face?" I asked, whirling on Vincent.

A strained chuckle left Jack, but it faded into the background as Vincent and I locked eyes. Everything clicked into place, and I let a slew of profanities fly. It made perfect sense. Lucas had been uneasy about this deal for as long as I could remember. They all had. And once they brought me in, Henry paid *too* much attention to my every move. It was something we had foolishly brushed off as him being a pervert.

"So, this whole deal..." Vincent trailed off, eyes narrowing to slits.

"It's been me the whole time," Jack told him. The look on his face was way too smug for someone who was minutes away from death.

Or should I have said seconds?

In one fluid movement, Vincent slid his gun from the table. He had already attached the silencer, so there was only a muted *bang* as he aimed it at Jack's forehead and fired.

No grand speeches.

No threats.

Just a hole right between Jack's lifeless, tawny eyes.

My stomach rolled, and I had to turn my back on the grotesque scene. Touching my fingers to my mouth to stop the reaction, I took a deep breath. Before I had even exhaled, two hands came down on my shoulders. Vincent's touch was gentle, applying just enough pressure to let me know I wasn't alone.

"I'll be okay."

"I should've warned you," he murmured, pulling me back so that I was leaning on him. "Let's get out of here."

He waited until I nodded, and then kept his hand on the small of my back as he led me from the room. Just before the door closed behind us, I glanced back. Jack's head had fallen forward, and one could almost think he was just passed out if they didn't know any better.

But I did.

He would never take another breath. He could never again terrorize the people I cared about. But there was still a pang in my heart for the man I had thought I had known.

"It's okay if you don't know how to feel, princess," Vincent murmured. When I turned my head to meet those steady forest eyes, he gave me a small smile. "They were both real. The man you knew and the man he turned out to be."

"I should be happy he's gone," I said, wrapping my arms around myself. "But I just feel numb."

"It's okay," he repeated, drawing me into his warmth. "The only thing that matters is he can't hurt you anymore."

"He can't hurt *any* of us anymore."

"I love you," Vincent said, tipping my face up to kiss me. I let myself fall into him for just a moment. When we pulled apart, I took a steadying breath. Then I squared my shoulders and headed for the steep stairs leading up into the warehouse.

There were people everywhere. Rarely had I seen the warehouse this packed, but today was a win for us. We were one step closer to being able to breathe easy again. A few more players to remove from the board before we were back in control again. Whatever our next steps were, they would define how things carried on in Valarian.

With the slightest pressure against my spine, Vincent urged me to head to the center of the room. The soft hum of conversation died out as all the attention swung our way. Vincent surveyed everyone gathered, and I noticed our closest friends moving to surround us. Every one of their faces showed a similar frown, but it was Angelica who caught my attention the most.

Our gazes locked, and I answered the unspoken question in her eyes with a nod. Her shoulders dropped, and she let loose a long breath. She let her gaze drift skyward, and my own eyes pricked as I realized what she was doing. Turning to face the others again, I let her say her last goodbye to Alana in peace.

"It's done," Vincent said, his soft statement sounding like a gunshot in the resounding quiet. Grim smiles rippled through the room, but he was quick to get to the matter at hand. "It's not time for celebration just yet. Jaxon Graham is dead, but we still have the issue of whoever his contact was. Juliette found out that it was Henry Kline."

Murmurs spread through the gang as the news sank in. I was still trying to digest the fact that Vincent had given me the credit for the information. It was just another way he continued to make it clear that I was in this with them. Just as much of a leader as he was. The gangs' eyes ran over me, taking in the blood that spattered my clothes and my hands. I hadn't even thought about it until now.

Blowing out a breath, I crossed my arms over my chest. "We need to decide how we're going to handle this situation. We're neck deep into this deal with Kline. You all have been working on it long before I came into the picture. But the fact remains that this betrayal cannot go unpunished. Ja–" I caught myself. "Graham, let us know he has been behind this deal since its inception."

"I killed him before we got anything more out of him," Vincent chimed in, stepping to my side. "But if I had to guess, I'd say their plan was to report the deal to the police when it was about to go down. It would have put me behind bars, and the entire operation in jeopardy just in time for Graham to come in and save the day."

"So, what's our plan?" Lucas asked.

Vincent looked at me. A test.

"We keep Graham's death under wraps for now," I said. The gang met my statement with more murmuring and a few outright protests. I held my hand up, and that chatter died. "I know what you all want. That you want nothing more than to make it known that we are still in control of this city. But we have the element of surprise on our side. If we play this right, Kline won't have any idea we know he's been two-timing us. He won't have time to escape."

"We go through with the deal as if nothing has changed," Vincent continued. His support radiated through me, and I had to tamp down the smile that wanted to break through. "We set up the exchange, and we wipe out Kline and his entire empire in one fell swoop. He's the last of the people that were loyal to the Graham family. This ends with him."

My eyes roved over those gathered, and I saw the determination set into every one of their faces. They may have wanted to stake Jack's head to the front of the building, but they knew we were right. The worst thing we could do to Jack now would be to let his legacy die with him. No fanfare, no mourning. Just another light extinguished in silence.

"Arkin?" The brunette looked up at the sound of my voice. "Find Sebastian Rathbone. I want him dealt with as well."

He nodded, and without a word, pulled out his phone and headed out of the warehouse. Sure, Sebastian wasn't as big of a player as Henry, but he was still someone Jack had considered a friend. He was the one who had actually taken the shot that killed Alana. He also knew one of my pressure points, and I wouldn't allow him the chance to push it.

Devyn walked up to me then, as if she had known I was thinking about her.

Vincent nudged me in her direction as he continued to talk logistics with the gang. The rest of the planning would be up to them. I needed to decompress.

Devyn wrapped an arm around my shoulders and angled me towards the stairs leading up to the apartments. Without a word, I leaned into her as we walked. Angelica fell into step beside us, and together we headed up to Vincent's.

No one said a word as I unlocked the door. Angelica made a beeline for the kitchen. Devyn didn't hesitate to continue on to the bedroom when I pointed her in the right direction. When we made it to the bottom of the stairs, I pulled away from her enough to lead the way. Her eyes took in the bedroom for the briefest of moments when we emerged. Not even bothering to say anything, I headed into the bathroom.

Devyn was with me again only moments later. Brushing past me, she turned on the faucet in the bathtub. She let the water run until steam billowed through the room, and only then did she take stock of what was sitting on the ledge of the tub. She spotted the bubble bath Vincent had bought me in my first few days here and poured a hefty amount into the water. The scent of lavender wafted around the space as the air turned balmy.

"Strip," she ordered, standing with her hands on her hips.

"Excuse me?"

Her eyes rolled so far, it tempted me to tell her they'd get stuck that way. "I've seen that vacant look in your eyes before. Strip. You need to relax."

Grumbling about how bossy she was, I did as she instructed. I tried not to think about how much blood was crusting up on my skin. Devyn moved to take every piece of clothing I peeled off. When I was completely naked, she nudged me towards the bath. Sighing, I stepped into the water and hissed at how hot it was.

"Suck it up," she told me, taking a seat on the edge of the counter.

"I really hate you sometimes," I muttered. Slowly, I lowered myself until the water submerged me up to my neck. My eyes slipped closed. Bless Vincent and his choice to get a deep soaking tub.

"Do you want to talk about it?" she asked, her voice soft.

"Not really."

"Well, if you do, I found Vincent's stash of liquor," Angelica said as she breezed into the room.

I cracked one eye open in order to see the bottle of tequila and the three shot glasses she was holding up like they were trophies. Devyn and I both chuckled as she came to sit on the floor between the two of us. A feline smile curved her lips as she lined the glasses up and filled them. Between when she had left us in the basement and when we had finally come back up, she had found the time to shower and change as well. Her burgundy hair was slightly damp, and not a speck of blood marred her skin. When I reached for the shot she offered me, bubbles stuck to my hand and arm. She handed one to Devyn as well, after making sure I wouldn't drop mine.

"Cheers, girls," Devyn chirped, raising her glass. "We made it."

"For now," I mumbled, before tossing back the shot. Devyn reached into the water just enough to flick some at me. I glared at her. "What?"

"Don't give me that."

"Jules is right," Angelica said, eyeing Devyn as she poured herself another shot. "This fight isn't over."

"Listen, I know I'm not as involved as the two of you, but I *am* still involved. And I'll be damned if I won't celebrate when we win. I know we've still got some shit left to handle, but that doesn't diminish what we accomplished today."

Angelica and I glanced at each other. She raised her brows at me, and I just shrugged before turning back to my best friend. Devyn's dark brown eyes were blazing, but I knew what she was doing.

"You can be pretty wise when you want to be," I teased, instead of calling her out for trying to cheer me up.

"Somebody has to be the sunshine with you two doom-and-glooms around."

"Hey!" Angelica exclaimed, reaching forward to swat at Devyn's knee. "I resemble that remark."

Devyn laughed, and the sound was so light and carefree that it helped a weight lift off my chest. Angelica passed out another round of shots, and once I could feel the tequila warming me from the inside out, I grabbed my loofah and washed away the left-over grime that was still clinging to my skin. Thankfully, it seemed like my clothes had taken the brunt of the blood. There was some caked under my nails that I scrubbed at, and before long, every last reminder of Jack was swirling down the drain.

Devyn reached over and flipped the hot water back on, adding more bubble-bath as the water refilled. Now that I was clean, I could just let the water ease some of my still-tense muscles. This wasn't the first time Devyn and I had done the bubble-bath therapy sessions. We had been naked in front of each other more times than I cared to count over the years. But it surprised me I felt just as at ease with Angelica around. As if she had always been there.

It made me wonder what our group would have been like if there was a fourth.

"If you're comfortable with it," I started, leaning my neck against the lip of the tub. "I'd like you to tell me about Alana. I've heard about her from Vincent, but I want to know about who she was outside of just his sister."

"She would have loved you," Angelica said, a sweet smile breaking across her face even as tears gathered in her eyes. "Anyone that could make Vincent light up the way he does around you would have been her favorite person in five seconds flat."

And then she launched into story after story about the woman that I would never get to meet, but desperately wished I could have. It was like a dam breaking open, and I wondered how long Angelica had been keeping these stories to herself. Wondered if she had ever shared any of them with Vincent, or if they had just shut each other out after they lost her. Too wrapped up in their individual grief to help each other through it.

My money was on the latter.

The story of how they met was such a meet-cute, Devyn couldn't stop herself from gagging a little. Angelica just made us take another shot for being a 'pair of love-hating assholes.'

"I'm sorry, you expect me to *not* roll my eyes at the fact that the first time she met you was when you *literally* caught her before she could face-plant coming down the stairs?" Devyn asked, pierced eyebrow arching.

Angelica's entire face went the same shade as her hair. "Heels and those old stairs didn't mix. It's why we had them redone."

Devyn snorted, and I flicked a healthy dose of water at her.

"And just *what* is going on in here?"

All three of us turned our attention to the doorway, where Vincent was leaning with one shoulder against the frame. His eyes found mine, trailing over the bit of skin he could see peeking out above the water.

"We're having girl-time. Get out," Angelica told him, a pout on her face. Her cheeks were still a little pink, though I couldn't tell if it was from embarrassment or the amount of tequila we had consumed.

"Angel, this is *my* bathroom. You get out." He may have been speaking to her, but his attention was on me. There was a heat simmering in his eyes, but the concern showing on the rest of his face outweighed it.

Devyn's gaze flicked back and forth between me and the man at the door. With a smirk, she grabbed the half-empty bottle of liquor and hauled Angelica to her feet. The red head stumbled a bit, and Devyn wrapped an arm around her waist to steady her. With nothing more than a wink sent my way, she eased Angelica from the room. Vincent broke our staring match to watch them go. Their quiet bickering drifted back to me, but I didn't try very hard to decipher it. Once the sound of the front door shutting echoed through the apartment, Vincent crossed the room to kneel next to the tub.

"Hi," I murmured, blinking as I gazed up at him. The buzz was hitting me with a vengeance.

"Hi," he responded, that familiar ghost of a smile dancing around the edges of his lips. "How're you holding up, princess?"

"I'm realizing I'm drunk, and they can officially charge me as an accessory to murder. I'm doing great."

The laugh that rumbled through his chest caused my thighs to clench. He cupped my cheek in one of his hands, running his thumb along my cheekbone in slow strokes. "You were incredible today."

"Now you're just trying to flatter me."

He shook his head before reaching for my shampoo. He moved so that he was behind me at the head of the tub and then pressed against my shoulder, urging me under the water. I didn't even hesitate. When I came back up for air, he gave me a moment to get resettled. I heard the cap on the shampoo snap open, and then close a few seconds later. When his fingers began massaging the soap into my hair, a low moan escaped my throat.

We didn't speak as he doted on me. And I didn't question it. Vincent somehow always knew when I needed him to comfort me, versus when I needed him to push me. He knew how much killing Jack was going to weigh on me. Just like Angelica and Devyn did. They were all taking care of me in their own ways, and I realized how immensely lucky I was.

Another soft touch had me dunking my head again. Vincent made quick work of rinsing out the shampoo before moving to work the conditioner through the ends of my hair as well. He laid my hair across one of my shoulders so it could sit, and then he leaned far enough forward to kiss my cheek.

"He had a dog," I murmured after a while, my gaze fixed on the ceiling.

"Who?"

"Jack." I swirled a bit of the bubbles around to have something to do with my hands. "Her name is Arya."

"Are you wanting me to find her?" There was amusement tinge-ing his voice, and I twisted so I could see his face. Mirth was dancing in his eyes. I nodded. "Consider it done."

"I love you," I told him, leaning up to capture his lips.

"As I love you," he said, pecking my nose before moving to sit next to the tub. He offered me his hand, and I took it within a second. "To the death, Juliette."

I grinned, leaning my head back as I let a sense of peace settle over me. "However slow or swift it may come."

FORTY-ONE

THE TRAP

"*What* do you mean, I'm not coming with you?" I asked Vincent, my arms crossed as I blocked the door out of the apartment.

He leveled me with a glare. "Juliette, I love you. And I know you can handle yourself, but Kline knows how much you mean to me. I'm not letting you get caught in the crossfire."

"After everything we've gone through together, after how much *I* have done and given for these people, you don't have any right to take this from me."

His forest eyes were blazing, that muscle in his jaw ticking. "I know. But you do remember that you nearly got blown up less than a week ago?"

"Of course I do," I seethed. My aching bones barely let me forget it. "But that doesn't mean I shouldn't be there. I should be at your side when we finish this."

"He asked if you were going to be there for the final trade off," he said, coming forward to rest his hands on my shoulders. "We've kept him at bay by using Graham's phone to make him think he's still alive. But I don't know what he has planned for you, and I don't trust it. Please, just let me end this for us."

I knew his heart was in the right place. And I also knew that I had done more than enough. More than I ever thought I was capable of. I had proven time and time again that my place was at his side.

But I was also impulsive, and I knew that was what he was most worried about. More than whatever plan they had for me, and I was as sure as he was that there was one. He was worried about what *I* would do to keep him safe.

Another rebuttal was on the tip of my tongue, but Vincent pressed his finger to my lips. "Do you remember that IOU I asked for when we took the lawyer home?"

"You have *got* to be kidding me."

"I'm calling it in."

Letting out a deep sigh through my nose, I dropped my stance. Fine, I could let him have this. Vincent's shoulders relaxed in answer.

"Who're you taking with you?" I grumbled.

"We're keeping it small. It'll just be Lucas and Brandon with me, and then a handful of others running backup."

"We'll take good care of him, sugar."

I about jumped out of my skin at the sound of Lucas's voice. The smile on his face was anything but kind when I whirled on him.

"Twenty-eight," we chorused.

"Make it twenty-nine," I hissed, aiming a punch at his gut. He sidestepped me with ease, chuckling as he caught me in a headlock. Not wasting a second, I spun out of his hold and tackled him to the ground.

We both knew I only took him down because he let me.

Vincent muttered something about working with children as Arkin and Brandon stepped into the apartment as well. They all stopped to watch as Lucas and I fought for dominance. With Jack being dead, Lucas was going to step in to continue my training. It would be nice to have time to spend with him again, but it was going to be even better getting to kick his ass now and then. He outmatched me in weight, but what Jack had taught me about using my size and speed to my advantage still held true.

Just not this time.

Lucas laughed as he pinned me. A heavy groan escaped my lips an instant before Lucas's weight vanished. Gentle hands hoisted me up, and Brandon glared at his cousin before checking me over.

"She's still recovering from a bomb, genius. Take it easy."

Lucas and I both rolled our eyes, but I let Brandon finish his inspection. When he was satisfied I wouldn't fall apart, he took a step back. He was still glaring daggers at the blonde, and I turned to Vincent and Arkin. I motioned to the two with a kind of 'help me' gesture. They just shook their heads at me.

Brandon opened his mouth, more than likely to spew something foul at Lucas, but I stepped in between them. Brandon's blue eyes met mine, and I raised my brows at him. He dropped his shoulders with a huff.

"You done?" I asked.

"You shouldn't be training yet."

"Spare me. What's the plan for tonight?"

Brandon dropped it, and they explained the trap they had planned for Henry. It was simple and solid. Nothing that I should worry about. Even so, something in my gut twisted. While Lucas and Brandon were talking, my eyes drifted to Vincent. He was studying the others, for once not focused on me. There was no tick in his jaw. No tension in his stance. If Vincent wasn't worried, then I definitely shouldn't be.

But I couldn't shake this feeling.

In what seemed like a matter of minutes, we headed downstairs so they could leave. I leaned against the outside wall of the warehouse as they loaded the cars with what they were taking from here. The rest of the shipment was already at the exchange point. A few of the gang said hello to me as they walked past, but I could barely manage to nod at them in return.

"What's wrong, princess?" Vincent asked, coming to a stop in front of me. He reached up and brushed a loose strand of my hair behind my ear.

"Something doesn't feel right."

"Nothing has felt right about this deal for a long time. But we're almost done. What more could happen?"

"You should know better than anyone not to say shit like that."

He grinned at me, forest eyes sparkling as he cupped my face. "I'm coming back to you. I promise."

I pushed up on my toes, claiming his mouth in a kiss. The softest groan rumbled through him, more purr than anything. When we broke apart, he pressed his forehead to mine.

"You had better," I said.

He left a soft kiss on my cheek before he headed to the Escalade and got in. The boys climbed in with him, and then they were gone, leaving only one more nondescript SUV in the parking lot that would follow behind them. The last group was waiting a bit to leave and would take a roundabout path to the exchange. That way, it wouldn't be as obvious that our side had brought back-up.

Arkin walked up to me and set his hand on my shoulder. "They'll be fine, Jules."

"I hope so," I muttered. He gave my shoulder a reassuring squeeze, and I placed my hand over his. I patted it twice before meeting his baby blues. "I'll be in soon."

Suspicion danced in his eyes, but he nodded before leaving me alone again.

I stared at the open hatch on the SUV for a minute as members filtered in and out of the warehouse.

Fuck this, I thought.

He's going to kill you, I scolded myself. *Vincent is going to lock you in a padded room and never let you out again.*

As I crouched behind the metal shelving, one knee digging into the concrete, I had a pretty good view of Vincent and Henry. It would have been safer for me to stay behind, but I *could not* shake this sick feeling in my gut. I had no way to explain it, but it hadn't dissipated the entire way here. How I had pulled off hiding in the cargo hold of the SUV *and* getting back out without detection was beyond me, but I wouldn't question it.

The men in the center of the room began arguing. Henry looked enraged. His weasel-like face was turning red and bordering on purple. Vincent, on the other hand, was the picturesque vision of calm. At least to the naked eye. But I knew him. I could see that muscle along his jaw pulsing as he spoke through clenched teeth.

A door in the back corner of the warehouse opened. As the person moved forward, that gut feeling finally made sense.

Sebastian looked almost jovial with that bounce in his step. Shrinking back from the opening I had been peeking through, I placed my hand over my heart. It was way steadier than I thought it should be. What the hell was he doing here? Arkin had been looking for him incessantly since Jack's death. We hadn't found a trace of him. Steeling myself with a deep breath, I inched back to where I had been sitting.

Lucas was the first to notice Sebastian. He nudged Vincent before nodding at the smiling man. If I thought Vincent was angry before, it was nothing compared to the rage I could see boiling up into his forest eyes. His jaw set into a hard line as his eyes narrowed the smallest fraction of an inch.

Please don't do anything stupid, I pleaded in my head.

Unfortunately, I couldn't hear them from where I was. But I knew the boys like the back of my hand. From their rigid postures and stoic faces, they were itching to get their hands on Sebastian. But we needed to play this smart. There was no way for us to know if either man knew about Jack's death. Or about how much *we* knew because of it.

Sebastian and Vincent were chest to chest. I had always thought that Sebastian was stunning, but seeing him toe to toe with the man I loved, and knowing what he had done, I couldn't find a single attractive thing about him. He made my stomach curl. As I watched, whatever conversation they were having deteriorated. Vincent's jaw was ticking faster and faster, and Sebastian's smile had long since vanished. I could see the malice sparkling in his onyx eyes from here. With a sneer, he leaned down and said something into Vincent's ear.

The room exploded into chaos.

Vincent's fist connected with Sebastian's cheekbone in less than the time it took for me to blink. Lucas grabbed Vincent, and they flattened themselves to the floor as Henry's men opened fire. My men scattered, searching for cover.

Cursing under my breath, I moved to the back of the row of shelves as a bullet pinged off the metal that was my only protection. In my haste to be a sneaky little shit earlier, I hadn't had the time to go back up to the apartment and grab my gun. But that could be remedied. Spinning on my heel, I ran back to where the cases of guns we had brought with us were still sitting. Sifting through them as fast as I could make my arms move, I finally located a Glock I was comfortable with.

The magazine was empty. A few more came up with the same result.

Why hadn't I known about *this* part of the plan?

Resisting the urge to scream, I threw the gun down and sprinted back to my previous post. Glancing around the end of the shelving, I saw the gunfight had slowed. Vincent peaked out from behind a stone pillar across from my position. Searching the rest of the room, I could see Lucas and Brandon creeping closer to the final two shooters: Henry and one of his cronies.

Where was Sebastian?

Frantically running my eyes over every inch of the room, I finally saw him. He raised his gun and aimed it directly at the back of Vincent's head as he slunk closer to him.

No.

The thought echoed throughout my head. I couldn't lose Vincent.

Not after everything we had been through.

I wouldn't.

My legs moved before I even gave them permission to. My body crashed into Vincent's with a *bang* before a sharp sting tore through my shoulder.

The sound was enough to gain the boys' attention. They turned their guns on Sebastian and fired without hesitation. I saw him crumple to the ground, but I couldn't bring myself to care.

"God damnit, Juliette," Vincent seethed. With a gentleness only he was capable of, he pulled me into his lap. He placed his hand on my shoulder and another stab of pain flew through me.

Had I hit the ground that hard?

Lucas and Brandon skidded to a stop and fell to their knees on either side of us. "Oh, no. Jules," Brandon murmured.

"Go get the car. Now," Vincent ordered in a harsh, strained voice. The boys nodded before hustling off. Once we were alone, his tear-lined eyes bored into mine. "Why, Juliette? Why couldn't you listen, just this once?"

"Because I'm not letting you do this shit on your own anymore, you idiot," I ground out. The adrenaline faded from my veins all at once, leaving way for the searing pain in my shoulder. The sheer panic on Vincent's face was the last thing I saw before darkness overtook everything.

"She passed out," Vincent told Brandon and Lucas a few seconds later when they made it back to him.

"I cleared out the back and put down the third-row seats," Lucas said.

"Good, let's go," Vincent ordered, cradling Juliette's limp body against his chest. Picking her up as carefully as he could, he walked with the other two to the SUV. Neither of them tried to argue with him when he climbed directly into the back of the vehicle and kept Juliette in his arms. They simply shut the hatch and hustled to the front of the car. It didn't take long for Vincent to feel the car move. He just thanked God that they weren't too far away from the warehouse.

He couldn't make out a thing that was blurring past the window, so he was assuming Lucas was speeding. Good. He just hoped that today wouldn't be the day the police finally pulled them over. That would be a grand story to tell.

The SUV came to such a sudden stop that Vincent lost his balance and fell to his side, nearly crushing Juliette in the process. His anger simmered, but he forced himself to stay calm. There would be other times to rip into Lucas about his horrible driving habits. It was only a few beats later that the hatch opened. Brandon held out his arms for Juliette, and Vincent hesitated.

"Let me do my job, Vince," the brunette coaxed. "It'll be easier for you to get out if I have her."

Nodding, Vincent placed Juliette in Brandon's capable arms and hauled himself out of the back of the car. It was tempting to take her back, but he knew Brandon was going to be the one to take care of her, so he just led them inside the warehouse instead.

The door slammed against the inside wall when Vincent shoved it open. He noticed the winces that crossed the faces of the people gathered in the sitting area, but he barely paid them any attention. The one thing that did register was the way their faces all crumpled into masks of worry once they saw Juliette. Saw the blood soaking her shirt and dripping onto the floor in their wake. Arkin was the first to move. He ran for Vincent's office and threw the door open, standing to the side as Brandon walked through. Lucas followed Brandon in, but Arkin caught Vincent's arm.

"What happened?" he asked, his eyes darting inside when a series of crashes sounded.

"She was trying to save me again," Vincent growled, looking into his office to find that Lucas had wiped everything off his desk. In any other situation, Vincent would have been furious. As things stood, he had been planning to do the same thing.

"Damnit," Arkin swore, blue eyes burning with panic as he stared helplessly into the office. Vincent knew it mirrored the same look on his own face.

"Not now," Vincent told him, setting a hand on his friend's shoulder. "Keep Devyn, Dante, and Angelica out of here until Brandon clears her." Arkin nodded before heading back to where the rest of the group were still watching them with anxiety painted expressions. Vincent gave one nod before ducking inside his office.

"I need scissors, tweezers, a needle, and thread," Brandon called, a look of concentration on his face as he lifted Juliette into a sitting position to remove her leather jacket.

Vincent looked to Lucas, and the blonde nodded before going to hunt down the first aid kit they kept on hand. Vincent rounded his desk and opened the top drawer in the meantime. He handed the scissors he kept there to Brandon.

"Is she going to be okay?" he asked, emotion clogging his throat.

"I won't know until I get a better look at it," Brandon said, taking the scissors. He made quick work of Juliette's shirt, cutting it to ribbons before ripping the shreds out from under her. They hit the ground, along with everything else that had previously occupied Vincent's desk. Her chest rose and fell evenly, but Vincent thought it seemed slower than it should. He sat in his chair and rolled it to Juliette's side before taking her limp hand and holding it in both of his.

Lucas burst back into the room and placed the first aid kit that they had amassed themselves onto the desk next to Juliette's hip. He flipped it open so that Brandon could access it easier. Lucas's face was uncharacteristically grim as he moved to the chair in the far corner of the room and sat down, running a hand through his hair. Vincent expected him to say something, but Lucas just placed his elbows on his knees and let his head rest against his clasped hands.

He looked like he was praying.

Brandon's lips formed a tight line as he rummaged through the kit. Once he had tweezers in hand, he moved to the side of the desk so that he had better access to Juliette's shoulder. With a deep breath, he placed one hand just below the bullet hole and pulled the skin to enlarge the opening. Juliette winced, but otherwise gave no other sign she had any idea what was going on. Vincent watched as Brandon took another breath before plunging the tweezers into the wound.

It took less time than Vincent imagined for Brandon to extract the bullet. It made a dull clunking sound as it fell onto the mahogany desktop. Once the obstruction was gone, the blood flowed anew onto Juliette's shoulder. The cloying copper smell permeated the air, and Brandon cursed before reaching for the first aid kit again.

"I need a towel or something," he said as he pulled the needle and thread from the kit. As he began threading the needle, Lucas stood and removed his jacket, followed by his button down, which he moved forward to place over the bullet wound. Vincent hadn't even had time to think of anything. Appreciation for the two men in the room flowed through him, but he couldn't force the words out.

Vincent was always the one with the level head, always the leader, but this was an entirely different scenario.

Brandon nodded to Lucas, and the blonde removed the shirt from Juliette's shoulder. The blood still pooled, but not nearly as much as it previously had. Brandon pinched both sides of the wound together, seemingly unaffected by the blood, and stitched the skin back together. Vincent held his breath, and before too long, Brandon was wiping the stitches down with an antiseptic wipe. He wrapped Juliette's shoulder in a bandage, and after securing it, he finally stepped back.

"I think she's going to be okay," he said, wiping away the sweat that had gathered on his forehead. "It doesn't look like the bullet hit any arteries. She got damn lucky. I'm surprised it didn't go clean through."

Vincent thanked whoever was watching over her and gripped her hand tighter. Lucas and Brandon shared a look before leaving without a word. The door shut with a soft click behind them, and Vincent's head sagged against the desk. The last few hours had utterly drained him. He was still trying to figure out whether he should be angry at Juliette, but he was so relieved she was alright that he couldn't bring himself to be mad at her. At least not yet.

When she woke up would be another story.

FORTY-TWO

LOOKING FORWARD

The overhead light was bright enough to blind when I forced my eyes open.

Cursing the pain in my head, I tried to sit up, only to get pushed back down. Startled, I whipped my head up and locked eyes with Vincent. Relief flooded his face as his hand constricted around mine.

"Thank fuck," he murmured, leaning forward to rest his forehead against mine.

My brow furrowed. "Well, hello to you too," I said.

"Do you remember what happened?' he asked, pulling back from me to sit down. It was only then that I recognized the walls of his office. Though, now that I looked around, I realized someone trashed it. Everything that normally sat on his desk was in a heap on the floor, as if someone had shoved it there. Considering I was lying on the desk, there was a high possibility that was exactly what had happened. "Juliette?" he called, reminding me he was waiting for an answer.

"No, I don't. I just remember shoving you out of Sebastian's line of fire."

"And putting yourself right into it," he snapped. My eyebrows rose at his tone. He sighed, pinching the bridge of his nose between his thumb and forefinger. "You took the bullet he had aimed at me."

As if his words were an incantation, pain blossomed outward from my shoulder. Wincing, I looked at the source of the offense. My stomach rolled at the sight of the blood-soaked bandage, not to mention the bruising creeping out from beneath it. Memories of how I had felt when I saw a similar bandage on Vincent's stomach made me even more queasy. Raising my opposite hand, I prodded at the dressing and flinched at the immediate throb of pain.

Okay, so moving was probably going to be difficult. Raising my arm had taken way more energy than I was expecting. And training was definitely out of the question for a while.

"Brandon got the bullet out and stitched you up," Vincent said, calling my attention back to him. "It's not the prettiest, and it's gonna scar, but at least it'll heal. And you won't die." He shook his head before walking around the desk to the chair that sat in the far corner. There was a flannel draped over it I could never in a million years picture Vincent wearing. He picked it up and tossed it to me.

Raising my arms to catch it on reflex, I cried out when my shoulder protested against the sudden movement. Before I even dropped my arms back to the desk, Vincent was there. His hands hovered around me as if he didn't know what to do with them.

Which would be a first.

"I'm fine," I ground out.

I could almost feel him roll his eyes at me. "Let's just get you dressed."

Glancing down, I blushed to find I was only in my bra. Locating the shreds of my shirt on the floor, I knew Brandon must have had to cut it off in order to get to the bullet. Huffing, I allowed Vincent to help me ease into a sitting position. His fingers were gentle as they drew the fabric up and over my shoulders. He traced the opening of the shirt to the first button, his touch just barely grazing my skin. Goosebumps spread as I shivered, and he smirked before making sure he fastened every single button. When he was done, he took me by the biceps and turned me to face him. With me still sitting on the edge of the desk, it was easy for him to nudge my legs apart and settle himself in the space created. His eyes were an even darker green than normal as they searched my face.

"Something wrong?" I asked, raising my good arm to cup his cheek. Even that was a strain.

"You mean besides you getting yourself shot? Not at all," he replied, leaning into my touch.

"If I wouldn't have been there, it would have been you. You would have broken your promise to come back to me."

His eyes softened. He raised his own hands to cradle my face. His thumbs pressed against the underside of my jaw, forcing me to tilt my chin and meet his gaze head-on. There was no escaping him, even if I had wanted to.

"That bullet clipped you in the shoulder, princess. I was wearing a vest. I would have been fine."

"He was aiming for your head."

"Then he would have missed."

"No, he wouldn't have," a familiar voice inserted. Vincent didn't let go of me, but he allowed enough movement to twist so I could see Brandon. He nodded at Vincent before turning his gaze back to me. "I spotted Sebastian just before she did. I was going to be too late lifting my gun because she's right, he had a perfect shot at the back of your head. But he hesitated. When she jumped for you, she distracted him, just for a split second. By the time he pulled the trigger, his aim was already off."

"See?" I asked. "You would have been dead. I saved you. *Again.*" I thought he was going to scold me. But it pleasantly surprised me to see that familiar ghost of a smile playing around the edges of his full lips.

"Is there a reason you're in here?" he asked Brandon, not bothering to look away from me.

"We wanted to see if she had woken up."

"Get out. Tell the others she's fine."

A low laugh left the brunette. He gave a quick, two-finger salute before slipping out of the office. He winked as he shut the door behind him.

"I'm livid with you for disobeying an order," Vincent murmured, his eyes trailing down to my lips. "But I am so glad that you're okay."

"I love you, too," I teased, pulling him down so I could press my lips to his.

He groaned. The sound vibrated through his chest, right into mine. It sent a flair of pain through my shoulder, but I didn't care. I caught his bottom lip between my teeth and nipped.

The chuckle that rumbled through the room was as much of a promise as it was a threat, and I could barely control the heat raging through me.

We had made it. He was alive. I was alive.

And all our enemies were dead.

At least for the time being.

My shoulder twinged again, but I ignored it as I stood. Vincent retreated enough to raise a skeptical brow at me. Grinning, I eased him down into the chair he had been sitting in. The same one I had sat in my very first night in this office. For a moment, I just stared at him. I took in the heat of his gaze and couldn't believe this was where we had ended up. If I had known then, would I have done anything differently?

I didn't think so.

The man before me had upended my entire life. But now, I couldn't imagine it without him.

"What're you thinking about?" he asked, reaching forward enough to catch my hands in his. He entwined our fingers before pulling me into the space between his spread thighs. Vincent was always gentle with me, but with the wound on my chest, he was treating me like I was glass. He released my hands in favor of cupping the backs of my thighs, his thumbs moving in lazy circles.

"Shouldn't we go out there? Announce our victory?" My hands settled on his shoulders as he continued to drive me mad with his feather-light touches.

"Lucas can debrief them."

I hummed, tracing my fingers up the column of his throat to tangle in his hair. The movement caused some discomfort, but my focus was on the man in front of me. I needed the distraction, and I think Vincent was picking up on it. His smile turned wicked as I pulled on the hair at the nape of his neck, angling his head up so I could slant my mouth back over his.

"You know," I mused, trailing kisses along his cheekbone until I reached his ear. "I seem to remember you once telling me that most people would be on their knees for you in this office."

With my shoulder, sex was off the table. But this? This I could do.

His breath caught. He pulled away from my grip, but only enough to meet my eyes. His pupils blew out, black swallowing green in a way that made my blood spark in answer. Giving him a coy smile, I dropped to my knees in front of him.

"Guess you weren't so wrong after all."

My mouth was otherwise occupied after that.

"It's healed! Look," I said, rotating my left arm. "I can go back to work."

The three men gathered in my apartment just gave me dead pan looks. My teeth ground together in frustration.

"Jules," Brandon started, running his fingers through his hair.

"No." I hissed, pointing at him. "It has been *four months* since I worked a shift. This has got to stop."

Dante and Vincent exchanged glances I didn't even want to decipher. Those two had become thick as thieves in the past few months, and I still wasn't sure how I felt about it. Dante had returned to 'retirement' as he liked to call it, but he still kept up to date with what we were doing. Still helped Vincent with any advice he needed for dealing with the other gangs in Valarian.

In *our* city.

We had wasted no time in spreading the news of the end of both the Graham and Kline families, once and for all. It hadn't taken the rest of them long to fall in line. If they had feared and revered Vincent before, it wasn't anything compared to how they looked at him now. And they knew which ring Dante had finally tossed his hat into. After years of staying neutral, he now had a vested interest in Vincent's success.

And no one doubted why that was.

Devyn and I were as good as family to Dante. With how deep we had entrenched ourselves in the gang, he really didn't have much of a choice.

Poor thing.

But *now*, it was time for me to go back to my life. Vincent had been paying for my apartment for long enough. I had done every single thing Brandon had asked of me regarding my recovery. But I was absolutely going to lose my mind if I didn't get back to work.

Did I still run things with Vincent? Yes. I was in on every meeting. Every decision. But that wasn't enough. It wasn't *mine*.

Tuxedo? That was mine. And I wanted it back.

The men blew out a collective breath as I crossed my arms over my chest and arched my brows at them. They weren't winning this argument this time, and I think they knew it. I had let them talk me out of it for long enough.

Brandon threw up his hands first. "Fine. You're clear on my end. It's up to your boss and your boyfriend at this point."

"Fiancé," Vincent corrected coolly.

My engagement ring suddenly felt heavy.

"*Fiancé*," Brandon mocked, rolling his eyes before heading for the door. He hooked an arm around my neck and pulled me in for a bear hug as he passed. My lungs sputtered for air as I hugged him back. "I'll see you guys later. Have fun."

Dante had a smirk on his face when I finally turned to him. His warm brown eyes sparkled, and he held up a finger the moment I opened my mouth. "You can come back on one condition."

"And what's that?"

"You train with me."

"For what?" I asked, brows drawing together.

"To take over. I'm not going to run that bar forever."

For a few heartbeats, I could do nothing more than blink at Dante.

"You can't be serious." Vincent laughed at my outburst, trying to cover it with a cough, when I turned to look at him. "Did you know about this?"

"Yes."

"Dante!" How dare he tell Vincent first?

This time, my boss did roll his eyes at me. "Jules, my plan has been for you to take over for *years*. Lord knows I wouldn't leave Devyn in charge."

"I can't–"

"You can," he said, cutting me off. "You've been working there for over a decade now. No one else has been there as long as you. There is no one I would trust more. And it would be beneficial to you both for you to be the one in charge. You're one of the most powerful people in this city. It's time to put your name on something of your own."

I was going to be sick.

Vincent moved to my side, and I sank into his warmth. He took my left hand in his, running his thumb over my ring. I could feel the smile on his mouth when he kissed my forehead.

"You've got this," he murmured, his lips brushing the shell of my ear.

My hand tightened on his as I looked up into the forest green eyes I knew so well. They were sparkling, crinkling at the corners in the way they only did for me.

"And you'll be with me?"

"Every step of the way."

Dante coughed. "That's my cue to leave. 3 o'clock sharp tomorrow, Jules."

Dexter chuffed from his spot on the couch, but didn't bother moving as the front door shut. Arya perked up for a moment, but lost interest just as quickly and buried her head back under her tail.

Silence settled over the apartment. It wasn't exactly uncomfortable, but after having the hustle and bustle of the warehouse for so long, it felt empty. My eyes roamed over the room. The place I had been ever since I set out on my own. For the first time since the day I moved in, it didn't feel like home.

"The offer still stands to move in with me," Vincent said, reading my mind as he wrapped an arm around my waist.

"I didn't want to consider it before today. This was enough." I flashed my ring at him, the single princess-cut diamond flaring in the late afternoon sunlight. "But this doesn't feel right anymore."

"So, what's your decision?"

"I don't want to live in the warehouse. Doesn't really scream 'married couple running an empire' to me."

He grinned, spinning me to fully face him. "There's always the house."

"That's your family home, Vincent."

"What do you think this makes you?" he asked, raising my hand to his mouth so he could kiss my knuckles. "You are my family, Juliette. We'll keep the apartment for when we don't want to drive out to the house after late nights with the gang. But you're right. It's better if we build something that's ours, separate from the warehouse." He grinned, a playful edge to it as his eyes trailed to the dogs. "Plus, there's plenty of room for those two to run out there."

"I'm not the decorator Alana was," I teased.

"That's obvious," he said, glancing around my home. For the first time at the mention of her name, there was no sadness that crossed Vincent's face. I swatted at him, and he caught my wrist.

He used my momentum against me and pulled me impossibly closer. "But we'll do this together. To the death, remember?"

I wrapped my arms around his neck, pressing a soft kiss to his lips. "However slow or swift it may come."

EPILOGUE

FOUR YEARS LATER

The music from the club pulsed through the office, and I dropped my head into my hands. There was a knock at the door, and I glared at it for half a beat before calling for whoever was standing on the other side to come in.

Devyn popped her head in with a smile on her face. "Hey there, boss lady."

"Shut up," I grumbled, rubbing at my temples.

Her tinkling laugh filtered through the room as she closed the door behind her. She leaned against it, crossing her arms before arching her pierced brow at me. "You doing okay?"

"Fine. I could just kill Dante. These records are a disaster."

"No wonder he wanted you to take over instead of me."

"We both know you wouldn't have wanted it, anyway."

"True. Assistant Manager suits me just fine."

My eyes rolled back so far, it surprised me I couldn't see my brain. "Don't make me regret asking you to take that role." She grinned, an edge of wickedness to it. I eyed her, wariness creeping into my veins. "What are you doing here?"

"I'm here to take over for the night." I just blinked at her. She pursed her lips. "Jules, do you know what day it is?"

"Thursday."

"What's the date?" I shrugged. She laughed under her breath before pulling her phone out and showing it to me.

My eyes tried to bug out of their sockets.

"Shit," I spat, jumping up so fast my chair rolled back and smashed into the filing cabinet behind me. Stopping for just a second to glance in the mirror next to the door, I checked my reflection.

"You look great, but you might not want to keep him waiting."

"I love you," I told her, throwing my arms around her neck. "You sure you have everything covered for the rest of the night?"

"I do," she said, laughing as she squeezed me back.

Grabbing my purse, I made a beeline for the doors leading out to the bar. When I burst through, the swinging door nearly clipped me as it swung shut again. I scanned the room for Vincent.

He was leaning against the bar, forest eyes already fixed on me. A slow grin spread across his face, and I took the time to admire him. Under the flashing neon, he looked even more dangerous than he normally did. His leather jacket pulled taught across his shoulders, and as I raked my gaze over him, I noted the single red rose he was spinning between his fingers.

Anthony and Ember occupied themselves on the other side of the bar as I made my way over to my husband.

Man, that was still weird.

"Took you long enough, princess," he said, mirth dancing in his eyes as I moved within earshot.

"I'm sorry," I replied with a wince.

"I know you've had a lot on your plate with the handover of the club."

"Still–"

He shushed me, grabbing my hand as he towed me out from behind the bar. He pulled me into his arms before presenting me with the rose. A small smile pulled at my mouth as I accepted it. "Are you ready to go?"

"Yes."

He nodded before lacing our fingers together. With a gentle tug, he led me through the bar and out the front door. The late October air was crisp, and I took a deep breath as it washed over me.

"You didn't wear a jacket today, did you?" Vincent asked, pausing as he turned us towards the heart of downtown.

"No. It was warmer when I left this afternoon."

He rolled his eyes, but pulled me tighter against his side so I could soak up his warmth.

"I have a surprise for you," he said after we had been walking for a while. We stopped, and I glanced up to see that we were at Scotti's, one of our favorite restaurants.

"Dinner?" I asked.

"Well, yes," he chuckled before leading me in. "But there's more."

The host gave us a warm smile as he pulled out two menus and instructed us to follow him. Scotti's was a small Italian hole-in-the-wall, but it had some of the best food in all of Valarian. In the three years Vincent and I had been married, we had come here any chance we got. Each table offered enough privacy for us to discuss anything we needed to. Legitimate business or otherwise.

From the look in Vincent's eyes, I knew whatever he had for me was going to fall into the *otherwise* category.

Once we settled and ordered our food, Vincent placed his hand palm up on the table. A subtle request, but one I indulged on instinct. His thumb ran along the back of my hand once I placed it in his, and that ghost of a smile I loved so much played at the edges of his lips.

"Well?" I prompted. He laughed, the sound sending a flash of heat through me even after all this time. He reached into his jacket with his free hand and pulled out a small, but fat, envelope. Placing it in front of me, he leaned back. His expression was expectant. "What is this?"

"Only one way to find out."

My brows pulled together as I picked it up. I recognized Vincent's handwriting across the front of the envelope, and my eyes widened at the name printed there.

To the attention of: Christopher Kenton

"What–"

"Happy anniversary."

With shaking fingers, I pulled out the stack of papers. It took me less than a heartbeat to recognize the man in the photos. A man I hadn't laid eyes on in over a decade.

Peter Vaughn. My dad's partner. The man I was sure had killed him.

My eyes raised to Vincent's, and he nodded for me to continue. I flipped through the papers, and my heart beat a little faster with each page.

This information was *damning*.

Correspondence between Peter and the people who had been involved in the original murders. More recent photographs from the past few years of Peter being spotted with everyone from Henry Kline, obviously taken before his death, to a few of our other rivals in the city.

"He's moved from homicide to narcotics," Vincent told me.

"How?" The single word was all I could manage as I continued looking over the information he had collected. My eyes raised to his, and for just a moment, I caught sight of the ruthless killer that lurked under Vincent's skin. "How did you get all this?"

"I have spent every spare second since the moment you told me what he did, having him watched," Vincent admitted, that muscle in his jaw beginning to tick. "I knew you said that you didn't know how high up the corruption went, so I found out. From everything I've gathered, it's only him and one of his direct superiors. I have a file on him as well back at the warehouse. Kenton said to reach out to him if we ever needed his brand of help. I think it's time we called in that favor, don't you?"

Chris helped me with most of the legal work when I took over the club. Over the past few years, he and his sister had become indispensable allies. We had rarely asked Chris to stick his neck out for us, even though he insisted he would do it when needed.

My lips parted with a harsh exhale. My hands started shaking, and I had to blink back tears. But Vincent nodded back to the information in my hands, and I took that as my cue to finish looking through it.

My breath stalled in my lungs.

I don't know how he had done it, but the brief note was enough to make the tears fall.

Take care of Gracen. Permanently.

The messy scrawl made my skin crawl. I had the kill order for my father in my hands. Or at least a copy. Raising my eyes, I met Vincent's again.

"Where did you *find* this?"

"Vaughn had it in a safe in his home office. I'm sure he was keeping it as insurance in case they ever wanted to turn on him. Smart, but stupid to keep it somewhere so obvious. Though I'm sure he never expected anyone to come looking for it, either."

"I love you," I breathed, clutching the papers like a lifeline.

"As I love you. I'd do anything for you, you know that."

"But this..." I couldn't believe he had done this. He'd had this in the works for years and had never uttered a word of it. None of them had.

"Was child's play. I wanted to make sure I had enough to bring them both down, the proper, legal way, before I gave it to you. I only went in and broke the safe a few days ago. Not like it's something he would've reported, but he went to the superior I mentioned. The information is only the first half of your present."

That piqued my curiosity. "What's the other part?"

Vincent grinned, sharp as a blade. He leaned across the table to wipe my tears away with feather-light touches. "After dinner. It's not going anywhere."

I took a deep breath before nodding. I had just placed all the papers back into the envelope when our food arrived. Anticipation thrummed in my veins as we ate. Vincent attempted to distract me with idle conversation, but it was hard to focus. What else could he possibly have done for me?

Before long, we had finished our meal and headed back to Tuxedo to grab the car. The silence that wrapped around us was comfortable, and I let myself bask in it. Threading my arm through Vincent's, I leaned against him as we walked. Valarian was in full swing around us, but I barely noticed. The man at my side, and the promise of something to top the news I had just gained, was enough to make me giddy.

"I didn't get you anything," I mumbled as we crossed into the back lot of the club.

"I get you. That's enough."

"You're such a sap." He shrugged, opening my door for me before bowing low. My eyes rolled. "Ridiculous."

"Only for you, princess," he said, a mischievous light in his eye as he helped boost me into the seat.

"Mom and Dad are home!" Angelica yelled, hurting my eardrums when I walked into the warehouse.

"Would you knock that off?" I asked, scowling at her.

Her smile was nothing short of feline as she lounged on the couch. "Absolutely not. I like that it's caught on."

Fighting against the urge to rub my temples, I allowed Vincent to tow me to the basement door. My brows raised, but my heart rate kicked up a few notches. He motioned for me to go down the steps ahead of him.

I had scarcely been down here since we killed Jack. Vincent had never pushed it. There was rarely a need for me to be a part of what went on below the warehouse, but sometimes I still went. Every time I ended up feeling sick for hours after.

When we made it to the small, cement block room, Vincent brushed past me to flick on the bare bulb hanging from the ceiling.

I had suspected, but seeing it was something else.

They had chained Peter to the chair in the middle of the room. His brown eyes squinted as light bathed the room. His black hair had matted to his scalp with the sweat rolling down his face, and his normally olive skin was washed out, looking like he hadn't seen the sun in months. Narrow chest heaving, he focused on Vincent for the briefest of seconds. Then, those cruel eyes slid to me.

"Juliette?" he croaked, relief slipping onto his features.

"Peter," I said, surprised by how steely my voice came out. My fists clenched at my sides, and I forced them to release. "It's been a long time."

"Jules, you've got to get me out of–"

Faster than I had time to process, Vincent punched him square in the nose. Peter's roar of pain echoed around the room, but it wouldn't escape these walls.

"I won't be getting you out of anything," I told him. The fear that crept into his eyes as they bounced back and forth between Vincent and me gave me a sick thrill. "I take it you've met my husband?" I asked, crossing to the man in question. His forest eyes were shining as they took me in, and I had never felt more in control than I did at that moment. Vincent turned to the table full of tools he had leaned against. The gun he handed me was familiar. It was the one he gave me at the start of everything.

"Husband?"

"Mhmm," I hummed, switching off the safety on the gun before turning back to the man who had haunted my nightmares for longer than I cared to admit. "You see, a long time ago, you took something very important from me."

"I never–"

"Are you really going to sit here and lie to my face?" I snarled. "After you threatened Mom and me, so we'd stay quiet?"

"Your father was poking his nose where it didn't belong," he said, dropping all pretense.

With one sentence, he had sealed his fate.

A low laugh escaped me, and I could feel a kind of calm slipping over me. After all this time, I had him. The knowledge that I had his life in my hands was a heady power. Even now, I sometimes forgot how much pull I had in this city. Between the connections I had made on my own, and those I had inherited when I changed my last name, I wasn't the same scared little girl I was the last time I had encountered this man.

I was Juliette Monroe, and this life debt was *mine*.

THE END
for now

BONUS

THE PARTY: JACK'S POV

Jack was taking a tremendous risk. He knew that. But Henry's intel had been good so far. He had been dancing around the edges of Vincent Monroe's detection for far too long. It was time he saw for himself where the loyalties of Valarian City had fallen after Monroe took over. After he had tried to murder Jack in cold blood.

Out of habit, Jack rubbed at the spot below his collarbone where the scar sat. The bullet should have killed him. It would have, had it been mere centimeters to the left. It would have hit him directly in the heart. The only reason Jack made it through that night was because he had been swimming since before he could walk. It had been almost too easy to stay under the water long enough for Monroe to think he was dead.

The rest was history.

He supposed he deserved it. Having Alana killed had been a coward's move. He could admit that now. But even back then, Monroe had been too powerful for Jack to go after directly. The only person who mattered to him had been his sister, and Jack thought it was almost poetic. Family for family.

Jack shook his head, focusing on the subject at hand. Which was sticking to the outskirts of this party. Monroe had somehow survived the attack he had orchestrated the previous week. Sebastian's protegee had sworn that slice to the gut should have ended Monroe. Jack should have been able to come back and claim the gang with ease. Yet no news of Vincent's death had spread. And then Henry had gotten a call about the bad shipment within forty-eight hours. Somehow, Vincent was up and moving as if nothing had happened.

Jack's jaw clenched as he forced himself to slink through the shadows of the room. There were more people here than he had expected, but it was working in his favor. He knew what Monroe was doing. This was more than just a chance to check in with everyone on his payroll. This was a hunt. Monroe wanted to know where the leak was, but he wouldn't find it.

No. Tonight Monroe was going to see a ghost walking amongst *his* people. And the paranoia would set in.

A familiar, warm laugh washed over Jack as he maneuvered closer to the bar. He allowed a small smile to creep onto his face as his focus switched to the brunette slinging drinks. It really shouldn't have surprised him to find out that Juliette and her friend were the ones working tonight. For a gathering like this, Dante would only select his best. However, he could admit that his pulse had jumped when he first spotted her.

And his wasn't the only attention she was drawing. Vincent and his inner circle's eyes kept drifting her way, and for good reason. She looked stunning tonight. Her light brown hair was curled away from her face in a way that accentuated her high cheekbones. Even from this distance, those doe eyes sparkled whenever she interacted with someone. As he watched, she laughed again at something her friend said as she passed Juliette.

He knew Juliette wasn't someone he could have. She had been spoken for from the moment she entered the studio. Whatever man held her heart, he was a lucky bastard.

Jack just counted himself fortunate enough to be someone she trusted. He may not have been a good person, but damn if being around her didn't make him feel a little lighter. At least for the brief moments they had.

Henry entering the room drew Jack's attention. They locked eyes for the briefest second, and the sneer Henry sent his way would have made lesser men cringe. As usual, the older man had slicked his dark hair back to the point of looking wet. At first glance, he wasn't someone most people would think twice about. It was something he used to his advantage. Henry had been in the game long before Jack, had worked side by side with Andras Graham until the day he died. Henry knew everything there was to know about the underbelly of this city. It was why Monroe had always begrudgingly kept business with the older man.

But Henry's loyalties had always stayed with the Graham family. So, when Jack had shown up on his doorstep over a year ago, back from the grave, it hadn't taken them long to devise a plan to take Vincent Monroe down.

It had been hard to keep the suspicion off of Henry. He was the first person Vincent looked into once things started going awry. But Henry had played his part well. Every alibi, every lie had fallen perfectly into place. Even that wench Angelica hadn't been able to figure it out, and Jack knew how capable she was. She was the one who had figured out he was behind Alana's murder.

But now, they were in the home stretch of the plan.

Jack took notice of the other bartender leaving the room, dragging one of Vincent's lackeys with her. His eyebrows rose, and he redirected his gaze back to Juliette. He had turned just in time to see her whip her towel at Lucas, the blonde who was Vincent's right hand. Jack smothered a smile. Of course, someone like Juliette wouldn't think twice about hitting a high-ranking member of a gang. Then again, he doubted she knew the truth of the people surrounding her tonight.

Lucas leaned forward, a flirtatious smile on his face. Juliette rolled her eyes in response.

Then Monroe walked up.

Jack's spine snapped a little straighter as Juliette and Lucas shifted their eyes to the gang leader. He took a deep breath before slowly letting it out. Vincent Monroe was a lot of things, but a threat to Juliette was not one of them. On top of Monroe's disgustingly high moral compass for someone in his position, Jack knew Juliette could handle herself. He had taught her, after all.

Vincent slid his empty glass her way, and she turned to grab the bottle. Once she turned her back, Vincent's eyes scanned the crowd again.

And then, *finally*, they locked with Jack's.

If Jack hadn't been studying Monroe for years, he would have missed the recognition as it flashed across those green eyes. A muscle in his jaw ticked as they held each other's gazes. Jack had the delight of watching a myriad of emotions play through Vincent's eyes. Though not on his face. Vincent had always had an impeccable skill for masking his expressions. But that was a murderous rage in his eyes as he stared Jack down.

Jack waited for the order. Waited for Monroe to alert his men that he was there. And then the hunt could truly begin.

What he didn't expect was for Vincent to turn away from him. His brows drew together as Vincent caught Juliette's wrist when she reached to fill his glass. In an instant, he had pulled the brunette towards him across the bar until his lips were at the shell of her ear. Jack's hackles rose as he took a step in their direction.

Maybe he had misjudged Monroe's moral compass. Plan be damned. He'd never let him lay a hand on her.

But something made him pause his advance.

Juliette's head dipped, just barely, as she eased back from Vincent. No harsh jerk to rid herself of his hand. No acidic glare. In fact, she didn't even raise her eyes, but he saw her lips move as she spoke to the gang leader. She finished pouring the drink and set it in front of him. To an outside eye, their interaction seemed innocent enough, but Jack couldn't imagine why she would have let him grab her like that. There had been no fight to her when she retreated from him.

Almost as if...

No.

Jack blinked as he examined them in a new light. Lucas had shifted so that his body was slightly between Juliette and the rest of the bar. Vincent's eyes were roving over the crowd from where he had initially seen Jack, only to be drawn right back to Juliette. As she was messing with the register, she let her own eyes casually peruse the room.

She confirmed Jack's suspicions when she turned back to Vincent to give him his money. As their hands touched to transfer the cash, Vincent entwined their fingers for only a heartbeat. But it was enough to make Juliette's shoulders drop. Enough to make the fake smile she had plastered on melt into something more genuine.

"I don't care about him," she had said that very first day in the studio.

"He's not the kind of guy to do things for someone with no benefit to himself. So, I don't know what he wants from me."

"So you're together?" he had asked her, mere weeks ago.

"Yeah." And it had been that same smile she was sporting now that had crossed her face as she thought of him. Of *Vincent Monroe.* And Jack had been happy for her. Because some of that haunted look that he had seen in her eyes on the day they met had been gone.

Of all the insane coincidences.

Jack's head was spinning. There was a tightness in his chest he hadn't felt since the night he learned his father was dead. He needed air, and he needed out. To hell with the rest of what was supposed to happen tonight. Vincent had spotted him, but it wasn't creating the paranoia he had wanted. Jack knew that with their history, Vincent would do everything in his power to keep Juliette safe. He had a reason to keep his head on straight.

And it was the same woman that made Jack's own traitorous heart warm every time she was near him.

What was he going to *do?*

BONUS

A New Kind of Crown - After the Epilogue

"Vincent!" I yelled, scowling as I looked through the fridge.

"Yes?" he replied, popping up in the kitchen's archway.

"Where is that bottle I had in here?"

"You're not supposed to be drinking, princess."

I shut the door, rattling the contents as I whirled on him. His forest eyes were alight as he watched me over the rim of his glass of scotch. I flicked my gaze over his shoulder, making sure no one was behind him. When I was certain our friends were still in the living room, I made my way over to swat at him.

"It was sparkling cider, you idiot. Devyn is bound to ask why I'm not drinking."

He laughed and hooked an arm around my waist before towing me back to the fridge. He opened it, and it took him about five seconds to find the bottle at the back of the top shelf. My eyes narrowed because I knew I hadn't put it up there. I was too short to reach it. He moved to our cabinet of glasses and pulled down a flute before filling it for me.

"If someone saw that in there, namely Lucas or Devyn, they would've asked why we had it. So, I hid it."

"Remind me again why our best friends are so damn nosy?" I muttered, taking the glass when he offered it to me.

"It keeps things fun."

"What does?" Lucas asked, appearing way too close to my back for my liking.

I jumped, the cider sloshing over the side of the glass as I went to take a sip. My eyes slipped closed as I took a deep breath. "Lucas?"

"Hmm?"

"Four thirty-nine."

"I can't believe you're still keeping track," he grumbled. I looked at him over my shoulder, and he gave me that damned kicked puppy look he knew got me every time.

"It's not too hard when you give her a reason to add to it at least twice a week," Vincent threw in, slipping past the blonde to replace the bottle in the fridge.

"It's not *that* often," Lucas protested.

"Close enough," Vincent and I chorused. My husband turned to grin at me, and I couldn't help but return it.

"C'mon, everyone is waiting for you two to do presents." Lucas huffed, ruffling my hair as he walked past me. "You'd think after five years you two could stop with the love-bird routine," he muttered before heading back to the living room.

A laugh fell from my lips as I held my hand out for Vincent's. He came back to me in an instant to entwine our fingers together. He kissed the back of my hand before pulling me in close and cupping my cheek with the other. "You realize he's going to lose it when we tell him?" he asked.

"They all are," I said, watching the same joy flash in his eyes that had when I told him four months ago.

"You're still not going to tell me first?"

"Nope."

He groaned but didn't fight me anymore. He pulled me up on my tiptoes to press a kiss to my lips, and then he led us into the living room.

My heart swelled at the sight of our loved ones gathered around the tree. The house had come a long way since we moved in before the wedding, and it felt more like home every year. Devyn and

Brandon were sitting directly in front of the monstrosity of a tree Vincent had talked me into this year, and they were just as enraptured with each other as they had always been. Lucas sat down next to his cousin, shoving him over so that he fell into Devyn's lap. Brandon lightly punched Lucas in the shoulder before twisting and beginning to sort out the presents. Angelica had sprawled across the armchair by the fire, practically purring as she bathed in the heat. Dante wasn't far from her, sitting on the loveseat that shared an end table with her chair. Dexter had his head in Dante's lap, and Arya was curled into her normal corner right next to him. Arkin noticed us enter, and he scooted to the end of the couch to make room for us.

I may not have had any family left, but this one made up for that tenfold.

"Took you two long enough," Dante grumbled.

"Don't be a grump," I said, picking the bow off one of my gifts and throwing it at him. It didn't even make it two feet before it fluttered back to the floor.

"He can't help it," Devyn said, a mischievous grin on her face as she glanced at him. "He's getting the cold shoulder."

"Sorry, I don't date old men," Angelica cooed, kicking her feet. Dante scowled at her back, and I wondered how long those two were going to pretend they weren't head over heels for each other. Vincent and I shared a look, and I could tell he was thinking the same thing.

Arkin shook his head before pushing a small, red-wrapped present into my hands. "You start, Jules," he said, a wicked twinkle in his baby blues.

Unease twisted my gut as I narrowed my eyes. The rest of the room focused on me, and a flush crept up my neck to settle in my cheeks. I set Arkin's gift aside for the time being because I had a feeling it needed to be opened later in the night. Arkin was too observant for his own good. Instead, I grabbed the smallest off the top of the pile that Brandon had pushed my way. The tag let me know it was from Devyn, and my eyes flicked to meet hers. Her smile was warm, and I took that as a good sign. It looked too small to be a vibrator, like last year.

Hopefully.

As I opened it, Devyn crawled over so that she was right next to me on the floor. The box contained a three-tiered necklace with an engraved silver bar on each chain. My eyebrows raised, and Devyn pointed to the date on the first bar. "This is the day we met, the day you took over Tuxedo, and obviously you recognize your wedding date." She pointed to each bar in turn, and my eyes watered when she finished.

"This is beautiful," I murmured, throwing my arms around her.

"I'm just glad you're not mad that I included myself as an important date."

"Of course you are," I said, pulling her in even tighter.

"Can't breathe."

I laughed, and we continued with everyone opening their gifts. Our tradition was getting everyone one thing, and you could always tell when someone left their buying until the last minute, hence the present from Devyn the previous year. But this year, almost everything brought me to tears.

I was blaming the hormones.

There were only a few exchanges left, and all attention shifted to the red head in the room. Angelica cut her gaze to Dante, eyeing the small box he had in his hand. If I didn't know any better, I'd say that was fear in her sapphire eyes. Dante cleared his throat before leaning forward and placing the package on the arm of her chair. She picked it up daintily and blew out a breath before opening it. Her brows quirked, and she tilted her head to glare at my old boss. He just grinned, teeth gleaming in the firelight.

"The peanut gallery would like to know why Dante is getting murdered tonight," Lucas said, flipping the scarf I had gotten him over his shoulder.

"I think Jules needs to open her last gift," Angelica said, snapping the lid on the box closed before stuffing it in the bottom of one of her bags. "I want to know what Arkin got her."

Stifling a sigh, I set down my glass and took the package from Arkin again. Checking the tag, I noticed his girlfriend's name as well. This wasn't the first year her family's Christmas had fallen on the same day we did ours, but it was their turn to get her. We were down Lucas's girlfriend this year too. She had been called away last minute because of work.

"Be sure to thank her for me too," I told Arkin as I tore the paper. It left me with a box just a bit smaller than my lap, and I removed the lid before gaping at the contents.

"What is it?" Lucas asked, leaning forward to see.

"How did you know?" I hissed, staring at the onesie nestled in tissue paper.

"I saw the list of names in your office a few weeks ago."

Because of course I had been stupid enough to leave that out, and now we had everyone's attention. Vincent glanced over my shoulder, and I felt the breath leave him as he stared at the little pink tiara adorning the onesie.

"We're having a girl?' he breathed, his words only meant for me.

But our friends caught it. Devyn was up off the floor in a blink, coming to get a good look at what was in my hands. Tears shimmered in her eyes as she flicked her gaze from the box to me.

"You're pregnant?" she asked, her voice catching. I nodded, and she squealed. She launched herself at me, and Vincent barely had time to move before we collided with the back of the couch.

"Devyn," Brandon scolded, peeling her off of me. "Take it easy."

"She's fine," I said, laughing as I sat back up. "But obviously, we had something we wanted to tell you all tonight."

Vincent's hand enclosed mine, and I watched as he took the onesie out of the box with his other. That was pure awe on his face, and when his eyes met mine, they were shining with unshed tears.

Everyone gave their congratulations, and I finally allowed my free hand to settle on my stomach. It was an urge I had been suppressing for weeks, and I was glad we didn't have to hide anymore. Angelica was the last one to hug me, her hold lingering longer than I expected. She squeezed me tight and drew back just enough to meet my eyes. "I hope you know that I'm still an aunt, blood or not."

"Ditto!" Devyn pitched in.

"God help us all," Dante muttered. "Let me know if you need any help with these two."

"Put your chicken hat on," Angelica said, glancing over at him. Devyn cackled, obviously pleased with her gift for our old boss. "At least then you'll look like a mother-hen as well." He glowered at her, and she just gave him a sweet smile before turning back to me. "Have you picked out a name yet?"

"I have." Vincent twisted to face me; one eyebrow raised. "As long as Vincent likes it, too. Genevieve Grace."

There was a beat of silence, and Vincent's entire face softened.

"Grace was Alana's middle name," Angelica murmured.

I didn't remove my gaze from my husband's. "I know."

It was also part of my maiden name. A way for us to honor everyone we had lost.

He pulled me over to him and kissed me. It was soft, mindful of our company. But when he pulled away from me, there was a storm of emotion flowing through those forest eyes.

"I love you all, but I think it's time we called it a night," he said.

Laughter trickled around us, and everyone said their goodbyes. Angelica and Devyn were already plotting the baby shower, and I was happy to leave them to it. Dante was the last to leave, hanging back as the rest of them trooped out.

"Don't forget your hat," I said, pushing the hideous thing into his hands. He let out a long-suffering sigh, and I fought not to laugh. Shaking his head, he pulled me into a tight hug.

"You have no idea how proud of you I am," he said, his voice low. "You deserve every ounce of the happiness you two have built here."

"I'm gonna cry again." His jacket muffled my voice as I held him tighter. His chest rumbled with laughter, and he ruffled my hair as he pulled away. "But you deserve to be happy, too."

"Working on it." He gave me a wink and pulled the door closed behind him when he left.

The silence of the house washed over me, and I basked in it for a moment. I could hear the fire crackling in the living room, and a floorboard creaked as someone approached. Vincent wrapped his arms around my waist, hands splaying over my stomach, before setting his chin on my shoulder. I placed my own hands over his and turned my head to press a kiss to his cheek.

"I love you," I said.

"As I love you."

"You ready for this?"

He snorted. "I don't think anyone's ever truly ready to become a parent, but I can't wait to do this with you."

"We're going to have to delegate a lot for a while. With the gang and the club."

"I have some people in mind."

"They'll kill each other."

Vincent laughed, the sound rich and warm, as he drew me back to our bedroom.

I went willingly, as I always had, and always would. I would love this man until the day I died, however slow or swift that may come.

SPECIAL THANKS

I won't lie. I never thought I'd get to this point. Publishing a book felt like a dream I wasn't sure I'd ever achieve. I started *Death of Me* in 2012. I finished my first draft in 2022, and it has been a whirlwind to get this copy into your hands. And there are definitely some people who deserve a little extra credit.

So, thank you to Abbie, Cass, and Zoeie. You three have read this book left, right, and sideways. You've dealt with me bouncing ideas off you incessantly. Answered late night texts about little and big things. This wouldn't have been nearly as fun without you all.

Thank you to Natalie and Megan. These girls and their *We Know How to Read* podcast were a significant part of what helped make this story gain traction in the first place. I can't thank you both enough for having me on your podcast and letting me dish about books for way longer than we had time for. And for giving a voice to this story in a way I hadn't even considered.

Thank you to my family for fostering my love of reading and writing at a young age. Thank you for taking my dream of being a published author seriously and never trying to steer me away from it.

Thank you to the thousands upon thousands of people who read the first draft of this story on my wattpad profile: *ErinxJacobs*. I have been writing on wattpad for over a decade. It's where I started, and where I truly realized I had a shot at this. I read every single one of your comments, and I have so much love for that community. I, honestly, could never have completed this without them.

And thank you to the rock that I have always broken myself against. Your unwavering faith was a driving force in my writing over these last few years, even if you didn't know it.

About the Author

Erin Jacobs has loved storytelling for as long as she can remember. It has been her dream to craft stories that stick with people since the first time she put a story to paper when she was eight years old. She currently resides in Ohio with her child and dog, and is working on the next installment of her debut series set in fictitious Valarian City.

Stay tuned for updates on Valarian City's resident golden retriever. He's about to have his world turned upside down by a black-cat woman with a badge.

TikTok: @.aiiry

Instagram & Threads: @xoxo.aiiry